As he fell, the ogre's spear tip swept around and caught the corner of Kerrick's hood, pulling the woolen shroud from the elf's head. Spinning on one foot, the Silvanesti sprinted after the fleeing slaves, trying to sheathe his sword and pull the hood back over his golden hair and pointed ear.

One more thing caused his heart to sink as he dashed away. It was shouted by a guard, loud enough to echo through the hall. . . .

"An elf!" came the cry. "An elf has come to Winterheim!"

ICEWALL TRILOGY
VOLUME THREE

Winterheim

DOUGLAS NILES

WINTERHEIM

©2003 Wizards of the Coast, Inc.

Distributed in the United States by Holtzbrinck Publishing. Distributed in Canada by Fenn Ltd.

Distributed to the hobby, toy, and comic trade in the United States and Canada by regional distributors.

Distributed worldwide by Wizards of the Coast, Inc., and regional distributors.

Made in the U.S.A.

Cover art by Brom
First Printing: January 2003
Library of Congress Catalog Card Number: 2001113264

9 8 7 6 5 4 3 2 1

US ISBN: 0-7869-2911-1
UK ISBN: 0-7869-2912-X
620-17850-001-EN

U.S., CANADA,
ASIA, PACIFIC, & LATIN AMERICA
Wizards of the Coast, Inc.
P.O. Box 707
Renton, WA 98057-0707
+ 1-800-324-6496

EUROPEAN HEADQUARTERS
Wizards of the Coast, Belgium
P.B. 2031
2600 Berchem
Belgium
+ 32-70-23-32-77

Visit our web site at **www.wizards.com**

Dedication

In loving memory of Millie Knappe

Friend, wife, mother, aunt . . .
she brightened the life of everyone
who was lucky enough to know her.

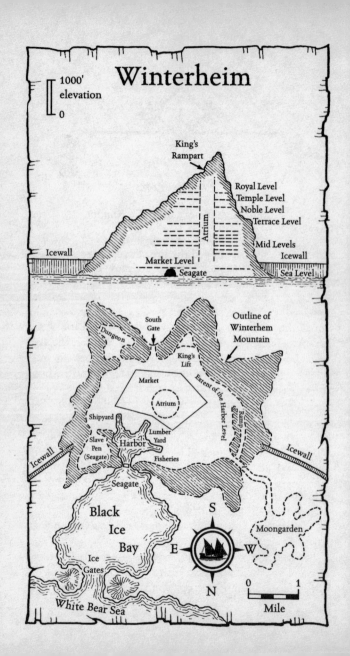

1

Two Kings

The mountain loomed above the still waters of Black Ice Bay, above the rim of the coastal foothills, above the bare face of the vast cliff spreading west- and eastward from the glacial skirts of the great massif. Though the smooth white barrier, the Ice-wall, towered a thousand feet above the sea, it was dwarfed by the greatness of that solitary summit, whose majesty seemed almost too big, out of scale.

The peak thrust into a realm of thin air, shrouded in ice and snow even now, during the last month of summer. Other heights jutted skyward to the right and left, but even the lower shoulders of the great massif rose far above the loftiest mountains of the White Range and the other saw-toothed ridges extending across the frost bound polar reaches. These lesser elevations were as mere cubs, gathered around the feet of a great white bear.

This mountain was Winterheim, and as great as it was, it was so much more than just a mountain.

As the ogre king returned here, to his home, he stared at the massif that was also his fortress, the capital of his kingdom. He drew comfort from the fact that this lofty vista, at least, remained unchanged. As he returned from an expedition that had claimed his mother's life, destroyed one of his two ships, and annihilated a proud bastion of his kingdom, he knew there were few constants in his world, but this mountain remained the greatest of those. For that he was grateful and relieved.

He remained aware that he was still a mighty king, could exercise his considerable power in many ways.

"Bring the prisoner up to the deck," he ordered, and several ogres of the Royal Grenadiers hastened to obey.

Grimwar was aware of his queen standing nearby, and though he felt her eyes upon him he did not deign to look at her. Instead, his gaze remained fixed upon that immaculate summit.

He heard a hatch open and the rattle of chains behind him, followed by a whip crack and the thud of a body being thrown to the deck. Only then did he shift his head to look down at the human who lay sprawled on the planking near the king's black whale-skin boots.

The man glared up at the ogre monarch, blue eyes icy with anger, mouth set in a tight line, but the human captive made no sound, even as a grenadier kicked him in the ribs.

"Kneel, slave!" growled the ogre warrior. "Kneel before your new master, the King of Suderhold!"

Instead the filthy, bearded man pulled his chained wrists together and slowly, awkwardly pushed himself to a sitting position. The grenadier drew back for another kick, but Grimwar Bane held up his hand, stopping the attack and allowing the chained human to rise to his feet. The king stared at his captive in frank interest.

The three weeks below decks had not done the man any good—he was sallow and thin, eyes blazing from sockets that seemed to have sunk halfway into his skull during the voyage. He squinted in the glare of the first daylight that he had seen in all that time. His movements were stiff, and he winced in pain as he forced himself to stand fully erect. He was a tall human, though still much shorter than the ogre king, and Grimwar well remembered the fellow's fearlessness in a hopeless attack, the frenzy with which he had wielded a lethal sword. No doubt the grenadier remembered, too, as a dozen of his comrades had been slain in that savage fight.

Grimwar Bane knew that the humans considered this fellow to be their king and a mighty king at that, and it amused the ogre monarch to see him debased like this. Since this summer's campaign had been an utter disaster, the ogre monarch had only this lone prisoner to show for his efforts and sacrifice, but the man was a valuable captive, and Grimwar tried to take some solace in that.

"A king, they called you," Stariz ber Bane declared scornfully, unable to remain silent any longer. The queen addressed the captive as she advanced to stalk a circle about him, glaring contemptuously down as the fellow utterly ignored her leering presence. "Now you will see the homecoming of a real king and a fortress that makes your petty castle look like a hovel on the tundra!"

Grimwar snorted his agreement, once again turning to glance at that massive mountain. The galley glided straight toward the base of the massif, where the plunging cliffs delved right into the deep, dark waters of the Black Ice Bay. The rocky face was smooth there, and as they drew closer the king nodded, pleased to hear the rumble of the massive capstan, the metallic clang as many tons of iron chain began to move. This was more proof of his power: a legion of slaves going to work because the king's approach had been observed. Slowly, almost imperceptibly, the great Seagate of Winterheim began to move to the side.

"There are five hundred of your fellow humans turning those gears," Grimwar noted casually. "If you were a less important prisoner, you might find your place among them, striving shoulder to shoulder with the mass of them until you die, but no—you are too valuable for that fate. We shall have to find a more exalted task for you."

The man's eyes narrowed, and the ogre king was not surprised to note a considerable depth of anger there.

The gap of shadow expanded, revealing the great cavern at the heart of Winterheim. The placid waters of the bay extended into the contained harbor, and as the opening grew wider sunlight spilled inside, brightening the vast, columned terraces of the ogre stronghold. Soon the gate was fully open, and *Goldwing*, propelled only by a few gentle, easy thrusts of her oars, slid beneath the lofty overhanging arch of stone and into the warm, moist air that kept Winterheim comfortable even during the most frigid depths of the sunless winter.

Stariz strode past the king to the edge of the deck, raising her arms and gesturing to Grimwar, drawing out a thunderous cheer from the great throng of ogres who had gathered to welcome their rulers back home. The king's subjects shouted from the docks of the waterfront and from the market plaza, the great square surrounding the wharves, the flat surface raised barely a dozen feet above the water level. More ogres lined the balconies of the massive atrium, the great chimneylike column that rose toward the summit of the mountain, providing the citizens of every level with a clear view down to the square and the harbor.

Even in the shadowed heights they stood and chanted their accolades:

"Grimwar Bane!"

"Long live the king!"

The galley eased gently into her slip. After the first roared greeting, the monarch took little note of the cheers or the assembled throng of ogres waiting on the waterfront plaza as the gangplank cranked down to the dock. This was as hollow a homecoming as he had ever experienced, and he felt the losses of the campaign so keenly that at first he could take little pleasure from the return to his great fortress city.

He was bred to this, and he would give his people what they desired. He stalked down the ramp and across the wharf with kingly bearing. To the assembled populace, he looked proud and regal, honored by their presence and pleased to be their ruler. He waved to the right and left and smiled, the gestures and expressions coming automatically, masking the darkness that churned within him.

The trappings of power, as they always did, helped to lift his bleak mood. He saw young nobles thumping their chests with clenched fists, the traditional hail of the bull ogre to his lord. Solid females lined the byways, waving bright pennants, smiling adoringly if his eyes so much as flicked in their direction.

"Take the prisoner to the Salt Caves," he ordered the captain of the Grenadiers. "His fate remains to be decided."

Some of his crewmen hurried to form an escort for the human, while twin ranks of palace guards, dressed in their scarlet cloaks and bearing huge, ceremonial halberds, flanked the approach to the lift that would carry the king and queen up to the royal level. The monarchs stepped inside the cage, turning to face the crowd as the door of metal bars rattled shut.

"Lift, slaves!" shouted an overseer, cracking his whip in warning. Instantly two dozen slaves put their shoulders to the gearlike teeth of a large crank. Chains clanked, and the floor beneath Grimwar's feet lurched then settled into a steady rise. More roars of approval rose from the ogre population, and the king treated his subjects to another wave.

Stariz, however, waited only until they were a few dozen feet up, out of immediate earshot of the guards and attendants. She had been surly and glowering during the whole voyage, but since the ship had been very crowded this was the first real privacy they had experienced since beginning the journey home from Dracoheim.

"How do you intend to recover from this disaster?" she demanded. "You have lost Dracoheim Castle and one of your ships—"

"Did you think I had forgotten?" snapped the king, his deep voice rumbling above the metallic noise of the lift.

"I wondered," she replied tartly, "yet if you had listened to me—"

Grimwar Bane was in no mood to hear his wife's rebukes though, as usual, his mood did not diminish the queen's torrent of words. Nevertheless, he felt the sting of those words with unusual acuity. Perhaps this was the reason that he responded not in an exasperated roar but in a rumbling growl—a tone that, at the very least, commanded her attention.

"Do you think I do not grieve for the loss of my own mother? That I do not understand that it was the humans who brought about this disaster? Do you think I forget that it was you who bade me go to Dracoheim to have the orb made! If blame rests in this palace, my queen, it falls upon your ample shoulders!"

Stariz snorted, and avoiding the king's eyes, turned to look outward through the gridwork of the cage door. The two royal ogres rose steadily through the great central atrium of Winterheim. The galley *Goldwing* rested in her berth below, illuminated by the sunlight that spilled through the still-opened harbor gates. The ship was scarred, battered and worn from a season of vigorous campaigning, looking as tired as Grimwar felt. The empty slip nearby, where *Hornet* should be docked, absolutely tore at the king's heart. That beautiful ship was driftwood now, timbers scattered on the rocky shores below fortress Brackenrock.

Stariz drew a breath—a sign that she was taking a rare pause before continuing her tirade. When she did speak, her own voice had softened, her tone as gently persuasive as she could manage.

"Why did you refuse to execute the prisoner on Dracoheim?" she pressed. "Your own men witnessed the destruction wrought by the humans. Did you not see that a display of royal resolution—and vengeance—might go far toward restoring their spirits? What is the value of one paltry slave brought back to Winterheim? He is perhaps a strapping specimen of a man, though still he is but one."

Even when her tone was gentle, the king reflected, it was as coarse as the growl of an angry she-bear.

"I saw that, and I saw, too, that this human is no ordinary prisoner. His value does not come from the fact that he is another slave—I already have thousands of the wretches! He is unique—you saw how his companion revered him! He is a king of the humans!"

"Why should that insure his life?" demanded Stariz.

"Perhaps it does not, but surely it is reason for consideration and planning. If he is to die, then his death can be wielded to good effect."

She surprised him by nodding in pensive agreement. "You may be right. How should he be killed, then?"

"I have not decided, yet," declared the ogre monarch, realizing that he had not decided because he hadn't given the matter proper thought. Until now, it had been enough to know that he held an important enemy leader. "I have been giving the matter much consideration," he declared breezily. "I will let you know when I have made my decision."

"He should be executed on the day of the equinox, at the ceremony of Autumnblight!" Stariz announced excitedly. "It will be a death witnessed by all the slaves in the city and will serve as a strong lesson to them, a reminder of your mastery!"

The king felt his temper rising again. "I have thought about this matter, and I will solve it my way, not yours!" he barked. "Now I desire to bathe and to garb myself in royal finery. Unless you have something important to say right now, I suggest that you depart for your quarters and do the same."

Stariz scowled, a wrinkled and dour expression that rendered her blocky face into an ugly smear. Her husband fought a powerful urge to smash his fist into her piglike nose. It was not the presence of the honor guard, royal troops assembled as the lift came to a rest on the lofty royal level of the city, that held his hand. Indeed, these ogres were loyal to him, and many had felt the lash of the queen's tongue. No doubt they would not be displeased by such a display of royal temper. Nor did he worry about the slaves, human men and women who stood respectfully back from the landing, waiting to garb the king and queen, to feed and bathe them. They were less than nothing—he didn't know how they would feel about a blow delivered by the king to the queen, but neither did he care.

In truth, acknowledged only in the deep pit of his belly, it was fear that restrained his blow—fear not of his wife but of the vengeful god who was her true lord. For Stariz Ber Glacierheim Ber Bane was not just the queen of Suderhold and mistress of Winterheim. She was the high priestess of Gonnas the Strong, seer of mystical truths and worker of dire magicks.

He was afraid that if his anger was released in violence, her reprisal—though certainly more subtle—would be far worse than a punch in the nose. Would his belly turn to fire in the night, wracking him with agony until his guts exploded to poison him? Would his eyes wither and dry, leaving him blind? Or his mind fail, turning him into a feeble, drooling fool who couldn't so much as ladle gruel to his own lips? Or would she think of something even worse?

These were questions he could not answer and had no desire to explore. He gave his wife a curt nod then let the guards fall in behind as he stalked regally through the palace gate and down the long, wide hallway leading to the royal apartments. The doors were opened by slaves, and at last he felt as though he could exhale as he entered the familiar comfort of the cavernous chambers. A fire burned on the massive hearth, and the several comfortable chairs arrayed about the room, each layered in plush white bearskin, offered instant soothing for his weariness.

Instead he turned immediately toward his bathing chamber where a tub of steaming water awaited. The waters relaxed and cleansed him, and the heat soothed the aches of the long campaign from his flesh. He lay there, half conscious, eating a loaf of fresh bread and five steamed ice-trout, and gradually his life seemed good again. He was clean, well fed, and found that he could think about more pleasant pursuits.

One pursuit in particular came to mind . . . for he knew that Thraid Dimmarkull, the royal mistress, awaited him with a greeting that would banish all of his remaining troubles to the far corners of his mind.

———◆◆◆———

Thraid Dimmarkull lolled against the railing of one of the city's lower balconies, excited and frightened at the same time. She would have loved to greet the galley in the harbor, to have run forward and clasped her beloved

Grimwar with all the affectionate power of her soft, enveloping embrace. Though it seemed terribly unfair, she knew that such a display would only make him mad.

The hardest part about being the king's mistress—secret mistress, for now—was that Thraid was required to be patient, and patience did not come easily to her. She had come to the railing because for the immediate present she had nowhere else to go. The king would debark then be busy for several hours . . . but she knew that he would soon be anxious to see her. She hoped he would like it, the little place she had prepared for them on the terrace level. It was discreet, perfectly private, and sumptuously appointed.

The best feature: a single tunnel rose from the rear of the chambers all the way to the royal section of the city, so the king would be able to come, perfectly unseen, to his tryst.

Thraid had entrusted her slave Wandcourt with a message for Grimwar Bane, detailing the arrangements. Wand was a human, but he had proved himself loyal over many years. Indeed, she trusted him more than any ogre for this task. Sooner or later, the king would come, and she would be there….

She watched as the queen marched down the gangplank, glaring around the city as if seeking reason for complaint, looking for signs of things that had gone wrong during the absence of the royal couple—an absence that despite the king's pledge to the contrary had lasted all summer.

Her heart, her very being, brightened as her Grimwar, the most handsome, strapping, powerful—indeed, beautiful—ogre in all Krynn, came striding off of the gangplank. She felt vicarious pride as the ogres who had gathered on the waterfront, nearly a thousand of them, burst into cheers at his arrival. He waved—he was always gracious to his people—but even from this height she could see that he was tired, discouraged, weary beyond words.

How desperately she wanted to take his broad head and nestle it between her breasts, to stroke his hair and murmur soothing words of affection. How he needed her! No doubt the long voyage, trapped aboard the ship with that hateful ogress, had taken a terrible toll on him.

Of course, Thraid had heard things, tales of a battle lost, *Hornet* destroyed, even rumors of some dire disaster on Dracoheim, but in the mind of the king's mistress, those things were of secondary, even trivial, concern. To look for the cause of Grimwar's fatigue she had to search no further than the presence of that awful queen.

At that moment Stariz turned and stared behind her, not at Grimwar but at something else, something on the ship. Thraid watched the rest of the crew trudge up from the rowing benches and plod wearily down the gangplank. One figure caught her eye: small among the ogres and golden haired. He was chained, but even in shackles he walked with a bearing of unbreakable pride.

A human, she realized—a captive taken by her Grimwar, brought back to the city.

The man glared around him, and somehow Thraid felt the dazzling ice of that glance, even as far above as she was. He was intriguing, this prisoner, and strangely appealing. Queen Stariz all but spat in hatred as she stared, and the ogress at the railing quickly saw that the human was the source of the queen's hatred.

Immediately Thraid wanted to know more about him.

As the ship was made fast to the dock, Strongwind Whalebone warily examined his new surroundings. Whatever fate held in store for him, he lacked the energy, the stamina, to put up much of a fight. However, his spirit remained vital, so he would look for ways to rebuild his strength, to study his enemies, and to plan.

He had welcomed his release from the hold primarily because of the chance to breathe fresh air. For two weeks the fish guts and whale blubber that mingled effluence in the deep hold of the galley had raised a stink that choked and nearly suffocated him. There, below the benches where ogre oarsmen labored, a heavy wooden hatch had sealed out any glimpse of sun or sea, rendering the little chamber into a smothering cell.

The lone prisoner had suffered in silence and immobility, since stout manacles secured his wrists, chafed his skin and held him awkwardly across a wide bench. Water, carrying an irregular and ever shifting array of flotsam, sloshed across the floorboards and kept his feet permanently cold. His wounds burned, while hunger gnawed at his belly and thirst parched his lips. Nevertheless, Strongwind Whalebone was determined to make no complaint, to offer no display of weakness that might give his captors a sense of satisfaction or reward.

Indeed, what complaint could he have made? What mere verbiage could possibly articulate the devastation that blackened his heart, rendering insignificant his own predicament? There was a greater truth that doomed his whole future, signaled the end of his dreams and visions. He knew this in the naked honesty of his own heart.

For the Lady of Brackenrock was dead.

When the ogres had shackled him and thrown him into this dank hold he had felt a sense of vague relief—not that he had survived but that he was locked away so that he could grieve in private. In that compartment he had cried like a baby until numb, bruised, and drained, he fell into a well of dreamless sleep. Whenever he was awake, he grieved, and for the weeks of the journey his only respite had come from fitful intervals of sleep.

In that solitary gloom he had come to understand something about himself, a surprising realization driven home by the insurmountable pain in his heart. Though he had pursued Moreen aggressively for years, making the case for their marriage as though he were proposing a political treaty—which, on the one hand, he was—he had never really considered the possibility that he truly loved her. Certainly he had desired her more than any other woman he knew, but this desire had been a feeling such as the hunter holds toward the prize stag. Moreen Bayguard seemed a trophy, valuable and even cherished but little more than that.

Now she was dead, and he saw how very wrong he had been.

He didn't count the days or nights; he knew only that it was a very long time later that the hatch opened and ogre guards came down the ladder, seized his chains, and hauled him up to the deck. He saw the mountain, forced his expression to remain bored despite the wonder of this place as they glided inside.

So this was Winterheim. He viewed the massive gate with a sense of detachment, didn't marvel at the enclosed harbor, barely recoiled at the great crowds of ogres cheering their rulers and jeering the new captive. As the shadows of the underground harbor embraced him, the king of the Highlanders looked up as the archway passed overhead, wondering if he was looking at the sun for the last time in his life.

That, too, didn't really seem to matter.

For the Lady of Brackenrock was dead.

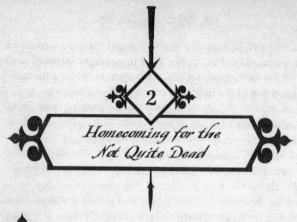

2

Homecoming for the Not Quite Dead

he Lady of Brackenrock and Kerrick Fallenbrine had to do something—fast—or they would drown together in the cold, deep waters of the White Bear Sea.

Just a moment ago their boat, the submersible craft that was the invention of the gnome called Captain Pneumo, had collided with the rocky gate of Brackenrock's harbor, crushing the cylindrical vessel's metallic prow and bringing water gushing inside with furious force. Kerrick, jammed against a collection of pipes and valves, felt a fiery pain in his right leg and guessed the limb was broken. Water poured around him, an icy torrent already surging up to his waist. Choking smoke and steam swirled through the tainted air, and the vessel lurched sickeningly.

"Head for the hatch!" cried Pneumo. "We're going down!"

The elf tried to force himself upright but was still stunned from the force of the collision. He was aware of the cold water rising past his belly, of the two gully dwarves bouncing against each other, one clawing to reach the ladder leading up from the control chamber, while the other strove irrationally to flee toward the boiler room in the stern. The first broke free to scamper upward and twist the valve, pushing the hatch open to reveal a tantalizing glimpse of sunlight, a precious waft of fresh air.

"Come on!" Moreen demanded, shaking her head groggily though her voice was strong. She forced herself to her feet and offered him a hand. "Stand up!"

"My leg!" Kerrick protested weakly, shivering under a dizzying onslaught of pain. The water was up to his chest now.

The chiefwoman seized the elf beneath the arms. She was not a big person, but her strength surprised him as she pulled him upright, dragging him toward the base of the ladder. Pneumo shouted, the gnome sprinting through the hatchway in pursuit of the gully dwarf who had fled to the stern. Kerrick shook himself and tried to stand, only to scream in agony as his leg twisted uselessly beneath him. Grabbing a rung of the ladder, he hung limply, teeth clenched as he forced himself to remain upright.

"You go first!" he barked.

Moreen looked ready to argue, which was a pretty standard look for her, but then she apparently decided that she could help him more by lifting from above than by pushing from below. She went halfway up the ladder in a single bound, then reached down to grab the scruff of Kerrick's shirt.

The elf looked up and saw the gully dwarf called Slyce pop out through the hatch. A gush of water followed as a wave swept over the low hull. Moreen shook the brine from her hair, then tightened her grip on Kerrick's collar. He grunted as she lifted, then did his best to pull upward, kicking and flailing with his good leg as he sought to stand on the cold steel rungs. Now the air was sweet and pure, spilling right through the open hatch, and the elf exerted every effort to drag himself along.

That sunlit sanctuary was elusive, apparently slipping farther away with each passing second. More cold blue water poured through the hole, blocking the daylight as the submersible slipped below the surface of the sea. Moreen cursed, and her grip broke from his collar as the force of plunging brine drove into them. Kerrick clung to the ladder with one hand, while with the other he pushed upward, pressing her against the current.

The boat was going down. Pneumo had led them this far, but he had been unable to steer between the rocky pillars marking the mouth of Brackenrock Harbor. Instead, he had rammed one of those reefs and doomed his invention and perhaps himself. Kerrick tried to see through the flowage, hoping to catch a glimpse of the gnome or Divid, the other gully dwarf, but there was only the foaming, churning sea. Once again he felt Moreen's hand on his shoulder, and he groaned at this proof that she was still within the steel hull. He couldn't let her die, especially not here, within sight of her home.

Resolutely he started to climb, allowing her to aid him, employing all of his strength in a battle against water pouring down. They were near the hatch now, but his broken leg was a dead weight, and the force of the current was too strong. The cold sea surrounded him, but he could feel no trace of the chiefwoman overhead—he could only hope she had escaped.

A sailor throughout his eight decades of life, the elf had faced nautical emergencies on many occasions and always had survived. He believed he could do the same here. A rational corner of his mind told him that he just needed to hold onto the ladder until water filled the sub then swim out through the hatch without having to battle the crushing pressure of the inward flow. The chances for the gnome and the other gully dwarf deep in the hull, sadly, were not very good—the water had them trapped far below, and he doubted they would make it out.

There was nothing he could do for them. Instead, he clutched the ladder and held his breath, feeling the current ease after another minute until it ceased altogether. He exerted himself no more than necessary, conserving the air in his lungs. When he released the ladder, the natural buoyancy of his body actually lifted him up, bore him out through the open circle of the hatch. He looked upward, toward the brightness that was not so terribly far away, and started to swim.

Again he felt the stabbing pain in his leg, agony that would not let him kick. A glimmer of panic took root in his mind. He strained with his hands, tried to kick with his good leg, but he rose very, very slowly.

Another hand took his. He knew that Moreen had dived under the surface, and the sensation gave him a strange sense of peace. She pulled, and he rode along with her. When they broke through the surface and he drew a breath, he saw a boat—a sailboat—and he knew that he and she had somehow survived the long journey home. Either that or death was a wonderful dream.

In another moment he felt strong hands pulling his arms, then the familiar feel of a deck under his body as he collapsed onto wooden planks. He saw people, including a familiar round face beneath a shock of black hair—Mouse, but what was he doing here?—and finally succumbed to a sensation of peace, warmth, and silence.

━━━━◆━◆━◆━━━━

Moreen Bayguard lay on the deck, too exhausted even to cough. That weariness was almost her undoing, as her breath gurgled in watery lungs and a pleasant darkness began to close across the vision of her one good eye. Her eye patch, the flap she wore over the ruined socket, had been washed away by the sea, and salt burned in the scarred flesh of her face.

Someone wrapped strong arms around her and squeezed with crushing force. The reaction was instantaneous: She spewed a gout of brine across the pine planks then drew a ragged, gulping breath. Again she coughed and again, and slowly the darkness pulled back. Weakly she rolled upon her side, looking up to see a young man's face, the brown skin furrowed into lines of dire concern.

"Mouse?" she said weakly. "I'm dreaming."

"It's me," said her tribemate, one of Moreen's most capable aides—and her lifelong friend. "Don't try to talk. Just breathe."

"What about Kerrick?" she tried to ask, ignoring his advice and paying for it with another bout of choking and gagging.

"Bruni's working on him. He's breathing. The little fellow seems to be okay, too."

The chiefwoman turned her head and saw the elf, prostrate upon the deck nearby, with the unmistakeably large shape of Bruni leaning over him, wiping his brow with a towel. The heights of Brackenrock rose just beyond, as the sailboat stood in the water just outside the entrance to the harbor. Just beyond she recognized Slyce, or at least the gully dwarf's hindquarters, as the stubby castaway was bending over to look through a hatch, his head and upper torso sticking down through the hole in the deck.

Questions churned in her mind. What boat was this? How had it come to be here, just outside the entrance to her homeport?

Again ignoring the young man's advice, she tried to push herself into a sitting position. The sailboat had to be Mouse's, she realized—his home-built craft, dubbed *Marlin*, which had been nearly ready for launch when she and Kerrick had departed for Dracoheim. Mouse had taken it onto the sea . . . and now she noticed that he had passengers, strange folk she didn't know.

She saw two burly men, unmistakably Highlanders, watching her suspiciously from the foredeck. One of these was huge, nearly as large as Bruni, displaying a gold tooth as he glowered and clenched his jaw. The second was an older man with hair and beard of gray. His expression was unreadable.

"Who are they?" Moreen asked Mouse, as he helped her to a bench in the sailboat's cockpit.

"The big one is Barq One-Tooth, the other Thedric Drake. They're Highlander chieftains, and I picked them up on the east shore to bring them to Brackenrock."

"What do they want?"

"They want to know what happened to Strongwind Whalebone. That is, they want their king back," the young Arktos sailor said grimly.

"Strongwind . . ." Moreen declared weakly, despairing anew at the bitter memory. "He was captured by the ogre king . . . he created a diversion, allowed Kerrick and I to get into the castle."

"The ogres have him now? They've taken him to their stronghold?" replied Mouse, his expression bleak.

Moreen nodded, then gestured to the two thanes.

"Tell them—" she began to say, then paused as another interval of coughing seized her. Even as she had started to speak, she hadn't known what she was going to say.

"Tell them that I am going to get him back as soon as I can get ashore and make a plan."

Kerrick looked around and quickly realized that he was lying in one of the nicer suites in the upper reaches of Brackenrock's keep. He could see the midnight sun through the south-facing window, low and pale over the distant peaks of the Glacier Range, the rugged mountains beyond the Tusker Escarpment. His first thought was that he was dreaming, but when he shifted in the soft bed he felt a twinge in his right leg and remembered everything: the voyage back to this fortress, the desperate escape from the sinking boat, and the miraculous appearance of a sailboat on the surface of the sea.

The next thing he saw was Mouse, seated on a chair beside the bed, studying him worriedly.

"How's the leg?" asked the Arktos sailor.

The elf blinked in surprise, stretching the limb that had been badly broken when he lost consciousness. "Not bad at all," he replied. "Have I been out for weeks, or did Dinekki have something to do with that?"

"Her healing spells are the best in all the Icereach," Mouse said with a smile. "She said you'd be jogging around by tomorrow. No, you haven't been out long—we brought you, Moreen, and that little fellow ashore just a few hours ago."

"Captain Pneumo was lost, and Divid, too," sighed the elf, feeling a weary sadness. "Still, if you hadn't been sailing past when you were, I don't think any of us would have made it to shore."

Exhausted, Kerrick leaned back and closed his eyes.

"I still can't believe it!" the young Arktos man said, shaking his head in amazement. "I thought I was the only boat on the sea, and then people start popping up on both sides of me. To find out it was you and the Lady . . . and that little fellow. What kind of a person is he, anyway?"

"A gully dwarf," Kerrick said with a grimace. "Not the most appealing folks of Krynn, but he was a loyal crewman, and . . . and he lost his best friend."

"He didn't seem too broken up about it. He was pilfering fish from the market down at the waterfront within a minute or two after landing. Moreen had to talk Old Cutscale out of throwing him into the harbor. Now he's drunk, I think—he found his way into the cook's beer barrel."

"Yes, that's Slyce," the elf agreed. "I'm glad he had the sense to climb up when the boat started to sink."

"You," Mouse continued, "how . . . why were you coming back underwater? What about *Cutter*?"

The very word, the name of his beloved sailboat, nearly broke Kerrick's heart. He looked at his friend, very possibly the only man in all the Icereach who could understand the depths of his attachment to the boat that had been left to him by his father.

"She sank," he explained, trying to hold back the anguish. "We accidentally rammed the same metal boat that brought us so close to Brackenrock. Staved in the bow, and she went down like a stone."

"All your gold . . . it was on board?" Mouse said, remembering.

"Aye. Eight years' work—and I would let it go without regret, if I could only have my *Cutter* back."

"She was a beauty," the man agreed. "Like a swan, while poor *Marlin* is at best a duckling."

Kerrick closed his eyes again. He didn't have the energy to think about his future—and now, without his boat, the course of his life seemed destined to be guided by forces, powers, beyond his control. He was in a land where the sun disappeared for three months at a time, where icebergs the size of mountains loomed in foggy ocean mists, where he had grown accustomed to surviving on hard bread and fiery, intoxicating warqat, on meat and fish and little more.

If he had been in a mood of fairness, he would have acknowledged that there was in fact much more to the Icereach than this. He had great friends among these loyal people, the Arktos—and among the Highlanders as well.

There were summer days of literally endless sunlight, vistas of sea and fjord to explore, places where neither elf nor human nor ogre had ever ventured. Above all things Kerrick Fallabrine was a sailor, and the Icereach, notably the coastlines of the White Bear and Dracoheim Seas, made as thrilling a nautical life as anywhere upon the world.

At least, they did when those waters weren't frozen solid, layered in mast-high snowdrifts and scoured by winds so bitter they threatened to tear flesh from bone. That was the side of the Icereach he pictured looming now, ahead of him a lifetime of such winters. Moreen would be gone after fifty or sixty of them—

He stopped short. This was a dangerous line of thought, and he had schooled himself never to go there. With his own elf blood likely to grant him five or more centuries of life, it would be foolish to nurture an attachment to any human. He had proven a useful companion, even ally, to the chiefwoman of the Arktos, and she in turn had been an ally and a friend to him. That was as far as it went, as far as it could ever go.

It did not occur to him to blame her for the loss of his boat or his gold. True, he had been bearing her upon a mission of her own devise—a mission that never would have been undertaken if not for her determination, the force of her will, and her courage, but he had gone willingly enough. At least, that's the way he chose to remember it now.

"What about Moreen? Is she all right?"

Mouse grimaced, and Kerrick felt a stab of fear. "What? Is she injured?"

"No, not yet anyway."

"What's wrong, then?"

"Maybe you remember those two men on my boat? They were Highlander thanes—I was bringing them here by sea, to join a dozen of their fellows who marched here overland. They wanted to talk to Moreen."

"And?"

"She told them that Strongwind Whalebone has been captured by the ogres that he's been taken to Winterheim as a slave."

"Yes—I'm sure they were unhappy to hear that their king has been taken by the enemy, but surely they don't blame Moreen for that?"

"Well, maybe not in so many words, but Moreen seems to blame herself."

"What do you mean?" asked the elf in growing alarm.

"Just that she spoke to the thanes as soon as she landed. She told them that she intends to go to Winterheim, to enter the ogre fortress, and to bring Strongwind Whalebone out alive."

Kerrick slumped back in the bed, staring up at the smoke-limned ceiling beams. He, like Moreen, had witnessed Strongwind's capture, and like Moreen he regretted it deeply, but he never would have considered such a mad scheme of rescue. No human who had ever been hauled off to Winterheim had escaped the ogre clutches, not in the long history of the Icereach. He chuckled, soon laughing out loud.

"Are you all right?" Mouse asked, concerned.

"Of course," the elf responded. "I wonder, has there ever been a leader like Moreen Bayguard?"

"I don't think so," the Arktos sailor replied, allowing a smile to cross his own features. "I'm going to go with her, of course," he added.

"I know you are," said Kerrick, "and Bruni, naturally, and all those Highlanders. Why, it will be a regular war party—a suicide march to glory!"

Mouse scowled. "I don't know about that. You must stay here, of course, and get better—"

"Stay here?" Kerrick snorted, laughing again. "I wouldn't miss this for the world!"

A fter his weeks in the hold of the ogre galley, the mere act of walking across the deck and down the gangplank hurt Strongwind. His muscles felt crippled, and the chains weighed him down even further. Like an old man in pain, he shuffled across the crowded dock, still aware of little beyond the clean air in this vast place.

He only vaguely noticed the attention falling upon this ship, the populace of Winterheim gathered to greet their returning king and queen. As a side curiosity, the crowd of ogres also examined this unkempt, bedraggled human prisoner—Strongwind heard murmurs of interest, a few snorts and chuckles of amusement, as he climbed the half dozen stone steps leading up from the wharf to the broad, flat expanse of the harbor square.

Something about the crowd infuriated him, and his first instinct was to raise his chained fists, to rail and curse at these ignorant brutes, yet he realized immediately that such a reaction would only entertain and amuse them. There was no way, at least not here and now, that he could frighten or even worry them.

For now he drew himself up straight, ignoring the pain that tried to twist his spine. He bent his arms into curls, showing them that the weight of the chains was not enough to drag him down. He stalked up the steps as if he were the homecoming king, his glare haughty and disdainful as he swept it around the vast, underground harbor.

Despite his façade, he could not help but be mightily impressed, even awed, by this place. The harbor consisted of an open circle of water connected by a wide channel that led out through the still-opened gates. Each of those massive slabs of stone was moved, he saw, by the labor of hundreds of human slaves hauling on cables that turned huge capstans. Those slaves were watching him now, and he acknowledged them with a slight nod of his head, all the while marveling at the engineering that allowed such unthinkable weight to be manipulated by such mundane means.

The sun, low in the northern sky, poured brilliant light across the placid water and broad waterfront. There were three great mooring slips in the harbor, each a gash in the dock wide enough to allow a large ship to slide in between a pair of bracketing wharves. *Goldwing* occupied the central of these berths, while those to the right and left were empty. Beyond the wharves a series of wide ramps and stairways led to the vast plaza, raised ten or twelve feet above the dock height. It was on this square that most of the ogres were gathered. They made a festive crowd, cheering loudly as the king and queen, who had been first off the boat, passed them by, then turning their attention to the crewman and their lone prisoner.

Strongwind heard a few jeers and catcalls but paid them no mind as he looked around, studying this place with a tactician's eye. He watched the two monarchs enter a cagelike enclosure and was amazed to see this compartment start to move upward. Scrutinizing the scene, he saw another group of slaves, a score or more of them, laboring to pull the chains that controlled some sort of geared mechanism.

He saw that a circular atrium rose high above. Though the heights of that vertical shaft were lost in shadows far overhead, it was easy to imagine it extending nearly all the way to the mountain's summit. The atrium was ringed by balconies, more of these than he could count, rising upward to form a vast chimney. The royal couple rose higher and higher, riding a wave of cheers toward the heights, and Strongwind had an idle thought: if those twenty slaves suddenly let go of their chains, would the king's cage come crashing all the way back down to the waterfront? It was an idea that might bear investigation in the future.

More onlookers were gathered at the lower levels, looking down upon the sunlit harbor. One of these in particular caught his eye. An ogress studied him from a balcony perhaps a hundred feet overhead, and he met her gaze with a cool inspection of his own. She was unusually voluptuous for one of her race—unlike the blocky and bearlike ogre queen, this one was graced with an impressive bosom, her shape tapering to a narrow waist. The whole was wrapped in a dress of bright red, a color that stood out rather shockingly from the white or brown fur and buckskin garments worn by most of Winterheim's populace. Her face was not bestial but was rather attractive in a full-fleshed way, and it creased into a sly smile as she met his gaze. She twisted one hand in a lazy, casual wave.

A prod in the back shoved the captive forward, and Strongwind staggered, rattling his chains, barely keeping his balance. He whirled to confront a leering guardsman bearing a wide-bladed, blunt-tipped sword.

"Keep moving," growled the ogre with a cruel sneer. "You don't wanna get walked on, you don't!"

Drawing himself erect again, Strongwind continued forward, following the escort of several royal guards—they were called Grenadiers, he remembered—as they broke away from the main body of returning warriors. The Highlander was taken into a lofty tunnel leading away from the harbor, where coldness and shadow once again settled around him. Conscious of the same bullying swordsman behind him, he managed to keep pace with his captors until they arrived at a large wooden door.

This was pulled open from the inside to revealed a torchlit cavern where a few ogres sat idly at a large table. These looked up with grunts of greeting for the arriving party. The human king guessed that this was some kind of garrison room for the ogre warriors. There were many benches along the walls, and swords and bucklers dangling from equipment racks.

Strongwind was pushed again, the blow this time hard enough to knock him down. He spun about on the floor, pushing himself to a crouching position, glaring into the face of the sneering guard.

That ogre raised his sword and rested it across his shoulder with a casual gesture, then gestured to another who came forward with a ring of iron keys.

"Take th' cuffs off," said the bully. "No escape chance for him no more, not from Winterheim."

Strongwind rubbed his wrists as the manacles were released then stretched his legs, allowing the chains to be pulled free. Only when he had worked out some of the kinks did he slowly rise, eyeing the sword-wielding ogre from the corner of his eye.

When he was standing, the Highlander arched his back and extended his arms, continuing the charade of loosening his creaking joints. Most of the other ogres from his escort were unclasping buckles, sitting down to remove their boots, or hanging their weapons from the equipment hooks. They chortled crude greetings to their comrades, exchanged a few rough clasps or thumping blows to each other's backs and shoulders.

Strongwind was, for the moment, left under the watch of his lone tormentor. Clenching his fist, the king whirled suddenly and sent a hard punch directly into the nose of the bully. That guardsman roared loudly, dropping his sword as he staggered back, both hands clutching his bleeding snout.

"That was for knocking me down," Strongwind said, calmly eyeing the sputtering brute.

The captive's coolness only seemed to inflame the beast. "He's mine!" he roared, waving back his comrades who were advancing to restrain Strongwind. "Insolent human scum—you could have long life here! You are too stupid for that—and now you die!"

The Highlander kicked the sword out of the way and flexed his knees, fists raised to meet the onslaught. There were worse things, he thought, than dying in battle with a bullying captor—and he planned to get in a few more good licks before he fell. The ogre put his head down and charged. Strongwind punched again, a roundhouse blow landing on the brute's ear. The human ducked away before the long arms could trap him then bounced up again, fists raised as he waited for the next rush.

"Hold!"

The roar came from the entrance to the guardroom where another tall ogre stood, glaring at the guard who still snorted in rage. Looking at the crimson flow from the smashed snout, Strongwind smiled tightly. In his mind, this ogre would forever be known as Bloodsnout.

"Lord Forlane!" shouted one of the guards, and the whole company snapped to attention—all except Bloodsnout, that is, who was trying to stem the flow from his nostrils as he knelt and groped for the sword that the Highlander had kicked across the room.

The arriving ogre was dressed in what Strongwind took to be noble finery. His bearskin cloak was clean and pure white, descending all the way to his calves. His boots of walrus skin were polished to a bright shine, and though his garments were mere tanned leather, they were clasped with a belt of solid gold, and many chains of the same precious metal dangled from a neck as thick as the trunk of a pine tree.

"The prisoner was to be brought here merely for unshackling!" growled the lord, who seemed to have fixed his attention on Bloodsnout as the source of his displeasure. "Why is it that I find you in the midst of a full-scale revolt?"

"He—he struck me," declared the bleeding ogre, with a wicked glare at the human. "I was making ready to defend myself."

"A sword is of better use in the hand than on the floor," snorted Lord Forlane in amusement. Several ogres chortled appreciatively, ignoring a murderous glance from their bleeding comrade. The noble turned to regard Strongwind shrewdly. "I have instructions t'bring you to the slaves quarters on the Royal Level. Will I need to shackle you to get you there?"

The Highlander king made a short, stiff bow, recognizing a change in his circumstances of which he was ready to take advantage. "It would be my honor to accompany your lordship," he said.

"Very well." Forlane's chuckle was deep, like gravel shifting in the belly of a gold-grinder. "Clean this mess up," he snapped at the sullen guard, gesturing at the red smears across the floor. "Wash your face while you're at it." He gestured to another guard. "Give the slave two lashes for punishment—he must learn that violence against our kind will not be tolerated."

Strongwind had no chance even to react as a whip snapped, slashing across the bruised skin of his back.

Fiery agony tore across his skin. He grunted and staggered forward but managed to brace himself enough for the second lash to hold his position. Though he swayed unsteadily and drew a deep gasp of breath, he did not fall to his knees. Instead, he glared at Lord Forlane with narrowed eyes and a new sense of appraisal. The noble seemed to be taking stock of the prisoner as well. He grunted a sound of amusement, like half of a chuckle then pointed to a pair of grenadiers.

"You two, come with me—keep an eye on this fellow."

Immediately they stepped forward, one taking each of Strongwind's arms as they started toward the door through which Lord Forlane was already departing. The Highlander felt Bloodsnout's eyes boring into his back as he followed the lord from the chamber. Strongwind resolved to be alert for that one. The bullying ogre seemed like one who would carry a grudge.

He felt certain there would be a lot of grudges and much cause for revenge in this place.

———————◆◆◆———————

"He will make arrangements to see that trollop again, probably within a matter of hours," Stariz hissed. "I want him followed—I want to know the place where they meet and how long they are together!"

"Yes, my queen, of course," replied Garnet Drake, her most trusted spy.

Garnet was a human, but he had been born and raised amid the slaves of Winterheim. The queen had no doubt of his loyalty, for her favor had given him a status among his kind. She saw that he received gifts of good food and beer, and in return, he did her bidding and brought her word of all that happened throughout the city of Winterheim.

Now, as usual, the object of her curiosity was none other than her own royal husband. For just a moment Stariz looked longingly at the tub of once-steaming water, the bath that had been drawn for her by her personal slaves. How good it would feel to immerse in that soothing warmth! She forced that thought, that longing, aside, recognizing it for the sign of weakness that it was.

No doubt her husband had already proceeded to his own bath, was no doubt dreaming of one or more of the fanciful pleasures that drew so much of his limited attention. For he was weak, Grimwar Bane, weak in resolution and determination, areas in which his wife was strong. For a moment she gave way to another kind of longing, an idle wish that the ogre king would acknowledge the precious strengths of his queen. How could he not see that it was her traits and intelligence that had carried them as far as they had gone together?

Indeed, Grimwar Bane—with his clever queen—had the potential to be one of Suderhold's great rulers, a truly historical figure. Stariz knew her history well and understood that this kingdom had once been great, a colony formed of the ancient ogre realm that had held sway over all of civilized Krynn. It had been thousands of years since those days, however, and that distant ogre empire had long since crumbled.

She thought bitterly of the second ship of the royal fleet. *Hornet* had been designed by an elf captive and built with the labor of human slaves, but Stariz almost cried as she remembered the blast that had destroyed that prize ship. She almost cried, too, recalling that her most powerful ally, Dowager Queen Hannareit, was dead. Now everything was up to her, Stariz ber Glacierheim ber Bane.

There was only one good thing about the recent disaster. Stariz was convinced that the Elf Messenger had perished in the blast. She knew he had entered Dracoheim, and her god had warned her that the elf was a harbinger of doom. Indeed he had been a bane of her existence since his arrival in Icereach some eight years earlier. The knowledge that he was dead brought her some small degree of pleasure.

Garnet Drake was still standing there, patiently waiting for his mistress's next words. He bowed as she raised her eyes to his.

"Does the trollop still maintain her usual apartments?"

"In fact, no, my queen. In the recent weeks she has been spending time preparing a new place, a terrace house overlooking the middle levels of the city. She has ordered new chairs, two dozen bear furs, a hundred lamps for the place, and . . ." Garnet coughed regretfully.

"Speak!" demanded the queen. "What?"

"She commissioned the carpenters to create a new bed . . . gave specific orders to the master slave that it must be delivered before the king returned from his campaign."

Stariz trembled, felt her face flushing. For a moment she couldn't speak, could only clench her teeth, jutting the twin blunt tusks upward from her lower jaw. "The impertinent wench!" she spat, finally. "Is there no end to her shamelessness?"

"Perhaps your majesty may take some comfort in the fact that, among the slaves and ogres alike, there seems to be no knowledge of the king's . . . indiscretions. At least she has been delicate enough to prevent the affair from becoming common gossip."

"That is no comfort!" growled Stariz, her withering glare fixing upon Garnet Drake, who could only bow in humble apology. "No comfort at all! Now, go, do your job!"

The spy slave departed to set his agents in motion. No move of the king's or of Thraid Dimmarkull's would go unreported, but in the silence of her chambers, alone with her thoughts, Stariz understood that it was no longer enough to simply maintain knowledge of her husband's acts. No . . . the time had come to for her to take action of her own.

Once more she looked at the tub, its waters growing cold. Her skin itched. The sea voyage had left her hair crusted with salt, and the crude accommodations of the ship's cabin made her feel filthy and unclean, but still the bath would have to wait, her comfort again overruled by priority.

Pausing only to take her mask and robe, symbols of her status as high priestess, from the stand where they awaited her, she left the royal apartment and started along the promenade.

She needed to go to the temple to pray and to meditate and practice the magic of her arcane lord. As always, she would let the will of Gonnas the Strong show her the way.

Grimwar Bane ambled down the corridor leading away from the royal quarters. There were others—slaves and ogres alike—about, but his wife was off to the temple and would be kept busy for a long time. That gave him, at last, his chance at freedom.

He kept his eyes on the human slave, Wandcourt, who was two dozen paces ahead of him. He knew that Stariz would have spies lurking, so Thraid Dimmarkull's slave and the ogre king were making it appear that they were not together. It was important that Grimwar observe the route that Wandcourt took, because that was the path to his goal.

The man turned into an alley, one of the many passages that gave access between the great stone edifices of Winterheim's royal level. This one followed directly below the outer wall of the palace. The turn was not unexpected, but the king ambled past that alley with apparent indifference—they had agreed that it would be too obvious if both of them turned into the same, little-used passageway.

Instead, Grimwar passed the next block of buildings, elegant shops where gold items and rare spices were purveyed, and turned at the alley beyond. He hastened along the shadowy passageway until he reached the even darker connecting route—generally used only by slaves—behind the sprawling edifices lining the Promenade. This passage was shadowy and littered with refuse, but the king took no note of these distractions. Instead, he sought and found the black space to his left, just where Wandcourt had said it would be. In another second Grimwar darted through, then heard a soft rumble as the secret door was closed behind him. Only then did the slave unmask his lamp, the pale beams of light revealing nothing more than a small landing and a steep stairway leading down through the bedrock of the mountain.

"Do you think we were seen?" whispered the king.

"I do not think so, sire," replied the human. "There was a shadow, as of one entering the alley behind you, but by that time you were already at the rear of the building. If it was someone following you, he will not know where you have gone from there."

"Good. Lead on," ordered the monarch, impatience adding an edge to his voice.

Immediately, the slave started downward, holding the light to illuminate the steps for the king, even though in the darkness ogre eyes were much more keen than a human's. Still, Wandcourt apparently knew this route well, for he proceeded with good haste and no stumbling.

They went down the stairs for a long time. The terrace level, after all, was near the middle of Winterheim's ascending layers, while the royal palace was at the very top. All the while the king could hear his heart pounding in his ears, and it wasn't from the exertion of the descent. His thoughts were churning, anticipation bringing sweat to his palms, rendering his very breathing feverish with desire.

Finally they came to another door, one that Wandcourt knocked on discreetly before pushing it open. Grimwar all but pushed past the man, who had enough experience with these trysts to step out of the way. The king took little note of his surroundings, rushing through a small anteroom as a door opened beyond.

She was waiting for him, as he had known she would be, and she was even more beautiful than he remembered. Her gown, that silken shimmer of crimson that was so unlike anything else in the city of Winterheim, did little to conceal the voluptuous curves of her body. Her lips were rouged in the same color, and her eyes sparkled with joy as the king stepped forward and swept her into his brawny arms.

"My Grimwar!" she whispered, pulling him close. Somewhere behind he heard a door close and knew that the slave had withdrawn. "How I missed you!"

Still clinched, the two lovers moved sideways into another room, the boudoir. Hastily the king kicked the door shut. He kissed her with crushing force, almost angrily, and she met his embrace with passion of her own. His hands cupped her flesh, and she moaned, still kissing him. His knees were shaking, and he needed to draw a breath, but he wouldn't release her. Instead, they remained together, moving slowly across the sumptuously appointed room. The king only cast a sideways glance for a second, just to make sure that he could find the bed.

The Temple of Gonnas was a sacred chamber, huge and dark, located in the highest quarter of Winterheim's Nobles Level, just below the royal palace. This was Stariz's favorite place in the world, the great room where she truly felt her own power and at the same time knew the might of one who was so much greater than her mere mortal self.

The image of Gonnas the Strong looked down at her, an immense statue of slick black stone standing three times or more the height of a large ogre. The Willful One was represented as a strapping bull of her kind, an image that bore an uncanny resemblance to the glowering visage of her husband, the king, but where Grimwar Bane was lazy and vacillating, subject to the temptations of the flesh and the distractions of an idle mind, Gonnas was implacable and stern.

These were two traits that Stariz admired very much and tried to emulate to the best of her very considerable abilities.

"O Gonnas my Lord, my Immortal Master, please forgive my failures. . . . I return to you now not with the victory that you so verily deserve but with a plea for guidance and wisdom, for knowledge of the truths you may help me to see and of the actions that I should take in your ever-awful name."

The high priestess pressed her masked face to the floor, to the smooth black obsidian that was as shiny and dark as the statue itself. Her great face-mask, the grotesque and exaggerated image of the god, seemed to meld to the flat surface, and she felt her robes spread out like oil across warm water. Even her flesh seemed to flatten and to merge, as if she was no more than a rug, worthy only to cushion the footsteps of her all-powerful master.

She felt the presence of Gonnas as that crushing weight came to bear upon her. A lesser priestess would have cried out in agony—indeed, many an acolyte had perished upon the first sensation of this blessing—but to Stariz ber Bane the pressure of her lord was a blessing, even an ecstacy. She gasped in pleasure as she felt the weight increase, and she knew that her god was pleased— with her, if not with all of his flock. The high priestess couldn't breathe, but that was no matter, for it was now the power of Gonnas that brought oxygen to her flesh and vitality to her mind.

She would remain thus as long as it pleased the Willful One, and every second would give her naught but pleasure. Her mind was vibrant and active, full of thoughts of glory, of the punishment of her people's enemies, and of the aggrandizement of her god and her land.

Slowly, with excruciating and tantalizing glimpses, the will of Gonnas became known to her. She saw the human slave, the king they had captured on Dracoheim, sliced open so that his blood might fall into the god's ever-hungry maw. The image grew within her mind until she saw that Grimwar Bane was watching, all the ogres of Winterheim, and all of the slaves as well were watching the sacrifice. Stariz knew that her first instinct was right, and she knew a flush of pleasure at that thought.

"It shall be as you will, my master . . . the human king will be sacrificed at Autumnblight . . . and all of Winterheim shall behold his suffering, his fate, and your unending glory. . . ."

There was another squeeze of power from her lord, and she cried out in sheer joy under the merciless pressure of his own pleasure. It made her heart swell with love to know that she had pleased the will of the powerful god.

Stariz almost lost consciousness, so consuming was the grip, the crushing might, of Gonnas. With an effort of will she kept her wits, murmuring words of praise and exultation, promising over and over again that the slave king would die on the altar of the great, summer-end feast known as Autumnblight. This was what she had wanted, and it gave her great pleasure to know that her own wishes were so in tune with those of her true god.

Only then, as the last tendrils of awareness finally escaped her, did the Willful One remind her of her husband, Grimwar Bane, whispering that he could become a great king of Suderhold, perhaps the greatest in a thousand years. She was the key to that greatness, for she was strong where he was weak, and only through her diligence and care could that majesty be achieved.

Though it tore at her heart to hear the command from her god, she understood the last inkling of his will, and vowed to obey.

For the ogre king must be watched, very carefully indeed.

4

The Pledge

Broadnose did not know how long he had been held in this cell, though it was many days now, more than all of his fingers and toes added together. The big ogre, once commander of an elite company of royal Grenadiers, had resigned himself to spending the rest of his life as a captive of the humans. He wondered why they were doing this, holding him here, locked up. They had made no move to hurt or kill him, which surprised him. Neither did they make him work, so he had to conclude that he was not a slave. They fed him and even cared for his wounds in order to keep him alive. Funny creatures, these humans.

Probably they would kill him when they got around to it, Broadnose figured. After all, he had killed many of them in his turn and had been intent upon further bloodshed when he had been captured in the Mouse-warrior's ambush. His raiding party had plundered villages, massacred farmers, destroyed homesteads, all as his king and queen had commanded. He had been captured by his enemies, after all of his own troops had been killed in the battle.

A door of steel-banded wood prevented him from making any move to escape, with only the narrow slit at the bottom sliding open once a day to produce a wooden plate of food and a small gourd of water. Aside from a few perfunctory nudges, he hadn't investigated the strength of that door—and besides, what would he do if he got out of this cell? His king was far away, and there was no one to give him orders. He contented himself with sitting here, looking forward to his next meal.

He reached up to his face, lifted the dried leather patch, and touched the rough scab that had formed over his missing eye. The wound no longer pained him, and he imagined that it would make him look fierce if he ever got out of this dark hole. There didn't seem much chance of that.

Every once in awhile a human woman came to visit him. She was large, almost the size of an ogress, and possessed of a strange kindness. She was called Bruni by her kind, and Broadnose thought of her as Bruni-warrior. Well did he remember her ferocity when she had wielded the captured Axe of Gonnas in defense of her fortress. He had great respect for her strength and her courage.

It was she who had led him to this cell after he had been brought here to Brackenrock, the only survivor of his ill-fated raiding party. Periodically after that she came to personally bring him his food, and she would talk to him for a little while. She seemed curious about Winterheim and willingly shared much about Brackenrock. Oddly enough, she seemed like a better companion than most of the ogresses he had known. Her round moon of a face, with those large, dark eyes, Broadnose found pleasant, even beautiful.

Those visits were rare, and the rest of his life passed in a daze of gloom and boredom. He wondered when they would kill him and how they would do it, but so far they hadn't even kicked or punched him. The skinny old shaman had even worked magic over his damaged eye to make sure that it wouldn't . . . what had she said? Become "affected" or something? His vision remained limited to his one good eye, but the wounded socket had ceased the burning and blistering that had started to become a real distraction.

His cell was far down in the fortress dungeon, and at the end of a long corridor. There was no one else anywhere near him, so when he heard footsteps approaching this day, he knew they were coming to his cell. He expected his usual feeding—indeed, his stomach growled audibly as the footsteps drew near—but was surprised when instead of the food slot moving to the side he heard a key turn in the lock.

The door opened to reveal the Bruni-warrior, and Broadnose brightened. She was accompanied this time by a small woman with dark hair. He remembered her. She, like himself, was missing an eye, though she wore a clean sealskin patch over the socket. She was the chief of this place, Broadnose recalled. Pushing himself to his feet, though he had to stoop in the low-ceilinged chamber, he grunted a noise of welcome.

"Hello, Broadnose," said Bruni. "This is Moreen, the Lady of Brackenrock. She would like to speak with you."

"I will talk to the lady," he agreed.

"Bruni tells me that you know much of Winterheim," Moreen began. "It sounds like a truly wondrous place."

"Big. And old," he noted, pleased at her flattering words. "The great Seagate is a marvel to see—opened by an army of slaves! The channel is deep enough for any ship, and wide enough that the galley oars can be extended."

"Surely there must be other gates," she suggested, "for when one or two ogres want to leave, they don't go out on the galley?"

"Oh, no," he said. "Many gates are on the mountainside. Lofty and stone, they look over the Black Ice Bay or the Icewall. Many ogres live at these gates. I was garrison captain of the Bearded Glacier Gate for many years."

"All over the mountain?" Moreen squinted pensively. "Is there one that is far away . . . that is not on the mountain?"

"Not to the city," Broadnose said. "Nope, the only way there is Icewall Pass. That goes into the Moongarden—still a long way from Winterheim!"

"The Moongarden. Sounds magical."

"Old magic. Stones glow in big cave, make sunlight for lots of stuff to grow. Slaves work there, keep the food coming even in winter."

"Where is this place? I would like to see it," Moreen said.

"It's under the ground," Broadnose said, shaking his head, trying to graciously conceal his opinion that this woman was clearly not very bright. "You can't see it, not unless you climb the Icewall and go in!"

"Climbing the Icewall . . . that sounds very difficult," she allowed. "There must be a way into this Icewall Pass?"

Broadnose grunted and nodded. "There is, but it starts from escarpment, where the tuskers live. Don't think they'd let you go there."

"No," said the small woman, her eyes narrowing as she thought about something the ogre captive didn't understand. "No, the tuskers wouldn't like that, not at all. . . ."

Kerrick stood upon the familiar rampart of Brackenrock and looked over the vista surrounding this proud, ancient fortress. He had climbed to the highest portion of the keep until finally he emerged onto a wall-top palisade flanked by two crennalated battlements. To his left was the courtyard, where people—Highlanders and Arktos together—went about their tasks in busy good humor. A small market buzzed to the sounds of barter, as produce, goats, tools, and leather goods were traded. There were tanning racks where Arktos were hanging pelts to dry and a long roasting trough where a dozen Highlanders, men who had spent the past few years living in the fortress, were making charcoal. Beyond the walls were more people, gathering and pitching tents and huts on the tundra as humans came from all across the Icereach, drawn by the summons of Moreen Bayguard's bold quest.

The elf looked to the right, where the vista was open and empty. He saw the green hills rolling away toward the south, leading toward the fertile lands known as the Whitemoor. The rugged horizon of the escarpment and the white outline of the Glacier Peaks rose beyond, just at the limit of his view, and he knew that still farther away the massif of Winterheim rose toward the sky. He had seen that mountain from the sea and had been awed by its majesty, its sheer size. His many journeys along the coasts of Ansalon had never brought him within sight of a comparable peak.

His leg was barely sore, so effective had been old Dinekki's healing spell. He had climbed this long stairway with ease, relishing the freedom to get about after the weeks of confinement in the tiny submersible. He loved the sight of clouds, of the broad vista of tundra and ocean offered by this lofty vantage. His thoughts were as light, as free as those clouds, and for a time they roamed the heavens, wandering across the landscape of his life. He thought of glorious, crystalline Silvanesti, of soft lute music and delicate elf ladies.

Naturally, his musings grew more focused, turning back to this place, to her. She was a remarkable woman,

Moreen Bayguard. The elf chuckled at the realization that he was glad of her new quest, glad that he had a cause.

Of course, on the surface it seemed as though she was mad—completely insane! She was down in the Brackenrock dungeon right now talking to the ogre prisoner Mouse had captured earlier that summer, seeking some idea as to how to enter the stronghold of Winterheim. Meanwhile, Highlander and Arktos warriors were gathering here, camping on the tundra around the fortress, awaiting the commands of their chiefwoman or the thanes. All came willingly and showed great courage in joining this desperate errand—though it was certainly hard for any of them to believe they even had a chance of success.

"I can't see how we'll ever get into the place, much less bring Strongwind Whalebone out alive!" the elf said aloud, staring into the southern distance as if expecting the landscape to respond to his statement.

"How do you know?"

The answer came from right behind him, so calmly and quickly that Kerrick almost jumped over the wall in surprise. Instead he spun about, recognizing the voice, certain that he was going mad.

There he was, leaning casually against the parapet, smiling nonchalantly as if he'd been walking beside Kerrick the whole way.

"Cor-Coraltop Netfisher?" the elf stammered, gaping dumbly. "But . . . but . . . how are you even here?"

"I asked first," said the kender, lifting his diminutive frame up to look between two of the stone ramparts, kicking his feet against the wall like an impatient child. "How do you know we'll never get into Winterheim?"

"Do you know what she's planning?" asked the elf after a moment, almost stunned into silence by the mysterious appearance of his old sailing companion, the kender whom Kerrick alone had ever seen—and then only aboard *Cutter*, when he had presumed himself to be alone, far from shore in the lonely ocean of the south. "How did you get here? I was afraid I'd never see you again when my boat sank!" Only then did he consider the kender's exact words. "Wait. Do you mean to say that you're coming along with us? To Winterheim?"

"Too many questions! To the first, yes I know what she plans—she's going to rescue Strongwind, to bring him home. I think that's pretty brave," Coraltop acknowledged. "As to the last, well, of course, thanks for the invite—I mean, a chance to see Winterheim! Who wouldn't want to go? A whole city inside a mountain, they say. Well, that's not the kind of thing you find just anywhere—not unless you hang around with dwarves, I mean, and who'd want to do that?"

"Not me," Kerrick chuckled. "I'm just as happy to have landed among humans. There are times I even prefer them to elves!"

"Well, of course. Humans are lots of fun. More lively, too. Elves can be so . . . well, serious. They don't laugh much, have you ever noticed? Present company excepted, of course."

Kerrick did laugh then, softly, so as not to break the mood of the moment. He relished this time with Coraltop and was certain that if someone else was to stir, the kender would perform his usual vanishing act. He felt a rush of affection for the little fellow.

"The Tusker Escarpment, too—of course you'll have to get a look at that. Though I'd be careful about that part—you might want to take some strong drink along."

"Strong drink? Why?" Kerrick asked.

The kender continued as though he hadn't heard. "Too bad I can't come with you for the whole way. You know I'm really pretty busy, have lots of things to do—"

"Of course," Kerrick replied, growing exasperated, remembering the art of conversation the way it was practiced with the kender—as if they were always talking about two different things. "Maybe I should ask where you've been. You disappear for years, then pop back up just now? No one else sees you, and they think I'm mad if I even talk about you! You're off doing those important things, no doubt?"

"Do you even have to ask? I have a life too, you know."

The elf shook his head again, turning to look over the rim of the parapet. "Yes, we all have our lives," he said quietly, "and she's counting on us to sacrifice ours, if necessary, to help her, and by Zivilyn, I mean to do just that!"

He heard footsteps and laughter, as several people made their way up the stairs, approaching the rampart. Kerrick turned around, looking for Coraltop Netfisher, but of course the kender was nowhere to be seen.

Barq One-Tooth actually had several ivory stubs jutting from his gums—at least five or six, Moreen estimated quickly—but it was surely the one incisor of solid gold that gave the rough-hewn Highlander his name. That tooth was in clear evidence as the hulking thane glowered at her from across one of the banquet tables that had been set up in Brackenrock's great hall. The chiefwoman watched that gleaming chip of metal as the burly, bearded man—clad in fur from his boots to leggings and his tunic and even his huge cloak—tore off a piece of bread and chomped down on it as if it were an enemy warrior's head.

Repulsed, she turned to the other thane who had emerged as a spokesman from the band of a dozen or more

Highlander lords. He, too, was seated at the chiefwoman's table for this hastily arranged banquet. Thedric Drake came from Seascape, one of the coastal realms. The Highlanders who lived near the sea, Moreen had learned, tended to have at least a civilized veneer, unlike the mountain-dwelling clans such as Barq's stronghold at Southhelm.

Many of both groups were here, as well as more than a hundred of her own Arktos people, men and women from her tribe and others. All of them had sworn to assist in her great cause and had gathered in the hall for this night of planning and farewells. Even the gully dwarf, Slyce, had insisted on joining the war party—in fact, he had volunteered as soon as he learned there would be beer and warqat at the departure feast.

The midnight sun was pale, almost touching the horizon now as summer drew to a close, and the soft light spilled through the hall's high windows, joining the fire smoke to shroud the room in a cloudy haze. Bruni and Dinekki were also here, and Mouse of course, and Kerrick. Moreen once again felt the warmth in her heart that came from the presence of these good, trusted friends.

"To Strongwind Whalebone—King of the Highlanders!" cried Thedric Drake, raising his mug of warqat and offering a toast. "May he breathe free air e'en before the next Sturmfrost!"

"King Strongwind!" The name was echoed around the great hall as more than four hundred folk, Arktos and Highlanders alike, joined in the accolade. Moreen was careful to take only a sip of the pungent beverage, though she noted that most of those in the hall were unwilling to practice such restraint. Already, though the evening was young, the level of noise and boisterousness was rising considerably.

Why not? She knew that all of these men and women were willing to gamble their lives embarking on a quest that offered little hope of success or even of survival. Let them drink on this night!

"To the bravest of the brave, Mad Randall!" Kerrick Fallabrine offered, more somberly. He was seated to Moreen's left and swayed slightly as he raised his mug. Abruptly the elf pushed back his chair, which fell over, and stood unsteadily. "The true warrior who fell to the ogres but took a dozen of the bastards with him when he died!" He turned and cast his glass into the fireplace, where the remnants of warqat whooshed into a burst of blue flame. The elf blinked in surprise, then laughed aloud.

"Mad Randall!" The toast became a cheer, with many Highlanders thumping on their tables. Even Moreen was swept up in the moment, her eyes tearing as she remembered the brave man and loyal friend. She took a long draught from her mug and gritted her teeth as the fiery liquid seared down her throat.

"We carry on the fight!" Barq One-Tooth roared, standing up and raising his mug so that warqat splashed across the table. "The ogres will learn to fear us—and they will die! Mad Randall will be avenged for all the High-lands!"

"Mad Randall will be avenged for all of mankind!" Bruni shouted, her voice roaring even over the cheers that greeted the thane's pronouncement. "He was a brave man and a true friend."

"For Aghar, too!" Slyce proclaimed, climbing up to stand on a chair next to the elf. He leaned over and whispered to Kerrick loudly. "Who Mad Randall?"

"For all of the Icereach!" This was Kerrick's addition, and Moreen almost laughed at the toast—he was an elf after all but had thrown his lot in with the humans of this land.

Her heart warmed at the thought, and when he happened to glance down at her, she smiled, and his face colored in a very un-elven blush.

"To the return of Strongwind Whalebone—may he once again sit upon his throne," declared Moreen, more quietly now, as she considered the words herself. "All of us, Arktos, Highlanders and elf, have lost a great friend—a strong leader and a loyal friend." Murmurs of agreement rumbled through the hall, as each person took the measure of his or her own determination.

"I should think that you, my lady, might have an especial cause to grieve his capture." Thedric Drake leaned in to whisper to her. The elder thane's tone was gentle, but his gaze was as sharp as ever.

"Why do you say that?" Moreen asked, though after an instant of reflection she knew.

"There were many among both our peoples, who thought that the wedding of our king and the Lady of the Arktos was the perfect compact, the seal on an alliance that has been too many centuries in the making. Surely you knew that he loved you?" Now the thane's tone was gently chiding.

"I know that he and I discussed such a marriage on several occasions," the chiefwoman replied uncomfortably. "The words that we exchanged are personal words, between the king and myself."

"You did not marry him, yet he still accompanied you, gave up his freedom in the service of the Arktos tribe."

"Yes. He came not as my future husband but as a loyal friend," she replied, "and now I vow to rescue him!"

"Or die trying!" This was Barq One-Tooth again, staggering up from his chair, waving his mug in another sloppy toast. He threw his glass into the fire—and had left a good slug of warqat in the vessel, judging by the sheet of flame that erupted.

"Die trying!" The thought was echoed across the hall, and Moreen shivered slightly at the grim toast, but once again she raised her glass and joined in.

Thedric Drake stood, mug in hand, and the room fell expectantly silent, awaiting another toast. Instead, he looked at Moreen, smiled in an avuncular manner, and gestured for her to rise. When she did, he spoke gently.

"Now that we have joined you in this quest . . . can you tell us your plan?"

Suddenly Moreen felt a little drunk. She knew her idea was crazy, yet it seemed to her sensible enough. These were such good people, surely they would understand!

"I propose to journey to Winterheim, to enter the ogre city, and to find and free Strongwind Whalebone," she announced without preamble. "To bring him and the rest of us out alive. If we can free more of the slaves, even all of them, we will do that, too."

Barq One-Tooth uttered a low whistle of surprise then toppled forward, his face falling into the gravy on his plate.

"I admire your courage and your will, but the important question is, how do you propose to do this?" Thedric asked quietly. "Have you even seen Winterheim, much less found a way inside?"

"I have learned of a way into the ogre city through a cavern called the Moongarden. We can march there overland, though it means we must scale the Tusker Escarpment then the Icewall. I believe this route offers at least a reasonable chance of success."

"How did you learn of this entry?" asked Thedric warily.

"We have an ogre prisoner, the only survivor of a raiding party taken on the Whitemoor. Bruni has gotten to know him in the past few weeks, and he has proved to be quite talkative. It is upon his words that I have made my plan."

"A prisoner? Surely you must suspect treachery?" the thane argued. "He has perhaps directed you right into the arms of a permanent garrison."

Moreen looked at Bruni, who shook her head. "I have to tell you that I trust him," the big woman said. "For one thing, I am pretty certain that he isn't bright enough to practice any such deception. He talked to us willingly and seemed to be quite content simply to engage in conversation. I believe I have been able to win over his trust. Furthermore, he clearly doesn't believe that we present any credible threat to his king's fortress—he believes no harm can come from whatever he has told us."

"But the Tusker Escarpment," suggested a Highlander thane Moreen didn't know, "there are a thousand walrus men living there!"

"Then we'll kill 'em all!" It was Kerrick, standing and swaying, lifting a new glass to right and left, some wine sloshing out. There was a moment of surprised silence, then a roar swept up from the gathering, echoing in the rafters of the great hall.

"Death to the tuskers!" The new chant swelled in the hall, and more glasses were drained.

"I will bring the Axe of Gonnas and smite the ogres with their own talisman!" exclaimed Bruni, gesturing to the sacred weapon, captured eight years ago and now displayed on the wall of the keep, above the great hearth. "Even the ogre god cannot stop us!"

"There are more things than gods to fear," Dinekki said, her frail voice somehow cutting through the noise of the gathering, "but there are gods on our side, as well—gods, men, and even an elf," she added, with a wink at Kerrick.

"How can we fail?" asked Bruni, who seemed to Moreen to be surprisingly sober. The big woman raised her mug, took a deep drink, and proclaimed aloud, "To the Tusker Escarpment!"

"Up the Icewall Pass!" Kerrick added.

"And through the Moongarden of Winterheim," Moreen chimed in. Three more glasses crashed into the coals, and the vapors of warqat again puffed into their azure flame, the explosion whooshing right out of the fireplace.

The room fell silent, and the chiefwoman felt all eyes upon her. She felt sober now, alert and hopeful and in the company of good friends. Slowly and somberly she lifted her vessel for one final toast.

"A pledge," she said. "I make a pledge to lead you, my loyal companions, to Winterheim. We will enter the ogre stronghold and rescue Strongwind Whalebone—"

"Or die trying!" Somehow Barq One Tooth had recovered enough to lift his bearded face, gravy smear and all, to make that last addition to the pledge.

"Or die trying," Moreen echoed, drinking deeply.

She meant every word.

5

Destiny of a Slave

You lost him? The King of Suderhold goes out for a stroll in his own palace, and you cannot follow where he goes?" The queen's tone was deceptively gentle, but she felt the growl rumbling in her throat, a menacing indication of her rising displeasure.

"Please, your highness!" cried Garnet Drake, kneeling abjectly, speaking in the direction of the floor. "There was nothing I could do—he followed the trollop's slave only for a short time, then their paths diverged. Naturally, I chose to keep your husband in sight."

"Not very effectively, it would seem," Stariz noted in a calm, unemotional tone. She was pleased to see the film of sweat beading on Drake's brow.

"Well, he turned into a narrow lane then made great haste. I followed him as closely as I dared, all the way to the Slaves' Way!" The man's voice was growing shrill, tremulous. "When I got there he was gone! There was no one within a hundred paces in either direction, though I raced back and forth with great urgency. It was as though he vanished into thin air! I suspect sorcery, your majesty—sorcery of black and sinister import!"

"Don't be an idiot," Stariz snorted, controlling her mounting anger only with the greatest difficulty.

She felt an urge to reach out and wring this useless wretch's neck—indeed, the act would give her no small measure of satisfaction. Her chief spy was not entirely useless—indeed, his loyalty had been proven many times over, and if she were to dispose of him, she would have a headache replacing him.

Instead, she squinted then murmured a prayer—a minor entreaty, really, to the power of her awe-inspiring god. Immediately the human cried out, clasping his hands to his face, looking up at her with fear and horror in his eyes. He gagged, turning to the side, retching messily onto the floor.

The queen stood still, unmoved as she watched boils emerge from the skin of his hands and his face—sores, she knew, that were erupting all over his body. Each welt grew quickly, festering and bubbling beneath the man's pale skin.

"Please . . . Highness . . . I beg you!" groaned Garnet, rolling in his own mess, thrashing and kicking. He choked, gagging and croaking as he strained to draw each agonizing breath.

Still she made no move but watched emotionlessly as the boils blossomed angrily then burst, one by one, to leave bloody sores. The spy groaned in agony, but each movement caused him even greater agony. After a while he lay rigid, staring at her in a mixture of horror and awe.

Five minutes later he was breathing a little more easily, sobbing abjectly, covered in sweat and specked with the blood that had marked his oozing sores. Slowly, he pushed himself to his knees and wiped a bloody palm across his face to smear away his tears. He would be disgusting to look at for a few days, but Stariz was satisfied, even pleased by the lesson she had taught him.

"Next time I trust you will be more diligent," she declared, and he nodded mutely.

She gestured at the vomit and blood on the floor, wrinkling her piglike nose in distaste. "Clean this up," she ordered, "and get yourself into some clean clothes. I want you to show me this place where the king of Suderhold disappeared."

Stariz placed no credence in Garnet's suggestion that the king had vanished through magical means. She herself controlled the most powerful magic in Winterheim, and there was none who would dare work such power in the face of her displeasure. She would not detect any spell casting nor residue of magic.

However, she had hopes that, with careful search, she might be able to discover a secret door.

———◆·◆·◆———

Strongwind Whalebone and the three ogres of his escort walked in silence for a long time, at first climbing a wide, circling ramp that ascended steadily, then moving onto a stairway that spiraled about the center of a long, vertical shaft. Twice they paused to rest, and each time the lord and the two guards took drinks of water from a cask that sat, apparently for that purpose, on the landing. Strongwind was so thirsty that he would have had no qualms accepting the dipper from the guard who had just swilled from it, but in neither instance was refreshment offered to the slave.

Throughout these halls they encountered other slaves, humans walking with their eyes downcast, dressed in plain garments of brown wool. These people quickly moved out of the way as the party approached, and one woman cowered abjectly when one of the guards raised a fist to hasten her out of the way. None of them was chained, Strongwind noticed, and for the most part they seemed to be moving about on simple errands without any direct supervision or restraint.

Finally the group emerged into a straight corridor, once more on a level floor. They passed a room where pots clanged and tantalizing odors—baking bread and steamed fish prominent among them—suggested a kitchen. Several times they passed groups of men and women, all of whom stood to the side and bowed politely as Lord Forlane passed. These slaves, too, kept their eyes downcast, though the human king noticed several of them sneaking glances at him after the ogre nobleman had passed.

Strongwind returned the looks surreptitiously and made a few observations: While none of the humans were exactly fat, they did not seem emaciated either. Unlike the slaves on the lower levels, they wore garments of dyed wool, and their clothes—as well as faces, hair, and beards—seemed relatively clean. They made a contrast to the miserable wretches the king had seen laboring at the capstans in the harbor. He suspected these were some of the advantages of being enslaved in the higher levels of the ogre fortress.

Finally, the lord arrived at a broad door upon which he knocked once then pushed open. He led Strongwind into an anteroom lit brightly with oil lamps. Several humans were at work here cleaning some long tables and, in one corner, sewing patches on a several old leather cloaks.

"Tildy!" roared Forlane. "Where's Tildy Trew?"

"Keep your boots on, your greatness!" came a peeved reply from one of the many doorways leading off of this large chamber. A moment later a stout, round-cheeked woman emerged to glare impatiently at the noble ogre. "Well? Don't you know we've got to get the king's welcome feast together? What do you want now?"

Strongwind was startled at the slave's temerity—in his

own castle, a servant who spoke thus might be subjected to a rebuke, even a slap. Lord Forlane chuckled agreeably, despite the stern frown on the woman's features.

"This one is to be present at the feast for inspection by the court. The king wants you to get him cleaned up, dressed for the occasion, and so forth."

"Oh, great," muttered Tildy Trew, squinting up at Strongwind. He had the impression that she was near-sighted. "Did you just come in on the ship?"

"Er, yes," he replied.

"Well, all right. Not as if I have any choice in the matter." She addressed the ogre lord. "You can tell the king that I'll do my best—though I can't say he's given me much to work with!"

As the ogre lord, still chuckling, turned to leave, Strongwind noticed that the Tildy was in fact somewhat younger than he had first suspected. Her clean, round face was unlined, and her hair was a rich dark brown, like good, fertile soil. She was much shorter than him, shorter even than Moreen he thought, and her green eyes glinted with something that might be good humor.

"All right, get undressed," she declared, as soon as the door had closed behind Forlane.

"I beg your pardon?"

"Gotta look you over for wounds, you know. Heal you up if you need it." She spun about and shouted, her voice as keen as the cry of a hawk. "Sherris! Draw a hot bath for our guest, here! Looks like we'll have to comb some lice out!"

Strongwind heard water pouring in another room as the command was obeyed. He shook his head—lice? On the King of Guilderglow? Anything was possible, he conceded, as Tildy took his hand and tugged him toward the adjacent room.

Besides, a bath didn't sound bad . . . not bad at all.

"Grimwie?"

He hated it when she called him that, but he was too comfortable, too satisfied to raise an objection. Instead he merely sighed and settled more deeply into the pile of furs that was Thraid's mattress.

"I saw you brought a slave back on *Goldwing*. Didn't you?"

"Mmpphh" he said.

"He looked like a good one, I thought, not like so many of these humans, dirty and scrawny and all. He looked strong, and he was tall . . . like you wouldn't be ashamed for people to see him, say, in your house. I was wondering something."

Another sigh. The king hoped she was about done talking—he really wanted to sleep.

"Grimwie, my king?" She kept going. Her hands were moving now, another unwelcome distraction.

"What is it, my cuddle?" He tried to sound patient, lacking the energy to endure one of her pouts. "What is it that you were wondering?"

"Well, you know that my house slave, Wandcourt, is getting old. Why, he and Brinda tell me that their children have had children somewhere back around the Moongarden. Perhaps you noticed when you followed him—he's not as spry as he used to be. I think he would sleep half the day away if I didn't invent things for him to do, so I thought I should have a younger slave, one to help Wandcourt with the chores . . . someone who is a little more capable, who is strong and would look acceptable in my livery."

"You want the human I brought back from Dracoheim?" Grimwar was immediately unhappy with the idea, though he wasn't exactly sure why. "I don't think he's right for a house slave, my sweet. He was a wild man, attacked a whole company of my guards, killed more than a few. No, he's quite dangerous—too dangerous for a house slave. Maybe the Seagate crew for him. With a back like that, he could do the pulling of two men."

The king was lying. In fact, he had considered the prisoner for a slave in his own house—there was a presence and dignity about the fellow that seemed beyond the typical human. Of course, the King of the Highlanders would have to face a different fate soon enough. Stariz had made her intentions clear regarding his death at the Autumnblight feast, and—since she had the clear will of Gonnas on her side—the king was not prepared to dispute her on that matter. Until then, however . . .

"Well, after he's tamed, I mean," Thraid pressed. "In fact, I could help tame him. Certainly Wandcourt and Brinda would be a good influence—they're about as perfect as slaves can be."

"I thought you told me they were getting too old," the king retorted.

"Well, besides that. I mean, they've always been loyal. And discreet—you know how important that is! This new slave would be just perfect. I got a good look at him that night when you had him paraded off the ship."

Grimwar reflected, remembering the argument that had erupted between Stariz and himself when they had discussed the slave's fate. He knew that she sorely wanted to kill him to slake her craving for vengeance over the disaster at Dracoheim. This prisoner was the only tangible remnant of those reckless saboteurs. Certainly he was doomed, eventually . . . but maybe there was some way the king could get some use out of him before he was killed.

Indeed, what better way to keep him out of the way and to gain Thraid's gratitude than to temporarily give him to his mistress? It would make Thraid happy, and that always led to pleasant consequences. Indeed, her playful fingers were no longer annoying him.

"All right, Cuddle," he said breezily. "I will send him to you, and you can look him over. Then you can decide if you really want him."

"Oh, Grimwie, thank you!" she declared, rolling over to give him a kiss on his jowly cheek.

"Enough talk," he said, reaching for her with both arms. "Time for me to get what I really want."

———◆———

"Can I have a little privacy?" Strongwind asked, longingly eyeing the stone bathtub filled with steaming water. The lice he hadn't even noticed before were now starting itch, and he was ready, even anxious, to disrobe, soak, and clean up.

"Privacy? You're a slave!" Tildy Trew snorted indignantly. "It won't be anything I haven't seen before. You think I don't know my way around with the lads?" she asked, glaring at him with her fists planted on her pleasantly rounded hips. "It's my job to see that you get cleaned up proper—I should think you'd show a little more gratitude. Take those bruises, now!"

"What?"

She was pointing at his wrists, where the shackles had enclosed him, and he grimaced to see the purple-yellow marks that extended halfway up his arms. "That's where I was chained!" he growled.

"Of course," she said, "and an unsightly blotch you've got from it. Now, if you'll let me take care of you, I'll see them salved and slimed so that you'll be whole again before you know it."

Strongwind tried to decide what to do. He had never

had another human being speak to him like this—although he had to admit that Moreen had come close on a few occasions—and he felt his temper rising. Tildy Trew was trying to take care of him, under awkward conditions imposed by their mutual enslavement, and he could not lose sight of the fact that he had many real and dangerous enemies here. It did not make sense to add to the list of his foes one who might otherwise be neutral.

He sighed in resignation and shrugged out of his clothes, turning his back to her and slipping into the tub as quickly as possible. Unfortately, the water was so hot that a very gradual immersion was all he could manage.

Acutely aware of his undignified position, he turned his head to find Tildy examining him with sparkling eyes and a wide grin. That was all it took—ignoring the near scalding heat of the bath, he slid over the edge of the stone tub and sank into the water up to his chin.

"Hmmm," she said. "Comb a few tangles out of that beard, trim the hair a bit, and you might have some promise. We'll have to deal with those bruises, though—an ugly lot on your back, as well."

"That's where they had me strapped over the bench," Strongwind informed her, trying to sound haughty but far, far too comfortable to pull it off.

"It looks as if you've already felt the lash a few times," she remarked, her tone softer and sadder than before. "What did you do to bring that on yourself?"

"I bloodied the nose of an ogre who tried to push me around," he replied, with some measure of pride.

She clucked in what sounded like sincere concern. "Best you learn to let them do that when the brutes are of a mind to. Otherwise, you won't last long around here."

"I don't know if I want to last," he answered sourly. "Tell me, what about all these slaves? It seems to me that we humans outnumber the ogres here in Winterheim."

"Oh, we do . . . by at least two to one in Highlanders alone. There are hundreds of Arktos here as well," Tildy said, "maybe more."

"Has there ever been talk of . . . well, of revolt?"

There was a long silence, and Strongwind finally looked up. He was startled to see Tildy's pert face white with anger, her lips compressed into a thin line. She shook off the hand that he placed on her arm.

"Don't even think about that!" she hissed, looking around frantically. Strongwind had been careful to speak when they couldn't be overheard, so he was taken aback by her reaction.

"Why not?" he demanded softly, meeting her eyes with his own scowl. "Has every memory of freedom been driven out of you people?"

He was surprised again when her eyes abruptly swam with tears. Strongwind waited for her to regain her composure.

"I don't want to make you cry," he said finally. "I just got here. I don't understand this place, not at all, but I thought that I understood Highlanders, and the Arktos as well. I would expect them to be working against their captors!"

When she looked at him, her eyes were dry and her tone level but serious. "It's the queen!" she said. "She has ways of knowing when someone is planning trouble. There was a man, Redd Dearman, who tried to incite a little resistance a few years back. He was discreet about it and careful—but they came for him in the night. He perished on the altar at Autumnblight, but not before the queen made an example of him that every slave in Winterheim would remember. Even the children—the little ones—were forced to come and watch!"

"I would think that's all the more reason to revolt," Strongwind said. "How can people live under such tyranny and cruelty?"

"We make do," Tildy said, looking at him earnestly. "There are some who would make trouble—like Black Mike, who works in the royal kitchen. I have heard of him, and that means others have, too. It will only be a matter of time before the queen's attention falls upon him. More's the pity."

"Who is this Black Mike? How is he making trouble?" The Highlander king asked, trying to disguise the eagerness in his voice.

"Quietly, so far," Tildy said. "I shouldn't even tell you—but he is trying to recruit slaves, men and women for a secret purpose. I don't know what size group he has formed, but I know that the danger to him and to many others is real." She took Strongwind's brawny forearms in her small hands. "Tell me that you'll stay away, that you won't give the queen any excuse to single you out."

"Hmmpf, I've always been good at taking care of myself—"

"Until you got captured and enslaved!" she retorted pointedly.

He stiffened. "I have no regrets about that. I made a sacrifice to help a friend, the woman I still mourn, who made an even greater sacrifice. If this is to be my fate, I can only hope to meet it with the same courage that she met her own."

"I'm sorry," Tildy said quickly. "At least heed my words enough to be careful—please!"

Strongwind Whalebone nodded. "I will not do anything rash," he promised. "Nor will I endanger others, but I do intend to keep my eyes open."

She nodded seriously, then dumped some soap and water over his head, scrubbing fiercely. She surprised him by turning and shouting toward the door of the bathing room.

"Hey, Barkstone!" Tildy called, so loudly that the king winced.

"What is it, beautiful?" asked a man, sticking his head in the door. His accent was familiar. He was of the Highlander clans near the king's own fortress of Guilderglow. Strongwind could tell that, though he couldn't tell much more because soap was dripping down over his eyes.

"Blondie here doesn't think I know anything about the lads, he doesn't. Told me so himself!" Tildy was indignant again. "Thought maybe you could tell him about us in the Moongarden, that time?"

"Ah, Tildy—those memories will last my lifetime and keep me warm though I live through a thousand winters, but it wouldn't be very gentlemanly for me to speak about them, now would it?"

"I tell you, he doesn't believe me!" declared the woman.

"Who is he?" asked Barkstone, coming forward.

"Someone just came in on the galley, as fresh as you were yourself nine years ago, when the ogres plucked you off the coast."

"Sorry to hear that, my friend," said the slave man. "We've a life here, but it's a pale imitation o' freedom."

"I agree," Strongwind replied, brushing aside the soap and looking up. He was startled as the man, whom he didn't recognize, took a step backward then dropped to one knee and bowed.

"Your Majesty!" cried Barkstone. "I canna believe that they took you!"

"Majesty?" Tildy Trew said crossly. "Nobody tells me anything." She glared at Strongwind, and he merely shrugged modestly. "Who are you anyway?"

"This is Strongwind Whalebone, Lord of Guilderglow and king of all the Highlands!" declared Barkstone.

"No kidding!" Tildy threw another bucket of water over him. "I'd better clean him up real good," she said, her eyes still twinkling.

6

The Tusker Escarpment

Four hundred and twelve humans, one elf, and one gully dwarf gathered in the courtyard of Brackenrock. Gray clouds hung low over the fortress, and by the time they were ready to march a steady drizzle had begun to fall. It was hardly the greatest omen for the start of a perilous expedition, and the weather—combined with about four hundred ripping hangovers—cast a pall of gloom over the war party's departure.

The gates of the fortress had not been repaired since the destructive attack earlier this summer, and the warriors filed through the gaping entrance in no particular order. They carried everything they would need: food, weapons, shelter, a nip or two of warqat for the cold nights. Many more Arktos lined the towers and walls of the fortress, watching in silence as the war party marched away. By the time they had gone a mile, Moreen looked back to see that the citadel had already vanished into the mist and rain.

The soggy weather continued, with drizzle more or less constant over the next ten days. Nevertheless, the war party made good time. Even old Dinekki, who of course had insisted on coming, hobbled along at a brisk pace. Mouse led the way across the Whitemoor, following the same route he had taken two months earlier when he had ambushed the raiding party led by the ogre Broadnose. The long file marched past the ruin of one hamlet after another, the skeletal remains of small huts, no more than a dozen or two for each village, standing as a stark reminder of ogre cruelty. As each little ruin faded into the mist and rain behind them, the Arktos and Highlanders felt anew the hatred of their ancestral foes and the desire for vengeance that had sent them on this mission in the first place.

Even Slyce seemed grim as they passed these sights, the gully dwarf apparently affected more deeply by this devastation than he had been by the accident that had claimed the lives of his comrade and his captain in the submersible boat. Moreen noticed the rotund little fellow sniffled sadly as they passed the muddy remnant of a village, and he looked down and saw the broken pieces of a child's stick-and-feather doll.

The terrain of the moors undulated gently, the landscape utterly treeless except for a few cedar groves in the most sheltered valleys. Mouse led the band along these streams for the most part, though when swampy marshes blocked the lowlands he took to the rocky ridges. Their bearing remained almost due south, the direction determined by Dinekki's instinct and confirmed by a nautical compass Kerrick had made from a bit of lodestone.

The months of the midnight sun were drawing to a close—now four or five hours of twilight marked the middle of the night, though even in the cloudy, gray mist it never got truly dark. The short period of dusk seemed to suit the marchers well. They stopped only long enough to stretch out on the driest ground they could find, each person covered by his fur cloak to keep off as much of the rain as possible. Some sipped warqat; others brewed small pots of bitter tea. After a few hours of sleep they rose, ate sparingly from the dried fish, kelp, and trail-bread provisions each warrior carried along, and resumed their march.

Moreen usually fell into step somewhere in the middle of the pack, holding her head up and slogging along among the rest of the Arktos and Highlanders. Most of them were men, and that included of the Highlanders, but several dozen women of the Arktos tribes had eagerly joined the band. Bruni was here of course, as well as several other female veterans of the long march to Brackenrock eight years earlier. Even slender Feathertail, who had been a mere girl then, now carried a bundle of spears lashed to her back and wore the heavy leather tunic that was the traditional—and only—battle armor of her coastal dwelling people.

Every day the chiefwoman regarded them proudly— and guiltily. For all of her life, and the lives of her parents and all of her other ancestors, the humans of Icereach had lived in fear of the ogres, running and hiding, and when possible, trying to defend against their raids and attacks. To reverse that lifelong relationship was like trying to change the very reality of the world in which they lived.

Moreen told herself they were doing something that needed to be done. So what if she had led her small tribe to Brackenrock and held that citadel against two attacks in the last eight years? What did that mean if in the next eight years the ogres were able to attack them two, three—perhaps eight—more times? All she would have done in the end is bought her people some time along a path that would lead to the same inevitable fate. Now, if they entered the ogre capital and brought out Strongwind Whalebone and who knew how many slaves, they might change relations between ogres and humans for the rest of history.

At last the rolling swath of the Whitemoor came to an end. The high tundra was pinched between the rocky shore of the White Bear Sea, and the lofty crest of the Fenriz range, the impassible mountains that formed the east boundary of the long glacier bearing the same name. The warriors gathered on the last height of the moors, looking across a flat valley about two miles across. A shallow river flowed from the mountains through the center of the valley to spill into the sea. Some distance past the valley a rugged ridge, partially visible in the shifting haze, rose across their path.

"This is the Breakstone River," Mouse explained to Moreen, Kerrick, and Barq One-Tooth. "That ridge beyond is the face of the Tusker Escarpment—maybe ten or twenty miles past the valley. Pretty much everything on the far side of the river is thanoi territory."

"Do you think the thanoi know we're coming?" asked the chiefwoman. She was not afraid of the dull-witted though fierce walrus-men, but she was annoyed at the prospect that they stood between her and her goal.

"Hard to say for sure, though I don't expect so," said the Arktos warrior. "We haven't seen any tracks on the moors. Still, I suspect that they're keeping an eye on this valley—you can see there's not a lick of cover in the place, so they're bound to observe us as we head across the river."

Kerrick squinted at the sky. "It's almost dusk. Do you want to camp here and go across at first full light?"

"I think we should keep moving," Moreen said. "The night will provide us with a little concealment—not as much as I'd like—but if we go on now, then they'll have less time to prepare a reception for us."

"That's the right idea," Barq said, surprising Moreen with a nod of approval. "Go forward right away, and damn the flanks and any poor tuskers who try to stop us!"

The warriors continued onward, following the crest of a gentle ridge as it descended to the flat ground of the valley, then moving forward at a fast pace. Throughout the long column, humans fingered their weapons, nervously eyeing the rise on the far side of the river, wondering if tusked enemies were crouching there, waiting in potential ambush. The twilight deepened, and by the time they drew near to the Breakstone the murky gray of the late summer night had closed around them, masking the heights on both sides.

Moreen soon realized that the bottomland that had looked so flat from the height of the moors was in fact crossed by numerous gullies and washes. These were typically no more than six or eight feet deep, but they were steep sided and muddy in the troughs, forcing Mouse to pick a circuitous route as they drew closer to the actual riverbed. It was midnight by the time they stood at the gravel bank and looked at the channel itself.

The murk had deepened to the point where they could see only about a quarter of a mile ahead, and this seemed to be about the width of the river. For once the sky was clear, and a few stars twinkled in the purple north, away from the direction of the sun lurking just below the southern horizon. Moreen would have been pleased to have some of the dense cloud cover, even the drizzling rain, but as it was they would have to settle for the late summer twilight of the midnight sun.

Much of the riverbed consisted of flat bars of sand and gravel, with strands of gray water rippling between these dry islands in channels of various depth. Some of these courses looked deep and dark, while others trilled over stony shallows.

"I've never been across here before," Mouse admitted. "I don't know of a good ford, but if we pick our way carefully we should be able to do it without having to swim."

"Lead on," Moreen said, confident in the man's eyes, and judgment.

They found a place where the bank sloped gently down to the shallows and started to wade across. Mouse and Barq One-Tooth went first, with Moreen, Kerrick, and Bruni coming next. Using a long spear, Mouse probed the depth of the water with the butt end of the weapon while the big thane held his great battle axe ready in both hands. The chiefwoman and the elf had their swords drawn, while Bruni held a cudgel at the ready. The head of the Axe of Gonnas, the golden blade shrouded in a leather sack, jutted upward from her backpack, ready in case of emergency.

Cold water spilled over the top of her boots as Moreen followed the two men across the channel. Their guide had chosen well, and for fifty yards they slogged through a flat-bottomed stretch of river that seemed to be free of jagged stones and other obstacles. Shortly they emerged onto one of the sand bars, where Mouse turned upstream and led them along dry ground, following the bend of the dry land to carry them farther across the broad riverbed.

Next they crossed a deeper channel, where the water came up to Moreen's waist. Here the humans and the elf linked arms, and thus supported by the presence of many comrades, fought through a current that would have swept a lone walker off her feet. Dinekki somehow held her own here, though Slyce was nearly carried away by the water that rose above his head. A big Highlander picked up the gully dwarf by the scruff of his neck and dragged him through the channel. They climbed out onto a wide shelf of gravel, and this they were able to follow past the halfway point of the riverbed to another stretch of shallow water that looked like the last obstacle before the low bank on the far side of the river channel.

"I'd like to spot a good way out of the riverbed before we do the last part of the ford," Mouse admitted, eyeing the bank with a scowl. "That's about six or eight feet high, I'm thinking, the perfect place for them to meet us with an ambush."

"Have the archers string their bows," Moreen suggested. "That way they can give us some cover if we have to fight our way out of the stream."

"Good idea," her guide replied.

About a hundred of the fighters, Arktos and Highlanders both, were armed with the short, double-curved bows of the Icereach hunters. Under the captaincy of Thedric Drake, who looked very martial in a silvery metal helm, they readied their weapons and arrayed themselves on the gravel bar. The rest of the party—Mouse and Barq still in the lead—started across the last stretch of the channel.

Moreen kept her eyes on the flat bank, trying to see through the low tangle of willow bushes lining the crest. Nothing seemed to move there, and as they drew closer she began to hope that the speed of their advance had surprised the tuskers. At the foot of that embankment Mouse held his spear ready while Barq reached over his head, grabbed a handful of willow branches, and started to pull himself up the steep, sandy surface.

Something rustled through the bushes, and Kerrick was the first to shout, "Look out!"

The big Highlander thane cursed and staggered backward as Mouse stabbed into the bushes with his long, steel-tipped spear. Barq, his shoulder slick with blood, where something sharp had chopped through the thane's heavy cloak, cursed and stumbled, before regaining his balance.

A snarling creature lunged into view, twin tusks jutting from its jowls thrusting like speartips toward the two men. Mouse stabbed again, and the thanoi writhed on the blade of the weapon that pierced its guts. The creature slid down the embankment toward the riverbed, dropping a bloody stone knife. Wielding his battle axe in one hand, Barq chopped down hard, and the walrus-man lay still.

At least a dozen other brutes rose from the brush, hurling spears at the column of humans. One of these missiles flew past Moreen, grazing her ear—and inflaming her temper. She rushed forward, scrambling up the bank with the aid of one hand, while with the other she stabbed her sword into the rustling bushes atop the steep crest.

She shouted a profane curse as something grabbed at her, but she didn't have enough of a grip to hold her balance. She toppled backward into the water, falling on top of Kerrick. Only then did she realize that the elf had seized her and pulled her away from the enemy.

"What are you doing?" she spat, sitting up in the shallow water, shaking her head to clear the drops of her eyes.

"Get down!" he snarled, his voice harsh.

She opened her mouth to argue, and he reached out with both hands to push her roughly under the water.

This time when she came up she didn't even try to speak. Instead, she clenched her fist and smashed a blow into the elf's shoulder. The thanoi were forgotten as she lunged at him, infuriated beyond words—until she realized that he was laughing at her.

"What's so funny?" she demanded, surprised enough that her rage dissolved.

"You would have gotten shot by your own archers if you'd made it up that bank," he said, rubbing his shoulder. He wasn't laughing any more. "That hurt!"

Startled, she remembered the enemy and whirled around to glare into the brush. Several thanoi were partially visible, slumping forward, arrows jutting from the motionless bodies. There was no sign of the rest of them. Even more telling, the sandy bank, right where she had charged, bristled with feathered shafts. Obviously, the archers had delivered a lethal volley.

"I don't think we got them all," Mouse said grimly, "but the ones that weren't killed ran as soon as the arrows came down. I expect they'll carry the word to their fellows—I don't think we've seen the last of these tusked bastards, not by a long shot."

Moreen reached down and groped through the water until she came up with her sword. "Sorry," she muttered to Kerrick, "and, um, thanks."

"Any time," he said breezily. "Thank you, too."

"For what?"

"For dropping your sword before you swung at me."

"Oh," she said. She didn't feel like explaining to him that at the time she hadn't realized she'd lost her weapon.

Kerrick walked along the perimeter of the camp, his eyes straining to penetrate the fog that had rolled in before sunrise. Some of the humans were sleeping, shaggy cloaks drawn over them to hold back the damp and penetrating chill. They weren't going to rest for long, but after nearly twenty-four hours of straight marching fatigue had forced this halt.

The elf, however, wasn't particularly tired. He had offered to join the first shift of picket duty, some fifty or sixty warriors who remained awake and—like him—patrolled around the outside of the dry hilltop where the war party had made its bivouac. The ground was rougher here than on the moors and climbed steadily toward the Tusker Escarpment, which was still eight or ten miles away. The fog had thickened quickly so that he couldn't see more than fifty feet in any direction, and he fought a sense of aloneness brought on by the mist.

He tried to focus on his surroundings, but his thoughts naturally turned inward, reflective. How odd it seemed that he, a sailor of civilized Silvanesti, should find himself here, near the very end of the world. An elf among men—that had become his life, and for the most part he had come to accept, even enjoy, that existence. Certainly he had no regrets about coming along on this expedition. There was no place on Krynn that he would rather be than with these brave companions in the service of the chiefwoman of Brackenrock.

The elf kept his eyes open, warily looking across the shrouded landscape. The expedition was camped at the crest of a rounded hill five or six miles south of the Breakstone River. The ground, like everywhere else in this part of the Icereach, was treeless, the last groves straggling out north of the river. The terrain was grassy and green, broken by patches of white, square-edged boulders. Kerrick paid special attention to those rocks, reasoning that if they were being spied upon, the outcrops would offer the perfect concealment to enemy scouts.

Unfortunately, elf eyes were no more sensitive than human when it came to seeing through this kind of murk. The shifting fog seemed to have a life of its own, growing thicker or thinner in the blink of an eye.

Was that something moving? He imagined a leathery, tusked figure crouching down beyond a nearby boulder. Most likely it was a tendril of fog, but he drew his sword and took a few steps down the hill. With a sudden spring, he dashed forward and found only a patch of green moss.

Now he could see even farther down the slope. A shape flitted across the limits of his vision and staring intently he saw more, dull figures hunched over to advance in stealth. Ten, twenty—no, a whole mob of them, more than he could count—were creeping stealthily up the hill.

Quickly the elf retreated, backpedaling toward the crest until once again he saw the comforting shapes of his fellow warriors. He shouted an alarm, bringing the Arktos and Highlanders to their feet—and at the same time provoking roars of attack from the encircling mists below. The human fighters shook off their slumber in an instant, forming a defensive ring around the crest of the hill. Still holding his sword, the elf took his place in the line, standing shoulder to shoulder with Moreen and Bruni, once more prepared to do battle with the enemies of his friends.

———◆———

The attackers came out of the mist in a wave, at first roaring and barking in the distance like unseen, angry ghosts. As they drew closer, the vague shapes resolved into an army of snarling, bestial thanoi armed with spears, knives, and stone-headed clubs.

The humans met them in time-honored fashion, a resolute line of warriors standing side by side, with nearly half of the force waiting in reserve in the center of the ring. Moreen kept her eyes on a large bull that bore a stout spear and charged directly at her. The creature's bloodshot eyes glowed with hatred, the grotesque face twisted by an expression of almost maniacal rage. Twin tusks of ivory jutted forward from the brute's upper jaw, and when it raised its head to utter a loud roar those two prongs drove directly at the chiefwoman's face.

She held her sword at her waist, her arm bent back like a coiled spring. The thanoi rushed forward with its fellows, sweeping up the hill with surprising speed and grace. As it drew close it sprang, using the spear like a third, lower tusk. Moreen ducked under all three prongs, for once grateful of her short stature. She thrust with the sword and drove forward on her wiry legs, puncturing the beast's belly and grimacing as a rush of gore warmed her weapon-hand.

The monster howled and twisted, trying to wriggle off the blade, finally collapsing back into the ranks of its fellows. Moreen followed up her success with a slashing blow to the side, slicing the razor edge of steel into the flank of another tusker. By the time that one fell away, the whole line was locked in a howling, thrashing melee. Many on both sides fell in the first crush, but the Highlanders and Arktos held firm. From somewhere she heard Dinekki chanting a prayer praising Chislev Wilder and seeking the blessing of the goddess against their enemies. The chiefwoman took heart from that blessing and felt renewed power as she lifted up her weapon for the next parry and attack.

After slashing, chopping and stabbing for a frenzied minute or two, the wave of brutish attackers staggered then broke backward in the face of this determined resistance.

They did not fall away any great distance. Instead, the tuskers backed up only ten or twenty paces, where they continued to roar and beat their chests with clubs and fists. The din was deafening.

"Archers—give me three volleys! Let them eat your arrows!"

Moreen glanced back, glad to see that Thedric Drake was rallying the bowmen in the middle of the ring of defenders. His metal cap, the only such helm in the war party, stood out like a silver beacon. He strode back and forth, gesturing and shouting. The archers showered the attackers with missiles, and in seconds a score or more of the walrus men fell dead, pierced by the lethal arrows.

It was hard to calculate the odds, but Moreen estimated that the enemy had them outnumbered at least three or four to one. The only hope for the humans was their tight formation—so long as they held their defenses, the walrus men could not bring their greater numbers to bear, but how long could that last?

Once again the tuskers roared forward, hurling themselves with bestial frenzy against the wall of steel and flesh. Bruni cracked the skull of a huge, feathered chieftain, while Kerrick wielded his slender blade with dazzling skill.

The chiefwoman fought against a pair of attackers, brutish creatures who lunged forward in unison, using spears to block her frantic thrusts. She dropped to one knee as a stone blade scratched across her scalp, and when the other raised his spear she saw death staring her right in the face.

Her elf companion would not allow the attack. Knocking aside his own foe with a blow to the head, Kerrick turned and lunged, hacking his sword across the thanoi's flank, scoring a deep, ghastly wound. The monster howled and staggered away, clutching both hands to its side in a vain effort to contain its spilling entrails. Moreen sprang upward again, stabbing her crimson blade through the guts of the other tusker. Her weapon began to feel like a lead weight, and she wasn't sure she could lift it again, but fortunately the wave of attackers fell back once more, leaving more than a hundred of their number bleeding and still on the battle-churned field.

She gasped for breath and let her sword tip rest upon the ground, waiting for the next press of attack. Someone tapped her on the shoulder, and she turned to see Thedric Drake.

"We can't hold like this all day," said the elder warrior, his face creased by deep lines of worry. He removed his helm to wipe the sweat from his scalp, and she was surprised to see how bald he looked.

"Do you have a better idea?" she asked impatiently.

"Yes—let's carry the battle to them! Attack, and we might break their morale."

She looked at Kerrick, who had been listening to the suggestion, and the elf nodded in agreement.

"At least we can push toward the south," he added. "Make the bastards realize that we're not running away. If necessary, we can fight our way right up and over the Tusker Escarpment!"

She saw the audacity of the idea, and she also perceived that the thanoi were as tired as her own people. Perhaps a show of resolve was all that would be needed to break their will.

"Let's go," she said.

The plan was spread quickly, the thanes, the chief-woman, and Mouse quickly explaining the idea to all the fighters. Five minutes later Barq One-Tooth raised his axe and uttered a howling battle cry, and the entire formation lurched into motion.

The big Highlander clove his axe right through the skull of a startled thanoi. Warriors to either side of him added their own blows. The tuskers in the path of the advance quickly scattered out of the way, though not before several more fell to the weapons of the angry humans. In a tight formation, a solid ring with the archers and a dwindling supply of reserves in the middle, the war party moved down the hill and along the floor of a valley that took them due south.

A small band of tuskers worked themselves into a frenzy and rushed the front edge of the advancing circle. These were cut down with brutal efficiency, the war party not even breaking step as the humans trudged over the bodies of their enemies. The rest of the walrus men continued to bark and roar, howling on both sides of the ring and surging along at the rear, but they made no further efforts to try and block the advance.

On the flank, Moreen and Kerrick kept their eyes on the enemy as the tuskers remained just out of arrow range. The thanoi kept them surrounded, but the circular formation, bristling with weapons, maintained a steady pace toward the south. For three or four hours they continued on in this fashion, occasionally brushing off the attacks of small groups of thanoi who harried them. The humans did not have to contend with the full weight of the enemy numbers at any one time, though a thousand or more thanoi remained in view on all sides, still raising a constant din. The war party thus followed the course of the valley throughout its length, taking advantage of the smooth floor beside a shallow stream. Finally the march slowed as the formation began to climb the gradual slope toward the headwaters.

"This is the foot of the escarpment," Mouse declared. "Not as steep as I thought it would be—though the summit looks to be a good cliff."

"I think I see a pass there," Kerrick noted. "We might be able to get through it without scaling a precipice."

Indeed, the stream they were following seemed to issue from a narrow cut in the rocks at the head of the valley, and Moreen wondered if the thanoi would try to make a stand there to prevent the expedition from moving over the escarpment and into the wild lands beyond. Instead, she was surprised to see the attackers fall back even farther as the humans climbed the slope. Finally, as the Arktos and Highlanders drew near to the crest, the thanoi ceased their roaring and stomping. Now the creatures gathered in a long semicircle, an arc around the tail of the formation. They were several hundred yards away, out of range even of the stoutest longbow, and seemed content to allow the war party get away.

The humans drew near to the steep-sided pass that seemed to offer a good route over the Tusker Escarpment. The ring of warriors compressed in order to pass through that gap, smoothly adjusting their formation into a column at the front, while still maintaining a line of defense against attack from the rear. Bruni, Kerrick, and Moreen joined the rearguard, keeping a watchful eye on the brooding thanoi, while Thedric Drake and Barq One-Tooth strode boldly at the front.

Abruptly the column came to a halt, and Moreen heard shouts of consternation from the leaders. She turned to look and gaped in awe as a monstrous figure shrugged off a tumble of rocks to rear up into the air, twenty or thirty feet high. It seemed to be a giant insect of some kind, with horrible bulging eyes and a mouth surrounded by a pair of sharp, clicking pincers. An insect easily the size of a whale, it buzzed angrily, taut and menacing.

Barq One Tooth uttered a fierce, ululating war cry and rushed forward with his axe upraised. Other Highlanders shouted too, and Thedric Drake urged them to charge behind Barq. The monster swept a spiked leg before it—it had many such limbs, jutting from a body segmented like a centipede's—and knocked the big Highlander to the side with a slashing blow.

The horrible head snapped forward and down, a lethal stab followed by a click of those jaws. Thedric Drake shouted one word—"Kradock!" the name of the High-lander god—and vanished into that awful maw. The beast lifted its head again, wriggled through an unmistakable swallowing gesture, and let out a roar of challenge and hunger.

Thedric Drake was gone.

An hour later Tildy Trew and his bath were merely pleasant memories as Strongwind again found himself flanked by a pair of big ogre guards, following Lord Forlane through the halls of Winterheim. They were on the highest level of the city, he suspected, judging from the view of the harbor he glimpsed from the edge of the great, round avenue that circled the central atrium. Above him there was only an arched stone surface, and he knew he was looking up at the bare bedrock of the hollowed out mountaintop.

The lord led him past several guards and through a large, stone door. Great hallways branched to both sides, and the walls were lined with woolen tapestries depicting hunts, landscapes, and several examples of glorious sailing ships and galleys. Strongwind guessed that this was the entrance to the royal palace. Two minutes later he was led into a room where Grimwar Bane himself was waiting to look him over.

The ogre king was feasting on a haunch of mutton, and his jowls were slick with grease. A dozen of his subjects, all male, were seated at the table with him. All were dressed in long bearskin capes such as that worn by Lord Forlane. Several seemed quite old, with wrinkled faces and withered arms, and one caught the human's attention simply because he was immensely fat. That one had a shred of stringy mutton dangling, apparently unnoticed, from one of his tusks.

Grimwar grunted in approval, apparently satisfied that Strongwind had been adequately washed. The other ogres looked at the slave with interest, and the king leaned back in his huge chair, gesturing expansively.

"Here's the one I brought back myself," he said. "Put up a real fight, too. He and his comrade killed a dozen of my Grenadiers." This description drew several whistles of astonishment and appreciation.

"Do you think he's still dangerous?" asked the fat ogre, his eyes wide as he looked Strongwind up and down.

"Yes, very," said the king, with a glance of contemptuous amusement at the huge lord. He gestured to the two guards. "These fellows will kill him if he so much as makes a move toward the table."

Grimwar Bane turned to Lord Forlane. "I have decided what to do with this slave, for now," said the king of Suderhold.

Forlane leaned in, and Strongwind watched them talk, wondering what fate had in store for him now.

———————•◆•———————

"I sent Garnet Drake to fetch that slave, the one we brought back from Dracoheim, and bring him to the temple," Stariz told Grimwar. "I wanted to keep him there in preparation for Autumnblight! My lord, that ceremony is only three weeks away!"

The king had just arrived home after a dinner with

several of the lords of the different city levels of Winterheim. He was full, a little drunk, and tired. He hadn't even had a chance to take his boots off yet, nor did it look as if he would get that chance, as his wife continued her verbal onslaught.

"Garnet was told that the slave had already been assigned—and he was unable to find out where the human was sent!"

Stariz glared at him, her hands on her hips. Grimwar faced that gaze, resentment building, wishing he knew a way to dam that torrent of words. His wife opened her mouth to speak again, and the truth washed over him: He didn't have to listen!

Instead, he plopped down into his most comfortable chair, ignoring her so blatantly that she stammered a surprised sound then clamped her jaw shut. He couldn't see her fierce expression as he lifted one foot at a time to allow the two slaves to pull off his walrus-hide footgear. He knew that she would be staring daggers at him, but he felt cloaked in a strange new sense of invulnerability. Why hadn't he made this discovery years ago?

In fact, the king decided that he had had just about enough of being cowed by his wife. There was much of which he should feel proud. The wasted campaign aside, his kingdom seemed to be doing very well indeed. All the gold mines were operating at full capacity, and his coffers were gathering wealth at an unprecedented pace. His mistress had been very good to him since his return from the summer's campaign, and he knew that she anxiously awaited his next visit. Thraid would undoubtedly be delighted and grateful that he had provided a slave for her amusement, at least until Autumnblight.

"I myself gave orders for the slave to be moved," he finally said, leaning back in the chair and gesturing the slaves to leave. Moments later king and queen were alone.

"I did not want you doing him any harm, not yet, in any event. He will be yours for the ceremony but not until then."

"I must prepare him, and you know that! The Willful One must be appeased, and what better way than to sanctify the blood of one who did him such grievous harm? You had no right—"

"I had every right, woman!" roared the king, pushing himself to his feet with a flex of his powerful arms. Stariz halted in mid-rant, eyes narrowed, watching him suspiciously.

He shouted again, delighting in the release of his temper. "Do not forget that I am king here—king of Suderhold! You hold your station only because I have placed you there! I am tired of arguing with you over matters that are my own decisions. You too often lose sight of your place—but I am the king! I am lord of Winterheim, monarch of Suderhold. I am your master!"

She recoiled from his words as if he had raised his fist to her, and he took great satisfaction from the expression of fear on her face. He lowered his voice to a growl and bared his impressive tusks.

"I see that you are afraid of me, my queen. Remember that feeling. It is one you should remember, for you will have cause to fear me if you do not do a better job of learning your own station."

"Forgive me, Sire," Stariz said meekly—more meekly than she had ever said anything to the king in all their years of marriage. "I shall remember your words, and I thank you for your kindness in giving me warning." She bowed her head, then astonished him with a curtsy!

The king was somewhat taken aback by her abrupt mood change. His temper evaporated and was replaced with a sense of bemused satisfaction. Turning abruptly, he stalked out of his apartment in his bare feet onto the promenade far above the harbor. He was well satisfied with his handling of the matter. The human slave would be forgotten for the next few weeks, and quite possibly his wife would be a little easier to live with.

If he chose to continue living with her.

That thought, daring and sacrilegious, came into his mind unbidden. He thought about his words to her. He had spoken the truth—he was the master here, and why should the master of a powerful realm not be the master of his own bedroom?

Of course, there were reasons for the marriage, all of them centering on politics—Stariz was from Glacierheim, a barony that was historically among the most restive of Suderhold's fiefdoms. As high priestess, she was the leader of the ogre religion, pre-eminent interpreter of the will of Gonnas, a fact that she had used to her advantage on many occasions.

As for Glacierheim, that frost-bound realm had been peacefully acquiescent for years, and he had more than enough might in his own royal guards to deal with any rebelliousness that might develop there. The religious aspect of his wife's influence was more worrisome. He knew that her clerical powers were real, that the god of her temple was a proud and willful deity, but Grimwar Bane honored Gonnas in his own way. It seemed at least possible that the powerful immortal would not bring down his displeasure merely to soothe the wrath of a scorned ogress.

More importantly, right now neither Glacierheim nor Gonnas seemed as important to the king as his own reborn sense of purpose. After all, there was precedent for the ogre ruler choosing his own desires over outside concerns. Indeed, his father had divorced his wife for a younger woman—that had been the cause of the dowager queen's exile to Dracoheim. Perhaps Grimwar Bane himself should take a lesson from that history.

As he thought about it, the idea began to make more and more sense. He imagined a life without Stariz sticking into his side like a venomous thorn . . . and with Thraid's lush body, instead, warming the royal bedchamber.

He was king, a mighty king. Why should he not have what he wanted?

"O Great Gonnas the Strong, Willful Master of Ogre-kind—grant me the wisdom to understand the danger and the power to act in your interests!"

Stariz, her face obscured by the great black mask of her station, prostrated herself on the smooth slate floor, heart-sick and frightened. The massive statue of her dire deity, obsidian and standing three times the height of any mortal ogre, loomed above her, silent and impassive. Always in the past she had found that massive presence comforting.

Now, however, the fear that gnawed at her would not subside.

Bitterly she recalled her husband's dreadful rebuke and the even more disgusting acquiescence she had pretended in order to mollify him, at least temporarily. How dare he speak to her like that? Didn't he realize the strength, and the wisdom, that she brought to their royal pairing? Didn't he fear her power?

In truth, she suspected that he didn't, at least not as much as he should. If it wasn't for her, Grimwar Bane would probably have been content merely to amass his gold and to live in his citadel, master of an ancient and steadily waning kingdom. It was she, Stariz, who had convinced him of the need to make relentless war against the humans, to drive them from their coastlines and verdant valleys, lands that rightfully belonged to Suderhold. It was she who was responsible for him bringing hundreds of slaves into the warrens of Winterheim, and everywhere in the Icereach the humans were on the defensive. She was the one who rooted out the potential rebels among the slaves, through her network of spies and the potent auguries of her god. She made examples of these recalcitrants—vivid examples—and throughout the king's reign there was no hope of inciting of even a modest rebellion.

The king was a fool! He would throw it all away, she knew, if ever she ceased pushing him, guiding him onto the paths chosen by their dark and warlike god. He had been seduced by a pretty ogress, one who was empty of mind and character, who offered nothing to the kingdom except carnal diversion for the monarch.

Stariz began to understand. The king was right about some things: He was powerful, too powerful for her to change when his mind was set upon a stubborn path, so she would not strike at the untouchable king. Instead, she would find someone else to feel the brunt of her wrath, someone close to the king but still vulnerable. Someone whose fate would serve a warning to the king.

Someone like the Lady Thraid Dimmarkull.

Once more Strongwind was led through the halls of Winterheim, this time back down from the palace, past many levels, until he guessed that he was near the middle of the lofty fortress-city. Lord Forlane led the way, with the two sturdy guards maintaining a vigilant escort. They emerged from the long, descending ramp to follow the wide street that seemed to occupy the ring around the atrium on each level.

Soon they turned into a narrow side street, following this back from the atrium and into the shadows near the outer mountain wall. Several lamps, presumably fueled by whale oil, brightened the narrow street and illuminated the entrance to a narrow courtyard that abutted a door at the very far end. Strongwind guessed that this structure, at the fringe of the city, lay up against the solid bedrock of the mountain itself.

One of the guards stepped forward and knocked on the door, which was quickly opened by a muscular human of middle age or slightly older—a Highlander, Strongwind judged, by the man's high forehead and blue eyes. The hair might have once been straw-colored, though it was now thin and wispy at the top and shaded to whitish gray in the fellow's beard.

"Lord Forlane, welcome," he said. "You must be bringing the new house slave our mistress mentioned." The elder human turned to look a Strongwind. His expression was unreadable.

"My name is Wandcourt."

"Call me Whalebone," Strongwind said as he entered.

Lord Forlane followed him inside. "Is the Lady Thraid in?" asked the ogre nobleman.

"Yes, my lord, expecting you both, in fact," Wandcourt replied with a bow.

The elder slave led the ogre and Strongwind through a stone-walled anteroom that seemed remarkably plain in its appointments, given the size of the chamber. The Highlander got the immediate impression that this place hadn't been occupied for long.

That notion was reinforced as they passed under a high stone archway into the apartment's great room. There was a large hearth in the opposite wall and several bearskin rugs in the center of the room, with a chair and a large divan arranged there. Several lamps burned in alcoves in the walls, but—like the anteroom—the rest of this chamber seemed barren, as if still awaiting more furniture. It called out at least for the softening touches of a few additional bearskins.

Only then did Strongwind realize that someone occupied the divan—an ogress who faced away from him and was partially screened by the back of the long, couchlike seat. Wandcourt led him around to face her, and he quickly bowed.

"Lord Forlane! What an honor to see you, personally," declared the ogress, in a voice like a purr—the purr of a very large, and very dangerous, bear. She pushed herself to a sitting position and extended a hand, which Strongwind's escort bent to take.

"My Lady, I would never pass up the chance to spend a few moments in your charming presence. When His Majesty asked me to see to the delivery of your new house slave, I marked it an opportunity for a visit."

"This is the slave?" Thraid murmured. Strongwind, still bowing, felt her attention shift to him, though he couldn't read her tone. "Straighten up and let me look at you."

He did as she bade and returned the inspection as she looked him over. He was startled to see a creature of softness and curves, with rouged lips, and eyelashes outlined in henna. He recognized her at once—she was the ogress who had watched him debark, had waved to him as he was taken off of the galley. She shifted slightly, leaning to balance on an elbow as she partially reclined on the divan. The slave king had a sense of helplessness, as if he were a small rodent being inspected by a cat, the feline pondering whether the snack had enough meat on its bones to make it worth the trouble of the kill.

He was tempted to make some remark of greeting but decided that his new status made it safer for him to wait until she addressed him. Again she purred, her full lips curving into a small smile.

"You look as though you will do quite nicely," she remarked. "How are you called?"

"I am Whalebone, my lady," replied Strongwind. "It is an honor to be considered for your service."

She chuckled. "Very nice, indeed. One cannot assume that such manners will be ingrained in all those of your countrymen. You are a Highlander, are you not?"

"Indeed, my lady."

"Of noble birthright, perhaps?"

Strongwind shrugged. "There are some who would say so."

"I have heard something of your battle prowess," she said, musing. "There was even a suggestion that you might be, well, dangerous, but I had a feeling that first time I saw you, when you came ashore from the ship . . . a sense that you would be a good slave, that I can trust you. Surely you realize—as Wandcourt or Brinda will tell you—there are many worse postings for a slave than in the house of a noble ogress."

"I do not doubt that for a moment, lady," Strongwind replied evenly.

Thraid Dimmarkull rose very slowly from her divan. She did not so much stand up as undulate into an erect posture. She was as tall as the Highlander king, and again he noticed the exaggerated contours of her shape. Her tusks were barely visible behind those full, pouting lips. She reached out a hand and placed it on Strongwind's shoulder. The king stood still, not knowing what to expect—but he was too astonished to resist when she suddenly pressed downward with a hammer blow of force, dropping him to his knees.

He grunted and strained to rise, but she held him down with one hand while with the other she took his chin and forcibly tilted up his face. Her expression was mildly amused—except for the spark of fire he saw in her eyes. Clearly, she was enjoying this very much.

"Pretty words," Thraid said, her lips pursing in an

expression that Strongwind couldn't read. "So long as you remember your place—and fall to your knees when I so command—you will do nicely."

She squeezed his cheeks, and Strongwind's temper flared, but he exerted all of his self control to mask his feelings.

"Wandcourt, show . . . 'Whalebone' . . . where he will be staying. You and Brinda take some time to acquaint him with the household and with his tasks. For now, leave me with Lord Forlane—I have important matters to discuss, things that are not for human ears."

"Very well, my lady," replied the elder slave.

Strongwind rose stiffly and followed him through the archway and down a smaller, darker hallway. The slave king resolved to pay attention, to learn what he could. Always he would remain alert, analyzing his new masters for the weaknesses that undoubtedly existed in Winterheim's tenuous relationship with its slaves.

The King's Rampart was the loftiest platform on Winterheim's outer slopes. Only the summit itself, ice-draped and sheer, rose above it. Several paths climbed to this flat, square surface which, by tradition, was intended only for the feet of the monarch of Suderhold.

Grimwar Bane stood alone here, wearing his black bearskin robe, staring into the northwest, where the sun was nearing the horizon, bringing the end to an early autumn day. He looked between the Ice Gates, across the bright stretch of the White Bear Sea. The air, even at this lofty elevation, was cool but not cold.

He thought fleetingly about his cloak, the only black bear pelt he or any other ogre had ever seen. He had captured it from what he thought was a simple village of

Arktos peasants nine summers earlier. His warriors had slain every man of that tribe, and with only a few females and young escaping into the hills, he had thought the band eradicated.

How ironic that it had been one of those women who had become his most vexing foe! It was she who had led her people to Brackenrock, reclaiming the long-abandoned stronghold from the savage thanoi who had taken up residence there. It was she who had made the place a true fortress, a bastion that stood against his most devastating attack.

The human woman was dead now, slain with her elf companion in the catastrophic explosion that wracked Dracoheim, yet she continued to fascinate him. This was one reason why the captive warrior, the slave he had sent into the house of Thraid Dimmarkull, was interesting to him. That man had been willing to give his life for the Lady of Brackenrock, and sooner or later the king intended to ask him why.

He had more important matters to concern him for the immediate moment. Indeed, he had many things on his mind, did the king of Suderhold.

One of these was paramount. The matter of his vexatious wife demanded resolution, a resolution that would allow the king to proceed with his life, his future, in a manner of his own choosing. If Stariz remained attached to him, she would be his doom, a cancer eating away his manhood and his rule until he was an emasculated hulk, a mere puppet for the priestess-queen.

He had blustered and threatened, pleaded and dealt with her, but ever she remained the same. For all this time he had sought a solution that would work with Stariz ber Glacierheim ber Bane. Now, finally, he could see the error of diplomacy. There could be no solution with her, for she herself was the problem.

He realized now that he had to send her away. He would wait until she had performed her ritual sacrifice at the ceremony of Autumnblight, then he would make his announcement to his wife and to his people.

His marriage would end, and the rest of his life would at last begin.

8

The Remorhaz

Kerrick shivered under a sense of revulsion so strong that he almost gagged. He had never seen a monster like the beast towering in the Escarpment Pass, never even imagined that such a horror could exist—save, perhaps, in the lightless depths of the ocean, where even the gods never looked. To find such a grotesque creature here, in the shadow of the Icewall, seemed like a defiance of life itself, of every order of natural law.

Thedric Drake, a brave man, and a solid and sensible leader, was gone forever, taken in the first slashing bite of the monster. A dozen more Highlanders lay on the ground where the beast had smashed them, some dead, others writhing in pain, clutching broken limbs or puking up blood and guts from insides wracked by smashing force. Barq One-Tooth, knocked aside like a toy by the monster's first rush, had struggled to his feet and managed to stumble away.

The creature seemed to barely be getting started. The elf watched as the monster rushed forward again, smashing through the front of the war party's column, crushing men under its multiple feet, jabbing this way and that with those horrid, slashing jaws. The humans had no recourse. To a man they turned and fled back from the gap in the ridge crest, spreading out, tumbling and falling, crawling on hands and knees in frantic attempts to escape.

Some of them made it, and others didn't. The monstrous head lunged forward again and again, each time striking some hapless person. Many of these victims disappeared in a single gulp, swallowed by the same fate meted out to Thedric Drake; others were cruelly cut, even bitten in half, until the ground at the mouth of the pass was littered with body parts and gore.

Kerrick spun around, having momentarily forgotten that the horde of thanoi remained in their grim, silent semicircle. He would not have been surprised to see that band rush forward to take advantage of the human's consternation. Instead, the walrus-men seemed content to watch and to wait. All along they had been waiting.

"Why not?" muttered Bruni, who had apparently taken note of the same thing. "The tusked bastards won't take any more losses, and what in Chislev's name can we do against that thing?"

What, indeed? The monster had a segmented body that was fifty feet or more long—indeed, the tail remained out of sight, buried within the cluster of rocks from which it had burst.

"We have to try to attack it!" Moreen declared. "Surely it can be wounded somehow!"

"I agree," said Kerrick, with another glance at the ominously waiting thanoi.

"Let's go," grunted Bruni.

She had dropped her heavy pack on the ground and now drew out the Axe of Gonnas, quickly pulling the leather shroud off of the blade. The metal gleamed in the pale daylight, shining with an internal brightness. The shaft alone was nearly six feet long, and the blade was as big as a barrelhead.

The Arktos woman hefted the weapon in her hands and started toward the notch of the escarpment, Moreen and Kerrick advancing stoutly at her side. Barq One-Tooth, bleeding from several wounds, joined them, and even old Dinekki hobbled behind. Others of the war party maintained the solid rearguard under Mouse's command, facing the walrus men, banging weapons and chanting, making a show of force that would keep the thanoi away.

More Highlanders joined the small party in the advance, until there were three or four dozen fighters making the charge.

"Kradock curse that thing—it can't be slain!" grunted Barq. "I landed a sharp blow on those chest plates, and me axe bounced away like I was smitin' stone!"

"That's because your blade, solid though it be, is but cold steel," said Dinekki, who somehow managed to keep up with the striding warriors. "That is a beast of the dark corners of the planes—as such, it must be pierced by metals that have been cast in forges of godly blessing."

"My blade was made in the ancient elven fires," Kerrick volunteered grimly. "I will try it against the brute."

"This axe is a talisman of the immortals—even if it was made in the name of an ogre god," Bruni declared. "Let those gods turn its edge against the monster."

Barq looked at the woman and the elf with an expression of grudging respect. "Well, I'll attack with ye—even if I can't hurt the thing, I'll give it worry!"

More and more of the Highlanders had fallen in with them as they approached the mouth of the pass. The monster seemed to be at rest, but those bulging, multi-faceted eyes were alert, shifting and glowing as it inspected the approaching force. Slowly it drew its sinuous foreparts off of the ground, rising to twenty, then thirty feet in the air. The grotesque jaws, gory with blood and bits of clothing and flesh from its victims, gaped.

"Feel that—the beast is hot," observed the chiefwoman in surprise.

Kerrick, too, sensed the heat against his face, a sensation as though he was approaching a large pile of glowing coals.

"'Tis a remorhaz—the polar worm," said Dinekki, with a low whistle. "A creature of legend it be, and never did I think I'd be looking one in the eyes. Beware those plates on its back—they are hot enough to sear your flesh, should you come close."

"Aim for the belly, then," said Kerrick, "and strike hard."

The attackers, two score or more of them, rushed forward in unison. Again that monstrous head snapped forward and a big Highlander right next to the elf screamed as the gaping jaws descended upon him. The sound was instantly muffled as the elf struck to the side, driving the tip of his blade through the plates armoring the monster's flanks. Kerrick needed all of his strength to pull the sword out when the creature twisted away.

When the beast reared back the hapless warrior's boots were left scattered haphazardly on the ground, the elf nearly gagging as he realized that the Highlander's feet were still in them. He pressed home the attack, lunging in to stab at the exposed belly. Again, he cut through the hard, scaly surface, but the sheer size of the creature insured that he could not strike very deeply. Barq, too, struck a blow, his mundane steel cutting open one of the plates, but neither did he do much apparent damage to the rampaging beast.

Bruni had a little more success—the Axe of Gonnas blazed fire as she drove against the monster's other side, and with a powerful blow sliced off one of the spidery legs. The creature shrieked and whirled toward her, but she fended off the jaws by waving the sacred axe back and forth. Kerrick and the others then attacked frantically, stabbing, chopping, even shouting invective, and finally the monster turned away from the big woman to snap at another victim. This time it was a courageous Arktos warrior who vanished into that insatiable maw.

When the worm reared back again, the elf and humans had to yield to the inevitable, retreating in a scramble to get out of the mouth of the pass. The remorhaz lunged but came up short. This time it clawed its way fully out of its rock pile, twisting the serpentine body and sending huge boulders tumbling this way and that. Kerrick felt a stab of panic as the creature came on in a startling rush, undulating the body as its many legs clawed across the ground.

Moreen sprinted next to the elf, and he held back, giving her the edge to get away. A Highlander tumbled and fell, then screamed horribly as those mandibles stabbed down and ripped him apart. A quick glance showed the creature gathering for another lunge, and Kerrick ran desperately, passing Dinekki. He stopped in shock as he realized that the slight, elderly shaman was standing firm and alone in the face of the monster.

She held up a skinny hand and barked out the words to a spell, a casting that Kerrick had seen her use once before.

"Chislev Wilder, born of flood—render bedrock into mud!"

The remorhaz roared forward, and at the same time the swath of mountainside in its path began to darken and sag. Kerrick saw an outcrop of rock melt like butter under a hot sun, oozing down. The monster's front end reached the soft terrain, and it fell in, sinking with a splat, throwing mud up in the air as it thrashed and fought. Slowed by the mire, it pulled backward and lifted its forequarters high into the air, shaking free of the muck, regarding the humans and elf with cold, baleful eyes.

Instead of resuming its pursuit, however, the polar

worm roared a shrill sound of triumph, spewing a cloud of sulfurous smoke. Several grisly objects, charred and unrecognizable, belched from those horrific jaws to bounce and roll across the rocks. Each of these was blackened and charred, still smoking. A couple bore ghastly resemblance to burned human skulls, while one bounced and clanged metallically, rolling all the way down to the surviving warriors.

Barq One-Tooth, his expression furious, kicked at the charred and sooty object, tipped it over to reveal a concave shape. "That is Thedric Drake's helm," he growled. "Half melted by that infernal heat—and now all that is left of a brave thane." His knuckles whitened around the haft of his axe as he glared at the monster, and Kerrick wondered if his rage would compel him to make a suicidal charge, but the big warrior, with a visible effort, gained control of his emotions.

"The tuskers are still keeping their distance," Mouse reported, climbing up to where Kerrick and Moreen were studying their monstrous foe.

"I'm not surprised," Kerrick replied

"So now they just wait here for us to starve," asked Moreen bitterly, "or does anyone have any better ideas?"

Something was rattling around in Kerrick's mind, an idea that maddeningly eluded his attempts to articulate it. What had Coraltop Netfisher said in their brief conversation atop Brackenrock's tower? They would need strong drink to get over the escarpment . . . but how could that . . . ?

In a flash, he understood.

"The fireplace!" he blurted, suddenly, to looks of consternation from his companions.

"What?" snapped Moreen in irritation.

"Warqat—we have lots of canteens of it along with us, right?"

The chiefwoman shrugged her drinking skin off of her shoulder. "Here, if yours is empty, take a drink of mine, if that will cheer you up."

Dinekki's eyes were glowing excitely. "The fireplace, you said?" she repeated.

"Yes. Remember, the banquet . . . the glasses thrown into the fire?"

"And the warqat puffing up into blue flame!" the shaman added.

"Look at this charred helmet. The inside of that worm is hotter than any coals. If we can get it to swallow a bunch of warqat . . ."

Kerrick turned back to the monster, which continued to gaze at them from its position astride the entrance to the Escarpment Pass. The many wounds inflicted by the warriors at the cost of a score or more of lives were mere scratches on the armored surface. It was hard to imagine doing any more damage than that, no matter how many men and women were willing to sacrifice their lives.

"Well," he was pleased to hear Moreen say, "it's worth a try."

———◆———

The polar worm drew back into the confines of its narrow pass and curled itself around the pile of boulders. The beast lay still and silent, but those bulging eyes never closed or blinked Moreen could feel them seemingly focused directly on her even when her back was turned. At least the monster seemed content to remain in place, as did the thanoi that closed the war party off from retreat.

All of them were exhausted, following the interrupted rest of the previous night and the day of constant battle and march. Reasoning that their next attack stood a better chance if the warriors were refreshed, Moreen and Barq ordered a bivouac on the mountainside. They posted pickets to watch the tuskers and others to keep an eye on the remorhaz, while a detachment of Arktos and Highlanders went around and gathered all the canteens and skins of warqat. Naturally, Slyce volunteered for this task, but his services were politely rejected. Instead, the gully dwarf sat and watched sadly as the containers of the potent liquor were collected into an ever-growing pile from which he was kept a safe distance.

The chiefwoman stood nearby and watched the monster, thinking of the brave men who had been swallowed whole during the frantic battle and of the many others who had been grievously injured or killed by the crushing mandibles, flailing tail, and slashing claws. Did she even stand a chance of defeating it? She murmured a soft prayer to Chislev Wilder and tried to convince herself that she did.

"That elf—he can be a clever one," Dinekki remarked, breaking into Moreen's reverie.

The shaman had come up behind her unnoticed, and now she reached up to take the chiefwoman's chin in her thin, but startlingly strong, fingers. Her eyes, of ice blue, stared into the younger woman's, and the elderly priestess clucked worriedly.

"Don't take all of this to heart, lass," she said kindly. "We lost good friends today, brave and true folks, but they were doing what they chose . . . the burden of their lives does not lie on your shoulders."

"Not on mine alone, perhaps," Moreen said, "but I can't help remembering that they came here because I elected to come."

"So did they—choose to come, I mean. If you carry on with those thoughts, you'll give yourself a burden too heavy for one person, man, woman or even elf, to carry along."

At the mention of Kerrick, she turned to look at him.

He was supervising the gathering of the warqat, giving directions as the canteens were arrayed on the ground.

"Do you think his idea might work?" Moreen asked.

She was distressed when Dinekki shrugged her shoulders noncommittally. "Who knows? At least he was thinking, and came up with a plan. Almost like he had the notion whispered into his ear."

"Yes . . ." The chiefwoman wasn't sure what to think.

"He has a god of his clan, you know, just as you do, lass," the shaman suggested. "Zivilyn Greentree and Chislev Wilder are in many ways cut from the same cloth, both true gods and wise. They will help those who have faith and who are willing to work to help themselves."

"It looks like they have all the warqat collected. Let us hope, Grandmother, that our faith is true and that our gods are with us."

———◆———

It was Barq One-Tooth who came up with the idea of the Warqat Man. This was a structure made from a framework of spear shafts, designed in the approximate shape of a human, at least insofar as it had two arms, two legs, a torso, and a place for a head. It was not an image that would have fooled anyone who cared to look closely, but Kerrick had hopes that the polar worm lacked that kind of discretionary ability. In any event, it seemed like the best idea they had.

To this framework the humans attached as many of their warqat containers as they could, draping them several layers thick over the chest and limbs, bundling three of them to make a crude approximation of the head. When the first effort collapsed from an excess of weight, they made a second, using double lengths of spear shafts for support, as well as a third, anchoring a leg that would extend off the back of the thing and form a tripod mount that would hold it erect. All this time they kept the Warqat Man out of sight of the polar worm.

To distract the monster, other warriors ventured closer to the remorhaz. Some of them shot arrows at the creature, which didn't even seem to notice the missiles, while others simply pitched rocks. One bold Highlander started to climbed the cliff flanking the pass, intending to drop boulders down onto the monster. Unfortunately, the creature—after apparently ignoring the climber's efforts as he scaled fifty or sixty feet up the nearly sheer cliff—abruptly shot up to its full height, lunging upward with those deadly pincers snapping together. The mandibles closed around the desperately kicking climber's foot and plucked the man from the wall. The remorhaz released its bite, and the hapless fellow plunged down, tumbling over the jagged rocks to come to a rest near the monster's serpentine body. He lay there, groaning piteously for several minutes, until the beast placed one of its segmented legs on his chest and pressed down slowly with life-crushing force.

It was a grim group of warriors who at last prepared the Warqat Man for his sacrificial task. Kerrick, Barq, Mouse, and Bruni formed a tight screen in front of the figure, while another half dozen Highlanders took the limbs and hoisted it just off the ground. A score or more of warriors spread out to each side so the group could advance in numbers that might make the decoy easier to conceal.

Moreen insisted upon coming along, though Barq was just as adamant that she remain behind. "Who'll take over this motley lot if we fail?" he growled. "You are the one they follow, the one who must survive! You can watch from back here!"

"My place is with the rest of you who are risking your lives!" she retorted. "I will not accept orders to the contrary!"

Recognizing the stubborn clench of her jaw, Kerrick leaned in and spoke to her quietly. "No one is giving you orders," he said reasonably, with a stern glance at the glowering Barq, "but it only makes sense that you stay back, at least for this attempt. After all, if we fail, someone is going to have to lead the next try, and that will have to be you."

She glared at him, her dark eyes ice cold with fury, her mouth opening as she prepared her retort. The elf was surprised when, with visible effort, she clenched her jaws together and didn't argue.

"Very well," she said finally. "Good luck—and may all the gods watch over you."

"Thank you—I think that they are watching," was Kerrick's reply. He saw that she was terribly afraid for them and felt a surprising—and very un-elf-like—lump in his throat. "Say a prayer," he whispered, leaning forward to give her a kiss on the cheek.

The warriors then turned to the worm, which had taken no visible interest in their preparations. Fanning out across a wide front, with the Warqat Man being carried along in the middle of the group, they started forward. When they came to the swath of ground that had melted under Dinekki's spell, Kerrick was surprised to see that it had hardened again into stone—though it retained the smooth surface into which the mud had flowed.

Moving across this, each warrior held a weapon ready and stepped carefully, ready to fight or flee as the situation demanded. Closer and closer they crept, and still the monster didn't react. Kerrick vividly remembered the creature's lightning quickness, however, and feared that, at any moment, it would spring to the attack.

Finally they halted, no more than one hundred feet away from the remorhaz. The elf heard activity behind him, knew that the Highlanders were setting up the Warqat Man. "Ready!" one of them whispered, finally.

Kerrick raised his sword and took a step forward. The others did the same, waving their weapons, shouting insults and curses at the monster. Several of them reached down to pick up stones, and these they hurled in an irregular barrage. At last the monster seemed to stir, lifting its ghastly head, glaring with those pale eyes. The elf watched and saw the many legs curl underneath the segmented body, perceived the growing tension in the rigid limbs. The wave of heat was palpable, as the internal fires of the remorhaz raged into life.

The jaws parted slightly, and he knew it was time.

"Now!" he cried, turning away from the monster, glancing around to see that the rest of the advance party wasted no time in heeding his cue. All of them, Arktos and Highlanders, sprinted away, every one running back toward the mass of the war party.

All of them, that is, except for the Warqat Man. The decoy figure remained standing where the warriors had left it, a lone challenge to the suddenly enraged monster.

The polar worm reared upward, hissing in fury. Kerrick glanced back, saw those widespread jaws looming as wide as a cave mouth, the serpentine body uncoiling like a spear shot from a bow. With one chomping bite the creature bit down on the figure of sticks and water skins, again rearing back and raising its head as it swallowed the bait.

For an interminable time—at least two heartbeats—nothing seemed to happen, then the elf felt the impact of a powerful, albeit muffled, explosion. The monstrous mouth gaped open, emitting a huge rush of blue flame, and the polar worm swelled, suddenly growing much fatter. The remorhaz thrashed violently, the lashing tail breaking loose chunks of the enclosing cliffs, and a howl of unspeakable fury and pain emerged from that great form. More blue flame jetted from between the chinks in its chitonous plates, and a billowing cloud of filthy smoke roiled in the pass.

In the next instant, the monster lay still, motionless except for the acrid smoke that continued to belch from both ends of the body as well as from several huge gashes along its segmented flanks.

The remorhaz was dead.

9

Priestess and Queen

I t gleamed in her mind like the sun, shining and golden, limned in fire. It was more glorious, more precious even than the life-giving orb in the sky, for it was the talisman of her master, the image of his power and the symbol of his omnipotent will. She could discern every detail, each carved symbol and immaculate, perfect facet. Once it had been hers, to hold and cherish, but she had failed her master, her god.

The Axe of Gonnas remained just out of reach, but Stariz tried—she tried desperately—to seize that magical haft once again. Her blunt fingers strained, but they were too short for the task. Her arm was inadequate, her great weight held her down like an anchor, and the glowing object seemed to be getting farther and farther away with each panting breath. Her feet were mired in clutching mud, and a strong brute—her husband, Grimwar Bane himself—held the ogress by her shoulders, bearing her down, holding her back from that which she so desperately desired.

She was soaked in a cold sweat when she awoke to gasp aloud in anguish, for she knew that the cherished trophy remained beyond her grasp. It was gone, lost—she acknowledged in the depths of her soul—by her own failure to kill the Elven Messenger when she'd had the chance. Though he was now dead, the axe remained unattainable, locked away in the fortress of humans.

Or was it? As her pulse ceased racing, she reflected more carefully upon her dream. The intense emotion, the brilliant colors . . . these were signs of more than just a mundane, sleep-induced fantasy. There had been a magical quality, a vivid presence that she could feel in the pit of her stomach. Truly, this dream had been sent by Gonnas himself.

For what purpose? What was he trying to tell her? What did he want her to do?

"Please, O Willful One, forgive my ignorance," she whispered. "Grant me the wisdom to understand."

The great sleeping chamber, her private sanctuary, remained lightless and silent, except for the measured sound of her breathing. The walls were cold, the lamps dark. Whatever the purpose of her god's dream, it remained for her alone to decipher.

The axe remained on her mind as she rose and went about her toilette, disdaining the services even of her handmaidens, since she desired solitude for reflection. Could it be that one of the humans had dared to use the axe for some new purpose? Had it been moved from the hall of Brackenrock? She would pray and meditate on this matter and hope for enlightenment.

One of the house slaves informed her that the king had already departed, intending to inspect his treasury. She believed this, for it was too early in the day for one of his assignations, and Grimwar Bane would know better than to try and deceive her with a lie she could so easily confirm or disprove.

Satisfied that she had some time to herself, the queen lit three candles around her table and focused her mental energies on the flickers of flame. The tiny lights amplified her thoughts, and the power of her brooding god allowed her to send a silent message through the ether of magical space. She was pleased—albeit unsurprised—when Garnet Dane arrived at the secret door to her apartments only a few minutes later.

"Enter quickly," she said. "The king is gone for the next hour, but I have much to do in these precious minutes of freedom."

The spy nodded humbly and nervously scuttled through the door, standing in the shadowy alcove near the back of her dressing chamber. He looked up at her with wide, fearful eyes, and she was pleased to see that her recent discipline had apparently made a lasting impression. Long ago she had learned that fear was an important tool, a key means to instill obedience in her subjects, even in her husband.

"There is a slave in the city, the man whom we brought back from Dracoheim, captured on that island," she declared curtly. "He is a savage fighter, a very dangerous man, and I think that my husband does not understand the menace he poses. Ten days ago the slave was placed somewhere in Winterheim upon the king's orders."

"Indeed, Your Majesty. I observed him debark from the ship and understand he came to blows with one of the overseers during his initial march to the barracks." The spy looked up at her slyly. "Do you wish to have him killed?"

Stariz snorted contemptuously. "What I wish is my own concern. I do not wish for you to kill him, however. I command you to locate him!"

"Of course, Majesty. Please forgive my impertinence. Am I to assume that he remains somewhere in the city?"

"Yes, certainly. My husband has posted him somewhere and will not reveal the location to me. I think it is safe to assume that he has not been sent off to the southern mines—we have plans for him, after all, at the ceremony of Autumnblight. Rather, I had the impression that Grimwar Bane had a place of relative safety in mind for this particular slave. I would not be surprised to find him in the upper city, in some private household. I don't expect him to be at the Seagate or in the fish market or the lumber yards."

"As you know, I have many contacts in the Middle Terraces. There is one woman in particular who is very well placed to provide information on matters such as this. I will go to work at once," pledged the spy.

"As I knew you would," the queen replied smugly. "Make your report to me as soon as possible—but for now, I do not want this man know that he is the subject of royal inquiry."

"Naturally, Your Highness. As ever, I maintain discretion."

"It is your best quality," the queen replied, her eyes narrowing to bore in upon the suddenly perspiring spy. "You might say that it is all that has kept you alive . . . so far."

The secret door closed behind Garnet Dane a moment later. The queen turned to other more mundane matters, certain that the man would do everything in his power to see that she was not disappointed.

"Whalebone—I am taking you to the Nobles' Market—you will carry back the salmon for this evening, two of them." Thraid Dimmarkull made the announcement with an air of excitement, the first enthusiasm she had displayed in the week or so of the slave king's service. She reclined on the fur-lined divan where she had spent the past few hours, now pushing herself to a sitting position.

"Yes, my lady," replied Strongwind Whalebone. He masked his own reaction, but he was glad to have an opportunity to get out of these stultifying rooms in which he had been confined.

"Brinda, fetch my walking cloak," commanded the ogress.

"Yes, lady."

Brinda was making bread in the kitchen. She stopped her mixing only long enough to wipe a strand of gray hair back from her forehead. Strongwind thought she looked tired, and he wasn't surprised. Every morning the slave woman was already working when he got up from his slave's pallet. She remained busy throughout the day and was still cleaning up when he and Wandcourt retired for the night. Now she went without complaint to get a white bearskin cape, trimmed in red fur. Her husband took it and reached to drape it over their mistress's shoulders.

Strongwind was anxious to get out and see more of this city. Thus far, his work had been confined to the apartments, where he had been ordered to build some storage shelves and perform mundane cleaning tasks. He had been hoping for a chance to perhaps meet and talk to other slaves, particularly in the area of the Nobles' Market. Wandcourt and Brinda had proved to be taciturn. They had bluntly discouraged any of Strongwind's questions about their voluptuous mistress. After a few perfunctory attempts at conversation, the king had learned to keep his thoughts and words to himself.

Thraid produced a supple length of chain and a metal collar, and Strongwind guessed that he would not have a great deal of freedom on this excursion. However, the new slave was willing to endure the humiliation of having the collar shackled around his neck if it would get him out of the apartments for a few hours. Still, he glowered at Wandcourt, and the elder slave shrugged in mute apology as he fastened the device. Thraid tugged roughly on the chain, yanking Strongwind to the side as she concluded that it was attached satisfactorily.

"I will walk along willingly, my lady," he said through clenched teeth. "You will not find it necessary to jerk me along."

"Oh, but I like to!" she said with a giggle, pulling hard enough that he fell to his knees. She smiled in delight, and as he stood again the man reflected with some surprise that it was not a cruel expression but more like the innocent happiness of a child with a new toy.

"Now come, Whalebone," she said.

They departed the front door, crossed through the courtyard, and went down the narrow side street that seemed to lead only to Thraid's house. Strongwind followed behind the voluptuous ogress, taking care to stay close. Even so, she tugged hard on the chain when they reached the corner.

"This way!" she exclaimed, pointing ostentatiously, drawing the attention of others within earshot.

They joined the stream of other slaves and ogres moving along the terrace promenade. Here, as on the other levels of Winterheim he had seen, the promenade was a great, circular avenue that passed completely around the ring of the city's central atrium. The humans tended to remain away from the balcony, walking close to the building fronts that lined one side of the wide avenue. The other, with its sweeping view down to the waterfront and harbor, was best left to the ogres who strolled with much less urgency than the humans.

Strongwind, tethered as he was, found himself walking among the ogres. He noticed sneering, contemptuous glances and imagined that the brutes delighted in his chained confinement. He ignored the looks and did his best to stay close to the Lady Thraid. Only gradually did he realize that some of the looks—especially the contempt of other ogresses—seemed to be directed at his mistress, not himself. He was surprised at that, since he had guessed that the king's personal interest in his assignment had meant that the lady was a favorite of the king himself.

The Nobles' Market was up two levels, and the ogress and the slave king climbed the ramp in long strides. Finally they arrived at a wide double doorway leading into a cavernous chamber where many slaves milled about and a few armed ogres glowered and shouted orders or fingered long, wicked-looking whips. There was a great hubbub of noisy conversation and a significant amount of jostling for position in several long queues.

"A smelly lot," Thraid sniffed, indicating the mob of humans. "I command you, slave, to get me two large salmon. I shall wait for you over at the plaza inn, where I will be having a mug of tea." She reached forward and used a small key to disconnect the chain from his collar, then pressed two gold pieces into his palm. "These are for the fish and nothing else. Do you understand? On your honor, return to me swiftly."

"Certainly, my lady." The slave king's expression remained blank, but his heart pounded at the thought that he would at last be turned loose among a great congregation of slaves—and in the Nobles' Market, the place he most wanted to visit in all the city!

He wandered through the door and looked around, grateful that his height allowed him to see over most of the crowd. Six or eight large alcoves opened in the wall around the perimeter of the big room, which had a temperature much chillier than the rest of Winterheim.

After a moment's inspection, the Highlander king deduced that these alcoves each opened into a large warehouse where different types of food were kept. The alcoves were used for disbursement. Wooden signs with crude pictures marked the locations. A fish, a flask of oil, and a loaf of bread were readily found, and with a little study he understood that salt, berries, and sea-greens were among the other offerings.

He would get the salmon, but first he would seize this moment to briefly extend his freedom. Remembering Tildy Trew's words, he joined the line at the salt alcove, waited for the half dozen slaves in front of him to have their sacks filled by a big, swarthy man—obviously an Arktos—who curtly gestured for the next in the queue to move forward.

"Can't give ya salt wit'out a sack," he declared, all but sneering when Strongwind arrived before him.

"I don't want salt," he replied. "I want to talk to Black Mike."

Though he hadn't known what to expect, the Highlander king was startled when the glowering fellow reached across the counter and seized him by the front of his collar. With a jerk of a sinewy forearm, the man pulled Strongwind forward and hissed at him a few inches from his face.

"Where'd you hear a name like that? What kind of a fool are you, to use it here?" The man's mouth was clenched into a tight line, and flecks of spittle flew from his lips as he all but snarled.

Firmly the king broke the grip, his own fingers twisting the salt vendor's wrist with unrelenting pressure as he leaned back and pulled his adversary halfway onto the counter. "Where can we go to talk?" he asked, conspiratorially.

The fellow's eyes narrowed to twin spots of darkness, and his black hair and beard framed the swarthy face in bristling fur. In that instant Strongwind knew: This was Black Mike himself.

"Garic, take over here," said the salt vendor, and another fellow—a lanky, long-haired Highlander—advanced from the recesses of the alcove.

Shooting a sideways, narrow-eyed glance at the two men, he took his place at the salt counter. The slave in line behind Strongwind was already pushing forward as the Highlander king stepped to the side then went through the door that opened for him, following the other man into a dark, cool room. Blocks of salt were stacked up to twelve or more feet high, enclosing the walls of the room and forming several corridors of small passages in the large chamber. Wooden stepladders were erected here and there, providing access to the tall stacks. To one side, near the counter, several male slaves were busy grinding a salt block into granules for distribution.

"I'm taking the new man back to the evaporation room," announced Strongwind's guide. They followed a narrow corridor between two towering stacks of salt blocks, turned a corner near what seemed like the back of the room, then passed under a stone arch that led to a wide connecting hallway. At the end of that hall was a door, which the man opened then stood back, gesturing to the king to proceed.

A sense of alarm prickled along the nape of Strongwind Whalebone's neck, but he had come too far to back out now. Indeed, he was encouraged that his question had provoked such an unquestionably genuine reaction. Balling his hands into fists, he stepped through the door and quickly looked to the right.

A man was waiting there with an upraised club, and the Highlander reacted immediately, stabbing a punch into the fellow's face, drawing a curse as the would-be attacker stumbled backward. A heavy blow smashed onto Strongwind's head from behind—from another club wielder lurking on the other side of the door—and Black Mike drove into his side with a charging rush.

The king went down, but not before he kicked the second attacker in the gut. His hands grappled for the third man, and when the two hit the floor Strongwind wound up on top. Only when he saw the two clubbers raise the weapons to either side did he release his grip, springing away to face the trio in a fighting crouch.

"What's this about?" he demanded. "I ask a simple question, and you try to bash my brains in!"

Slowly he became aware that other men were in this room, a dozen or more surly-looking fellows advancing from the shadows to surround him in a menacing ring.

"I'll have the truth from you one way or another. Where did you hear that name?" demanded Black Mike.

"Your name?" Strongwind acted on his guess and saw by the man's widening eyes that he had hit the mark. "A slave woman told me—made it sound like Black Mike was somebody I'd like to talk to."

"You're awfully careless, then," snarled Black Mike. "Why shouldn't we kill you right now?"

"Because I don't know the rules of slave life in Winterheim? I've only been here for ten days, so forgive me if I come up short on some of the finer points of rebel etiquette."

"Ten days?" One of the other slaves, a muscular, stocky Highlander, spoke up. "Are you the bloke that came in on the galley with Grimwar Bane? You're the king?"

"That's me," Strongwind replied.

There were several appreciative whistles from the men. "Well, they put you to work, I see—for now," said one of them, with a grim chuckle.

The Highlander wondered what the fellow meant but didn't take the time to ask. Another slave nodded, apparently impressed. "I had it from some of the grenadiers that you gave them a pretty good licking before they took you.

Those bastards would have loved to have your head on a pike. So you're really the king of Guilderglow?"

"I was a king. It seems I am a slave, now, but I am still a man, and they have not broken my pride."

Black Mike was scrutinizing Strongwind with a more intrigued and markedly less hostile glare. He rubbed his throat where the king's fingers had throttled him. "You're a fighter, I'll grant you that, but what do you want with me? Why did you come asking after Black Mike?"

"I want to get out of this place. I want to break the backs of these slobbering ogre lords. I want to see our people free to live, to go where they will, not as slaves of brutes who can barely remember the symbols of their own civilization. The woman I talked to suggested you might have some of the same desires."

"Those are dangerous words in Winterheim," Black Mike said, shaking his head. "You're not the first man to think them—all of us have done the same—but you should know that anyone who's tried to act on them in the past has ended up dead, quickly and unpleasantly. What makes you think you'd be any different?"

"As you said, I'm a fighter, but I'm not a fool. I want to find other men, fighters like me, and see what we can do together. I might be able to help—I've got a position in the house of an ogress noblewoman."

"There's lots of slaves in houses like that," Black Mike snorted. "Most of them are pretty well tamed. Who is your mistress?"

"Thraid Dimmarkull—the lady Thraid Dimmarkull," Strongwind replied. He hoped that the name would carry some meaning, but he was surprised by the grunts of appreciation from some of the men and saw a couple exchange nudges in the ribs or mutters of coarse humor.

"Now that is interesting," said Black Mike, "and unique."

"Why?" asked the king.

"I guess you're too new here to know what's going on. You'll be interested to hear that you're serving the king's own private whore."

Grimwar Bane was running out of patience. His wife had been watching him like a hawk these past few days, and he had been unable to so much as get a message to Thraid. Yesterday, he had been obliged to inspect the treasury and as a result a splendid opportunity—six whole hours, when his wife was distracted by the training of temple acolytes—had been wasted.

Now, again, Stariz was off to the temple, and he knew she would be busy for most of the day. Though he had not communicated with his mistress, he was determined to take advantage of this chance and surprise her with a visit. He left the palace for a stroll and quickly turned around the corner into the Slaves' Way. Certain that no one was looking, he pushed through the secret door, lit the lamp, and descended the long spiral of stairs toward the terrace level. His feet drummed on the stones, a pounding cadence that bore him farther and farther downward.

Finally, panting for breath and covered with sweat, he arrived at the terminus of the secret passage. Here discretion demanded that he be careful, so he settled for a thumping knock on the panel, knowing that he was the only one who usually came to her this way. Nothing happened for several seconds, so in his growing agitation he knocked again, harder.

He was just preparing for his third signal, which in all likelihood would have knocked the door from its hinges, when the portal was pulled open to reveal Wandcourt looking at him, his eyes wide with surprse.

"Your Majesty!" said the slave, bowing deeply. "Forgive me. We were not expecting you!"

The king bulled eagerly through the door, through the room beyond and out into the apartment's main chamber. "My lady!" he called in a hoarse whisper, "I have come to you!"

"Er, Sire," Wandcourt said, hesitantly.

The king was busy looking around, realizing that there was no sign of Thraid Dimmarkull. He turned his attention to the elder human.

"What is it? Where is she? Speak man!"

"Not here, Your Majesty—though she will be terribly distressed to learn that she missed your visit. She has taken the new slave, Whalebone, to the Nobles' Market."

"She took that slave out in the city?" demanded the king, appalled.

Surely he had insisted that she keep him out of sight! Hadn't he? He growled softly, realizing that, perhaps, he had failed to make that point clear. No doubt Stariz would soon learn of the slave king's whereabouts. Still, the fellow wasn't here now, and that might be a good thing. Discretion, Grimwar Bane knew, was still important.

"Did she cloak him, hide him under a robe or something?" the ogre monarch asked hopefully.

"Not exactly, my lord king," explained Brinda, who had emerged from the kitchen to stand at her husband's side. "That is, I think she wanted to, well, show him off."

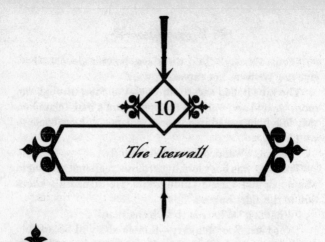

K aryl Drago ber Glacierheim was an immense ogre, even by the standards of that immense race. Indeed, it had been said by others of his kind that he was too big—as if such a thing was possible in an ogre warrior. It was not in his fighting ability that his size was viewed as a liability. On the contrary, Karyl's prowess with his great, stone-headed club was legendary. He easily twirled around a weapon that a normal ogre would have trouble lifting from the ground. He had never been defeated in combat, not by human slaves, thanoi foes, or ogre opponents. Once he had broken the neck of an ice bear in an arena contest, just for the sport of it.

Unfortunately, the strength of his musculature and his grace with that mighty club were not matched by a sense of ease in the presence of other ogres, nor, most notably, did he possess even the rudimentary manners needed to master the confines and rituals of Noble Winterheim.

Karyl Drago had been born and raised in the remote outpost of Glacierheim, where by the time of adulthood his reputation as the barony's pre-eminent warrior was well established. Even there, in that mannerless, practically barbaric community, his lack of social graces had marked him as an outcast.

At the drunken brawls that passed for the baron's celebrations, no one wanted to sit next to Karyl Drago. Not only did he take up enough bench space for any two normal ogres, but he jealously and aggressively reached for every scrap of food, every tankard of beverage, that came within reach. Since his arms were as correspondingly huge as the rest of him, this inevitably resulted in a scouring of the banquet table that left very few tidbits for the other ogres in the immediate area.

Any attempt to redress this matter would inevitably provoke the great brute to violence, and no one—or two or even three—wanted to face up to Karyl Drago when he was enraged. Also futile was the effort undertaken by the baron himself to speak to the ogre after such incidents. Drago would willingly agree to behave himself next time, and he certainly meant those words, yet he would just as certainly forget his promises when once again subjected to the temptations of roast bear haunch or seasoned warqat.

When the baron's daughter, Stariz ber Glacierheim, had been summoned to the royal capital by the former king, Grimtruth Bane, as a suitable match for his son, Grimwar, the baron had sent a score of warriors from his own garrison as an honor guard to accompany Stariz to Winterheim and to stay with her in the city. He took a great deal of pleasure in assigning Karyl Drago to this detachment.

Drago's own reactions to this move were straightforward. He did as he was ordered, of course, and indeed he looked forward to life in Winterheim, which was widely known as the center of all ogre culture in Icereach. In fact, Drago had a secret fascination with all things gold and knew that Winterheim was the greatest magnet for gold in the world—at least, in all the world that was the Icereach.

There he hoped to find some pretty toys that he could gather to himself and cherish.

As for the soon-to-be queen Stariz, with her mysterious rituals and undeniable influence with the Willful One, she frightened him, just as she frightened almost everyone else. In fact, there were rumors that her own father found her to be such an ominous presence that he had vigorously sought the match with the king and had agreed to a surprisingly miniscule dowry—a few silver mines and a hundred human slaves—in order to ensure that she would be shipped off to the capital.

Whereas Stariz had really found her element in Winterheim, quickly assuming mastery of the great temple there even as her husband ascended to the throne, Drago was even more out of place in the great city than he had been in the less cultured land of his birth. His first experience with a royal banquet had been nearly disastrous when he had elbowed the obese Lord Quendip out of the way in a lunge for a prime rib—all the ribs, actually—of beef. The lord's six handlers had tried to intervene, and they had ended up with one broken arm and two dislocated shoulders. Lord Quendip had demanded exile for the offending lout, but the king—who knew a good fighting man when he saw him— declared instead that the hulking Karyl would be assigned to the garrisons of the outer palisades.

His first post had been at the South Gate, where the roads to the vast gold mines converged upon the city. Drago had been part of a hundred-ogre garrison charged with careful observation of all who entered or departed the city, as well as with the operation of the great stone gate itself. Karyl's strength was a great asset in the gate-opening—he could turn the massive winch alone, though it had previously required the efforts of a half dozen stalwart ogres. Here too, however, his uncouth behavior led to suspicion and dislike from his barracks-mates. There never seemed to be enough food or drink for both Drago and the ninety-nine other ogres who shared his quarters.

It was at this posting, however, that Drago really began to develop the love that was to last the remainder of his life. It was not an emotion extended toward any other being, male or female, that welled up in his mighty heart. Instead, he began to truly nurture his fascination and fondness for the golden metal itself, the product of the rich mines that had always captured his fancy.

Not that he was greedy or inclined to thievery or the amassing of wealth—far from it. Drago's worshipful affection for gold was a purely aesthetic expression. Quite simply, he liked it because it was pretty to look at. He loved to study the metal, caress golden objects in his huge hands, feel its good, solid weight against his chest. His favorite items of gold were not the solid ingots that were imported so steadily into the city. Rather they were the small ornaments, the rings, chains and medallions, even the children's toys sculpted into the shape of seals or bears. To most ogres, these lacked the value of the solid gold bar, and Drago had no difficulty amassing quite a collection of such trinkets. When he was not working he would sit in his room in the barracks, surrounded by his toys, admiring them.

In the end, as it had been in the palace, it was an incident with a noble that rendered the assignment at the South Gate unworkable. A certain duke, Greckan Marst, was charged with administering nearly half of the royal gold mines. On one occasion, he decided to make journey of inspection and to do it incognito so that his charges would have no advance warning of his arrival. Leaving the city on foot with merely a dozen slaves to bear the provisions required by the duke on his three-day tour, Grackan Marst led his entourage through the gate that had been opened by Karyl Drago.

The last slave in Grackan Marst's entourage captured the eye of the hulking gatekeeper, whose appetite had been enhanced by the exertions of wheeling aside six tons of solid granite. A carelessly wrapped leg of venison jutted from the hapless human's backpack, and Drago reacted without thinking. He reached and tugged, freeing the deer meat but inadvertently breaking the slave's neck in the process.

The duke's mission had been thwarted by the subsequent delay though his wrath was soothed by a royal payment. Once again Drago was reassigned. This time he joined the overseers of the many hundreds of slaves at the Seagate, the massive portal allowing access to the city's subterranean harbor. His work was good—he terrified the slaves into certain obedience, but since this was the route by which all the salmon fishers brought their goods into the city it was only a matter of time before trouble resulted there as well.

Finally the king decided upon the perfect assignment for Drago. There was a lonely gate into the Winterheim Warrens, far from the city and removed from nearly all ogre citizens of either noble or common birth. It was such a small and unimportant outpost that it required but a dozen ogres to guard it, so long as they were led by a warrior of stout courage and battle fitness. In other words, it was the perfect place for Karyl Drago.

He was assigned to the gate at the summit of Icewall Pass. He watched the narrow aperture throughout the sunlit months of the year, withdrawing into the city only during the fury of the Sturmfrost and the three months of frigid night that followed that epic, annual blizzard. Bears and seals were not uncommon around the Icewall, and Drago and his men were allowed to kill and eat as many of these as they desired. They had an ample supply of coal for cooking, and every few months a caravan of slaves would bring them a new keg of warqat from the city's distilleries.

The ogres of his garrison were as uncouth and barbaric a lot as one could find in all the Icereach. They respected him as their master and allowed him first pick of all sustenance, be it in solid or liquid form. In return, he gave them freedom to drink, hunt and gamble unfettered by the restraints of civilized society.

He never bothered any other ogres because he never saw any other ogres, and the king gained the security of knowing that the Icewall garrison was commanded by as fit a warrior as any in his service.

Karyl brought his golden trinkets with him, of course, and on days when his henchmen watched the sea and the land, he spent much of the time in simple play, admiring the sleek coat of a little golden seal or imagining the growls of a rearing golden bear. He made jangling necklaces of his medallions and rings, and he found the music of that metallic tinkling to be the most pleasant sound in the world.

For ten years Drago had held this post. On many sunny mornings he took the guard duty himself and beheld the dazzling expanse of the White Bear Sea extending far to the north from the base of the Icewall. When the weather was cloudy or foggy he patrolled the steep, narrow pass relentlessly, assuring himself that no intruder ventured there. For ten years there had been no intruders, save for the hapless bears that occasionally and fatally mistook the entrance to the Icewall Gate for the mouth of a sheltering cave.

Despite the lack of any real threat, Karyl Drago's vigilance never waned. His loutish appearance might have suggested a certain simplicity of intellect, but—except when it came to matters of self-control—he was in fact a rather intelligent example of his race. He knew every inch of his pass, each approach to the narrow entrance that did, indeed, resemble the mouth of a natural cave. Though wafts of natural steam warmed the shelter and the entire interior of the cavern, he never shirked the duties that drew him outside to study, inspect, and patrol. His men came to respect, even to love him, for he was fair and willing to work as hard as any of the guards under his command. Also, he could smash the skulls and break the bones of any two of them without breaking a sweat, and to an ogre warrior this was an attribute demanding high honor and complete obedience.

Thus it was on yet another sunlit morning, with the mountainside slicked by early autumn frost, that he decided to look upon his world. He called in Squint-Eye, who had had the duty through the pale dawn, and Drago emerged alone to look down the steep slope toward the always-empty tundra. He stretched, yawned, and scrutinized—then hesitated. Was that something down there? He stared and blinked, rubbed his eyes, and looked again, wondering if his vision was playing tricks.

His eyes were accurate. There was a file of people down there, either humans or thanoi, since they were too small to be ogres, and they seemed to be marching directly toward the base of Icewall Pass. As the disbelieving Drago watched, he studied the posture of the marchers, noted that they wore fur and wool clothes, and lacked the characteristic tusks of the walrus men. This could only confirm his first suspicions: There were humans coming toward his pass, his gate. The mighty ogre warrior crouched low in the crest of that pass and watched. He estimated that there were several hundred potential intruders.

To left and right the Icewall rose as a perfect precipice, a barrier to all land-bound creatures. Only here, where the great cliff was notched by the pass, was there a place for passage, so Drago knew at once that they would be coming up to the gate that it was his solemn duty to protect.

The big ogre lifted the club from his back, withdrew from the lip of the cliff, and settled down to wait. He thought about rousting his garrison but decided to wait. After all, there were only a few hundred humans, and they had a very long climb in front of them before they could really begin to make trouble.

◆◆◆

"You have a care now, y'hear?" warned Dinekki, squinting in concern as she looked up at the steep, smooth face of Icewall Pass. "I've got an ache in my bones that tells me there's danger here—real, nasty danger."

"Thank you for the warning, Grandmother," replied Moreen, seated on the narrow strand of gravel beach at the base of the steep incline. She was draining her boots, which had gotten soaked as the war party had been forced to wade through shallow water to skirt the foot of the Ice-wall. "It's the gateway to an ogre fortress—I'd be more worried if your bones told me there was *no* danger here."

The warriors, numbering around three hundred after casualties from battle with the tuskers and the remorhaz, were still filing through the placid water, following a gravel shelf where it was only a foot or two deep. They gathered in this shallow and calm cove at the very southern end of the White Bear Sea. A few gulls cawed and circled overhead. Aside from the birds and an occasional seal, the companions had seen no sign of life along this barren and desolate shore. The looming bulk of Winterheim rose twenty miles or more away, down the coast and along the Icewall. The summit rose high into the clear air, trailing wisps of clouds draped over the peak like royal pennants.

The old shaman clucked in irritation. "I don't mean just general trouble. There's something up there watching and waiting."

"I take that very seriously," Kerrick said. He stood beside Moreen, stringing his bow as he studied the impressive height. "Whatever is guarding up there has all the advantages. There's no cover on that pass, and it looks slippery enough that we'll have to really watch our step. A well-placed rockslide could bring this whole mission to an end before we even get started."

"Bah," snorted Barq One-Tooth contemptuously. He held his great axe in his hands and scowled at the slope as if it was a sentient foe. "This is nothing to deter a Highlander. You seashore types wait here, and I'll take care of it meself. I'll tell you when it's safe to come up. You'd better be right about finding a cave up there!"

Kerrick ignored the blustering human, turning to look at the next member of the party, Bruni, as she waded ashore. Her large pack bulked high, rising even over her broad shoulders. Jutting from the top of that pack, with its golden blade still wrapped in dark sealskin, the Axe of Gonnas seemed to wave like an exotic headdress.

"You might want that somewhere you can get it out easier," noted the Highlander thane, pointing to the big weapon.

Bruni hefted her walking stick, a stout piece of knobby cedar that was more than six feet long. "I have this. As to the talisman of the ogre god . . . let's just say I'm saving it for a special occasion."

Kerrick was glad of this. He knew that she had used it, reluctantly, against the remorhaz, but he agreed with her that it was best to keep it out of sight and quiet as much as possible.

"I think a few of us should go ahead and scout out the pass," said the chiefwoman. "That slope is terribly exposed. I don't like the thought of our whole war party getting caught there."

"Good idea," Barq said quickly. "I'll lead the way. You pick who's to come along behind."

Moreen declared that she would come too, and Kerrick and Bruni quickly insisted upon joining the scouting force. The chiefwoman's hand went to the hilt of her sword, the weapon dangling freely from her belt. She clenched, almost drew the blade, then relaxed her grip. "I think I might need both hands just to climb this thing."

Still holding his bow, Kerrick was wondering the same thing. Though this notch in the Icewall had been termed a "pass," it bore no resemblance to any kind of pass he knew about. True, the top of the massive precipice dipped significantly here. It was perhaps eight hundred or a thousand feet above them, as opposed to nearly twice that elevation for much of the barrier. However, there was no discernable path or road leading from this narrow beach to the gap atop the wall. Instead, the slope ascended steeply at an angle approaching forty-five degrees.

He corrected his first impression of a featureless slope, however, when he saw that the wall was in fact scored by a series of parallel gullies or ravines that ran like vertical stripes from the summit all the way down to the shore. While this barrier was termed the Icewall, he saw that the terrain was mostly rough bedrock. Long strips of ice and hard packed snow had accumulated in the beds of the gullies, adding to the appearance of stripes.

"I think we can stick to the rocks and get fairly decent footing," he said.

Barq One-Tooth had not waited for this observation to commence his own approach. Swaggering across the beach, he went up to the same gully the elf had been eyeing as the most promising route. The Highlander stepped onto a rock, used his free hand to reach for another handhold, and quickly started to pull himself up. He didn't look back.

Moreen scowled in exasperation, but Kerrick merely smiled and patted her on the shoulder. She glared at him then started after the Highlander.

"Give him a little room," the elf suggested, sauntering behind the chiefwoman, with Bruni bringing up the rear. "If he knocks a rock loose, you'd like to have enough time to duck out of the way."

Heeding his advice, Moreen waited another minute before starting onto the slope. Kerrick did the same before following. He was impressed to see that Barq was actually picking out a fairly decent route up the steep incline. It was more like climbing a stairway than walking along a path, but many of the stone "steps" had flat tops, and all of them seemed firmly anchored to the mountain. Working steadily, placing his feet with care and using his hands when necessary to aid his balance, he moved upward.

Kerrick was surprised when a half hour later he looked down to see that the warriors gathered along the beach had dwindled to the size of ants next to the placid water. They were drying off, resting, wiping salt off of their swords and spearheads, and watching the progress of the four scouts. Kerrick chuckled as he saw Slyce get slapped away from a Highlander's pack. The gully dwarf was still bemoaning the loss of the warqat they had expended in attacking the remorhaz. He had displayed considerable ingenuity in trying to pilfer the loads of the fighters, who as a consequence had become vigilant in looking out for him.

Pausing to catch his breath, the elf enjoyed the sparkling expanse of the sea, with a few rocky islands barely visible on the northern horizon. He watched Bruni climbing steadily toward him and saw that the big woman advanced with measured strides. Despite her heavy load—she and Barq both carried huge packs—she didn't seem to be tired. When she looked upward, he saw that her face was slicked with sweat, but that didn't stop her from smiling broadly as she met his gaze.

"Nice stroll through the hills," she remarked, drawing deep breaths as she slowly climbed closer to the elf.

"I agree—I wish all of it would be this pleasant," he replied.

They resumed the climb after a brief rest, the four of them separated by intervals of fifty or sixty feet. At the foot of the pass, some of the warriors were starting to come up after them, but they were still giving the scouts lots of room. Looking up, Kerrick guessed that the Highlander must be drawing near to the summit, though the actual top of the slope couldn't be discerned from his position on the side.

He heard an abrupt crash, stones striking stones, then he caught a glimpse of something—a huge brown bear?—on the mountain above Barq One-Tooth. The elf squinted, trying to see what was going on. The hulking shape, more manlike than a bear, dropped from the elf's view, but not before Kerrick could see that a number of stones were tumbling down the steep slope. Barq shouted an alarm, then grunted and toppled backward as he was knocked from his perch on the steep slope.

"Hold on!" cried Kerrick. Above him, Moreen threw herself flat against the mountainside, her hands clawing for grip on the rocks as she braced her feet. Several rocks tumbled past, a few stones rolling right over her, but her position was secure.

Not so for the big Highlander. He had landed on his back and kept rolling, kicking and flailing as he plummeted past Moreen, and still building up speed, falling straight toward Kerrick. The elf braced his feet and one hand, and reached with the other, clasping a fringe of Barq's bearskin cloak. The jerk almost tore Kerrick's arm from his shoulder and produced a sputtering curse from the Highlander as the cape's clasp first tightened around his throat, then snapped apart.

Kerrick was left holding the white bear pelt as Barq continued his fall, sliding headfirst down the gully. More noise clattered as rocks tumbled after, and the elf instinctively crouched against the mountainside, pulling the bearskin up as protection for his head. He felt the pummeling blows of fist- and skull-sized stones but was able to maintain his position in spite of the barrage. Moments later the last of the rocks had passed, the rattle of noise dropping away below.

A quick glance above showed that Moreen still clung to her own handholds. Turning his attention downward, the elf saw that Bruni had flung herself sideways and somehow wrapped a big hand around Barq One-Tooth's ankle as the thane tumbled past. She was splayed across the slope, feet braced on big rocks, her uphill arm stiffened into a beam of support while she strained to keep the heavy man from falling farther down ravine. Rocks banged into her shoulders, bounced off her pack, and tumbled away, and still she held firm.

Cursing loudly but possessing enough sense not to thrash against his rescuer's grip, Barq swung himself around to get his own feet under him. Satisfied that the Highlander was not going to fall farther, Kerrick looked toward Moreen again and beyond the chiefwoman as he saw that huge shape moving across the mountainside again.

It was definitely not a bear. It seemed too large to be an ogre, but whatever it was, it was now lifting a gargantuan club and slowly, carefully, descending the gully toward the Lady of Brackenrock.

Spy and Slave

Strongwind was on his way out of the salt block storage room when he felt a firm hand on his shoulder. He turned to see Black Mike, dark brow furrowed with concern, peering at him closely.

"One more thing. I'm going to be keeping my eye on you," declared the swarthy rebel with no hint of apology. "I don't like that you heard my name so soon—or the way you came looking for me."

"I am a man of direct action," the slave king replied. "Your secrets are safe with me—and as I told you, I think I'm in a position to help your movement."

Mike snorted. "Movement? Bunch of skulking around, pretending something might happen? Not much movement going on, but we're still alive, and we want to keep it that way."

"I may have misjudged you," Strongwind said, his tone intentionally harsh. "A lifetime of slavery is intolerable, but people make adjustments. Maybe you've adjusted more than you want to let on?"

"You watch your tongue!" The brawny hand on his shoulder tightened its grip, and the Highlander shrugged it away, quickly snatching Black Mike's wrist in his own hand, squeezing until he felt the bones start to shift.

"I am used to watching my tongue," replied Strongwind, conversationally. "I never say anything unless I mean it."

The rebel stared into Strongwind's eyes for a long beat, as if studying him. Finally he spoke again. "If you're speaking the truth and you want to do something, see if you can learn how the king gets to the Lady Thraid. We know that he has a way to do so, but none of us has been able to track him. He is the monarch of this entire city, and it cannot be possible for him to hide—yet somehow, he does."

The slave king nodded, his expression cold. "I will keep my eyes open," he said.

He turned his back on the glowering slave and made his way through the salt alcove into the great room of the market. The line at the fish booth was long, but he stood patiently waiting until he was able to collect the two salmon requested by Thraid Dimmarkull. The two large fish were whole, though they had been gutted, and they were wrapped in a blanket of fresh kelp. Carrying the load awkwardly in both hands, he started toward the gateway leading back to the promenade.

"Hey, Big Guy—where have you been keeping yourself?"

"Tildy—hello!" He was delighted to see the short, sturdy slavewoman, who had come up beside him unnoticed. Her cheeks were bright and rosy, and her eyes sparkled as she smiled at him.

"Looks like they've got you loaded down, already."

"I guess so," he said. "What are you here for, fish, salt, or something else?"

She laughed, and brandished a piece of parchment. "All that, and more, but I don't have to carry it. I just bring a list, and they send it up to the Posting House. They keep us pretty well supplied." Her expression grew more serious, and she looked at him carefully. "How is it for you? Have they given you a decent station?"

Strongwind shrugged. "A nice enough house, and the duty is not too hard. I think I might go mad if I had to keep at it for more than a month or two, though."

"A noble lady's house, Lord Forlane said. Who is your mistress?"

Strongwind hesitated momentarily, yet he quickly remembered that Tildy was the one who had, indirectly, put him in contact with the rebels.

"Her name is Thraid Dimmarkull," the king replied, smiling as Tildy's eyes widened. "I take it you've heard of her?"

"Heard of her and seen her. Her house is better than lots of places you could have ended up, I'm thinking."

The slave king started to look around as they emerged from the great market hall, afraid that his encounter with Black Mike had taken long enough that Thraid would be irritated or even suspicious

"You! Slave!"

He turned to see a strapping ogre in the uniform of the King's Grenadiers bearing down on him. The brute's mouth was set into a cruel smile, but it wasn't until the ogre rubbed a hand across his nostrils that Strongwind recognized him as Bloodsnout, the guard he had punched in the first hour of his stay in Winterheim.

"Careful," Tildy whispered, somewhat unnecessarily.

"Here—can you hold these for a moment," replied Strongwind, handing the two salmon to the slave woman.

"I look for you," snarled the ogre, stomping closer.

"Glad to see you got that nosebleed cleared up," said the man breezily.

Bloodsnout roared loudly, tucked his head, and charged with his long arms outstretched. Remembering the lash across his back, Strongwind skipped out of the way as the ogre rushed past. The enraged brute stumbled and nearly fell, finally lurching to a halt in the doorway to the market. Dozens of slaves scattered out of the way, many of them looking open-mouthed at the infuriated ogre and his calmly taunting adversary. Shouts came from the ogre guards in the market, but the throng crowding in the doorway prevented them from rushing out to intervene.

Strongwind was preparing to dodge another assault when he saw that Bloodsnout was hesitating, looking past the slave at something on the promenade.

"Whalebone! It's about time!"

He actually felt a rush of relief to see the noble ogress come trundling toward him. He pivoted and bowed deeply.

"Yes, my lady." He quickly took the two salmon, which Tildy held out for him. "I am returning with the fish, as you requested."

"You were dawdling!" she sniffed, with a contemptuous glance first at Bloodsnout, then at Tildy Trew. "I was waiting for you too long!"

"My apologies, mistress," he said humbly. "There were a great many slaves in the queue, and I did not press forward as aggressively as I might have."

"Humph!" Thraid snorted. She extended the chain and fastened the lock to Strongwind's collar while he stood still, biting back the anger he felt at the humiliating bondage. He was ready for her to pull on the chain, and when she did he was already moving, so that she didn't yank him off of his feet.

"Come along, then!" she snorted, stomping away, with another jerk on the chain.

He took the time for one glance backward, saw Bloodsnout glowering at him, and caught a wink and amused smile from Tildy Trew. Strongwind fell in beside Thraid, who set a brisk pace along the promenade.

"Did you speak to the wench who is your informant?" Stariz asked, glowering at Garnet Dane in the temple where they met. He cringed as he advanced, then dropped to press his face to the floor before answering. "I want to know what my husband has done with this Highlander slave!"

"Yes, your majesty. My contact had good information. She tells me that the Highlander prisoner has been assigned to none other than the Lady Thraid Dimmarkull as a house-slave."

"What? What! My husband intends to hide his prize away in his lover's house?"

At first, her reaction was pure outrage—how dare he? Anger surged at the thought of this further humiliation, certainly done to cater to some whim of the wench. However, as she stomped around and thought about it, a tight smile gradually creased her square face. There were ways this might be turned to her advantage. This might not be such a bad thing, not so bad at all.

"So it would seem, my queen," replied Garnet Dane. "Do you wish to command any further action on my part or upon that of my agents?"

She looked at him, eyes narrowed shrewdly. "No. For now it is enough to know where he has been placed. I think that his spirit will still slake the vengeful thirst of our god at the ceremony of Autumnblight, though he may have other uses before then. Tell me, this informant of yours—do you trust her? Is she well placed to maintain contact with the slave?"

"I can say that she has been a trusted source of information for many years, your highness. She seems very well placed in the human slave circles, with access to many different people, and I get the impression that she is trusted by all of them."

"Who is she? What is her station?" asked Stariz bluntly.

She was surprised when her spy straightened up, regarding her with a fearful but determined, gaze. "I cannot tell you that, my queen—this is one of those few matters where I must maintain my own counsel."

"You are audacious besides impertinent," she said coldly. "Have you forgotten so soon my punishment of your failure?"

"Nay, Lady Queen, nor shall I ever forget. Please know that I shall allow no failure to occur again, but there are some secrets I must maintain solely to ensure that my own value is . . . understood."

The queen nodded slowly. Despite herself she admired this little show of self-protection. Besides, the identity of the spy's agents did not seem to be a matter she needed to pursue immediately.

"Very well. See that you remember your pledge, and maintain your ties with this informant. Caution her that she must continue ultimate discretion, for now she is to watch and wait. When the time is right, we will take action."

"It shall be as you command, My Queen," replied the spy, his face still pressed to the floor. "Do you have more instructions for me now?"

"No. You have done well this time. Now, leave me— I have rites to peform, then I must return to the royal apartments."

The spy hastily withdrew, and the priestess queen turned to don her ghastly mask. Quickly she entered the sanctuary with its looming black statue and knelt at the feet of the monstrous image.

"My willful master," she began and immediately was pressed flat upon the floor as the immortal weight of Gonnas came to bear full upon her flesh. She gasped from the mixture of pleasure and pain and sobbed out her acquiescence to her lord's every command.

"What is it you wish of me, O Gonnas?" she gasped, fighting to push the air from her throat.

The response was not verbal, but she immediately sensed images of danger and menace, images of fury and volence, storming through her mind. She quailed at a sense of barely contained rage. She pictured a bull ogre in chains, frantically raging against his bonds and coming very near to breaking free. This was her god, both thrilling and terrifying. She quivered at the thought of the unspeakable power, the massive destruction, that might be wrought by the Willful One, should his anger be fully unleashed upon the world.

A bear lurked amidst her vision this time, the bruin followed by a leaping deer, and she recognized these two sigils of the human gods. Kradok, the god of the Highlanders, was often viewed as a bear, while Chislev Wilder—deity of the Arktos—assumed the guise of a deer, bird, fish, or other wild animal at will. As she watched, the bear loomed up to embrace the deer, and the two creatures fell to the ground, rolling together and soon merging into the flesh of one animal.

"I understand, lord," she murmured. "I know thy enemy, and she is mine as well."

Now she was pressed with a savage weight, far more painful than before, and she groaned and screamed in agony. "How have I failed you, master?" she cried, begging for an answer.

The response came in the form of another vision, an image of a leafy tree sprouting from the barren tundra. Limbs spread wide, and verdant greenery expanded in utter defiance of the snow and ice that spread in all directions. The tree seemed to have a light of its own, an internal brilliance that drove back the wintery dusk that should properly have shrouded such a scene.

This was the sign of another god, Zivilyn Greentree, she realized, and she took the vision as a warning. A warning of what? This was a god not of humans nor of the Icereach. Rather, the green tree was a god of seafaring elves. . . .

She felt fear, then, as a cold, angry pain took root in the pit of her stomach.

———◆———

"I will wait for the Lady Thraid here," Grimwar Bane sourly told Thraid's two slaves.

"Of course, Sire," said Wandcourt, the male. He arranged a fur and several pillows on the large, sturdy divan, and the king made himself comfortable. "I would expect the Lady Thraid to return within the hour."

"May I get Your Majesty a mug of ale or warqat?" asked the female, Brinda.

King Grimwar nodded distractedly, then gestured to the man as his wife went to fetch him a drink. "The lady's new slave . . . ?"

"Yes, Sire?"

"As regards the matter of discretion, I should like the slave to remain ignorant of my presence here. I want you to summon two of my grenadiers from the Terrace Level watch station and post them outside the door. They are to see that the slave remains outside when your mistress returns home."

"It shall be done, Your Highness," said the man, bowing then leaving the apartment.

———◆———

"You were flirting with her, I saw," Thraid remarked grumpily to Strongwind, as they made their way back down to the Terrace Level.

"With whom?" he asked, startled.

"That Trew woman. I know her. Brinda has warned me that she is an untrustworthy wench."

"We were not 'flirting,' " retorted the slave king stiffly. "She was kind to me when I was first brought to the Posting House. She merely asked how my life has progressed since then."

"Oh? What did you tell her?"

Strongwind bowed deferentially. "I explained that I had been assigned to the house of a great noblewoman and that I was bringing fish from the market—and just then I was accosted."

"That Grenadier? Why did he attack you?"

"Because I punched him, Lady, on the day I was brought off the ship. He was a bully, and he made me angry."

She looked at him slyly, her lips pursed as she considered his words. "I was warned that you could be dangerous. Would you ever dare to strike me?"

"No, I wouldn't. You are not a bully," Strongwind replied, realizing to his surprise that he was speaking the truth.

She smiled, apparently pleased with his words, and let the chain hang slackly for the rest of their descent. Soon they reached the Terrace Level, and ten minutes later they turned down the street leading away from the Promenade. Whale oil lamps, as always, kept the avenue brightly lit, though it seemed to Strongwind that there were fewer pedestrians about than would usually be found here during the middle of the day.

Thraid's apartment was at the far end of this street. He had noted before that the lady's chambers abutted the mountainside at the periphery of Winterheim's hollow core—she had mentioned once that this helped to ensure her privacy as well as eliminate the problem of noisy neighbors.

Bearing his fish-load into that courtyard, still trailing the ogress, Strongwind was thinking about nothing so much as a cold glass of water, about putting down the load and catching his breath. He was taken by surprise when two large ogres, both dressed in the scarlet livery of the King's Grenadiers, accosted them before the apartment's front door.

"Mistress Thraid, welcome," said one, with a deep bow.

"I thank you, but why—?" Abruptly a flush came to the ogress's round cheeks, and she pressed a hand to her lips. "Oh my!" she declared. Quickly she stepped between the two guards, pushed open the door, and vanished into the apartment. His leash left dangling, Strongwind made to follow.

"Where you goin', slave?" demanded one of the grenadiers, placing a rough hand on Strongwind's shoulder, stopping him in mid-step.

"This is the house of my mistress," he replied levelly. "I am on an errand for the Lady Thraid."

"Yeah? Well, she's got a different errand now fer herself."

"What should we do with 'im?" hissed the other guard.

"Oh, he can't go far. You just find somethin' else to do, and come back in . . ." The ogre looked at his companion, who winked and grinned.

"Better make it two hours," said the first guard, with a deep chuckle of amusement.

"Very well," Strongwind said, puzzled—until, in a flash, he understood the guard's odd grin. "I will leave this fish here and return later."

The guards nodded carelessly, moving back into the shadows where they couldn't be seen by the few passersby who came back this far from the promenade. Strongwind Whalebone turned his back and sauntered away until soon he was around the corner and out of view. There he found a small alcove in the side of the street where he could remain hidden. Making himself as comfortable as possible, he settled down to wait.

And to watch.

 sk—I knew something was bad about this," Dinekki noted tartly. "Not that these youngsters ever listen to me!"

Mouse was standing on the shore beside the shaman, squinting up the bright, sunlit slope. He could clearly see the huge, menacing figure, brandishing a club and descending slowly toward the much smaller shape of Moreen, who was clinging to the steep slope.

"What is that thing up there?"

"Trouble," retorted the old woman, not too helpfully he thought, but Mouse knew better than to distract the shaman as she rummaged through her pack and quickly pulled out a small circlet that seemed to be made of twigs and seaweed.

She whistled, loudly, and the gulls that had been swirling above the cove abruptly swept close, one of them coming to land on the ground at the shaman's feet. To Mouse it sounded as if Dinekki was mimicking bird sounds. She clacked and cawed as the bird watched her with dark, glittering eyes. Finally the woman extended her hand, and the gull snatched the thin wreath in its beak. With a flap of its white wings it flew across the beach, skimmed the surface of the water, and still bearing its odd burden, started to climb.

"What did you tell the bird?" Mouse ventured to ask finally, feeling sick to his stomach as he saw the giant, club-wielding creature advancing down the slope toward Moreen and her precarious perch. From his angle it was hard to see how far apart they were, but he could tell that the brute was descending steadily, and Moreen didn't seem to be moving.

"Just asked it for a little help on behalf of Chislev Wilder. I guess we'll have to watch and see if it understands."

Karyl Drago was pleased that his initial rockslide hadn't swept all the humans down the slope and into the sea. Though the end result would be much the same, the avalanche lacked the fun of the bone-crunching melee he so looked forward to. It looked as if he were going to be able to get his club wet and flex his muscles a little bit. Truthfully, the big ogre admitted in a tiny corner of his mind, since this was the only action he had seen in ten years, he wanted to stretch things out a little, to really enjoy himself.

To that end, he made his way cautiously down the steep terrain of the gully. His feet were too big for most of the footholds, so he balanced his heels on the steps and used his free hand to help him keep his balance. His tree-trunk of a club he hoisted easily in his other hand, ready to swing it as soon as one of the intruders came into range.

Despite their advantage in numbers, he didn't think these humans would provide much sport. His best hope was that they carried some pretty golden things with them so that when they were dead he could look through their belongings and claim a new prize or two for his collection.

The closest human was now looking up at him, and he recognized her as a female. Surprisingly, she didn't seem terribly afraid, not like most of the human slave women he had encountered, who would run away screaming if he so much as furrowed his brow at them. Instead, she glared at him with a look of cool appraisal, holding tight to the mountainside as he made his way downward.

She was some distance below him still. He knew that he could have smashed her off the mountain by throwing a well-aimed rock. Even if he missed with a few tosses, there was nowhere for her to hide. The big ogre shrugged. He had decided to use his club, and use his club he would.

Something hissed past his ear, surprising him. He heard a clattering on the stones above and behind him, and he turned to look, seeing a broken arrow lying next to a nearby boulder. Blinking in surprise, Karyl looked farther down the slope and saw that another of the intruders had pulled out his bow and was even now aiming another feathered missile.

That one sped upward, and the big ogre hunched to the side, feeling a pinprick in his shoulder as the shaft stuck there, quivering like a living thing. Karyl was impressed. After all, he wore a stiff shirt of dried leather and two layers of bearskins over that. For this archer to penetrate all of that in a steep, uphill shot was no mean feat. He left the arrow jutting there for inspection later. Though he could feel the scrape of the head against his skin, he knew that the missile had done no real damage.

At first Karyl didn't notice the gull winging past, but when the bird wheeled around a second time he took note of this curiosity—because the seacoast birds rarely bothered to fly this high. He saw that the creature had something clutched in its beak, and his mind registered dim surprise when that circular object was dropped. He chuckled, amused by the odd impression that the bird was actually aiming at him!

It was a small ring of kelp and threadlike strands, he saw, as the wreath landed lightly on the stones below his feet. Curious, he reached to touch the thing—then reared back as it vanished from sight. Not just the wreath vanished—everything did! Somehow a dense fog had materialized, vapors so thick that he couldn't even see his own feet. The ogre waved his club menacingly through the damp air, watching the tendrils of mist swirl and float. He could feel the moistness on his skin, in his hair, on the stout wooden haft of his weapon.

Ogres are not the most imaginative of creatures, but Karyl Drago deduced that the fog had somehow been caused by that thin wreath, no doubt through some kind of magic. He doubted he could make it go away, so instead he paused to think about what he should do next. His duty was clear, of course. He was determined to guard the entrance to Winterheim at the Icewall Pass. He had ventured out of that entrance to confront the intruders who were approaching.

Now, however, he could see nothing of those intruders. He suspected that they were still below him, but it occurred to him that they could be sneaking past him, a dozen feet away to either side, and he might not even know they were there because of the fog. He wasted no time regretting that he hadn't squished them all with a landslide, but his duty was clear.

Retracing his route along the gully, the big ogre slowly made his way back to the summit of the pass. The gap between the lofty shoulders of the Icewall Pass was narrow, barely a twenty-foot-wide notch between two massive balustrades of icy rock, and he had no trouble reaching out with his hands to identify first one, then the opposite side of the familiar embrace of the gap. Just beyond and to the right was the entrance to the cave.

He felt the warm air of that aperture as he drew close, smelled the familiar hint of brimstone that he had come to associate with Winterheim's natural steam heat. Two more steps took him into the cave mouth, though even here the strange fog seemed to have penetrated, and he had to feel with his hands to make sure he was in the right place.

Now it was time to roust his garrison. He clumped into the chamber a hundred paces from the entrance to the Icewall Gate, where the twelve guards maintained their lair. Roughly he kicked a couple who were sleeping and grunted a cryptic warning to the others.

"Humans come."

Quickly the ogres picked up their clubs, spears, and axes, and followed their leader into the main passageway.

A short distance from the entry to the gate, a narrow shelf constricted the passage into a ledge beside a deep crevasse. Karyl deployed his men in several shallow niches on the side of the wall away from the crevasse, bidding them to remain there until he ordered them to attack. Finally, he turned to face the outside. He sat on a square boulder that had served as his guardpost seat for the past ten years, rested his mighty club across his knees, and waited for the humans to come to him.

———◆◦◆———

Moreen knew she had Dinekki to thank for her miraculous reprieve. Once before the shaman's magic had helped them to hide from ogres by raising a curtain of impenetrable fog. She didn't know how the old woman had gotten the spell up to the summit of the lofty mountain, but she murmured a soft prayer of thanks just the same.

She strained her ears, listening for some sign of the monster's advance. She didn't dare move, certain that if she did she would make some sound that would betray her own position. However, she did shift her posture slightly, freeing up her right hand so that she could draw her sword. The cold steel of the blade, wet with droplets of fog and bare inches from her face, gave her at least an illusory sense of security.

Finally she heard a footfall on the rock, a dislodging of a few pebbles. With relief she understood that the sound came from below, and in another instant Kerrick was stretched beside her on the steep face of rock, his own sword in his hands.

"What was that thing?" he whispered. "Did you get a look at it?"

She nodded but shrugged. "Some kind of giant, I guess. It could have been a huge ogre, but I've never seen one that size. The face was pretty frightening—it had tusks as big as a bull walrus!"

"Any sign of it now?"

"Not since the fog came up."

"Nice trick, that," Kerrick said. "Saved us all, for the time being, anyway."

"What about Bruni and Barq?"

"They're coming along behind," the elf replied. "We split up as a precaution, but all three of us kept climbing. The rest of the war party is following cautiously."

Moreen wanted to ask him what they should do now, but she knew that her guess was as good as his. Her guess suggested that there was no point in doing anything but continuing with their mission.

"Let's keep climbing," she said, "and hope this fog hides us until we get to the top."

Kerrick nodded. The fog was extremely disorienting, but the slope was so steep that they had no difficulty fig-

uring out which way they had to go. Handholds appeared
through the mist a few feet from their faces, and they
slowly inched upward.

It seemed as if the whole day had passed, though in reality it was probably little more than an hour before the
slope abruptly leveled out. For the first time since they
had started climbing Moreen stood up straight. She and
Kerrick held their swords ready, but nothing moved into
their view nor made a sound within their hearing.

She felt a gust of wind against her cheek and shivered.
Slowly the mist dispersed, carried through the pass by the
moving air. Soon they could see Barq One-Tooth and
Bruni just below them and to either side, and they waited
for their two companions to join them in the notch of Icewall Pass. The rest of the warriors came into view farther
below, Mouse leading the band. Slyce was scrambling
along beside him, and even Dinekki was somehow making
the ascent, disdaining any offers of help. Soon they began
cresting the ridge, a dozen, then a score or more fighters
joining the four companions.

Within a few minutes the last of the magical fog had
dispersed, revealing once more the sun-speckled expanse
of the White Bear Sea. For the first time they could see
beyond the Icewall, and Moreen was stunned by the vista
of glaciers and snowy summits arrayed before her, an expanse of landscape as inhospitable as anything she could
ever have imagined.

"Well, we made it this far," growled the Highlander
thane. He nodded at Bruni a trifle sheepishly. "I owe my
life, or at least my unbroken bones, to the wench—er, the
woman—here. She made a nice catch."

Bruni smiled benignly. "You'd do the same for me, I
trust," she said.

"Aye, that I would," replied Barq. He glowered at Kerrick and Moreen as if challenging them to dispute him.

Instead, the chiefwoman nodded then turned to the gap. "Where to from here?" she wondered.

"Right there," Kerrick said, pointing to the mountainside. Moreen saw a wisp of steam there and only then perceived that there was a narrow crack in the face of the rock.

"Do you think that giant—or whatever it is—is waiting in there?" asked the chiefwoman, as she examined the narrow cavern mouth leading into the bedrock at the summit of Icewall Pass.

"I think we have to assume that it is," Kerrick replied. "We may as well just call it a giant. That club he carried was as big as a tree!"

"Bah—giant or ogre, they both bleed, and they both hit the ground hard, when they fall," growled Barq One-Tooth. He held his great battle axe in both of his hands. "I have a score to settle with the brute. I'll go first."

Bruni held her cudgel, and Moreen and Kerrick had their swords drawn as they gathered behind the brawny Highlander and peered into the dim recesses of the Icewall Gate. The rest of the war party assembled behind them, some still climbing. A hundred or more fighters had reached the top of the pass, and these brandished their swords, spears, and bows, pressing forward in the confined space. Steam wafted in small wisps from the entrance, and they could all feel the warmth emanating from the hole in the ground.

"It must be like Brackenrock," Moreen suggested. "Heated from within by the ground steam of the world."

"I don't care how it's heated," Barq snorted. "I want to see how they guard it. Don't see any sign of that big bastard yet, but it gets dark in there pretty quick."

"Here." Bruni pulled from her backpack one of the many torches that the party, knowing they would be traveling underground, had brought with them. Kerrick struck a spark from his tinderbox, and in moments the oily head of the crude light sprang into flame.

"Ready those brands back there," called Kerrick to the men who were making ready to enter the cavern. "One for every four or five people should be good—and you who carry the fires make sure to hold them high!"

"Aye—hold it high," ordered Barq, starting forward into the shadowy passage. The walls pressed close to either side, barring them from walking side by side, so Bruni came next, followed by Kerrick holding the burning brand aloft.

Moreen, behind these three, could only clutch her sword and wish that she could see around her companions. She rubbed at the patch over her ruined eye, suddenly and acutely feeling the lack of adequate depth of field. There was nothing for it but to advance and to be ready.

Abruptly she heard Barq yodel a battle cry. She saw the thane's axe raised high as he charged forward, the other companions racing to follow. The Highlander's shout was almost instantaneously overwhelmed by a bestial roar emerging from the depths of the cavern.

The passage grew wider here, and Moreen darted to the side. She saw the monstrous form of the gate's guardian rising, towering high over Barq One-Tooth, seeming to fill the entire passage with his massive girth. The Highlander was nothing if not courageous, and she was awed by the sight of his fearless charge. He slashed with his axe, but the giant's massive club swung around and swatted the big warrior to the ground as if he were nothing more than a pesky child. Barq rolled to the left, tried to claw to his knees, then disappeared with a shout of alarm.

Bruni closed in next, while Kerrick lunged beside her, driving forward, stabbing both with his keen steel blade and the flaming torch. Light flared, illuminating tusks and eyes that glittered brightly—Moreen was certain she saw an expression almost of rhapsody there as the battle was joined. The massive gatekeeper swung his huge club again, and Bruni raised her own cudgel in an attempt to parry the heavy timber. Moreen groaned as she saw the blow bat her friend's weapon aside. The giant's heavy stick smashed into the big woman's shoulder, slamming her into the cavern wall, where she slowly slumped to the floor.

The chiefwoman hesitated, looking for an opening, and men pushed past her. Two Highlanders charged in a frenzy. They closed on the monstrous creature with axes whirling, but the guardian of the gate let loose a gleeful howl and smashed them both to the side with a single blow. They rolled after Barq One-Tooth and in an instant they were gone, having utterly disappeared.

Only then did Moreen realize that a wide crevasse yawned to the left, a deep and shadowy gap that had swallowed Barq One-Tooth when the Highlander had rolled off the lip. In the flaring torchlight, as more fighters came forward, she saw his fingers, clinging to the lip of the precipitous drop, and she threw herself prone on the ground, grasping each of the thane's hands in one of her own.

Kerrick, meanwhile, danced back from the gigantic defender's next blow, though not before the elf's blade scored a fierce stab into the creature's massive thigh. This strike drew a roar loud enough to rumble in the bedrock underneath Moreen's belly. She felt acutely exposed as she pulled on Barq's hands—a single downward blow from that mighty club would almost certainly break her back or smash her skull.

Kerrick wouldn't let that happen. The monster took a step forward, and the elf lunged in again, sword and torch dancing in a whirling pattern. Again the brute swung that club, and once more the elf ducked out of the way. The stout timber cracked into the cavern wall with a sound of splintering wood, sending a shower of wooden daggers across the floor. The end of the club bounced past Moreen and vanished over the lip of the crevasse. It was several seconds before she heard it banging against rocks far below—and even then it continued to fall, ricocheting violently into the subterranean depths.

More Highlanders came on in a furious charge. Arrows whooshed through the air, mostly clattering off hard stone, though several jutted from the stiff tunic of the huge warrior. Swords flashed silver in the shifting torchlight, and the beast bashed his club back and forth, driving a dozen warriors away. Only then did the creature seem to make a decision, throw back his head, and shout a guttural command.

"Hargh, me garkies!" he cried. "Come to fight now!"

Moreen saw a surge of ogres, ten or a dozen of them, come rushing into the fight, emerging from niches and gaps along the cavern wall. Many Highlanders fell in that first rush, smashed to the ground by clubs and spears wielded by these newcomers or pushed right back to the rim of the precipice by the momentum of the sudden charge. With roars and howls the fresh attackers swept into the melee, the fight now surging through the level floor space between the wall on one side and the lethal drop on the other. Two men fell, screaming, while other humans united to push a charging ogre off the edge. Another guardian came lumbering forward, but Mouse knelt and extended his spear as a trip bar. The ogre stumbled across the obstacle and fell howling into the chasm. Moreen kept her grim hold on the thane's hands, praying that no ogre would see her in her helpless position.

Barq One-Tooth, in the meantime, managed to fling one of his legs up and over the edge of the precipice. The

Lady of Brackenrock reared back, tugging hard, slipping on a floor growing slick with blood. A heavy body—another ogre—thudded to the ground beside her, a spear jutting from its neck. She used the twitching corpse for leverage, wrestling with all of her strength to pull Barq to safety. With a grunt and a curse the big man rolled his body onto the floor.

The chiefwoman spun around and picked up the sword that she had dropped in her headlong dive to save the thane's life. She looked up at the cave's gigantic defender, who was snarling like an angry bear and looming over Kerrick, like a mountain towering over a village temple. This was indeed a mighty ogre, she concluded, as the torchlight reflected again from those two blunt, yellowed tusks. The creature's belly swelled outward, bulging over a crude leather belt, and each foot was encased in a boot that seemed to be the size of a full-grown walrus.

Other defenders were smaller, but tough, smelly ogres. A knot of Highlanders pressed the attack, and one hulking ogre pitched one over the edge. Another ogre rushed in to help, and Moreen stabbed that one in the flank, drawing a howl of pain and sending the brute tumbling to the floor. A human killed him with a single chop of his axe, as the chiefwoman turned back to the giant, looking for a way to help Kerrick.

The elf flailed with the torch, fanning the flames with rapid, swirling swipes, but the ogre leader pressed forward, swatting at the fire as if it were an annoying fly. The wall rose up beside him. Kerrick was clearly running out of options. The creature was wielding only half of his original cudgel now, but with its bristling cap of splinters the broken timber looked even more menacing than the original.

Kerrick darted forward one more time, slashing with his sword, carving another slice into the ogre's massive thigh, drawing another bellow. The elf skipped to the side, darting past the huge guardian, as the monster spun around. Heading farther into the cave, Kerrick turned to face the monster. His back to the rest of the battle, the ogre leader seemed completely focused on this lone attacker.

Bodies were strewn everywhere across the cavern, and men and ogres stumbled and tripped as they frantically maneuvered over the increasingly tangled floor. Barq was scrambling to his feet to charge forward when Moreen grasped his wrist. Scowling, he froze as he saw Bruni pushed against the nearby wall. All three exchanged a look.

The massive ogre leader lunged after Kerrick, smashing the floor with the splintered end of his cudgel, just missing the elf. Kerrick saw the other three watching him, caught a signal from Barq, and retreated another half dozen steps. Still pursuing, the monster lumbered forward, the crevasse yawning a half step away to his left.

The trio charged forward in unison, making no sound except their feet scuffling across the floor. At the same time the ogre made a vicious sidearm slash, a blow that Kerrick ducked. The momentum of the swing left the monster overbalanced, staggering to the left to recover his footing.

Bruni and Moreen hit him in the right side, at the same time as Barq grasped the fellow's bearskin cape and jerked the hulking creature toward the left. The chiefwoman punched as hard as she could, using the hilt of her blade to knock the brute in the side. One huge foot slipped from the rim of the deep pit, and the ogre seemed to remain suspended in a weightless dance for a moment.

He recovered with amazing nimbleness, squatting to regain balance, then planting the outward boot firmly on the lip of the crevasse. With a mighty shrug he tossed Bruni and Moreen off. The chiefwoman flailed with her sword, scraping the bulging arm before she sprawled roughly along the cavern floor.

Spinning, the ogre punched Barq One-Tooth in the face. The Highlander's head jerked backward, and he staggered away, uttering a long mournful groan. Finally he fell onto his back, right at the edge of the crevasse, and lay still. Blood gushed from his nose.

Moreen also lay on her back, clutching her sword. She saw the monster loom overhead. That bestial face looked down at her, and the ogre hesitated. Slowly, it closed one eye—she had the strange impression that it was examining her eyepatch, mimicking her injury by blocking the view from one of its own eyes. In that instant of respite, she rolled to her side and bounced to her feet, backing against the cave wall opposite the crevasse.

She stumbled over a dead ogre, saw a knot of men—four or five of them—grappling with another of the brutish defenders. The whole seething tangle perched precariously on the lip of the crevasse, and toppled like a writhing creature. Screams and howls rose from the darkness, ogre and human voices mingling for shrill seconds before they terminated in brutal, violent smacks of flesh against stone.

Bruni knelt nearby, fumbling with her pack, pulling out the wrapped Axe of Gonnas. The big ogre glanced at her then looked deeper into the cave—clearly it was still concerned about the elusive elf. Kerrick crouched in the darkness, long sword extended. Barq hadn't moved, and Moreen prayed that the brute wouldn't notice the bleeding Highlander, since one shove would have been enough to send the man over the edge.

Finally, Bruni pulled the huge axe free. She tore away the leather shroud in a single gesture, then raised the weapon and twisted the hilt. The feeble light of the dying torch reflected on the golden blade, and the ogre's eyes widened as it saw that sheen of pure metal. Bruni lifted the haft, and immediately flames sparkled into life, bright fire outlining the edge of the golden cutter. With an almost bestial roar the big woman charged forward, swinging the weapon. With the impetus of her blow the flames erupted into a roaring ball of fire, rushing straight toward the ogre's head.

Those huge eyes remained widened, more in awe than fear, Moreen thought. The monster uttered a surprisingly plaintive moan as Bruni lunged closer, the fire searing the shaggy breast of the ogre's cloak, but instead of retreating the creature reached out a hand as if he would grab that fire, that golden blade, draw it close, and crush it. Bruni pressed the attack, jabbing with the fiery blade, and at last the brute took a step back.

There was no floor behind him. The human woman maintained the thrust of her assault, and this time the ogre was too far gone to recover his balance. He swatted a great fist toward the head of the golden axe, missing by several feet as Bruni pulled the blade out of the way.

The ogre toppled into the darkness and was gone.

13

A Premonition

Stariz sat on the floor of the temple, a film of sweat damp on her brow. She was trembling, breathing heavily, trying to reconstruct the fragments of an unsettling vision, a sweeping experience of godly power that had left her drained and unconscious on the floor. Anxiously she stood on the smooth obsidian surface, casting a spell that brought light to the sconces posted on both sides of the great chamber.

"What is it, O Willful Master?" she murmured. Her mind was bright with an image of gleaming gold, an immaculate and sacred expanse. She recognized the memory: the Axe of Gonnas, the cherished talisman that she had lost more than eight years ago. It was a burden of guilt that bore heavily upon her conscience, even to this day. She had felt that loss anew when she had dreamed about the axe two weeks ago.

Why would she see this vision now, again, and in such a vivid fashion? It was as if . . . perhaps it was not lost forever.

Now she could really believe that the Axe of Gonnas was near. Whatever the means of its transport, it called to her, and not from terribly far away. Someone was bringing it to her, carrying it into Winterheim.

Where, once again, it would belong to the high priestess and queen.

———◆———

Strongwind waited in his alcove for longer than two hours, but nobody came out of the Lady Thraid's apartment. Finally, the two guards ambled past, chortling in private amusement over some crude joke. They did not see the Highlander, and he waited until they had turned the corner before he emerged.

The man looked at the exit, the only exit, from the courtyard. He had been posted where he would have seen anyone coming or going from here, and his vigilance had never waned. No one except those two guards had passed while he watched and waited.

He advanced to the door and knocked tentatively. A short time later, Wandcourt opened the door, and Strongwind entered without comment.

"So there you are," Brinda said, coming out of the kitchen.

"What is that? Did Whalebone come in?" Thraid called from the bedroom.

"Yes, my lady!" Brinda said, with startling urgency. "I will put him to work cleaning up the supper mess."

"Let me see him," Thraid said. The door to her sleeping chamber opened, and the ogress emerged.

Strongwind glanced up and froze a mental image in his startled mind, then quickly looked away so that he would not be perceived as staring. The truth was plain in the smearing of the lady's lip gloss and fact that her dressing gown hung wide open across her otherwise naked body.

Clearly the ogress had just engaged in a tryst with her

lover. The presence of the royal guards seemed to confirm the rumor he had heard from Black Mike, that Thraid's paramour was none other than the king himself. The final detail was proved by his watch over the only known approach to this place. He wasn't sure what he could do with such information, but he knew it was valuable.

For now he knew beyond any doubt that there must be a secret passage connecting Lady Thraid's new apartment to the royal quarters of Winterheim.

"Will my lord king be eating dinner in the royal apartment tonight?" asked Stariz solicitously.

"I don't know!" snapped Grimwar Bane. "Why do I have to decide everything right away?"

"I beg Your Majesty's forgiveness," said the queen demurely, casting her eyes downward. "I meant no offense—merely hoped to have the pleasure of your company at the evening meal."

"Well, yes, I will eat here, tonight," the ogre king declared, guilt and irritation mingling to darken his mood. "First I have to go out—the grenadiers are drilling, and Captain Verra asked me to inspect the ranks."

"Very well, my lord. May Gonnas watch over your footsteps."

"Yes, may he do so," Grimwar replied, hastily throwing a cloak of white bearskin over his shoulders and making his way toward the door so quickly that the slave on duty there barely had time to pull it open.

Once outside, on the King's Promenade, Grimwar Bane drew a deep breath, angry with his wife and with himself as well. A week ago, when he had made up his mind to cast Stariz out of his life, he had felt grand and imperial, commanding and masterful. That feeling had lasted only until he returned to the apartment to find his wife offering him a comfortable pair of whaleskin slippers and a chilled glass of the finest vintage warqat.

Why did she have to be nice to him all of a sudden? He didn't need her ministrations, didn't even want them. Now that he had made up his mind to act, he resented her very presence, and it would have been much easier if she had treated him coldly, arousing the feelings of antipathy that had been so common during their decade of marriage. Instead, it was as if she were trying to prove herself a good wife.

Well, it was too late for that! Making long strides along the paving stones, he pushed through the crowds of lesser ogres like a great ship gliding through a flock of bobbing seabirds. The citizens of Winterheim drew their cue from the expression on his face and quickly moved out of the way, bowing and murmuring honorifics but making no effort to meet his royal eyes or to draw him into any conversation. This was as he desired it, and he began to feel better as he descended the long ramp to the Martial Level.

Once he entered the grenadiers' barracks compound, he was almost back to his old, confident self. Certainly the matter of Stariz would have to be addressed, but he would postpone that until after the ceremony of Autumnblight. Until then, the best thing was clearly to avoid her as much as possible. That was when he remembered that he had just told her he would have dinner with her tonight.

"Your Majesty—thank you for honoring us with your presence!"

Captain Verra of the grenadiers rushed forward and bowed as the king approached. They were in the great, square training room, where the ogres practiced their weapons drills, as well as marches and other ceremonial pursuits. Several of the red-coated warriors were in here now, and they had snapped to attention at the king's entrance. The others, Grimwar knew, would be polishing weapons or tending to their equipment in the many smaller rooms adjacent to this drill floor.

"Yes, of course," barked the monarch. "Proceed with the review at once!"

"Certainly, my lord—right away!"

Verra, who was a stalwart ogre veteran of many raids and campaigns, spun on his heel and roared out the order to assemble. More than two hundred grenadiers spilled from the dozen or so doorways along the far wall, adjusting tunics, buckling boots and helmets as they hurried forth.

Watching them gather into their ranks, the king couldn't help but be impressed. These ogre warriors were the pride of Winterheim, he knew, and they made a fine-looking formation indeed. To an ogre they were trim and muscular, avoiding the tendency to bulge in the middle that was a trademark of most adult ogres, including—if he was honest enough to admit it—the king himself. Each carried a long-hafted halberd and wore a wide-bladed sword at his belt. Those belts, as well as their boots and the many straps festooned across tunics and helmets, were polished to a gleaming black.

The grenadiers did more than just look impressive, the king was pleased to note. They marched to and fro in perfect unison, turning to the right or left as sergeants-major barked commands. Their heavy boots thudded against the floor with a cadence that stirred his heart. When they ceased their movement, the ranks were as crisp and precise as they had been at the start of the drill.

Several detachments advanced for weapons demonstrations, and this part of the display helped to lift Grimwar further from his bleak mood. He relished the slashing of the halberds, the clash of blade against hilt in tightly choreographed routines. In one impressive maneuver, two ranks of a dozen ogres each roared loud challenges, then rushed together to meet in an apparently frenzied melee. With stylized movement they wheeled around the floor, advancing and retreating in precise lines.

The final aspect of the drill was a contest of sword play in which sixteen skilled fighters were paired in duels. Unlike the careful precision of the halberd drills, which were designed to look furious while following prescribed forms of attack and defense, the sword matches were actual contests—though the edges of the blades had been dulled for the occasion. The first set of matches yielded eight winners and several bruises and broken bones among the losers. In short order the eight were pared to four, then to the best pair of fighters in the esteemed regiment.

At last, these final two swordsmen came together to put on a dazzling display of combat, slashing and clanging at each other in a duel that carried them back and forth across the wide floor. The watching grenadiers shouted encouragement to their favorites, and many gold pieces changed hands as bets were placed and paid off. At last the victor, a lanky sergeant who used his long arms to great advantage, knocked his foe to the ground and drove the blunt tip of his sword right up to the loser's throat.

"Bravo!" cried the king himself, as the ranks of ogres erupted in cheers or groans—depending on the wagers placed. Grimwar Bane himself placed a heavy chain of solid gold links around the neck of the winner, then retired with Captain Verra to his office, where they shared mugs of warqat.

"I commend you on the training of the regiment," said the king, raising his tankard in a toast.

"Your Majesty is very gracious," replied Verra, "but I confess, these good ogres do make me proud." The officer looked hesitant for a moment, then cleared his throat. "May I speak frankly, Your Highness?"

Feeling expansive, Grimwar waved the ogre to continue. He liked this soldier and trusted him. Now, he watched curiously, wondered what the captain wanted to say.

Verra's jaw was set firmly, his twin tusks jutting upward a good inch or more in a fine display of ogre masculinity. His shoulders were square, and his eyes showed a depth of curiosity and understanding far from common among the males of Winterheim. He fixed those eyes upon his king.

"I worry for the safety of the realm," Verra began. "I train my men to do the best that they can, but we are not enough. The citizenry of the city has, by and large, become complacent concerning the existence of a great threat right here in our midst."

Grimwar growled softly. "By 'threat,' you mean the human slaves that necessarily dwell among us in such numbers," he suggested.

"Aye, Sire, I do. Have you noticed how, in many families—even among the higher nobles, those who should have a sense of history—the slaves are granted a great deal of freedom. They make decisions, plan menus, establish schedules . . . as if they are the masters."

"It has always been thus, has it not?"

"I suggest, Sire, that the situation is becoming extreme. My men have reported to me rumors of another uprising, a cabal of slaves that seeks to overthrow your regime, our whole populace, and claim Winterheim for themselves."

"I appreciate your bluntness," said the king. "Indeed, a conversation such as this is all too rare. Usually, those with whom I speak are only interested in telling me what they think I want to hear. Surely you know that it has always been thus—there are a few rabble rousers among the slaves. When they are caught, as they inevitably will be, they become but examples to all the rest of the folly of resistance."

"Indeed, Sire, this is how it has gone in the past, but my sources indicate that this group of rebels is especially pernicious and cunning enough to have avoided discovery up to now."

"Do you have specific information? Where are these slaves posted—what is the nature of their plans?"

The king began to sense an opportunity here. One of his queen's most valuable functions had been to discern these types of plots, and if he could put her onto the trail of something like this, it would provide the perfect distraction through the next week until the ceremony at Autumnblight.

"The best indication is that at least some of the rebels are posted in the Nobles' Marketplace. I wish that I could give you more specifics, but alas, I have none to offer. However, the rumors indicate that the movement is widespread and continues to gain support."

"Captain, I thank you for the valuable information," said Grimwar Bane, rising to make his farewells. "I will bring this matter up with the queen. Perhaps we shall be able to offer some compelling sacrifices this year in the ceremony of the Autumnblight."

"Your Majesty does me great honor," Captain Verra replied. "I thank you for hearing me. It is my most sincere hope that these rascals can be publicly brought to justice."

"Yes," agreed the king, as he departed. "I think that would be a happy ending for all concerned."

———◆———

Thraid relaxed in the tub of steaming water, pleasant memories of her lover drifting through her mind.

It especially pleased her that the king had seemed just a little jealous of her new slave when he learned that she had taken him to the Nobles' Marketplace. She enjoyed teasing him about things like that, but it only seemed fair.

Didn't he know that she got jealous, knowing he had to go back to that cow of an ogress every night?

Yes, indeed . . . it was a rare pleasure to be able to turn the tables. She giggled quietly as she sank deeper into the tub. Was her water getting a little cool? It didn't really matter, come to think of it.

"Oh, Whalebone?" she called, sitting up a little, so that the upper globes of her massive breasts emerged, slick and shiny, from the bath.

"Yes, lady?" he asked, discreetly remaining on the other side of the door.

"I need some more hot water. Bring it to me, at once!"

"Of course," he said. She heard the scrape of a pot as he put it on the stove to warm. In a few minutes, she would have him pour it into the tub.

Perhaps she would ask him to scrub her back.

"In the temple this morning . . . I had a vision of the Axe of Gonnas," Stariz announced to Grimwar Bane as they dined together at the long table in the royal apartments.

The king suppressed a sigh. He had had a very pleasant day and thus far had escaped any meaningful conversation with his wife. Now he would have to feign interest in this most tiresome subject. He lifted his head from his haunch of beef to look at her and nodded in what he hoped looked like a thoughtful gesture.

"Indeed. Was it unusual?" he asked.

He knew the queen's bitterness over the loss of that treasured artifact. She tirelessly grieved over it. However, since this was one of the few difficulties in her life that she had never been able to blame on him, he allowed himself a perverse pleasure as she discussed it.

"Yes!" she said, her eyes flashing with excitement. "That's just it—it was a hopeful message, a sign from the Willful One! I believe we have the chance to regain the axe!"

The king's expression immediately darkened. "If this is a dream that sends me to Brackenrock again, I'm not going!" he warned. "How many hundreds of my warriors must die before you're content? Besides, winter is closing in—"

He was somewhat surprised when she shook her head, cutting him off.

"No, the axe is near. The axe is coming to us!"

"Did your vision explain how the axe is traveling?" he asked, more tartly than he intended.

She didn't seem to notice his skeptical tone. "Someone is bearing it. Mostly he keeps it masked, or I would sense it more strongly, but twice now he has used it, pulled the cover away from it. I could hear it calling to me, full of promise, crying for vengeance. It is the will of Gonnas, my lord!"

This conversation was getting more disturbing with each utterance. "What about the elf? Did you dream about the Elven Messenger?"

That, of course, was his great nightmare, that he would again be tormented by the creature who had been behind his problems for eight years. It was the elf who had taken the axe, who had led the Arktos across the sea to Brackenrock, and it was he who had drawn the king on his last, fateful adventure to Dracoheim. Although there was no evidence, he had hoped the elf was dead.

Stariz shook her head. "No, I saw no suggestion of any specific person. I think we are safe in the knowledge that he was killed in the explosion of the Golden Orb."

"Yes . . . he must be dead, and that woman, too, the chieftain of Brackenrock, but then who else has the talisman of our god? Who is bringing the Axe of Gonnas to Winterheim?"

"That is what I intend to find out. I shall go to the temple again in the morning. There I will pray to the Willful One and hope that he favors me with illumination. My lord husband, I am convinced that this is a real opportunity. Trust me, the axe is nearby!"

"I trust you," he said, lying. "Let me know as soon as you learn anything else."

"Certainly, Sire, I will," she replied, bowing her head meekly.

"Very well. Now, I intend to retire early tonight," he said, pushing back his chair, rising to make his escape. It was only then that he remembered the subject raised by Captain Verra, a matter that could benefit from his wife's unique skills. "One more thing, my queen?"

"Yes, Lord King?" Stariz waited expectantly.

"Have your contacts reported any rumblings about unrest among the slaves—more than the usual, I mean? Do you have any indications of a possible uprising?"

"I cannot say that any such reports have come to my attention, not in the immediate past," she replied. "Of course, there were those treacherous smiths I discovered in the foundry last fall, but we put them to death at the Sturmfrost feast, you recall. Why do you ask this? Have you heard a rumor?"

"Just something from one of the grenadiers—a good officer. He said that there was some unusual activity in the Nobles' Marketplace, and he wondered about some of the slaves there."

"Interesting. It is a place where the humans mingle with little supervision," Stariz said. "I agree, it's a potentially dangerous situation. I will look into the matter at once."

"I knew you would," said the king, content that the

issue was in capable hands. He exited the dining room with a bounce in his step, ready to get a good night's rest.

After the way Thraid had been working him, Gonnas knew, he needed it.

———◆◆◆———

Strongwind waited until everyone in the apartment was asleep. Brinda, the last to retire, had blown out her lamp a half hour earlier, and he could hear the measured breathing coming from behind the curtain where she and her husband shared a pallet. Slowly, quietly, the High- lander rose to his feet and padded out of the slave quarters into the great room. He pulled the outer curtain closed over the slaves' alcove, and ignited a small oil lamp.

Next he pressed his ear to Thraid's door, satisfied to hear the sonorous snores that meant his mistress was drowsing deeply. He was relieved that she had demanded a drink after her bath and that he had had the foresight to make it very strong. He hoped she was sleeping very soundly.

Finally, he looked around, wondering where to start his search for the secret door. He ruled out the walls of the kitchen, since they fronted the courtyard. Likewise Thraid's bed chamber—one wall of which abutted the street outside.

One possibility was the great room, another was a wall of the social parlor, and a third was the storeroom. All of these abutted the bedrock of the mountainside and could provide cover for a hidden passage.

He started in the great room, holding the light close to the wall, grateful that the furnishings were still spare and that nearly the whole stone surface was bare. He spent a long time going back and forth, probing with his fingers, studying each irregularity, looking for some evidence of a crack, a breach, any kind of opening. After a half hour he was forced to conclude that the surface was solid stone.

Next he moved into the storeroom, pulling the door shut behind him, then turning the lamp wick up to its full height. He repeated the inspection on the two walls of the chamber that allowed possible connection to the city's mountainous bedrock and once again failed to find any indication of a concealed passage. After refilling his lamp from the barrel in this chamber, he turned to the small parlor.

The parlor had three walls joining other rooms of the apartment but one surface adjacent to the mountain. Once again he pulled the door shut behind him and turned up the lamp to full brightness. The room was un-furnished and—in his estimate—hardly ever used. His at-tention was immediately drawn to the bearskin hanging on the wall, the only decoration of any kind in here.

As soon as he pulled the pelt aside, he knew he had found his secret panel. The outline of a door was faint, but he could clearly see a deep crack.

The portal seemed securely set in its frame, but he knew there had to be a way to open it. He turned his at-tention to the small alcoves set in the wall, perches for the lamps that were a feature of every house and every room in this subterranean city. There were two of them here, each with an iron bracket mounted in place. He reached into the alcove closest to the door, took hold of the bracket, and gave it a twist.

Immediately he heard a rumble of grinding stone, and with a touch to the bearskin he felt the wall behind the pelt sliding away from him. After a few seconds the sound, which was too faint—he hoped—to rouse any of the sleepers, ceased. Pulling the skin to the side again, he observed a narrow hallway revealed, extending only a couple of steps before it became a steep, narrow stairway leading up.

Quickly Strongwind adjusted the bearskin then turned the bracket to slide the door closed again. He was certain the route led all the way to the top of Winterheim, to the Royal Level, possibly the king's own apartments. He didn't know yet how he would take advantage of his discovery, but he doused his lamp and went to bed on his own pallet feeling that he had learned something very important, something that would prove to be quite useful indeed.

14

Paths of Stone and Shadow

Kerrick limped past a row of dead humans, the bodies arranged by the survivors with as much dignity as they could manage. The elf was sore, badly bruised in many places on his body, but he could not ask Dinekki for help. Her precious store of healing magic was expended on those with broken bones or ghastly wounds, and in this way she saved the lives of a score of valiant warriors before she collapsed from utter exhaustion.

"How many more are hurt badly?" asked Kerrick, looking first to Moreen, who shook her head, still trembling from the aftereffects of the fight. Next he turned to Bruni, who was carefully re-wrapping the Axe of Gonnas, handling the artifact with great, even reverent, respect.

"A few bruises," the big woman said, moving her left arm through a stiff circle. "Nothing's broken, though."

Other warriors were moving around, bandaging wounds, collecting scattered arrows. The humans had quickly realized that those who had fallen into the chasm were utterly lost, the bodies beyond retrieval.

The survivors of the war party had all filed into the cavern. All of the ogres had been slain and their bodies dumped into the crevasse, but the cost of victory was dire. Some thirty-five humans had lost their lives in the frantic fight. Three more were terribly wounded, unable to walk, and though it broke their hearts the others knew they could only leave them behind to die. Each of the three had declined the shaman's healing magic, knowing that it would be better used to restore some wounded fighter to health than to merely allay the suffering of those who were inevitably doomed.

The elf knelt beside Barq One-Tooth, who still lay flat on his back beside the crevasse. The Highlander thane was breathing, but his eyes were closed, and his face and beard were sticky with blood. Kerrick took a bit of water from his canteen and sprinkled it on the man's face, eliciting a grunt of awareness. Carefully the elf tried to rinse away some of the blood.

"I think his nose might be broken," he noted. "He took quite a punch to the face."

He did his best to pull the thane a little farther away from the drop-off. A few minutes later Barq was sitting up, mopping his bloody beard with a rag, shaking his head groggily.

Kerrick grimaced at the sight of the burly Highlander's face. The thane's nose was smashed nearly flat, while bruises had extended to black circles around both of his eyes. His lips were puffy and swollen, like two ragged sausages plastered across the gateway to his mouth.

He snorted in reaction to Kerrick's expression. "Haven't you ever seen anyone who lost a fight before?" growled Barq.

"We won—and that was a brave charge you made," the elf remarked.

"Never took a hit like that before," Barq grunted. Only then did he look around curiously, finally standing up and hobbling to the edge of the precipice, staring down into the shadowy depths. "The big one—he's down there?"

Kerrick nodded.

"How did you do that?" wondered the thane.

"I needed to use the Axe of Gonnas," Bruni said. "The flames startled him as much as anything, and he lost his balance."

"Did you notice the way he stared at it?" Kerrick asked. "It was entrancing to him—as if he loved that axe!"

"Not for long, he didn't," Moreen remarked wryly.

Barq nodded again, soaking in the information. "Nice work," he acknowledged, finally, "all of you."

"You, too," Moreen said. "We make a good team."

Barq didn't seem to be listening. His eyes widened as he probed his gums with his tongue then reached up to feel inside his mouth with his broad, blunt fingers. He exclaimed something that sounded like "Ai oof!"

"Looking for this?" The chiefwoman leaned down and picked up a golden chip that was lying on the stone floor, holding it. Barq One-Tooth groaned as he saw it, holding it up close to his face and examining it glumly.

"We'll have to call you Barq No-Tooth for the time being," Kerrick observed, drawing an angry glower from the hulking Highlander.

Apparently he lacked the spirit to argue, however, for he simply placed the loose gold tooth in a small belt pouch and went about collecting his backpack, which he had cast aside early in the fight.

"Here—spread this across your nose and your cheeks." Moreen gave him a small jar of the healing ointment Dinekki had brought. They had a small supply of the stuff remaining, which was useful mainly for minor wounds.

The fighters were exhausted from their long climb and the intensity of the brief battle, but they loaded up their gear, re-ignited their torches, and started to follow the cavern that curved and twisted away from Icewall Pass. Bruni led the way, followed by Kerrick and Moreen, with the limping and bruised Highlander joining the rest of the warriors in the shuffling column. Barq cast frequent glances behind them, sharing Kerrick's irrational dread that perhaps the monstrous ogre guardian might not be dead.

It was a weary and dispirited group that made its way farther into the cavern. Dinekki was carried by Bruni, who supported the elder shaman like a baby, cradled against her chest in both of her brawny arms.

For an hour they made their way deeper into the Icewall cavern, following a fairly wide passageway with a smooth floor that was, thankfully, free of any further obstacles. Finally exhaustion compelled a halt, and at a wide spot in the corridor the weary warriors stretched their bedrolls on the floor and tried to find space to rest. However, many of the men and women sat staring, eyes fixed upon remembered images. Sleep proved to be a very elusive comfort.

The torches sputtered and failed until only a few of the brands still flickered. Kerrick found himself restless and uneasy, and as he had on the faraway hill before the Tusker Escarpment, he pushed himself to his feet and wandered along the periphery of the war party.

He heard an annoyed shout and turned to see a big Highlander holding the gully dwarf, Slyce, by his neck.

"Little bugger just stole the last of me warqat!" growled the man. "I oughta punch him clear back to the White Bear Sea—knock the lights out of him!"

"Looks like he's already pulled the shades," the elf remarked, seeing the little fellow's eyelids close droopily.

"Hmmph," snorted the warrior, his rage apparently dissipating in weariness, or despair. "Stone drunk—wish I could join him there."

He cast the gully dwarf against the wall, where Slyce collapsed and started snoring noisily. The Highlander ended up stretching out next to the pudgy little fellow, and using his chest as a pillow, he was soon snoring his own accompaniment.

Here, in the underground passage, Kerrick probed ahead of the group, allowing his elven eyes to penetrate regions of pure shadow, places that would have been utterly dark to the humans. It was a relief to get away from the torches, which sizzled and flared in his vision annoyingly.

The elf wandered on, looking for something, anything, to distract him along this twisting passageway. He saw signs of serious excavation and knew that the ogres—or more likely their slaves—had labored hard to create this route through the mountain. Steps had been carved into the floor to ease the passageway in places where it descended or rose. Narrow corridors had been widened, the walls showing the marks of countless chisels and picks, so that even at its most constricted point the corridor would allow the passage of four or five ogres walking abreast.

Before he knew it the elf had wandered a good distance away from the rest of the group. Behind him the torchlight was invisible, the faint sounds of sleep swallowed by the twists and turns of the circuitous route.

"Nice fight," said Coraltop Netfisher, who was leaning against one of the cavern walls, a dozen paces in front of the elf. "You really know how to use that sword."

Kerrick snorted bitterly. "Now you show up? It would have been too much trouble to help out, I suppose."

If the kender took offense, he didn't show it. Instead, he ambled forward then reached up to rummage through Kerrick's belt pouch. "No warqat left, huh?" he said, disappointed.

The elf blinked in surprise. "No . . . but that was a good tip, to carry strong drink up the Tusker Escarpment. How did you know to tell me that?"

Coraltop shrugged. "Know to tell you what? I thought you'd drink the stuff—never thought it would go to waste inside of a polar worm!"

"Well, it was good advice, anyway," Kerrick noted, "but we've lost nearly half our men, and we haven't even made it into Winterheim yet. Now what do we do?"

"How should I know?" asked the kender, with maddening indifference. He brightened, though, even smiled. "I guess it's going to start getting interesting now!"

———◆◆◆———

Kerrick awoke with a start, sitting up on the cavern floor, his hand instinctively going for the sword that slid soundlessly from its sheath to gleam coldly in the lightless space. He was alone in a wide stretch of the underground passage connecting from the Icewall Gate, and he had somehow dozed off while sitting against the wall.

"By Zivilyn!" he gasped in a breathless whisper. "I can't believe I fell asleep like that!"

He had. Anything or anyone that had come along could have killed him, and he would have been utterly defenseless.

"Coraltop?" he asked, remembering that he had been talking to the kender in his last moments of wakefulness.

He was not surprised to receive no answer, but when he placed his hand on the stones where his seafaring companion had been sitting, he was startled to feel that the bedrock was still warm. Perhaps he hadn't been as defenseless as he first thought.

"Thanks, old friend," he said quietly.

He was stiff and uncomfortable when he rose to his feet and felt like an old man as he hobbled back to the war party, only gradually working the kinks out of his joints and limbs. The battle with the monstrous ogre had taken a toll on him that he would feel for days, he felt certain.

He found the group of warriors stirring, though most of them, too, seemed to be suffering the aftereffects of the fight—all except Slyce, who moaned under the influence of an obviously thudding hangover.

"That'll teach you to steal good warqat!" snapped the Highlander.

"Never no more," agreed the gully dwarf lugubriously.

"Ah," the warrior said, his tone softening. "It'll wear off with a few good miles under your boots."

"We go on the same way?" Barq asked, squinting into the dark passage Kerrick had scouted.

"No other choice," Moreen said. She addressed Kerrick. "Will you lead the way?"

"Sure," he agreed as Bruni fired up a torch. All along the file other brands flared, until the war party looked as if it were escorted by a legion of huge, smoky fireflies.

With his back to the blazes, Kerrick found he could see pretty well. The walking was easy here. The passage was obviously a natural cavern, with stalactites on the ceiling and stalagmites rising from the floor in many places. Here and there the walls showed signs of chisels and hammers, where the ogres—or their slaves—had widened the route to allow for easier traversing. The floor was for the most part level, though not infrequently there were periods of steep descent. These were invariably carved with steps that, even if they were a little tall for a human's stride, made for relatively easy descent.

Nowhere did the cavern narrow to the constricted route that had marked the entrance. Kerrick speculated that the mouth of the gate had been left thus to make it easier to defend, while the interior had been widened and made smooth to allow for easy marching, possibly by a large contingent of ogres. The air throughout was warm and moist, much like the air in the caverns below Brackenrock. They knew this was the result of subterranean heat sources that would—also like Brackenrock—ensure that Winterheim maintained a comfortable and constant interior temperature even during the worst ravages of the Sturmfrost and the sunless winter.

For hours the party trudged along, mostly in silence, though there were occasional hushed observations from some of the humans, awed by the vast sweep of a chamber ceiling or an exotic column of stone that seemed to have been formed from solidified mud. They came to the longest stairway of the route, a series of thirty steps that carried them steadily downward, with a broad landing after each ten tiers. At the bottom they entered a very large chamber, and Bruni and the others held their torches high. The light barely reached the walls but reflected back from enough slick surfaces to reveal a cavern that was nearly the size of Brackenrock's great hall.

The air was slightly cooler in here, and it felt moist against Kerrick's skin. He looked around in a moment of silent awe and heard the gentle trickling of water. Crossing the room he found a small pool, with a stream flowing into it from a gap in the opposite wall and a little channel leading away, eventually passing through a hole in the far side of the cavern where it undoubtedly continued its descent toward the sea. Beside the pool was a wide, flat expanse of fine-grained sand. Here they decided to take an extended rest.

"Look—blindfish!" Moreen exclaimed, pointing into the shallow, clear pool.

Kerrick saw a number of the cave dwelling swimmers, including a pair that were a good foot and a half long. Quickly he nocked an arrow into his bow and with a few well-placed shots was able to pull two of the largest fish out of the water. The shiny creatures wriggled and flopped until, with a few swipes of his knife, he filleted and cleaned them. Bruni gathered pieces of driftwood that had collected here.

Several Highlanders took up positions along the river-bank with light spears, while others held torches, the light reflecting in erratic glimmers from the rippling surface. In short order they had plucked dozens of fish from the stream, while still more of their comrades set about cleaning and cooking the aquatic delicacies. They grilled the fish and ate some of their dried bread, while sharing a few companionable sips from their dwindling supply of warqat.

Moreen and a dozen Arktos offered to stand the first watch, giving the others a chance to sleep. It was hard to tell how long they remained here in the lightless grotto, each of them standing a turn at the watch, but some time later they were all awake, refreshed, and ready to continue.

Barq gently probed his battered face. "Doesn't hurt as much now," he said. "Still swollen, though. Right?"

"No, really, it looks much better," the elf suggested, disingenuously. He didn't say better than what.

They continued along the cave. The party formed a long column, each warrior staying within a few paces of those marching before and behind. They passed through an array of caverns, some narrow with low ceilings, others vaulting high overhead. Water became common, mostly in small streams or clear pools.

"How far do you think we've come?" Moreen asked when they stopped for what they guessed to be a midday rest.

"Hard to tell with all the winding around, but counting yesterday, I think we've gone at least ten miles," Kerrick speculated. "That must be half way to the main citadel, judging from where we saw the mountain outside."

"We'd better stay alert," Barq noted grimly. "There's bound to be more of those big brutes waiting up ahead. They ain't gonna let us walk right into their city like this."

The others nodded, though Kerrick was not so sure. He was beginning to think that the ogre Broadnose had been right, that this was pretty much a forgotten and remote route into the ogre citadel, not a place that any citizen of Winterheim would use for a practical purpose.

"We should be coming to that place, the Moongarden, somewhere along here," Moreen said. "Do you suppose we'll know it when we find it?"

In another hour their question was answered as they came through a narrow arch in the cavern passage to find themselves in a chamber much, much larger than any before. There was no way for the torchlight to reach even halfway across the huge cavern, but neither was it necessary. Indeed, Bruni quickly extinguished the light, and the companions looked around in awe.

"It's like a forest of mushrooms," Moreen said, gesturing to the floor of the cavern some fifty feet below them. Everywhere grew massive clumps of fungi, some the size of bushes or boulders, others as big as cottages.

Throughout the clumps of mushrooms they could see streams, some rippling over rapids, others swirling or marked by still, deep pools. Flying creatures dived and spun through the air some distance away, and Kerrick pointed out that they looked like bats—a swarm of a thousand or more.

"It's underground," Moreen said, gesturing to the lofty ceiling rising to a shadowy definition overhead, "but we can see everything!"

"The walls," noted the elf, inspected the stone surrounding the arch through which they had entered. "This is a glowing lichen here, and it seems to extend all the way around this place."

Indeed, the illumination was soft, greenish in tint, and very pleasant to the eyes. It cast no shadows but instead provided a gentle and uniform light that resembled a summer night, when the skies were clear and the white moon full with the solstice light. It struck them all at the same time, as they looked at each other and nodded in understanding. It was Barq One-Tooth who articulated the general realization.

"I think we found the Moongarden," he said.

———————◆◆◆———————

There was a stabbing pain in his right side. Vaguely, over a long time, he realized that his arm was twisted behind him, almost impossibly bent. Probably it was broken, he thought glumly.

Karyl Drago had very good cause to be glum. He was wedged between the walls of the crevasse, an unknown distance far below the lip.

The big ogre uttered a groan and tried to shift his body around. It was his massive belly that had lodged him here where the chasm walls leaned close together, he realized. In so doing his great girth had saved his life. He had thrown enough loose rocks into this crevasse over his years of duty here. He well knew that it was virtually bottomless. If he had slipped past this spot—he could feel by kicking his legs that the gap was much wider just below— he would have plummeted an unknown, fatal distance.

How had they managed to knock him down here? He reflected on the question, not used to analyzing his own failures following a lost fight. Indeed, he had never been beaten before, though in his time he had battled a half dozen bull ogres at once.

It was that axe! He remembered the fire that had exploded before his eyes, dazzling him, filling him with wonder. The brilliant golden-edged blade had been the most beautiful sight he had ever seen, a miracle that warmed his soul and entranced him. He had been consumed by such a sense of awe that he had gone weak in the knees just from the sight. That weakness had been enough to doom him.

Or was he doomed? With a little more determination, he wiggled around, realizing that his arm, though wrenched, was not broken. Using all of his strength, he pushed on the walls to either side and ever so slowly began to inch upward. After ten minutes he had climbed out of the narrow choke point that had pinned him and was able to support himself with his legs widespread, massive feet braced one on either side of the chasm.

He looked upward. The crevasse was not terribly wide, and he wondered if he might be able to brace himself like this all the way to the top. Grimly he pushed, lifting himself another few inches before he had to shift his feet to new perches. Now he knew he was not trapped here, not doomed.

He chuckled, a rumble echoing through the deep chasm. The chuckle boded well for him and ill for those who had left him here. He would climb out of here and go after them. It was his duty, of course, and he would not let himself fail. He had another secret reason as well. He absolutely *had* to have another look at the wonderful, beautiful, axe.

Experience had taught Stariz ber Bane that in the most secret matters of the human heart— that is, the insatiable desire for freedom— normal procedures of intelligence gathering rarely applied. Slaves who were inclined to gossip casually about trysts and alliances, who would gladly discuss thievery and betrayal in matters of lust or greed, became unreasonably tight-lipped when it came to matters of rebellion. Even bribery or torture was of little use once they clamped their mouths shut.

Thus, neither bribery nor torture was the favored tactic of the high priestess as she sought to investigate the sedition in the Nobles' Market. Oh, certainly Garnet Dane, with his wily ways, might be able to discover a useful bit of knowledge, perhaps even a name, but when it came to learning the full truth behind such a movement, the queen of Suderhold would have to put her trust in a higher source.

Besides, she had a more important use in mind for her spy. The time was near for that crucial task, and she did not want him distracted by mundane matters.

She would pray. Her acolytes, young ogresses sworn to the service of the Willful One, came forward with her tall mask and her sleek black robes. She stood still while they climbed up onto stools around all sides of her. Two of them lowered the obsidian visage over her head, until the comfortable weight rested upon the queen's square shoulders. She could barely see through the narrow eye slits of the mask, but it was not her eyes that would serve her best now. When she felt the fullness of the robes draped from her back and her bodice, the smooth wool rustling against the skin of her arms, she was ready.

The acolytes withdrew silently, except for one who tripped and dropped a stool. Stariz stiffened but didn't turn. The others would identify the clumsy wench, and the high priestess would deal with her later. Instead, she fought for a return to the focus and serenity that had accompanied her donning of the ceremonial garb. Soon she was breathing deeply, seeing only slits of firelight through the mask, but aware of so much more beyond her clothing, beyond the room, the realm, and the world.

She advanced with measured steps, feeling the rumble in the floor as the great door to the inner sanctum rolled to the side. Her strides remained steady as she continued forward, until finally she stopped before the massive black statue that was, in Winterheim, the physical representation of her mighty god. Her heart filled with awe and devotion for her mighty god.

The image of that great bull ogre, carved from shiny black stone and rising more than twenty feet high, loomed in her mind. She imagined the stony eyes turning down to look at her, and she perceived the curiosity, the strength there. More than that, she knew her god was pleased with her, and she silently, solemnly pledged that he would always be pleased with her.

"O Great Gonnas," she began, "Willful Master of this humble ogress, may it please you to open my eyes and my ears, to fill my senses with the knowledge that will protect your people from the basest of threats."

With great dignity she slowly knelt on the floor, relishing the feel of the smooth stone against her knees. Carefully she leaned forward to brace herself on her hands. The mask, with its formed shoulder brace, rested firmly over her head as she lowered herself to lie flat upon the floor.

"Please give me a sign, O my Great Lord . . . a sign that I may use to work against those who seek to do your people harm. Let me know where I may find them, how I may know them. . . . I will do the rest in your name."

She lay still, her face pressed to the floor, her vision nothing but blackness. Gradually, however, this impenetrable veil became shot through with stabs of light, flashes that originated in the center of her mind and seemed to radiate outward in pulsing and brilliant waves.

"You are real, O Willful One, and I feel your strength," murmured the high priest.

The lights pulsed brighter, swirling now, remaining within the confines of her awareness instead of blasting away into nothingness. The flashes merged into a whole, a whirling image of white, and the high priestess held her breath, sensing that revelation approached.

Fear stabbed through her bosom, her guts, her loins—fear of powerlessness, of failure. She was pierced by the knowledge that her king was trying to abandon her, that he would try to escape her—and that if he did, she was finished. This was a warning, clear and direct from her deity. Her worst fears would be realized if she did not do something drastic.

Yes, indeed, it was time for Garnet Dane to perform his task.

She was prepared to rise, to put her plan into motion, but she felt the pressure of the Willful One's presence forcing her back down for another message. She lay flat again and opened herself to communication with her god. At once she saw there was more to this vision.

She fought for the serenity, the clarity to understand. At last, there it was: an image as clear in detail as it was murky in meaning. Stariz studied that picture, memorizing every detail, unconcerned with the fact that she didn't, as yet, understand. Full knowledge would come later after she had time to digest and analyze the vision bestowed upon her by her god.

When the image faded at last, once again leaving utter blackness, she remained prostrate for a long time, breathing slowly, reflecting, remembering. At last she pushed herself to her feet, and walking somewhat shakily, she withdrew toward the door that rumbled open to allow her egress. She stood alert without speaking, puzzling over the image she had seen.

She knew what to do about the matter of the king; that plan needed only one final command. As to the rebels, perhaps she would consult with her husband about this matter, for the significance of the sign continued to elude her. She knew there was truth there, but what? How?

Why had her god shown her an image of a dozen blocks of salt?

———————◆◆◆———————

Grimwar Bane made his way back into his apartment, grateful that Stariz was gone. He allowed his slaves to disrobe him and draw him a bath, and as soon as it was ready he settled into the steaming water, allowing the warmth to soak into his body. He left instructions with his two bodyguards to guard the door and prevent him from being disturbed, even if it meant angering the queen herself.

He thought about Thraid, shaking his head in amazement. He had told her only yesterday about his intentions to send Stariz away. Her delight had been thrilling and her gratitude so intense that he had been left weak in the knees. In those moments of ecstacy the king saw beyond any doubt that he was making the right decision. He had promised to return to her tomorrow, as soon as he could get away, and already he was anticipating that delightful encounter.

The matter of explaining this new reality to Stariz was an unpleasant detail that he would continue to relegate to the future. He had begun to wonder if perhaps he might be rushing things a little too much by speaking to her immediately after the ceremony of Autumnblight, only five days away. There would be plenty of good opportunities as the season waned toward the end of the sunny days in which he could break the news to the queen, informing her that her royal presence was no longer required.

Of course, he would see to it that she had a chance to make a life for herself. Probably he would send her back to Glacierheim. Her father was baron there and in his dotage, but the king would send along a gift—a generous gift—of gold, and count on that to soothe any injured diplomatic feelings. He had two things in his favor: Glacierheim was a long distance away; and the baron's army was barely a tenth of the size of King Grimwar's, should it come to that.

Though they did raise some ferocious warriors in Glacierheim, the ogre monarch reminded himself with a shiver. He remembered one particular brute who had come to Winterheim with Stariz a decade before. That fellow, Karyl Drago, was the largest ogre Grimwar Bane had ever seen, strong enough to break the necks of any two normal warriors in a fair fight. Drago had been a strange contrast, brutal in battle yet reduced to a happy sigh by the sight of a little golden mirror or some trinket made from the precious yellow metal. He had actually caused some problems with his uncouth behavior. Fortunately, they had found a post for him some place very much out of the way. At least, the king consoled himself, they couldn't have too many brutes of Karyl Drago's size, not in Glacierheim or anywhere else.

He emerged from his bath feeling much refreshed and was pleased when he went into the great room to find that though Stariz had returned, she had waited for him to come out instead of trying to barge in and disturb his reverie. She did have a matter that she wanted to discuss, and his mood was pleasant enough that he was happy to indulge her.

"Do you remember we discussed the slaves in the Nobles' Market?" she asked him.

"Of course. Did you learn anything?"

"I believe so," Stariz replied. "That is, the will of Gonnas was revealed to me. After I meditated upon the vision, I could discern what our immortal god in his wisdom was trying to tell me."

"These rebels? Where can we find them?" Grimwar pressed.

"I think you will find them in the warehouse where the salt is stored. There are many men working there, and I think the proper course of action is to have all of them arrested and killed. It might be hard to sort out the rebels from the ordinary folk, but bad apples spoil the barrel, you know."

The king stroked his chin. Like so many of Stariz's tactics, this one seemed drastic. On the other hand, if she had this problem to distract her, that would take her attention away from the king, Thraid Dimmarkull, and the Highlander slave.

"Interesting thought," he declared, putting on an air of great contemplation. "Of course you would perform these executions at the ceremony of Autumnblight."

"Hmmm. I had not carried out my planning to that level of detail, but yes, that would make perfect sense. As always when dealing with sedition, our ideas are in concert, my king. These enemies of the state can be drawn and quartered in different sections of the hall so that everyone can get a good view. The slave king can be gutted at the climax of the festival!"

"Yes, that would make a nice climax," agreed the king, as he began to think about his dinner. What would the chef be making tonight, he wondered. "It shall be done. I will give the order myself."

"Good. They can be taken soon, then?"

"I will send a whole company of grenadiers, my queen. They will be taken like fish caught in a strainer net."

Stariz stood and smiled at him almost tenderly. "Excellent decisiveness, my lord. That is what makes you such a splendid king."

For once, Grimwar Bane agreed with his wife.

———◆◆◆———

Stariz summoned her spy after her husband had retired for the night, and as usual he wasted no time in arriving at her secret door. Garnet Dane's eyes flickered nervously as she invited him to enter her chambers, even offering him the unprecedented courtesy of a glass of warqat. She was almost giddy and enjoyed the nervousness tinged with excitement that she saw reflected in her human slave's eyes.

"You wonder why I have summoned you here so late, do you not?" she said.

"Yes, Your Majesty, I do," he confessed, "though I

should be eager to answer your call, no matter what the time or the cause."

"That is what I thought. Tell me, how sharp is your knife?" she asked him bluntly.

Garnet Dane's eyes widened slightly, but he didn't hesitate to answer. "In your service, it is a razor, my queen."

"Splendid," she said. "It is time for you to use it."

He leaned close, his thin lips creasing into a smile as she outlined her orders.

"Whalebone!"

Strongwind heard the snap of Thraid's fingers as she summoned him into the great room where she indolently lay as usual upon her divan. It was late morning, but she had slept late on this day, as was also usual.

"I need you to make a trip to the market for me, but there is no hurry."

"As you wish, my lady," he said. "Am I to fetch anything in particular?"

"Yes . . . make it a lamb, this time." She fished several gold coins out of a purse. "Do not come back until this evening."

"Of course, mistress," he replied.

Strongwind was delighted at the timing of the request and relieved to get away from the voluptuous ogress for a few hours. Her attentions to him had been unnerving. She had insisted that he help her with her bath, an experience leaving memories that would require gallons of warqat to wash away.

Now he had important news about the connection between Thraid Dimmarkull's apartment and the royal palace and was eager to report his discovery to the nascent rebel group. He went immediately to the market and made his way to the window at the salt alcove. Black Mike was at the counter, and when he saw the Highlander approaching he quickly called for a replacement, then moved sideways to open the door so that Strongwind could join him in the evaporation room.

As before, they made their way through the aisles of stacked salt into the storage room in the back. The slave king noticed other men throughout the room setting their tasks aside and gradually, casually converging on the room.

A few minutes later the band had gathered, perhaps twice as many men as the dozen Strongwind had seen on his first meeting here. The group circled close, regarding him with interest as Black Mike folded his arms and waited.

"Well, did you learn anything?"

"Yes. The king did come to visit the Lady Thraid. There were guards—the King's Grenadiers—outside her apartment, and they wouldn't let me pass." Some measure of modesty caused Strongwind not to mention the disheveled appearance of the ogress when later he had returned to the apartments.

He was about to describe his search for the secret door when one of the men at the back of the throng held up his hand and whispered urgently, "Hsst! be silent!"

They all heard the thump of heavy boots. There were cries of consternation from the market, screams of frightened humans mingled with harsh ogre commands. Something heavy crashed to the floor outside of the room, and guttural roars bellowed above a growing din of panic.

"Out the back!" declared Black Mike. "Move!"

Strongwind was carried by the throng, as the men surged toward the shadowy nether reaches of the room. The Highlander could make out a door there and saw one slave pull it open.

In the next instant a spear darted into the opening, striking the man in the chest and erupting from his back in a shower of gore. Gasping, he tumbled back into the room, kicking weakly, dying very slowly.

There was light beyond the doorway, but that illumination only served to outline the shape of a hulking ogre, one of the red-coated grenadiers. He reached forward to retrieve his weapon, shaking the spear contemptuously to cast the corpse aside. With a rumbling chuckle of deep amusement, he advanced into the room, while more of his comrades followed behind—a dozen huge, armed ogres blocking the escape route.

At the same time the door on the other side of the room burst open. Strongwind was not surprised to see more ogres there, the rest of the company apparently. They separated, weapons raised, as the human captives stood frozen. One man fell to his knees and started to cry.

"Shut up!" Black Mike ordered, and the fellow's blubbering ceased. The slave leader cast a murderous glare at Strongwind before the ogre captain came swaggering through the two ranks of his men.

"Search them for weapons and lock them in chains," he barked. Grenadiers came forward to begin frisking the rebels, while others followed with heavy coils of iron chain. The captain looked at his ragged captives, tusks bared in a lip-curling sneer of disdain. "You lot are coming with me—we have a little appointment with the queen."

He chuckled, a sound like a bubbling vat. "No doubt she will have some of you talking—soon, while you still have yer tongues."

❖━━◆━━❖

Things were going pretty well, thought Grimwar Bane, leaning on the railing of his lofty balcony, admiring the view of the harbor far below. *Goldwing* was sparkling again, fully repaired and freshly painted. The sight of his gleaming galley made him happy. A small mountain of timber was stacked nearby in his shipyard, and he idly considered the notion of building another ship, a vessel to replace the lost *Hornet*. Perhaps that work could begin this winter?

He was happy to see slaves toiling busily in the lumber yard as well. Hundreds of humans bustled back and forth under the eyes of a couple of whip-cracking overseers. Elsewhere there were more humans, throngs of them carrying goods to the marketplace, selling and buying alongside ogres.

His wife was busy with her own little projects, staying out of his way. Indeed, he had been able to visit Thraid twice in the past three days, a state of affairs he found very satisfactory. There were plenty of advantages in the current arrangement. Idly, he wondered if there might not be some way to keep his wife as queen and his mistress as his lover. Certainly Stariz had her uses. It was hard to imagine Thraid being much help in tracking down sedition among the slaves, for example. There she had acted decisively. Just an hour ago he had learned that two dozen slaves had been arrested in the Nobles' Marketplace . . . she worked quickly, did Stariz ber Glacierheim ber Bane.

Nevertheless, he shook his head at the thought of both ogresses competing for his attention. He had been living that misery for too long, and he had made up his mind, yet there was no sense of urgency, no reason for him to act prematurely. The execution of the salt-cellar slaves from the Nobles' Market would provide splendid entertainment at the Rites of Autumblight. That was another task for which Thraid, for all of her voluptuous qualities, was clearly not suited.

Ah, but those qualities she did possess, she possessed in such abundance! The memory of those charms made him smile, stirred him deeply. In fact, they were much on his mind, because he knew that she was waiting for him in her suite. She had sent her slaves away and promised to be alone. Soon he would be there, in her arms.

Stariz had informed him that she would need more time to interrogate the prisoners—she would be occupied thusly for the rest of the day. The king nodded in satisfaction. No doubt she would get to the bottom of this latest insurrection. In the meantime, he had some time to himself.

He sauntered down the passage leading around the edge of the royal palace, walking casually, nodding to a couple of ogresses who waddled past. They were bedecked in gold and black sealskin furs and giggled happily at the royal attention. The king stopped to chat with the grenadier who stood guard at the next intersection. Another glance around left him feeling fairly certain that he was not being followed, so he turned down the alley and darted into the Slaves Way.

In a minute he was at the secret door, his heart already pounding as he turned the now-familiar latch to slip the portal open. Quickly slipping through, he pulled the door shut behind him and took the oil lamp that Wandcourt had left for him in the little alcove by the door. A spark ignited the wick, and he started down the long, winding stairway that in recent days had taken him so many memorable times to the Terrace Level and to the delights of his mistress.

Long strides carried him down the steps, anticipation building as he spiraled through the descent. His voluptuous ogress was waiting for him at the terminus of the long, secret stair. He relished the little circle of light around him, the pleasant glow of the lamp that was like his own little sun.

At last he was there, stepping off the bottom step, crossing the last few steps to the second secret door, the passage into his lady's chambers. Feeling very gentle, he touched the wall almost affectionately, working the metal lever that caused the portal to slowly slide toward him.

He stepped through, relishing the familiar surge of desire, taking his time to let the feeling grow within him. The apartment was quiet—good, she had followed through on her promise to send her slaves away. With soft footfalls he crossed the small room and entered the large central chamber. Nothing stirred here, though several lamps burned in the wall sconces, providing a soft and romantic illumination. The king uttered a low, affectionate growl as he realized that his mistress awaited him in the bedroom.

Gently he opened that door. He could see the outline of his lover's body on the bed, the soft curves actually making him short of breath. With trembling hands he moved the door mostly shut, allowing just a sliver of light into the room. This dimness was the perfect illumination for lovemaking, he knew.

"My pet?" he whispered.

Ah, the coy wench was playing with him, lying still. Hesitancy gone, he crossed the room in three long strides, sat on the edge of the bed and touched her shoulder.

"I am here—" he began then stopped.

Something was wrong. His touch had provoked no reaction, not even the trembling playful stillness she sometimes affected, knowing it increased his desire.

"Thraid, my lady," he said, shaking her gently.

No response. In growing confusion he pulled the blanket back and rolled her from her side onto her back. He saw those red lips, so carefully rouged for him, but there was more redness, too, a horrible crimson gash through her throat, the wound gaping like some ghastly caricature of her sensual mouth. Blood soaked the sheets and her sleeping cloak, still sticky but already cool to the touch.

He gagged and staggered across the room, crashing into the wall. His hands flew to his face, but they could not stifle his moans, could not wipe away the cruel truth.

The Lady Thraid Dimmarkull was dead.

16

The Moongarden

I t's hard to believe a place like this can exist under a world of ice and snow," Moreen said, unable to take her eyes off of the wonders around her.

She, Kerrick, Bruni, and Barq had descended the gently graded trail down to the floor of the Moongarden, and now they walked, entranced, among the stands of giant fungi, along the stone-lined bank of a rippling stream. The rest of the warriors were trailing behind, each stopping for a moment to gape in awe at this vast and illuminated garden.

At Kerrick's suggestion, the fighters lingered behind in the shelter of a small grotto while the four companions scouted ahead.

"This Moongarden is huge—several square miles I'd say," the elf ventured. "I see passages, a half dozen or more, going off to either side. Who knows where it all leads."

Moreen nodded. She was thinking about all the food represented by these mushrooms, which resembled the little caps and stems that were so common in the groves and meadows of the Icereach. They grew almost overnight during the warming days of spring, and for three or four months they were gathered to form a staple of the Arktos diet. Her people even dried them so they could be stored throughout the cold months.

But here! She imagined that just one of the bigger mushroom-trees would have provide sustenance to all of Brackenrock for several days.

"It's no wonder they can support a whole city underground," she said. "They must farm this place, use it as a food warren all year around."

"If this is a farm," Bruni said, raising a hand in caution, "don't you think we might run into some farmers?"

"Good point," Barq agreed, scowling into the shadows of a particularly thick grow of giant fungus. "They might be watching us right now."

"They might," Kerrick said, "but I don't think they are. I've been looking around, and—at this end of the Moongarden at least—I don't see any sign of tending or cultivation. It's as if all of this stuff just grows wild here."

"It's so big that maybe they don't have to come this far to get what they need," Moreen speculated. "After all, we have to assume that the city lies somewhere beyond the far end of this cavern, don't we?"

"It has to be in that direction," the elf agreed, pointing. "We haven't come far enough from Icewall Pass to reach the mountain of Winterheim yet. I'm certain that we're underground, maybe right under the Icewall, but still someplace between the pass and the city."

"Well, we're on the right path," the chiefwoman declared. "We just have to keep moving."

"How's your face?" Bruni said, speaking to Barq as they ambled along. "Do those bruises still hurt?"

The big warrior put his hand to his nose and wiggled, then shook his head. "The old lady's ointment's good stuff. I can even breathe with my mouth closed again."

"The power of Chislev Wilder," Moreen remarked. "Dinekki has long been in favor with our goddess."

"Perhaps we should find a place to rest while we're still in the wild part of the Moongarden," Kerrick said. "This might be our best chance to gather our strength and have plenty to eat, before we try to push on into Winterheim itself."

"Good idea," Moreen said. She turned to Kerrick and Bruni. "Over there looks like a nice grotto. It's out of sight from the main cavern. I see signs of a waterfall, and it might be large enough to give us all some soft ground for sleeping."

She led them along the bank of a rapid stream. Nearby, the uneven floor of the cavern rose from the ground level into a ten- or twelve-foot embankment, a ledge that would serve very well to conceal them. The clearing was small but flat, and a layer of lush moss cushioned the ground.

"This looks like a good place," Kerrick offered. "There's enough space for all of us to stretch out, make a camp, and still be out of sight."

"I'll have a look around," Barq One-Tooth said. "Make sure we don't have any neighbors."

"Be careful you don't meet the neighbors," Moreen warned.

"No chance o' that," the Highlander snorted.

He stepped across the stream on several small, dry-topped stones, showing surprisingly nimbleness for his size. Three steps later he had disappeared between the trunks of the mushroom trees in the nearby grove.

In a few minutes the two Arktos women and the elf had dropped their packs and shucked their heavy boots. Moreen sat down and relished the feel of her feet immersed in the cold spring water flowing past. Nearby, Kerrick found a pool of comfortably warm water in which he quickly washed his hands, feet, face, and hair.

Bruni, meanwhile, was delegated to go back to get the rest of the war party. Rolling her broad shoulders, stretching after she relieved herself of the heavy load of her pack, she lumbered toward the entrance where Mouse waited with the others. Kerrick made himself comfortable, dropping on his back and closing his eyes.

Moreen felt refreshed and invigorated but not yet ready to bed down, so she decided to take a walk along the shore of the stream. She scrambled up a steep stretch of jumbled rock beside the small waterfall where the water spilled over the embankment.

She stopped in shock when she saw movement a short distance away, someone walking in a meadow beside the stream. Ducking down, she recognized the rounded shoulders and hulking size of a bull ogre. The creature, who carried a heavy whip, stopped suddenly and planted his hands on his hips.

"All right, Tookie, you get out here!" he barked.

Moreen gaped as a human girl suddenly stepped from the cover of the fungus grove, barely ten feet away. The youngster's eyes flicked in panic to the chiefwoman, who was still concealed from the ogre's view. The child turned to the ogre and stepped out of Moreen's sight, but the Lady of Brackenrock could hear her clearly as she spoke .

"Yes, Master Harmlor. What do you want from me?"

The chiefwoman drew farther back, leaning against the stalk of a giant mushroom, her pulse pounding. She couldn't see the girl any more but knew that the child had spotted her. Would she reveal the presence of intruders to the whip-wielding ogre? There was no way to know.

Turning back to the grotto, Moreen skidded down the stones of the steep embankment, dropping the last few feet into the meadow where her elf companion rested.

"Kerrick! Wake up!" she whispered urgently, kneeling beside the elf, nudging him.

A seasoned campaigner, he awakened without a loud expression of alarm and quickly snatched up his long sword. Moreen spotted Bruni off a short distance away, where the big woman had apparently stopped to wash up, and waved at her in agitation. Bruni came lumbering back, whispering "What's wrong?" as she drew close to her companions.

"There's an ogre up there—and a human girl, a slave. She saw me then got called away by the ogre."

The elf was already climbing, his sword held in his right hand. A few steps from the top he froze, and the chiefwoman looked past him and gasped.

The ogre she had observed moments before stood there, looking down at them with a wicked grin. The little girl was at his side, her arm clasped in his meaty hand as she tried to squirm away. His other hand held the long, sinuous whip in a relaxed, ready grip.

"What do we have? Mice or rats?" asked the ogre with a deep chuckle. He tossed the girl away contemptuously; she landed among the rocks and started to cry.

"You bastard!" Kerrick snarled, lunging.

The ogre was faster. The whip curled out and snapped loudly. Kerrick cried out and stumbled back, clutching his hand, as his sword dropped from his grip to fall between several of the jagged boulders.

"That's enough o' that," barked the ogre. "You three waits right here, and ol' Harmlor keeps an eye on ya. There'll be help comin' soon enough, then we'll find outs where you needs to go."

Bruni moved to the side, and the whip cracked again, snapping in the air before her face. "That's enough, girl. Say, you're a big one, aintcha? Kinda pretty, too—not a scrawny bag o' bones, like most o' you human wenches. You must get sick o' these puny slave fellas."

He laughed, an obscene bark of sound, and Moreen felt fury overwhelm her. She started forward, and when the whip came up again she glared at the ogre in defiance. Pointing at the whimpering girl, she spoke.

"I'm going to see if the little one's all right."

"Tookie? She's fine, but go ahead. Just move slow."

The chiefwoman reached between the rocks and lifted the girl free. The youngster cried out as her arm twisted, and Moreen saw that the bone was broken.

"I've got something that'll help that," she said.

"D—don't hurt me," sniffled Tookie. She glanced up at the ogre, her eyes wide with fright. "He made me show him where you where."

"We won't hurt you," replied the woman, leading her to the pack containing Dinekki's ointment. "Here, sit down."

Moreen glanced up again and saw that Harmlor was watching her with amusement. She saw something else too and had to exert all of her will not to react as Barq One-Tooth came into view, advancing stealthily behind the hulking overseer. The Highlander had his axe in his hands, the weapon raised high as he crept closer with measured, deliberate steps.

Some scuff of a footstep gave him away, and at the last minute, the ogre spun about and roared. That whip snaked out, but the Highlander was too fast, charging forward in a bull rush, swinging his axe in a blow that slashed across Harmlor's face and chest. With an incongruously high-pitched scream the ogre toppled backward, falling down the embankment to crash awkwardly onto the rocks.

He thrashed there, trying to get up, as Kerrick reached between the rocks to snatch up his dropped sword. At the same time Barq leaped down, following his first blow with a sweeping downward slash. The elf stabbed at the same time, and the ogre kicked once and died.

"You killed him!" gasped Tookie. "You can't do that!"

"We had to do that," Moreen said, "but I told the truth when I said we wouldn't hurt you."

"Why—why not? What do you want?" asked the girl tremulously.

"Well, we want to get into Winterheim," replied the chiefwoman. "I wonder if maybe you can help us?"

Karyl Drago plodded tirelessly through the long, winding cavern. It had been years since he had gone all the way to Winterheim, but he remembered the way. Fortunately, there were only a very few alternate passages, most of them short dead ends. He checked each of these, determining that the intruders were not hiding there before lumbering back into the main cavern.

He found the remains of one camp, bones of many blindfish on the cavern floor and the cold ashes of their cookfires. Sniffing the bones, he ascertained that the bits of meat remaining there had not yet spoiled. He was no more than a day or so behind them.

Thoughts of the golden axe infused him with a growing sense of urgency as he continued on. That fire—those beautiful flames! The image burned freshly in his mind. The human woman who had wielded the axe was an enigma. She had displayed a fury and determination worthy of an ogress, and Karyl Drago could not bring himself to hate her. Though she as well as her companions had attacked him and had forced him from his duty, she deserved special attention—after her cohorts were killed, of course.

The big ogre's thoughts did not go much deeper than this, but they burned hot and bright . He would find that axe, and then . . . he didn't know what he would do. Worship it, perhaps? That seemed right.

He didn't have to decide now. Instead, he simply plodded onward, winding through the long cavern, knowing that before long he would reach the Moongarden. The city was not far beyond that fertile warren. Even now, contemplating those wonders and glories, he could only think of that wonderful axe.

"I never saw a person kill an ogre before," Tookie said to Barq One-Tooth, who muttered an awkward and unintelligible reply. "I've seen ogres kill people before. I don't like to see that, but it happens. Old Harmlor, he mighta killed me, I think, when he threw me down."

The girl rubbed her arm, which Moreen had liberally smeared with Dinekki's healing ointment. "It doesn't even hurt any more! Was that stuff magic? I never had any magic touch me before! I only see magic when the queen does it, and then it's pretty scary."

"Yes, this is good magic," the chiefwoman said gently. "It was made for us by a nice lady, a grandmother of our tribe." She tousled the child's black hair, noting the dark skin and deep brown eyes. "Your tribe too, I think. You're an Arktos girl, aren't you?"

"I don't know," Tookie replied. "I'm a slave girl, I guess."

"Are your mother and father slaves, too?" Kerrick asked.

She shook her head. "They're dead is what they are. My mom died when I was born, and my father . . ." Her eyes teared, and she sniffled, then tossed her head and glared at the elf as if challenging him. "He was killed by an ogre."

"I'm sorry," Kerrick said, placing a hand on her shoulder.

"How come your ear is so big, the one, I mean? The other looks like it got cut off or something."

The elf flushed. Moreen knew that he had been scarred by his own king on the night of his exile from Silvanesti, stricken with a sword that sliced away half of his distinctive elven ear. The chiefwoman didn't even notice the mark any more, but now and then she noticed Kerrick touching it, his face an unreadable mask.

"It was cut off," he replied, still keeping his tone soft. "The other one is long because that's the way an elf's ear is supposed to look."

"You're an elf?" Tookie's eyes widened. "I thought elves were scary!"

"I can be scary," Kerrick insisted, scowling for a moment before breaking into a smile, "but I like you."

"I guess I like you, too. That was pretty brave the way you stabbed that ogre." She turned back to Barq, who was still scrubbing ogre blood off of his axe blade. "You too. If you hadn't fought old Harmlor, all of you would have been in big trouble."

The girl paused for a moment, looking at the companions one at a time, then turned to Moreen. "You know, I think you still might be in big trouble. They're going to notice when Harmlor doesn't come back to the garrison."

"Yes, we were thinking that too. Do you know, is there some way we could get away from here so that when they come looking for Harmlor they don't find us here?"

The girl nodded quickly. "I could take you to the slave barracks at the warrens." She frowned. "Everyone would know you were strangers, though. Some of them might tell the ogres."

"That wouldn't do—and we don't want to get you in trouble, either."

The girl's eyes fell to the ground. "Actually, I'm already in trouble. Harmlor, he was looking for me. You see, I'm not supposed to come in here on my own, but I just like the Moongarden so much. It's my favorite place in the world. The masters want me to run errands all the time, back and forth, to the Posting House, mainly. That's so boring. I wanted to come in here and wander around in the fungus forest."

The elf knelt before Tookie and looked the girl in the eyes. "What about this Posting House? Is that in Winterheim?"

"Yep. Up in the middle. It's where they bring all the slaves when they first come here or when they get old enough to be sent off to a job. Tildy Trew is the boss up there, and she's nice."

"Do you suppose you could take us there? Without us having to talk to ogres on the way?" asked Kerrick.

"Well, I could try. There's a path from the Moongardens that goes into the city, and it comes in right by the Posting House. I go there a lot, taking messages. If you were with me, I could say you were slaves, but you'd have to hide your swords and stuff."

"We could do that," Moreen said. "There are more of us over there near the cave leading in." The chiefwoman had another thought. "We're looking for a new slave, a man who was brought to Winterheim a few weeks ago. His name is Strongwind Whalebone. Have you seen him, or anyone that might be him?"

The girl's face wrinkled in concentration as she gave the matter some thought. "I don't think so. I didn't see any new slaves come in this summer, but I don't see lots of things, since I live in the Warren Barracks."

"Is the Posting House where they bring new slaves?" pressed the chiefwoman.

"Yes. Tildy Trew might know about this Strongwind Whale. Shall we go to see her?"

"As soon as we can pack up our equipment, yes," Moreen said. "Tell me, could we hide our weapons somewhere too?"

"Sure. Come with me to the other end of the warren—there are food baskets that we use for harvesting. You can put your stuff in them and hide it pretty good." She pointed at the Axe of Gonnas, the blade wrapped in burlap as it jutted from Bruni's pack. "I don't know about that big hatchet, though."

"Well, please take us there," Moreen said. "Bruni, will you go back and tell the others. They can hide in the grotto while we try to work out a plan. Tookie, are you ready to go now?"

The girl nodded with great dignity, then watched seriously as they packed up their gear, hoisted their packs, and made ready to go. "Aren't you going to hide Harmlor?" she asked.

"Good idea," Barq said. Tookie watched impassively as Bruni and Barq pulled the big corpse down the rest of the rocky embankment. They rolled several large rocks over the ogre's body.

"This way," the girl said. "You follow along behind me a little bit, okay? I can let you know if someone's coming and you have to hide."

"She's just a little girl. Do you think we can trust her?" whispered Kerrick to Moreen as they started out.

"Yes, I do," the chiefwoman said. She was impressed, even awed, by the child's casual courage as the waif led them out of the Moongarden.

17

The Slave Girl

"Wow, I didn't know there were so many of you!" Tookie exclaimed, as Bruni returned with Mouse, Dinekki, and the rest of the war party filing along behind. If the girl was frightened by the appearance of more than two hundred fur-clad, armed warriors, she gave no indication, but she shook her head at the prospects of maintaining secrecy. Her brown face creased into a scowl.

"I don't think we can sneak you all into the city, not right now anyways. I mean, I can go in with a few of you dressed like slaves, and I can show you where it is and everything, but we have to go right past the ogre barracks. They'll notice if there's so many of you."

"Is there a place in the Moongarden where the war party can hide while a few of us go into the city for a look around?" Moreen asked.

Tookie scratched her head and frowned as she looked around, scrutinizing several of the side caverns that broke off of the main chamber of the great underground warren. Abruptly, she brightened, pointing to one alcove about halfway through the huge cavern. "You could hide up

there in the Port Grotto. That's where they grow these big
mushrooms that take a long time. Nobody will go in there
until the winter when they're ready to harvest. There's
lots of space, soft moss in the meadows where you can
rest, and even blindfish in the stream."

The suggested alcove was about thirty feet above the
main floor of the cavern. A thin waterfall trailed over the
lip, dropping through a white plume to splash into one of
the many little brooks gurgling across the floor of the
Moongarden. There was a clearly defined path, almost as
a steep as a stairway, leading up to the alcove and disap-
pearing between the trunks of several massive, wide-
capped fungi.

"Is there another way in or out of there?" Kerrick asked.

Tookie shook her head. "Nope, just that path going up,
the one you can see from here."

"Well, they'll be able to keep an eye on the rest of the
cavern," the elf noted. "It would be easy to defend, if the
war party gets attacked there."

Moreen turned to Mouse and Barq One-Tooth. "Will
you two take the rest up there and get everyone settled
and concealed? Keep some guards posted, but try to let
everyone get some rest and food. We'll scout the approach
to the city and try to get back here as soon as we can."

The big thane shook his head stubbornly. "I'm going
with you," Barq declared. "Thane Larsgall can take command of the Highlanders, but I want to find out what they
have done with my king."

Moreen was about to object then nodded. Larsgall was
a young, strapping warrior from the eastern shore of the
White Bear Sea, and she knew him to be a level-headed
commander, well respected by the men.

"Very well. Bruni, Kerrick, you, and I will go along
with Tookie. The rest of you wait and watch. I hope it
won't be for very long."

The plan was acceptable to all except Slyce, who wanted to tag along into the ogre city. The chiefwoman informed him sternly that he was staying behind, and though he sulked, he eventually accompanied Mouse, Dinekki, and the others as they made their way toward the hiding place. Moreen watched as the fighters crossed the central stream on a ford of dry rocks then vanished into the fungus forest.

Tookie led the four companions deeper into the Moongarden. They followed a narrow trail through a thicket of tall mushrooms, a route the girl had told them was less heavily used than the main path in and out of the barracks. Concealment was easy as they stuck mostly to the shadowy reaches below the wide caps of tree-sized mushrooms.

For two hours they walked in silence, marveling at the vast stands of fungus around them, the smooth meadows lined with verdant moss. All of it was illuminated by the soft green light that seemed remarkably consistent. As they neared the far end of the cavern, they saw more alcoves branching off of the main cavern. Most of these were dark, though one gleamed with the harsh light of torches and lanterns. Several balconies overlooked that wide passageway, and Moreen saw an ogre lolling casually there.

"This is the work barracks up ahead," Tookie explained in a hushed voice. "It's where the slaves live who work in here."

"Are there guards nearby?" Kerrick asked.

From here they could see a wide-mouthed side cavern, deep and shadowy. It was fenced off by a stockade of timber, but the gate was open, and there didn't seem to be any ogres in this immediate area.

"Well, they have their own barracks over there," the girl replied, pointing to a ledge higher up on the cavern wall, "but they're always coming and going. You see, past there is the ramp up to the city."

Kerrick and the others could observe that wide, smooth route, as broad as a grand street, curving along the cavern wall. The ramp inclined upward at a gentle grade before turning away from the Moongarden to vanish into a wide tunnel. The orange glow of oil lamplight glowed from within that passage, a harsh contrast to the soft green illumination of the great, verdant cavern.

Tookie led them closer, halting within the cover of the last of the giant mushrooms. "Why don't you wait here and try to stay out of sight, most of you," she said. "I'll sneak in and get some slaves robes so you don't look so out of place. We can get baskets for your stuff."

"Can you carry all that?" wondered the elf.

"I might need a little help," she admitted, turning to look up at Barq One-Tooth, who was gaping around. "Can you come along and help me?"

The big Highlander looked nonplussed at the question, but something in the girl's expression seemed to move him. He cleared his throat gruffly then nodded.

"Sure, girlie," he replied. "Just tell me what to do."

Stariz inspected the ragged lot of prisoners with contempt. There were two dozen of them, all male, universally sullen and surly. The guards had chained them in pairs, and despite their bluster and bravado she could see their eyes were wide with fear. She could smell the stench of terror in their sweat. They were doomed, and they knew it. She was pleased, anticipating great suffering before these men finally met the release of death.

One man caught her eye, and she pointed to him. The guards unclasped him from his fellow prisoners and pushed him forward. The slave was tall and blond-bearded. The queen recognized him by his icy blue eyes and sandy hair. It was as her spy had told her, barely two hours before. This prize would be among the group of captives, if she acted quickly in sending the grenadiers. Still, she could not quite believe her good fortune.

"You are the Highlander, Strongwind Whalebone, who was captured on Dracoheim, are you not? You have a knack for causing trouble."

The man shrugged his shoulders, a contemptuous gesture that provoked one of the guards to shove him hard from behind. Stumbling to his knees, the slave glared up at the queen with an expression of pure hatred.

She snorted in amusement and spoke loudly so that all the slaves as well as the company of grenadiers could hear. "There is no need for you to respond. I recognize you, Highlander King. At the time of your entry into Winterheim I pronounced you a dangerous soul, and now the proof is in your company. Still you were sent into service as a house slave—to the apartments of Lady Dimmarkull, as I understand."

Looking around the great throne hall, the ogre queen saw that her words had been heard by all in attendance. That was good, another piece in her clever plan falling into place. She sneered down at the prisoner, flicking him away with an outward gesture of her fingers.

"Take him out of my sight. Take all of them away! Lock them in the royal dungeons on the harbor level, and do not bother to feed them. It is only necessary that they live a little longer, until the ceremony of Autumnblight three days hence."

The grenadiers trooped the hapless rebels away, while Stariz glared coldly after them. As soon as the door to the throne room slammed shut, she hurried toward her own, private exit.

She expected that it would not be long before she heard from her husband, and she expected the king to be in a very bad mood. She had an explanation ready, and she felt confident that she would be able to get him to believe her.

The Port Grotto was a big cavern and well hidden from the main chamber of the Moongarden. Quickly the fighters of the war party found places to stretch out and rest, though several men remained on sentry duty, hidden along the edge of the alcove. Slyce volunteered for this important job, but Mouse ordered the gully dwarf to remain in the back of the group and assigned two alert warriors to keep an eye on the little fellow.

Mouse realized that he hadn't seen Dinekki in a while and went to look for her. He found the shaman kneeling beside a pool of still water in a narrow niche of the cavern wall where the light of the phosphorescent fungus was muted. The liquid was still, reflective as a mirror, but he had the sense that she was peering at something far beyond the surface of the water.

"Are you all right, Grandmother?" he asked. "I didn't want to interrupt—"

"Help me up!" she snapped crossly, extending a frail-looking hand.

He did as she asked, unsurprised by the wiry strength in those thin fingers. He could not help noticing that she wobbled unsteadily as she rose then held his hand for an extra moment, as though fighting against a wave of dizziness.

"What is it?" he asked worriedly. "Did you see something amiss?"

The old woman sighed, for once displaying every one of her eight or nine decades of life. Her shoulders slumped, and she seemed to exert great effort just to raise her head to look at him.

"Trouble," she replied, with a shake of her head. "Trouble on all sides of us."

Karyl Drago paused at the entry to the Moongarden, taking in the view from a high ledge above the cavern floor. There was no place like this in all the world, he was certain. It gave him a special feeling of pride to know that he was entrusted to guard this place from the outside world. Of course, he had failed this duty, he recalled with more than a twinge of shame, and he ceased his gawking to once more take up the trail of those who had thwarted him, killed his garrison, and left him for dead.

He descended the steep trail to the cavern floor, looking for signs of the intruders. He was not terribly worried when he didn't immediately find any tracks. The ground was mostly hard stone, and besides, there was no other way that they could have come.

Now that he had reached the Moongarden, he knew that he would have to be diligent. This place was huge, with many concealed groves and grottos as well as side caverns in a half dozen places that were huge caves in their own right, each a place where a party of dangerous intruders might hide out, watch, and wait. They could be anywhere, and it wouldn't do for him to wander past and leave them undiscovered.

He paused long enough to take a drink of cold, fresh water. He was still sore from his drop into the crevasse and noticed that several large scabs had developed on his belly. These were starting to itch, and he remembered that there was a soothing pool of warm water very nearby. That would be just the place to wash the wounds.

Soon he was wallowing in comfort, rubbing away the grime and grit from his wounds. He was filled with thoughts of the fiery, golden axe. With a sigh of contentment, he leaned back and let the waters caress his battered flesh. It wasn't until he emerged and shook himself dry, that he noticed something odd about the water running past his little pool. It was discolored, tainted as if by mud or some kind of rust-colored dye. Curious, Karyl Drago followed the stream to the place where it spilled over the embankment. Here he saw that the dye was coming from beneath a pile of rocks. Several bare patches of dirt nearby seemed to suggest that these rocks had recently been moved.

A minute later the big ogre had pulled one of the boulders out of the way and found himself looking down into the slashed and lifeless face of one of the Moongarden ogres who worked as overseers of the slaves.

Clearly he was on the right track of the human intruders. However, his mission took on a new urgency. Again Karyl Drago felt a surge of shame. If he had done his job properly at the gate, this ogre would still be alive.

He picked up the splintered end of his club and scrambled up the embankment. It wasn't too far to the watch station, he knew, and it seemed time for him to start to spread the alarm.

Grimwar Bane smashed open the front door of Thraid's apartment with a single blow from his clubbed fist, sending splinters flying as the great wooden slab broke from its hinges and slammed into the ground. The echoes still resonated as he stormed through the courtyard and into the street beyond, bellowing at the top of his lungs.

"Murder! Assassination! Guards! Gather to me, warriors of Winterheim! Bring arms, and stand ready to fight!"

By the time he had crossed the promenade, his roars had raised a commotion. Slaves ran away from him in all directions, ducking into their houses or anywhere else they could find shelter. Ogres came running, including several wearing the red coats of the grenadiers. The king shook his fist at the mountaintop overhead and bellowed his rage.

"What is it, Sire?" asked one grenadier, kneeling before the enraged monarch.

"The Lady Thraid has been murdered, stabbed in her bed," declared Grimwar Bane, forcing his breathing to slow down, pushing out each word with an effort of will. "I want you to seal off her apartments and stand watch." He saw others of the royal guard running along the wide promenade. "As you get reinforcements, put them to work! Talk to everyone in these houses, and see if there are witnesses who observed anything! Shake the information out of them if you have to!"

"As you wish, Majesty!" pledged the guard, quickly gesturing to several of his fellows and starting toward the lady's rooms.

His emotions roiling, Grimwar believed he already knew the culprit. It was obvious. Perhaps Queen Stariz had not wielded the knife herself, but the king had no doubts that whoever had committed this foul murder had been operating under her orders.

He charged up the ramp, scattering ogres and slaves alike, passersby of both races who stared, slack-jawed, at the unprecedented sight of their king sprinting wildly up the sloping avenue. His feet pounded the stone, fists pumping as he lumbered up and up the many tiers of his city. Despite his exertion, he was barely out of breath when he reached the throne room on the Royal Level where the queen was supposedly interrogating rebels. The attendant guards barely had time to pull the door open as he barged in.

Grimwar Bane stalked into the great hall to find his queen seated on her own throne, a granite chair slightly smaller and less grandiose than his own. She was engaged in animated discussion with several of the grenadiers and looked up in surprise as he approached.

"My lord—" she began, then halted when she beheld the fury etched on his face.

"Out!" he roared at the guards, pointing to the door. In seconds they had raced from the room, the attendants discreetly pushing the doors shut.

"What is the matter?" asked Stariz, her square face furrowed in concern—mock concern, the king was sure.

"This time, you hateful creature, you have gone too far! You will be punished for this, punished like any treacherous assassin who dares to lurk in my halls!"

"My King!" she protested. "What has happened? Why are you so angry?"

He sneered, unwilling to consider the possibility that she didn't know what he was talking about. "I am talking about murder, murder founded on jealousy, carried out by treachery!"

"Murder of whom?" she gasped. "Whatever do you mean?"

"You insist on these protestations of innocence?" he growled. "You know perfectly well that the Lady Thraid has been slashed to death. No doubt you even know who wielded the knife! I will have the truth from you. I will draw it out with sharp hooks if I have to! I will see that you and all of your accomplices die a slow death—a death that will give you ample time to ponder your many sins!"

"My lord, no!" she gasped, in a display of innocence. Her face drained of color, and her jaw worked reflexively, though for once no sound emerged from her mouth. "I do not know of this!"

"Enough treachery!" He stepped close, saw her shrink back into the throne, her face distorted by fear. Abruptly, her expression changed, a light of understanding dawning in her features. The king hesitated, surprised and puzzled.

"It was the slave! It must have been!" protested the queen. "The captive Highlander warrior that we brought from Dracoheim. He was captured in the salt room with the other rebels! He was one of the conspirators! Undoubtedly, this was the first act of the insurrection! How many more ogre nobles would have perished by now had we not caught these perfidious rebels when we did?"

Grimwar Bane had not been expecting this. He scowled and shook his head stubbornly. "Why would the rebels kill a harmless noblewoman?" he demanded, still looming close, studying this horrible creature who was his wife, and his queen.

Stariz stood up and approached him, reaching out a hand that he slapped away. She pulled her arm back but glared at him stubbornly. "Is it true that you assigned him to the Lady Thraid—as a house slave? He was arrested with the other rebels! You can ask the grenadiers," she insisted. "Captain Verra himself saw the man taken."

The king turned his back on his wife and stalked across the throne room. He didn't believe her, but neither had he expected her to make this situation so complicated. Surely she was lying!

How could he prove it?

He was about to summon the guards, to have her thrown into the dungeon, when he heard a ruckus. Stepping out of the palace doors, he crossed to the railing over the atrium and glared at the sight of several guards running across the waterfront plaza far below.

One of them raised a brass horn, and several loud notes brayed through the city, rising up through the atrium, carrying all the way to the king's ears on the Royal Level. The cry was repeated, and Grimwar Bane strained his memory. He knew it was an important trumpet call, but he couldn't remember what it meant.

It was Stariz who interpreted for him as she burst out of the throne room and raced over to him with most unqueenly haste. "My lord!" she cried. "Do you hear?"

"Yes!" he declared, sternly. "The alarm sounds!"

He wished he could think of some way to mask his ignorance, but he failed. In frustration, he was about to ask her what the horn meant, when she spoke first.

"Intruders!" she gasped. "It is almost unbelievable, but that is the signal that intruders have forced their way into Winterheim!"

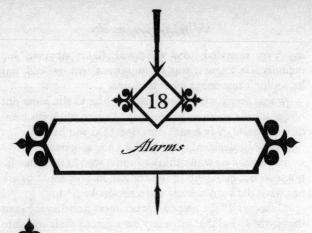

Alarms

The tunnel leading out of the Moongarden was wide and brightly lit, oil lamps burning in wall sconces every ten paces or so along both walls. After the soft illumination of the vast cavern, Moreen found the flaring wicks to be glaring and unpleasant. Furthermore, they seemed so bright as to render her disguise almost useless—she felt as though she were walking naked, fully exposed to any ogre who happened a glance.

It took all her will to keep her head down and to follow Tookie's casual pace, as they passed under the balconies of the ogre guardroom. Several of the brutes were up there, and she could hear them talking, even smell the stench of their sweat. She was grateful at least for the large basket she bore on her head, and in moments she and her companions were safely past, following the young girl along the broad, mostly empty corridor toward the ogre city.

Fortunately, the girl had done a good job in providing them with disguises. Moreen glanced at Bruni and Barq One-Tooth, behind her, Kerrick bringing up the rear. All of them wore brown hooded robes that Tookie had informed them were the outfits of the slaves who bore goods from the Moongarden to the various markets in the city. They carried baskets, individual loads for Moreen and Kerrick, while Barq and Bruni shared a long, almost coffin-sized, container in which they had placed the Axe of Gonnas.

"Just get out of the way if ogres come by," said the girl, her tone matter-of-fact. "They probably will."

For some time they made their way toward the city, meeting small parties of slaves, occasionally stepping to the side as an ogre or two ambled past. The ogres strolled along with no apparent sense of urgency. None of them seemed to take any interest in the small party of slaves.

Moreen almost dropped her basket, however, when the braying notes of a trumpet began to ring through the hall. The three rising notes originated behind her in the Moon-garden and were repeated many times. Soon they were picked up by other trumpeters, and in a few minutes the notes were ringing throughout the halls of this vast under-ground city.

"I think they must have found Harmlor already," Tookie said, her dark eyes serious. "You'd better just do your best to look like slaves. There's gonna be some excitement now, you can bet."

True to the girl's prediction, the corridor they followed soon echoed with lumbering footsteps, and the five of them pressed to one side, allowing a band of heavily armed ogres, a score or more, to race past.

"Uh-huh, they're going to the Moongarden," Tookie said. "Here . . . we're almost up to the city now."

She led them through a wide archway, and Moreen looked up in amazement. The size of the place yawning before them almost defied comprehension. Clearly they were inside a great mountain. A hundred feet below them was a wide plaza, and the smell of the sea was strong in her nostrils. She saw the ogre king's galley, *Goldwing*, berthed at one slip in a large harbor and realized that the whole port was enclosed within the mountain. A channel led up to the great gates, providing access to all the seas of the Icereach when those gates were opened.

Above, the ceiling soared away, up a long shaft encircled by numerous balconies. All these seemed to be filled with ogres gathering, on ledges, along the railings, peering down and up, gesturing in agitation, roaring out to each other with questions and speculation. Torches flared throughout these levels, and grotesque shadows were cast on the walls as the citizens of the city raced about in confusion and consternation. On the waterfront, several ranks of red-coated ogres were forming with military precision, responding to the orders of a silver-helmed captain.

"This way," said Tookie, leading the four intruders onto a wide, curving ramp, a climbing surface that led them away from the harbor and into the interior of the great city. Soon they had left the view of the central atrium behind. It was again as if they were wandering through a network of caverns, only this passage seemed to lead higher and deeper into the city of ogres.

The chiefwoman couldn't put the danger out of her mind. There were so many of ogres. How could they ever hope to succeed, now that the enemy was alert to their presence?

They had to stop and wait as yet another troop of guards rushed past, these too apparently heading toward the Moongarden. Everywhere slaves were gathered in small groups, whispering, looking around nervously, and the chiefwoman felt acutely exposed.

A voice boomed out, as loud as thunder, and Moreen froze in shock.

"The axe of fire—there it is! They try to hide it, but its glory is revealed!"

She spun around, astonished at the sight of the massive ogre they had battled at the Icewall Gate. There he was behind them, mud-splattered and bloody, pointing unerringly at the long basket borne by Barq One-Tooth and Bruni. A score of ogre guards were with him.

Astonishingly, that basket was glowing brightly, yellow light flaring beneath the wicker frame. The top seemed to quiver and dance, and the brilliance of the golden axe was the brightest thing she had ever seen.

———◆———

Strongwind leaned back against the cold stone walls of his cell. He was chained in here with the rest of the men who had been taken in the salt room. It was ironic, when he thought about it—those chains were probably all that was keeping him alive right now. From the looks of hatred and contempt on the other rebels' faces, especially Black Mike's, he had no doubts but that the men would have killed him if they had the chance.

He had told them again and again that he was innocent of treachery. He thought of trying one more time. They had to believe that he had not been the one to reveal the plot to the queen and to call in the royal guards.

It was pointless. They refused to even look at him.

Besides, he was too tired right now . . . he was too tired for anything except to just sit here and wait to die.

———◆———

Grimwar Bane paced fretfully back to the throne room, his wife trailing behind. Six grenadiers stood around with their halberds raised, swords loose in their scabbards, watching the doors with narrowed, squinting eyes. The king looked up when someone pounded on the doors. One of the guards, after checking through a viewing slot, opened the portal to reveal Lord Forlane.

"Well?" demanded the king. "What is the nature of the intrusion?"

The lord spoke rapidly. "The guard at the Icewall Pass gate reports that a great number of humans attacked him. He was ashamed to admit it, but apparently they bested him and killed his entire garrison. They caused him to fall into a crevasse where they left him and made their way into the Moongarden. There it seems that they made further progress by killing an ogre guard, one of the overseers of the warren slaves."

"And the guard in command at the gate—he is not dead?"

"No, Sire. You may remember him: Karyl Drago, the, ahem, very *large* warrior who came here from Glacierheim in our queen's entourage."

"Yes—I was just thinking of him the other day. You say he was overcome by these attackers?" Grimwar Bane found that hard to believe.

"That is what he says, Sire, and he seems to be speaking the truth. There was a small army of them by his report. He says that they used a golden axe and that the magic of that blade felled him. Nevertheless, he climbed free and pursued the intruders. It was he who discovered the overseer's body and subsequently issued the alarm."

"Golden axe? What kind of description do we have of these intruders?" demanded Grimwar Bane. He wished Stariz would venture some suggestion, but she watched silently, white-faced and trembling.

"It seems they are humans, Sire," Lord Forlane reported. "Both Arktos and Highlanders, by the report. Oddly enough, there were two women with the leaders. One was small and dark, the other was much larger. She is the one, according to Karyl Drago, who bore that axe of gold, the blade of which burst into fire before his very face."

"Then it's true! It is the sacred axe!" declared Stariz, her face transfixed by an expression of fierce joy. "It returns to me!"

"The Axe of Gonnas . . ."

All too well Grimwar Bane remembered his wife's dream of some nights before—at least at the time, he had dismissed it has a dream—that the sacred axe was near and was returning to her temple.

For the first time since discovering his lover's body, he began to wonder if perhaps the humans really were to blame for all his troubles.

"Very well. We must act at once," declared the king stoutly, suddenly seeing exactly what needed to be done. "Forlane, I want you to find Captain Verra. Command him to muster all the grenadiers. He is to watch the approach into the city from the Moongarden as well as keep an eye on the slaves at the Seagate and in the lumber yards. We don't want to take any chances. If he notices any signs of an insurrection, he must act quickly and without mercy to contain the slaves."

Suddenly that nightmare possibility, the notion he had discussed as a hypothetical with Captain Verra just a few days before, seemed a real danger. Had the slaves of Winterheim, the humans who outnumbered their ogre masters by two or three to one, somehow organized a revolt?

"Aye, Sire! It shall be as you command!" declared the noble ogre.

"What about the higher levels of the city?" asked the queen, her eyes wide.

"I myself will take command up here," said Grimwar Bane. "I will send the entire palace garrison to guard the ramps, to make sure there is no chance for intruders—be they Arktos or Highlanders . . . or rebellious slaves!—to work any mischief in the upper reaches of Winterheim!"

"Make haste! Make haste!" barked the queen. "Find the Axe of Gonnas and bring it here to me at once!"

The lord looked at the king for confirmation. Grimwar grimaced but then nodded.

"Yes!" he ordered. "Do as she says!"

* * *

"Mouse, there's something bad going on out there!"

The Arktos warrior sat up groggily, shaking the sleep from his mind. It was Feathertail, he saw, and she was speaking quietly but with undeniable urgency. He remembered she was one of the warriors who had stayed on guard duty while he settled down to get some much-needed rest.

Without a word, he followed her to the lip of the grotto where the human warriors had concealed themselves. They both crawled forward, peering between a pair of massive fungi stalks, to peer into the great breadth of the Moongarden. They had seen a huge ogre go through a few hours before, coming from the same direction the war party had taken, and Mouse had even speculated on the resemblance between that gigantic creature and the monstrous guardian at the Icewall Gate, the brute who had vanished into the crevasse. There had been no unusual activity since then, until the braying of the horns that had coincided with Mouse awakening.

Now Mouse immediately saw a group of ogres, a dozen or more of them, moving across an open field at a jog. The brutes wore cloaks of red and carried spears in both hands, the weapons' gleaming tips angled before them aggressively. One, apparently a captain, shouting and gestured, and several of the ogres broke away from the main group to charge into a narrow, shaded trail between the groves of giant mushrooms.

"They're looking for us, I think," Feathertail whispered. "There are three or four groups of them running around like that."

Mouse felt a stab of fear. "Some kind of alarm has gone out." He thought of Moreen and her companions and sent a silent prayer to Chislev Wilder pleading for their safety. What should he do now?

Thane Larsgall came rushing up to them, sliding to his own perch on the lip of the drop off. The waterfall plunged nearby, noisy enough that it would cover any slight sounds they made.

"Sooner or later they'll make their way up here," the Highlander noted.

Mouse nodded. "I guess we'd better keep our weapons handy and get ready. At least they won't take us by surprise!"

———◆———

Stariz watched her husband through narrowed eyes. The king had momentarily forgotten all about Thraid's murder—a good thing too, since it was proving hard to convince him that the slave king was the culprit. Thus, the distraction of the human intruders could not have come at a better time, for Stariz had almost begun to fear for her life. Now that the king was involved in this new crisis, she could set aside the problem of the dead mistress and later find other ways to win him over. In fact, she could use clerical magic to fog his mind if it became necessary.

Hmmm, that was a good idea.

Right now there was one thing more important than all else, only one truth that dominated her thoughts and infused her with hope and passion.

The Axe of Gonnas! These intruders had it with them. It was only a matter of time until it was returned to her!

———◆◆◆———

The huge ogre had honed in on Bruni and Barq, barking and jabbering as he pressed them against the wall of the corridor. They shielded the basket containing the golden axe, which momentarily stayed his attack. Kerrick, Moreen, and the slave girl edged outside the ring of other ogre guards and for the moment were ignored in the confusion.

The elf saw Moreen's hand slip under her robe and knew she was making a move for the sword she wore concealed there. He stepped into her roughly, taking her elbow in a firm grip, pushing her away from the throng of ogres converging around Bruni and Barq. From the corner of his eye, the elf saw Tookie also scamper away, avoiding the melee.

"Let me go!" demanded the chiefwoman, her voice a hiss of fury.

"No," he replied, levelly.

Forcefully he pulled her to the side, where many other slaves were gathering to watch the unfolding events. He turned them around so they too could watch Bruni and Barq but kept his hand firmly on her arm. This time she didn't try to break away from him.

"They're caught," he whispered. "We can't do anything against twenty ogres! The worst thing we can do is to get taken with them—then all our hope is gone!"

More guards converged from before them, and the two big humans were flattened against the wall of the corridor with nowhere to go. Barq and Bruni stood back to back now, the basket containing the axe on the ground behind their legs. They had the good sense not to flourish their weapons against the score or more of ogres who had them trapped.

The biggest ogre, Kerrick realized with astonishment, was the very monster they had battled in the gateway, the giant who had tumbled into the crevasse, where they had assumed, mistakenly, he had perished. His face was scratched and bloody, and streaks of mud marred his cloak and tunic, but his voice was as strong as ever as he shouted, "They bear the golden axe, and they fought through my gate. They are intruders into Winterheim and must be brought before the king for judgment."

He shoved them aside and knelt to grab the Axe of Gonnas, from the floor. His eyes were wide with wonder as he lifted the blade of solid gold, and for several long heartbeats it seemed as though he had forgotten everything else—the prisoners, the mob of ogre guards who seemed to be waiting for some kind of command, the throng of slaves who cowered nearby.

Kerrick noticed Tookie coming back, wiggling through the crowd until she came to a stop beside Moreen. She took the chiefwoman's hand.

"We have to help!" Moreen insisted, but the slave girl shook her head. The chiefwoman looked to Kerrick for support, but he nodded in agreement with Tookie.

"Tookie's right. The best thing we can do for our companions now is to try and keep from getting captured."

Angrily she pulled her elbow from his grasp, rubbing the skin where, no doubt, he had clutched her hard enough to leave a deep bruise. She stayed rooted to her spot, watching in anguish.

"Take these prisoners to the royal dungeon," cried the huge ogre, at last tearing his eyes free from the entrancing axe. Abruptly, he spun about, his big face contorting in concentration as he started to look over the throng of slaves that included Kerrick, Moreen, and Tookie.

"There were more humans, lots, with them," grunted the ogre. His big hand came up, a finger as large as a sausage extending in the general direction of Moreen.

"You there!" he barked, suddenly. "Take off your hood."

In that instant Kerrick he knew that he had to act. He gave the woman a shove, relieved as Moreen and Tookie joined the rest of the slaves in sprinting away, racing up the corridor toward Winterheim. Instead the elf lunged forward, drawing his own sword, slashing the weapon as he rushed at the hulking ogre warrior.

Another one of the brutes stepped into his path, raising a spear to block the lethal blade, but Kerrick was too quick, lancing under the parry to stab his long sword right into the ogre's guts. With a howl the creature fell backward, tumbling into his oversized comrade, knocking several other ogres off balance.

As he fell, however, his speartip swept around and caught the corner of Kerrick's hood, pulling the woolen shroud from the elf's head. Spinning on one foot, the Silvanesti sprinted after the fleeing slaves, trying to sheath his sword and pull the hood back over his golden hair and pointed ear. Knowing that he had no chance to save Bruni and Barq did nothing to assuage his misery as he abandoned his two loyal companions in the grasp of a half dozen ogre warriors.

One more thing caused his heart to sink, as he dashed away. It was shouted by a guard, loud enough to echo through the hall and confirm that he had been identified.

"An elf!" came the cry. "An elf has come to Winterheim!"

19

A Meeting in the Dark

You go in here," said the ogre, roughly pushing Bruni through a low doorway. She ducked so that she didn't bump her head and found herself in a large, stone-walled room where several dozen humans sat listlessly on the floor. Most, possibly all of them, were chained to the walls, though it was hard to make out many details in the near total darkness of the large cell.

She heard a burst of violence behind her and turned to see Barq One-Tooth struggling in the grip of another of their captors. The big Highlander tried to throw a punch but instead took a hard blow on his head from the hilt of a grenadier's sword. Groaning, he staggered and was pushed unceremoniously through the door to sprawl heavily on the floor.

The large woman knelt beside him, touching his head, feeling the sticky ooze of blood. Barq groaned and sat up, rubbing the wound then pulling his hand away to look at his bloody fingers.

"You'd think I'd learn to pick my fights better," he growled in disgust.

"It was a nice gesture," Bruni told him, "hopeless but nice."

"Bastards!" snarled the man, glaring at the metal door that clanged shut across the dungeon entrance.

He turned his attention to their surroundings, blinking in surprise as he saw the other men in the cell, all of whom seemed to be watching them with interest. There was a rattle of iron from one of the corners as one or two prisoners tried to stir. As she squinted into the darkness, Bruni perceived that many, perhaps all, of these men were secured in place with heavy chains.

"Where are we?" Barq One-Tooth demanded.

"The queen's own dungeon," muttered one fellow disgustedly. "We're locked up here till she finds the time to kill us. Don't worry—it shouldn't be long now."

"Cheery thought," Bruni said. "I know what we did to get tossed in here, but what about the rest of you?"

"Don't talk to her!" snapped one of the men, a swarthy fellow who was chained to the wall by both wrists. "She could be a spy—just like Thraid's lackey, over there!"

The prisoner spat contemptuously at another of the captives, a thin, bearded man in the far corner of the room. He, too, was chained and was gazing at the two newcomers with a strange expression.

Bruni thought the man looked familiar and was trying to place him when Barq One-Tooth cried out. He crossed to the prisoner and knelt before him. "Sire! May Kradok smite those who would dare to restrain you thus!"

"Strongwind Whalebone?" Bruni exclaimed in wonder. "Is that truly you?"

Their words provoked a startled reaction among the prisoners, several of whom whispered among themselves or muttered words of disbelief. The man was thin and haggard, bedraggled enough that he looked like a different, much smaller monarch than the noble Strongwind she remembered, but those eyes and that tight smile were un-mistakeable.

"Aye, it is, Bruni of Brackenrock and my old thane Barq One-Tooth. How did those ogre scum-lords acquire you two?"

Bruni was about to counsel discretion, at least in what they said within hearing of the rest of these prisoners, but the Barq spoke bluntly.

"We came to rescue you," he said, shaking his head miserably. "The Lady of Brackenrock brought us here, she and the elf and a small force of volunteers, but Bruni and I were taken as we tried to penetrate the city. My Lord King, we have failed you! May all the gods strike me down as just punishment!"

Strongwind's eyes all but bulged out of his head. Impatiently he waved off Barq's continuing efforts at apology. "The Lady—Moreen Bayguard is alive?" he asked. "She survived the disaster at Brackenrock? How? That's wonderful news!" He glowered, suddenly and looked askance at Bruni. "Was she captured as well? Where is she?"

"She and Kerrick avoided capture when we were taken, as best as I could see. Barq and I were carrying the Axe of Gonnas. It was hidden in a basket, but somehow it gave us away."

"You dared come to Winterheim to rescue me? That's mad!" Strongwind said in despair, still looking at Bruni.

"I came because Moreen was coming," the big woman said tartly. "There was nothing I or anyone else could say that would have deterred her from the path she had chosen. She felt responsible for your capture. It was the honorable course of action."

"How did she ever think she could succeed? No one has ever been rescued from this place!" Strongwind shook his head in agitation. "It is a hopeless quest!"

"I fear, Sire, that I must bear some blame for that," Barq said, hanging his head in shame. "Some of the thanes . . . led by myself . . . well, we were all set to accuse the lady of treachery when you failed to return from Dracoheim. Of course, we realized that she was a true friend to you when she declared for this quest. There was not a man from all the Highlands who would not have gone along with her."

Strongwind Whalebone slumped back against the wall, his eyes closed. When he spoke to Barq it was not in anger but in a tone of disappointment that Bruni suspected might cut even deeper than rage.

"Mad Randall and I . . . we gave ourselves willingly on Dracoheim to allow Moreen a chance to succeed in destroying the Golden Orb. Randall perished, and I was taken by the ogres. Even now that I know that the lady lives, I have to judge that day a success. What a blow . . . to learn that my own capture has led to her undoing! This is too heavy a burden to bear. It were better I died that day than to have drawn her into this ice-walled trap."

"Sire, don't say that!" Barq pleaded miserably. "She still lives, and we'll find a way out of here, you watch. That elf is a brave one, and he has a million tricks, too. There is still the party of brave warriors who came with us, and they're not done yet!"

"More madness," said the slave king, with a dejected groan. "I cannot be the cause of so many deaths. I am not that important!"

Bruni looked around at the other prisoners, who were watching with expressions of amazement. The swarthy captive who had first spoken so accusingly of the High-lander spoke up again.

"Is it true, then—you really are Strongwind Whale-bone, the king of Guilderglow? When we were captured,

I thought that was a ruse to win our trust, but the heir to the Whalebone kings is here, rotting here in an ogre dungeon?"

"It's true," Bruni replied testily. "He is as brave and true a man as you will find in all the Icereach."

The man cried out as though in physical pain. "Forgive me, Majesty. I accused you of the basest form of treachery. I am a fool!"

"You're a brave man," Strongwind said kindly, "and a suspicious one, as you were forced to be. Had our positions been reversed, I no doubt would have been wary of you as well."

"Is there any way out of here? Can we try to fight our way past the guards?" asked Barq One-Tooth hopefully.

Strongwind shook his head. "There are steel doors holding us here and plenty of guards on the outside."

"It is up to Kerrick and Moreen, then," Bruni said. When all the men looked at the floor, she added, "There are no better allies to have at a time like this."

"Pray to Chislev and to Kradok and to all the gods, then," said Strongwind solemnly. "May our friends be stricken with true inspiration and no shortage of good luck."

"Aye, and amen," said Bruni, bowing her head and adding her own hopes to that prayer.

"Sire!" The ogre courier was panting, his face slicked with sweat. He burst into the throne room without so much as a bow or word of permission from the guards at the door. Staggering forward wearily, he threw himself on the floor at Grimwar Bane's feet.

"What is it? Speak, man!" demanded the ogre monarch.

He loomed over the fellow, stifling the urge to deliver a swift kick to get the man's tongue going. Stariz made a move to step forward, as if she would deliver the blow herself, but a glare from her husband bade her hold in place a dozen paces away. Her eyes were bright as she stared at the courier, and Grimwar was irked at the thought that she, with her powers, might already have intuited the ogre's news while he himself lacked even a clue.

With great effort the messenger pushed himself to his hands and knees and drew several deep, rasping breaths. Finally he lifted his head to meet the king's eyes.

"Your Majesty, the Axe of Gonnas is reclaimed!" he gasped.

"I knew it!" crowed the queen. "Behold the will of Gonnas! His talisman is returned to his rightful house! Where is it?" she demanded, stalking forward to stand over the messenger.

"Karyl Drago himself brings it here, Highness!" explained the panting ogre. "I came from there now, from the Moongarden Road. There he discovered two humans bringing the axe into the city. They are prisoners now, and he captured the axe for you." The fellow blinked suddenly and looked back at the king. "That is, for *you*, Your Majesty."

"Do not forget who your monarch is," growled Grimwar Bane. He was looking at the courier but speaking to his wife.

"Certainly, my king. It was Karyl Drago who found the humans and took them with the aid of a party of grenadiers. He would let none other than himself hold the axe, which he clutched to himself most carefully. He bade me race ahead with news while he follows with the axe itself."

"You mention two captives? I heard a report of a small army of intruders coming through the Icewall Gate. Is that all who were taken?"

"Aye, Majesty—just the two, for now. One was a High-lander warrior, the other a large woman, apparently Arktos. A third was spotted, and he attacked in an effort to free the two. I regret to report that he made his escape out of the Moongarden tunnel, losing himself in the warehouses above the harbor."

"That is regretful," agreed the king. "Did anyone get a look at this third rogue?"

"Indeed, Sire. One of the guards stabbed at him and ripped his robe away. From Drago's description—this is hard to believe, I know—it is possible that one of these intruders may be an elf!"

Grimwar Bane's world suddenly grew dark around him. He staggered over to the great throne, collapsing into the stone seat as though he had suddenly been drained of the strength to stand.

"Did you say . . . 'an elf'?" he croaked.

"Er, yes, sire. Drago noted that he had only one full ear, an unusual ear, long and pointed; the other was stunted or scarred. Also, his hair was an unnatural gold color and his eyes large and green."

"Just one ear?" Nightmares were swirling up from his subconscious, memories of a cursed threat that had been vanquished—certainly destroyed—in the disaster at Dracoheim. "Was there a woman with him, a small creature with dark hair?"

The messenger looked surprised. "Indeed, your Majesty. Drago reported that two of the attackers were women, and one matches the description you just gave me."

Suddenly the king had to sit down. He was beginning to feel sick to his stomach. He shook off the feeling and looked around him with grim determination.

"Summon the prisoner to me," he ordered, "the human woman. Also, have the guards bring up the slave king,

Strongwind Whalebone. I would speak to both of them and try to learn what is going on."

The conversations among the prisoners ceased abruptly as a key clanked in the door of the cell, and the metal barrier creaked open. Four heavily armed ogres came in, swords raised threateningly. A fifth, apparently an officer, entered and gestured to Bruni and Strongwind Whalebone.

"We are taking you to the throne room. The king and queen want to have some words with you." He chuckled wickedly as Strongwind Whalebone pulled at his manacles, struggling in vain against the ogres who hauled upon his chains, pulling him roughly to his feet and dragging him toward the door. "The queen'll probably want to thank you. Maybe she'll even give you a reward," he said mockingly.

"What do you mean?" the Highlander king demanded.

"Well, I think you did her quite a favor, when you killed the Lady Thraid Dimmarkull. Quite a slice that was, right through her throat. She must have bled for an hour!"

Bruni saw Strongwind's face go pale with shock, then she was turned and roughly pushed out the door, the troop of ogres coming right behind.

Dinekki had spent much time beside the small, dark pool, muttering over incantations, casting her knucklebones, and otherwise seeking some sign via the pathways of Chislev Wilder. Occasionally Mouse saw flashes of light bursting between the stalks of the giant mushrooms or heard rumbles of noise that sounded very much like thunder. The rocks shivered under his feet.

The Arktos warrior had for the most part kept his eyes on the cavern. The ogres were searching systematically out there. Thus far their patrols had been busy on the far side of the central stream, but he knew that it was just a matter of time before they would cross that waterway and make their way up to the Port Grotto.

Finally Dinekki came out of the cave with her wrinkled face darkened by a frown of deep concern.

"What is it?" asked Mouse.

"Trouble," the shaman said cryptically. "Can't tell exactly what's gone wrong, but the signs are clear: Moreen and Kerrick have run into some bad luck, and it's only likely to get worse."

"What can we do?" Mouse wondered, staring in frustration at the marching column of ogres amid the green, fertile cave.

The ubiquitous bats were circling, diving to the canopies of the great mushrooms, sometimes ducking even between the stalks before they again circled to the heights.

"Well, don't know for sure one way or t'other, but I guess I'd better go and see what I can find out." The shaman clucked her tongue crossly and glared at the vast cavern as if it had somehow offended her.

"You mean, sneak past all those guards?" blurted the Arktos warrior. "No, Dinekki! Even you can't do that."

"Not in this body, fool," snapped the old woman. "Do you think these old legs could outrun even a one-legged ogre?"

"Well, no."

"Then don't be talking about stupid ideas."

"Then . . . how?"

The old woman made no answer. Instead, she went down into her little niche again and came out with a white shawl wrapped around her frail shoulders. "You wait there," she told him.

Mouse sat behind the stalk of a giant mushroom as she muttered, chanted, and prayed in the midst of the war party. He couldn't see her but heard her call out, making strange animal noises again.

He noticed the bats growing agitated, several of them flying toward him, fluttering close over his head. More and more of the tiny creatures swirled around.

Abruptly the bats winged away in unison, flying low across the serene cavern, then flapping briskly, gaining altitude. Most rose quickly, though one lagged behind the others, clearly straining to keep up. He watched them fly away, vanishing in the direction of Winterheim. The silence was eerie and oppressive, and at last he decided to risk the old woman's wrath.

"Dinekki?" he called.

There was no reply. Quickly he leaped up to the edge of the cliff, fearing that the old woman had come to some harm.

The lip of the precipice was empty. Frantically he looked down, afraid that perhaps Dinekki had fallen, but there was no sign of the woman or of her white shawl on the mossy rocks below.

Only then did he understand, looking toward the place where the bats had flown. Dinekki was not here . . . not on the rocks . . . the answer was clear.

She had flown away with the bats.

———◆———

Stariz brought Garnet Dane to her private sanctum, the small, incense-sweet room behind the great temple sanctuary. She saw by his tight smile that he was pleased with himself, and she decided to allow him this small pleasure.

Indeed, he had done well.

"The Lady Thraid is dead," she remarked matter-of-factly. "You have performed the task that I required of you adequately."

"Thank you, gracious queen," said the man, pressing his face to the floor.

"Did you enlist your female accomplice in the act?"

She was curious about this human woman Garnet Dane had alluded to, wondering who this person was who could perform such bloodletting and yet remain concealed among the ranks of her slave kind. Sooner or later, the queen would have to learn her identity, for she could prove to be very useful.

"Indeed, my queen. She had better access to the lady, so it was she who wielded the knife. She serves you willingly and loyally."

"I shall need the use of her again soon. I will trust that she will serve as well as she did in the matter of the Lady Thraid," said the high priestess.

"Yes, Majesty." Garnet Dane's eyes were bright with the lust for another killing. "How may we serve you this time?"

"There is an elf loose in the city. He will undoubtedly try to link up with the rebellious elements among the slaves. I do not know where he is, though it seems he entered from the Moongarden."

"I will have all of my ears alert, looking for any word or sign of such an intruder," said the human, groveling. "I will report at once, should anything come to my—"

"Fool!" she snapped, relishing the involuntary flinch in the man's craven frame. "I do not seek information. As soon as you or she finds him, make sure that he dies!"

20

That Kender Again

H ere—you can hide for a time, while I try to find out where the ogres are taking your friends," Tookie said, pushing open a door and leading Moreen and Kerrick into a small, dark room. Moreen was out of breath, her heart was pounding, and her palms were slick with sweat.

"What is this place?" asked the elf, sniffing cautiously.

"Well, it used to be a brewery for warqat," the slave girl replied. "Now I think they just store the barley and stuff in here. Nobody comes around this way any more, so you two should be safe here for enough time for me to go and look for Tildy Trew. She's the one who will probably know where your friends are being taken. She knows a lot for a slave. Wait for me right here, okay? I'll see if I can get her or someone else to help."

Moreen knelt and took the child by the shoulders, looking into her tear-stained face. "You have been very brave, and you've helped us a lot. That big ogre came after us because we fought him two days before we met you. You have to help us a little longer, but I'm sorry, for getting you into danger."

"Danger?" the girl snorted. "This is the most fun I've had in my whole life! Don't worry. We'll find where your friends are . . . and . . . and do something!"

"You are a great friend," Kerrick said, touching her gently on the shoulder, "and Moreen is right, you are very, very brave. We owe you a lot already, and we thank you."

A moment later Tookie had slipped out through the storeroom door, leaving the elf and the chiefwoman in the large, shadowy chamber.

"I'm frightened," Moreen found herself saying, surprised at her own admission. "I can't stand waiting here! We have to try and do something!" She paced a short distance, turned back in agitation, then glared around at their surroundings.

"I'm frightened too," replied Kerrick. "Seems like a pretty natural reaction to our situation, wouldn't you say? Let's have a look around and take our mind off our troubles."

To Moreen the chamber looked almost midnight dark, though Kerrick assured her that his elf eyes could make out some details. He removed one of the torches from their equipment basket and ignited it, sending flickering yellow illumination throughout the cavernous room.

They found several stacks of massive kegs and judged them to be empty by the hollow sounds when they tapped the sides. Much of the floor was covered in a layer of tangled straw, and several alcoves with raised floors branched into different directions from the three interior walls.

"You take the torch," Kerrick said. "Check out those rooms over there. I'll have a look on the other side."

The chiefwoman was reluctant to separate from her old friend, but she agreed and investigated the first two alcoves. These seemed like additional storage rooms, smelling dank, musty, and vaguely sweet. A few crates and barrels were stacked about, and there was a heavy layer of dust over everything. She found no sign of a doorway or any connecting passage in either place.

Carrying her torch back into the main room, she was startled to hear soft voices coming from behind one of the stacks. She crept forward, trembling, hoping that it was only Tookie coming back. Her hand tightened around the hilt of her sword, ready to attack if this was a threat.

She recognized the elf's voice, but he didn't sound frightened or agitated. Leaning closer, she tried to hear what he was saying.

". . . hiding in here, for now, but we've got to do something. We're both going to go crazy if we just have to sit around and wait!" the elf declared.

"Well, then find something useful to do," replied the second voice, with a sense of mild exasperation.

The tone was childlike, but it wasn't Tookie. Instead, it was male, and though high-pitched it sounded vaguely mature.

"I'm open to suggestions," Kerrick declared sharply.

Moreen came around the stack, holding up the torch. Kerrick chuckled shyly as he saw her and shook his head apologetically. "Oh, sorry. I didn't find anything. Then, I guess the dark just kind of got to me—I was having a quiet conversation with my imaginary friend."

"Coraltop Netfisher?" the chiefwoman said in awe, looking wide-eyed into the shadows past the elf.

"I didn't mean to upset you," the elf replied. "I know it makes me seem kind of crazy . . . what is it?" he asked, seeing her expression of amazement.

"If he's imaginary," she replied quietly, "why can I see him?"

Captain Verra paced restlessly on the edge of the market, looking at the tangle of docks. Crates and barrels were stacked up, great lengths of rope coiled, and all manner of nets and oars piled haphazardly here and there. In time of peace they were useful for all manner of nautical tasks, but he had no care for that.

Right now, each of them looked like a potential hiding place for an elf intruder, or any number of rebellious slaves.

Farther along the wharf long racks of fish hung to dry over beds of charcoal that had yet to be ignited. The sawmill hummed in the lumberyard as slave labor turned the heavy gears, whirling the blade through one after another log of fresh pine, splitting the timbers into boards. Stacks of wood were growing in the vast storage yards, but all he could thnk of was the slaves moving to and fro. He wondered what they were planning, feeling.

He had received the king's orders via a message tube that had been tossed down the city's atrium to land, with a loud splash, in the waters of the harbor. One of Verra's men had fished it out with a long pole, and the captain had quickly read the directive, and acted on it.

"Elf loose in the city . . . potential uprising of slaves . . . human war party penetrated the Icewall Gate and Moongarden . . ."

How could this be happening?

Verra was grateful that he had warned the king of a possible human insurrection only a few days earlier, yet now that he was confronted with the reality he felt woefully unprepared. He had three hundred ogres under his direct command here in the main square, with hundreds more scattered in detachments around the harbor level, but there were so many humans!

In agitation, he reviewed what he had done so far. First, he had secured the Seagate slaves in their vast warren. The humans in there numbered nearly a thousand in total, and they were now locked behind double doors of heavy steel, with hinges anchored several feet deep into the bedrock of the mountain. A dozen ogres stood guard at the second, outer door, while an equal number had commanding positions over the corridor, which the humans would have to traverse if somehow they managed to break out. Verra was satisfied that the Seagate slaves were safely locked away.

The slaves in the lumber yard numbered nearly an equal amount, but he had been unable to curtail them as effectively. For one thing, that vast work site was busy with cutting the timber that had been hauled across the tundra by the summer work parties. Much of that wood was needed for the Ceremony of Autumnblight, only two days away, and Verra had been reluctant to halt the work based on mere suspicions, so more and more boards made fresh piles, slaves carrying the planks from the saw to the storage racks.

Since he could not close the yard, he had posted an extra company of grenadiers—fifty veteran ogres—to reinforce the three score overseers who usually maintained order in the area. The odds were not unfavorable, but he had instructed his troops to be quick with the whip and vigilant.

The other work sites on the harbor level—the fish house and tanning factory, notably—only housed a few hundred slaves apiece. Verra had increased the guards at each of these and had given instructions for extra caution and discipline. He had ordered his troops to report anything the least bit out of the ordinary and had impressed upon them the seriousness of the situation. Now he could only wait.

He shuddered nervously, unable to shake the fear that he was forgetting something that might prove to be very important.

"You're Moreen Bayguard," declared Coraltop Net-fisher. The diminutive fellow advanced with a wide smile and an outstretched hand. "It is a real pleasure to meet you. I mean I've been hearing about you for, oh, I don't know how many years. It's great to meet you!" He took her hand and pumped it, his small fingers wiry and strong in her own grip. "You came here to help Kerrick, of course. I'm glad. I try to give him a hand now and then, but Zivilyn Greentree knows I can't do everything!"

"Um . . . likewise, it is a pleasure to meet you. I have heard very much about you over the years, too," replied the chiefwoman.

She was stunned to see this little person, talking to Kerrick. He could not have entered through the door of the warehouse without attracting her attention. She was just as certain that he was really, truly, standing here in front of her.

"Where did you come from? How did you get in here, and find us?"

"Oh, I keep pretty close tabs on Kerrick here," said the kender. He looked just as the elf had so often described him, wearing a plain green tunic and soft deerskin boots. His hair was tied in a long topknot that gathered at the crown of his head then flowed like a mane down his back. He leaned close and winked at Moreen. "I don't know if you noticed, but he has a way of getting himself into trouble. I've tried to help him out, whenever I can. I guess you do that too. He doesn't know how lucky he is to have us! Why, there was a time he was sailing along, barely paying attention, and he just about smacked into a dragon turtle! If I hadn't come along just then—"

"You were stranded on the dragon turtle!" Kerrick declared indignantly. "I rescued you, remember?"

"Not much of a mind for details, you know," Coraltop said with another wink. "Still, he's kind of likeable, just the same, though as I was saying, trouble seems to follow him around."

Moreen shook her head grimly. "I think I'm the one who usually gets him into trouble. Take now, for example. Our two companions have been captured, the ogres have got the Axe of Gonnas back, and we're hiding out here, depending on a little girl to help us."

"Tookie? She's really something, that one," said the kender enthusiastically. "You're lucky you met her." He looked at Kerrick and nodded sternly. "See what I mean—you keep coming across these good friends, and they all do their best to get you out of trouble."

"You're right about that," Kerrick said, with an audible sigh.

"Well, I really am delighted to meet you," Moreen said, smiling in spite of her anxious mood, "and you're right about Kerrick making friends wherever he goes."

"Kind of unusual for an elf that way," the kender said, leaning close and whispering very loudly. "Most of them are anti-social, but not our Kerrick Fallabrine!"

Kerrick glared at the kender, clearly vexed. "Is there anything else you want to say?" he demanded.

"Well, I wonder why the ogre queen wants to see your friend Bruni," Coraltop said with an elaborate shrug. "She seemed pretty interested in talking to her. The king too, I guess. They're quite a pair, you know."

"Who?" demanded the elf, mystified by that segue.

"Why, the king and queen of the ogres. Both kind of fierce, but personally I think that she's the really scary one. Anyway, the guards will be taking her upstairs any time now."

"What do you mean? Bruni is going upstairs? To the high part of the city?" Kerrick asked.

"Well, yes, of course." Coraltop looked at the elven sailor as he might scrutinize a slow-learning child. "Would you expect to go upstairs to the lower part of the city? Anyway, do you want me to show you the way?"

Kerrick snorted in exasperation, leaving Moreen to answer. "Yes, please take us there—right away!"

"I thought you'd never ask," said Coraltop Netfisher, turning toward the door, then addressing the elf. "You'd better pull your hood up, though. I don't think they see too many elf ears in Winterheim."

Strongwind shuffled along, the chains restricting his steps. He was determined not to fall, so he kept up with the guards and with Bruni, who trundled along right behind him.

"I still can't believe you all came here for me," he declared, shaking his head in misery. "There has to be a better purpose to all this! So many will get killed because of me. I can't bear it!"

"Well, we were going to try to rescue as many slaves as we could," she replied softly. Apparently the ogres didn't object to their conversation. At least, none of the guards said anything to intervene.

"There were some who were ready to rebel," the Highlander continued in despair. "They've all been captured now—they're doomed, too! Doomed, probably because they had the misfortune to encounter me! Why couldn't you all have just stayed away!"

How many of his friends and allies, his comrades and subjects, would die because of this mad quest? He meant it sincerely: He wished he could have perished on Dracoheim and spared them all this insane undertaking.

Now they would die, and he had only himself to blame.

Dinekki's shoulders were sore, and she found herself wishing she had thought to rub some of her walrus-blubber ointment on her joints before she had taken off. She loved to fly, yet as with so many other things, getting old complicated the whole procedure.

How many years had it been since she had worked the shape-change spell, taking on the form of a creature with wings? More than she could remember in truth. Still, the enchantment had come easily, the familiar blessing of her wild goddess warming her with the power. Normally she would have shape-shifted into the body of a bird, but the bat seemed to be more appropriate in this vast cavern. She found that the technique of flying remained pretty much as she remembered, though instead of the easy glide of a feathered form she had to flap her wings constantly to remain in the air.

Still, the fur lining her limbs looked sleek and soft and felt wonderful, and the skills needed to fly came back to her the instant that she had thrown herself from the ledge in the body of the tiny bat. At first exhilaration had filled her heart as she soared upward, chasing the flight of her fellows, winging past the fungus forests and those glowing, lichen-encrusted walls, fluttering over cold, clear streams.

She still had a long way to go when she first felt the cramps starting in her shoulders then extending through her back and her wings. The other bats had flown on or scattered, moving too quickly for her to keep up, but that didn't matter. She didn't need their company. She just needed to find the strength to make it farther into the vast, underground city.

Fatigue had started to drag her down, but now at least she was in the wide tunnel. She had gained some altitude in the early part of her flight, and now she swooped down near the floor, trying to ease the strain on her muscles.

Lower and lower she dropped until she was nearly skimming the stone surface. She had to work constantly, however, for she had no more room to descend.

Finally the vast gateway loomed high overhead. The elderly shaman used her last strength to fly up through the high arch. She saw a ship docked in the middle of the harbor, a tall mast rising from the deck. With a few more wingstrokes she lifted herself up, slowed, and came to rest upon the crosspiece high on the mast.

Here she panted, trying to catch her breath, and started to look around to see what was happening and where she should go from here.

———◆◆◆———

"We can't stay here and wait any longer!" Mouse declared.

He studied the ogre patrols that were sweeping back and forth through the Moongarden. At least four of them were making circuits around the huge cavern. Each detachment numbered a couple of dozen enemy warriors, but the Arktos warrior reasoned that if the humans attacked fast they might be able to overcome at least one or two detachments. If all hundred or so ogres banded together, he knew his little force would have a very tough time of it.

"We have to do something," he stated to Lars and Feathertail, who stood on either side of him. "It's only a matter of time."

"Better to be on the move and attack them on our own terms," agreed the Highlander thane.

"What should we do?" Feathertail wondered.

"I think we should hit 'em hard and just keep moving," counseled Thane Larsgall. "Make for the city and see what kind of damage we do before . . ." His voice trailed off.

Feathertail looked at him then turned her large, dark eyes to Mouse. "Before we die, he means, doesn't he?"

"Yes, but we have to try something, don't you see? It's better than waiting here like rats in a trap, waiting for them to find us and rub us out!" He looked into those gentle eyes, and his heart nearly broke.

To his surprise, this Arktos maiden whom he had teased as a girl, and watched grow into the most beautiful woman in the tribe, nodded in agreement and understanding.

"Yes," she said. "We have to try at least."

Mouse reached out and took her hand. He wanted to tell her so many things, but he found that he could not speak.

"Let's hurry then," suggested Thane Larsgall.

A few minutes later they had gathered the war party. Every man and woman clutched a weapon, swords and spears in the front, those armed with bows consigned to the rear. Grateful for the protection of the waterfall's noise, Mouse nevertheless spoke softly as he outlined the plan.

"Our plan is to head directly to Winterheim," he said. "Right now, most of the ogre patrols are down in the far end of the Moongarden, where the passage to the Icewall Gate leads out. We're not going to worry about them. There's one group, twenty or thirty of the brutes, that's up in the near end of the cavern. They're down there in a fungus forest now, looking around. They'll see us and get in our way. We're going to attack, kill or cripple every one of the bastards and keep moving. Does everyone understand?"

There were no questions. He was glad that no one asked what they'd do after they got to the city, because he was afraid he would blurt out his honest opinion: Truthfully, he never expected them to get that far.

21

Return of the Messenger

Grimwar Bane paced restlessly in his throne room. Stariz, fearing his explosive mood, had departed to dispatch her spies. He hoped they would prove useful. For now, he was glad to have her out of his sight.

He was startled when the doors opened and a file of grenadiers marched in. They brought the slave king, the man's hands shackled before him, a ring of iron around his collar. Two burly ogres held chains connected to the collar. Behind the first prisoner came a tall human woman with a round moon of a face and a long mane of black hair. Immediately he recognized her.

"You are the one who wielded the Axe of Gonnas at Brackenrock, are you not?" he asked in surprise. "You stopped my army when we were on the verge of victory."

"I only regret that I couldn't have buried that blade in your black heart!" she snapped at him.

One of the guards raised a fist to cuff her, but the king lifted his own hand and stayed the blow.

"You are a unique creature," he said, "one of the greatest fighters I have ever seen, and a woman to boot. I have never seen an ogress fight like you."

"I will take that as a compliment," she said, looking at him with her eyes burning. She drew a breath and shook her head with great deliberation. "You are not quite the uncouth ogre I expected."

"Nor are you the intruder I anticipated," the monarch replied.

Indeed, he found that his mood of a few minutes earlier—a mingling of rage, grief, and distrust—had mellowed swiftly. He was exceedingly curious about this woman. Now that she was captured, he didn't fear her, nor did he hate her. Instead, she fascinated him. There was much more to her than simply her outward appearance, no matter how impressive he found that. Indeed, she was similar to Thraid in shape and features.

As if cued by his untoward thoughts, Stariz chose that moment to stride through the throne room doors and remind him of her existence. "Has Karyl Drago returned with the Axe of Gonnas?" she demanded.

"Not yet," said the king, irked by her manner.

He wanted more time with the prisoner, to talk with her, to gaze at her. He wondered, vaguely, what she thought about him, whether she found him handsome. Unconsciously, he sucked in his gut as he turned to glare at his wife.

"This is the blaspheming wench who dared to wield the sacred talisman of the Willful One?" the queen asked. Turning to her husband she bowed her head in a gesture of respect. He watched her warily.

"When the axe is brought here, you must allow me to use it to separate her head from her shoulders," she continued. "Only thus can the honor of our god be redeemed." The queen gestured to a square block of stone on the throne room floor. "That will be her fate!" she pronounced.

"No!" Grimwar Bane roared, his voice a blast of sound that brought all activity in the great hall to a stop.

"My king—" Stariz began.

"Silence!" shouted the monarch, with enough force even to mute his wife. "There has been enough bloodletting for the moment! We must wait and talk to this prisoner. When we decide what to do, it will be a thoughtful choice, not an orgy of revenge! She came into the city through the Icewall Gate—she knows about a whole war party, an invasion that has the potential to incite all our slaves to revolt. If you have any role in this investigation, my queen, it will be to learn what this prisoner knows, that we may use that knowledge for the defense of our kingdom! Do I make myself clear?"

"Aye, Majesty, perfectly," said the queen demurely. Again she bowed, but Grimwar could see her look sideways at the human woman. Stariz's eyes narrowed to slits of burning hatred.

As for himself, he was startled by the depths of his own feeling. When Stariz had suggested slaying this woman, this enemy prisoner, Grimwar's reaction had been one of stark, heart-stopping fear. He meant what he said. How much killing must there be before the queen would be satisfied? In the privacy of his mind, he knew that there was not enough blood in the world to fully slake her thirst for violence and vengeance.

"You came here with the Elven Messenger, did you not?" spat the queen, turning again to confront the female prisoner.

The big woman's eyes widened slightly, and though the prisoner shook her head contemptuously, the king knew that his wife had struck at the truth.

"How is it that he was not killed on Dracoheim?" asked Grimwar Bane, genuinely curious.

The woman looked at him and drew a slow breath. He thought that she would remain silent and saw his wife tense with anger. The king was surprised when the prisoner answered him with quiet force.

"He escaped because he is a favorite of the gods—not just his own god of the Green Tree but Chislev Wilder as well. I believe that the gods have sent him to watch over the Lady . . . and he's doing a damned good job of it."

Mouse came around the corner of the winding path at a dead run, leading the file of warriors through the mushroom forest. They all trotted silently, weapons ready.

The captain of the ogre patrol was right in front of the Arktos warrior, just where Mouse had expected him to be. Mouse stabbed with his spear, piercing the ogre's throat and dropping the surprised brute to his knees. With a gurgled cry of alarm, the ogre toppled forward, the weight of his body driving the spearhead right through the back of his neck.

The next ogre in line gaped in shock, and the Arktos warrior slashed him across the face as he drew his sword. Mouse hacked with all of his strength. Thane Larsgall sprinted past the second ogre, crushing the skull of another brute with a mighty downward blow of his steel-headed hammer. The humans attack came in eerie silence, and they flew past the enemy formation, stabbing and chopping with ruthless efficiency.

In seconds the dozen or so ogres of the patrol had been slaughtered to the last one. Mouse was surprised to see Feathertail, who was running with the second wave of attackers, pause to drive her light spear through the throat of a writhing, wounded ogre. The brute kicked reflexively, grasping at the pronged weapon with two flailing fists for several seconds before he grew rigid and died.

The young woman jogged up to him. "I saw you stab that other one in the neck. That was smart."

"Can't you stay in the back?" Mouse pleaded, but

Feathertail ignored him, pushing past to continue her part in the attack.

The war party raced through the fungus forest of the Moongarden. The other ogre patrols had already passed them, and the humans—as well as the gasping, panting Slyce, who was forced to keep up—headed pell-mell toward the far end of the great cavern and Winterheim.

The trail ascended through groves of giant mushrooms and carried them across wide, mossy meadows beside a roiling, whitewater stream. They came upon a few ogres in one of these clearings, and the surprised brutes howled and chucked spears at the humans. The big missiles fell short, but the twenty or thirty arrows launched by the human archers found their marks. These ogres, too, fell dead, looking like a misshapen, bloody pincushions.

Breathing a little harder now, the war party approached the wide ramp leading up and out of the vast food warren. They saw slaves milling around in a great pen at the base of the ramp, with several ogres gesturing in agitation from platforms overlooking the route. One raised a brass horn, but before the instrument touched his lips he was pierced by a dozen arrows. The bugle fell from his nerveless fingers, and the ogre sagged forward, balancing for a moment on the railing before toppling over to plop heavily onto the ground twenty feet below.

Mouse looked up at the ramparts and windows. He judged this to be a large garrison house, but only a few ogres materialized, buckling on armor, hastening down to form a thin line across the ramp.

"Others are behind us," Larsgall said, pointing to the ogres forming a line of defense. "They're all spread out for now."

"Let's not give them time to regroup," the Arktos warrior said.

"Wait!" It was Feathertail. She pointed at the great fenced corrals, with hundreds of slaves pressed to the palisade, looking through the gaps between the stakes. Only three ogres were visible there, nervously standing guard at the closed gate. "Free the slaves!" urged the woman.

That idea was inspired. Mouse looked at the defense, no more than a dozen and a half ogres standing across the ramp leading to the city. If they could swell their ranks with a thousand rebellious slaves free in the Moongarden, the ogre king's problems would multiply considerably.

"All right," he said, pointing to the three guards at the gate of the slave pen. "Let's chase those ugly buggers off and let these people go."

———◆———

Kerrick led Moreen out of the storage room, both of them concealed in the Moongarden slave robes. The elf turned to hold the door for Coraltop Netfisher but was not surprised—not very surprised, in any event—when there was no sign of the kender coming after them.

"Where did he go?" Moreen asked, her eyes wide.

"Your guess is as good as mine," the elf replied with a thin smile. "I expect he'll be around somewhere. He has a way of showing up when he's needed."

"For all those years I thought you were losing your mind," the chiefwoman said.

"Just because my imaginary friend is real doesn't necessarily prove me sane," Kerrick said with a wink.

They hadn't taken more than a couple of steps when they spotted Tookie approaching with a sturdy, apple-cheeked, human woman in tow. The adult regarded the two intruders with intense interest.

"You were supposed to wait for me," said the slave girl, with a worried glance around.

"I know," Moreen replied, "but we looked around some and learned where Bruni and Strongwind are—now we're going to see if we can find them."

"Strongwind Whalebone, King of Guilderglow?" said the woman with Tookie. "Do you know him?"

"Yes—we came here to rescue him," Moreen said pointedly, assuming that anyone Tookie brought to them must be trustworthy. "I take it that you have met him as well?"

"Yes. I'm Tildy Trew. I run the Posting House where all the new slaves are brought to be cleaned up. Before they get sent to their posts, that is." She looked at Kerrick, so appraisingly that the elf felt as though he was one of the new slaves subjected to inspection by a prospective owner. Finally she nodded with the hint of a smile.

"Hey, you're a handsome one," she said warmly. "A little skinny—and with those big eyes! Not like any man I've seen before."

Somehow he found himself trusting her. He tilted back his hood just enough to show his sole, distinctively pointed ear. "Have you ever seen an elf before?" he asked.

She shook her head, the smile growing broad. "Pleased to make your acquaintance."

Moreen spoke up. "How was Strongwind when he got here? Was he hurt?"

Tildy shrugged. Kerrick wondered if there was an edge to her voice when she replied, speaking directly to Moreen, "He was bruised and hungry. Gave himself up to capture in order to help a woman, he said . . . he thought she died on Dracoheim, and he was pretty broken up about it."

Moreen's face went pale. "She . . . she didn't die," she said dully.

"It was you, wasn't it?" The slave woman nodded appraisingly. "Mistress of Brackenrock and all that. Why did you come here?"

"Because I couldn't let Strongwind stay here, any more than he could let me go into Castle Dracoheim without his protection."

"Well, you sure caused a ruckus. There are patrols all over the place, and I hear that the queen is fit to be roasted. She'll just as soon skin a human as look at him when she gets into these kind of moods."

"Do you know where Strongwind is now?" Moreen demanded, her face growing pale.

"Yes, I think I do." Tildy Trew nodded decisively. "He was locked in the same cell with your friends—the dungeon, down on the harbor level."

"Can you take us there?" asked Moreen urgently.

Tildy Trew nodded again and gestured for them to follow. The slave woman led them along the ramping passageway until they once again came out on one of the broad floors in the center of Winterheim. There were a hundred ogres walking about within a stone's throw of their position, but Kerrick noticed that many humans were dressed in the same type of robe in which he and Moreen were disguised. He kept his head low and followed Tildy and Tookie to the edge of the vast central atrium.

In a few minutes they were crossing a wide street. The slave woman pointed downward as Kerrick and Moreen looked in amazement.

From here he could see down into the central harbor and up through the rings of ascending levels. Several of the connecting ramps were visible, and Tildy pointed to one of those. They saw a file of red-coated guards marching along. The company turned in unison to start climbing a wide stairway that led toward a landing with a single, closed metal gate.

"That's a company of grenadiers, the king's own regiment. Like I said, your arrival has been noticed and created a bit of a stir."

Even as they watched, more guards emerged from through a gate that opened atop the wide stairway. Kerrick caught a glimpse of Bruni's black hair amidst the golden helmets of the ogre guards. Moments later the gate slammed shut, with four burly guards facing down the stairs.

"Seems like she's being taken up to the palace," Tildy said, with a worried shake of her head. "Not much chance of us getting up there. They're sure to search every slave going anywhere near the Royal Level."

"What about Strongwind?" asked the chiefwoman.

"He might still be down there. Worth a look, anyway."

"Then let's get into the dungeon, if we can," Moreen said.

"All right," Tildy said with another sharp look at the chiefwoman. "I know where we can get some help. We might be able to get him out, and I guess he'll be very glad to see you."

———◆———

Captain Verra ordered his grenadiers to form close ranks. At least his troops moved with alacrity. He had been ordered to send the two prisoners up to the royal level, and the captain had decided to send three dozen ogres as an escort. That left him dangerously thin down here.

He glanced about at the lumberyard, concerned to see all those slaves moving around and the relative paucity of guards. He tried to think: Where could he get some reinforcements? In agitation, his eyes roamed around the harbor and market levels . . . past the Seagate garrison, the various factories, the royal dungeon. . . .

There! He knew that some thirty or forty ogres remained in reserve on the dungeon detail. Most likely they were eating and gambling in the barracks room, deep within the bedrock of the mountainside.

The duty staff of at least a dozen turnkeys was more than enough to beat back any attempt by the prisoners to escape. Those other ogres were simply being wasted now when their value was acute.

Verra gave the orders, dispatching an eager sergeant to carry them out. He watched in satisfaction as the extra guards trooped out of the dungeon, some of them casting surly glances in his direction but all of them obeying his orders. They carried their weapons and their armor over to the lumberyard, and went to join the overseers on duty there.

Verra was still nervous. He couldn't stand still, so he lumbered down the steps to the docks. He would go over to the Seagate slave warren and make sure that everything was secure there.

Tildy Trew rejoined Kerrick and Moreen on the plaza near the waterfront, where she had left them to wait for her a few minutes earlier. She was joined by six strapping men, each carrying a stout wooden pry bar—tools Kerrick saw that could quickly be converted to weapons.

"These are some friends of mine taking a little time off from work in the lumber yard. That's the entry to the dungeons," Tildy said, nodding at a dark cavern mouth leading away from the waterfront. "We caught a break. They just sent all the extra guards over to the lumber yard, to keep an eye on the slaves there. The bad news is that Strongwind Whalebone, as well as your friend, Bruni, have been taken out of the dungeon. Seems they're on their way up to see the king. Your other companion,

One-Tooth, is still in there, together with Black Mike and a few other rebels who didn't have the sense to keep out of the queen's clutches."

The slave woman shook her head wonderingly and continued. "They're accusing Strongwind of killing his mistress, a noble ogress."

"Why would he do that?" Moreen asked.

Tildy shook her head. "He wouldn't, I think. His mistress was hated by Queen Stariz, and I suspect that she simply found a way to eliminate her rival and blame it on someone else."

"What about Tookie?" Kerrick asked.

"She wanted to come along, but I insisted that she stay safely behind in the shipyard," Tildy said. "Things might get a little rough." She looked at the faint outlines of the swords that the chiefwoman and elf wore under their robes. "Sure hope you know how to use those things."

They were sauntering casually across the plaza as they talked. Kerrick's hand tightened around the hilt of his sword, which was now concealed under his robe. He saw Moreen doing the same thing.

As they drew near to the two guards outside the dungeon entrance the pair of ogres stood straight and leaned with their halberds to form a giant X across the passage. "Go away," one of them growled, "or come with an officer."

"I have a pass," Kerrick said, stepping forward. His sword was in his hand in that instant, and he stabbed, feeling cold and vicious as he pierced the heart of one of the guards. The other gaped, then toppled as two of Tildy's slaves bashed him with their poles. Moreen's blade put an end to him before he could utter a warning.

"No time to waste, now! Go!" cried Tildy, standing back as the elf led the rescuers into the tunnel.

They ran down a long, dark passageway and burst into a room, surprising a half dozen ogres at a table where they were gambling and drinking. The elf dropped two with rapid thrusts, vaguely aware that his companions were slaying the others.

Tildy snatched a ring of keys from a hook on the wall and quickly turned one in a heavy iron lock.

"Hey!" growled a startled ogre as the door flew open. "What's the meaning of this?"

He got his answer in the form of cold elven steel. Twenty seconds later, the humans and elf were pulling open a large door, another barrier Tildy had unlocked. Kerrick and Moreen charged into the room and saw two dozen or more men looking up at them in mixtures of hope and alarm.

"Barq!" cried Moreen, racing across the dingy cell. Tildy came after, still carrying the ring of keys.

The pole-wielding slaves had spread out through the other passages of the dungeon, and Kerrick heard sounds of violence from several directions.

"Hurry!" he cried, as the woman freed one after another of the prisoners from thir manacles. They stood unsteadily, rubbing chafed wrists, then stumbling out the door of the cell to look for weapons. "Where do we go from here?" the elf called to Tildy Trew.

"Let's head for the Seagate," she said. "I think we've got a rebellion on our hands, and the capstan slaves will be more than happy to help us out."

The escapees burst from the dungeon a few minutes later, abruptly encountering a party of half dozen ogres who had gathered in consternation around the bodies of the first two guards. They were trampled by twenty or thirty infuriated slaves, as horns of alarm sounded higher up in the atrium of Winterheim.

Tildy was right, Kerrick decided. Like it or not, the slave rebellion was under way.

Stariz left the throne room, wringing her hands in agitation. The elf! Gonnas curse him—where was he? That was just one of many questions for which she lacked the answer. She could only hope that Garnet's accomplice, the treacherous slave woman, would find a chance to stick a knife in his back before he caused any irreversible disasters.

Something powerful and appealing grabbed her attention. The Axe of Gonnas was near! She felt it, looked up, and saw the immense ogre, Karyl Drago, striding out of the ramp from the lower city. He bore the prized talisman in his great hands, and his face was rapt as he stared at that gleaming, immaculate blade.

The queen stood, her hands on her hips, watching him approach. She remembered the great oaf, an uncouth fool from her own homeland, but she felt pride that it was he who had recovered this talisman for her.

As the immense ogre strode closer, however, it became apparent that he intended to step around her, to proceed into the palace on his own.

"Give that to me!" she demanded.

"I give this to the king," the big warrior declared, shaking his head stubbornly.

"It is mine!" she declared, stepping in and reaching for the weapon.

To her surprise and consternation the ogre yanked the axe away and glared at her as though he might dare to strike her. Rage swept through Stariz, a wave of heat that left her trembling, and she raised both hands, fingers outstretched as if to envelop the massive Drago.

"*Gonnas paralaxsis!*" she cried, bringing forth the magic of her god in a wave of pulsing power.

Karyl Drago halted in surprise as she reached forward to touch his burly forearm. The spell was cast in that touch, and the brute slumped to the ground as if he had been felled by a blow to the head.

The high priestess smoothly grasped the Axe of Gonnas as the big ogre fell, making sure that the device did not come into contact with the floor. Satisfied, she spun about to return to the throne room, leaving Karyl Drago unconscious, breathing very slowly, on the floor.

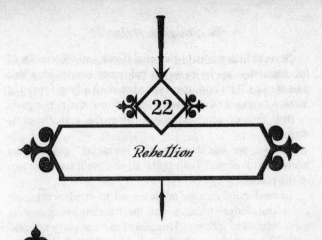

The Moongarden slaves spilled out of their cages as soon as Mouse and his warriors opened the latches. Some of the humans stopped to kick and spit at the corpses of the ogre guards, bristling with arrows, that lay just outside the portals. Others charged into tool sheds and work stations, emerging with all manner of picks, hammers, pipes, and other tools.

"Up to the barracks!" shouted one burly Arktos, gesturing to Mouse. "They have an armory up there—lots of weapons—and most of the ogres have gone into the Moongarden on those patrols."

"At least one of those patrols won't be coming back this way," the warrior said grimly. He clapped the man on the shoulder. "Lead on!"

The war party, now augmented by hundreds of slaves, rushed up the ramp that led into the wide, torchlit tunnel to Winterheim. Mouse saw Slyce, short legs pumping, running to keep up, and Feathertail, up among the vanguard. He put on a burst of speed to stay ahead and keep an eye on her.

Several heavy spears clattered down into the midst of the humans, cast by ogres on balconies overlooking this passageway. The humans responded with a fierce spray of arrows, driving the guards back from their ramparts twenty feet or more overhead, atop the smooth stone walls.

"Those are the doors to the barracks!" pointed the burly Arktos slave. "Bash them in, and we'll have the run of the place!"

Immediately, dozens of slaves set to work with their picks and sledgehammers, and the wooden barriers were soon reduced to splinters. Humans of the war party mingled with liberated slaves as they charged through the ante-rooms and tore into the few ogres guarding the area. Mouse was shocked at the frenzy of the slaves, some of whom used their fingernails and teeth as they surrounded the terrified ogres, dragged them down, and killed them. Even then, the vengeance didn't cease as the gory corpses were spat upon, stomped, and otherwise abused.

More slaves were breaking open equipment rooms, and in moments big spears and heavy axes were being passed among the rampaging rebels. There were huge shields, too, but these they left behind as they were too heavy for human use. Still more men had discovered a great keg of warqat, and they rolled it into the center of the room. One big Highlander smashed the cork off, and the freed slaves took turns lying down, placing their heads under the stream of biting liquid, letting it pour into their mouths.

Mouse was not surprised to see Slyce squirm through this pile. When the much larger humans pushed him away, the gully dwarf settled for licking the floor where the considerable overflow had started to spread in a wide pool. Acutely conscious of time slipping away, the Arktos warrior looked around, wondering how to mobilize this large, bloodthirsty, but temporarily distracted mob for the charge on Winterheim. It seemed clear that, given their choice, these people would stay here, get drunk, and become easy fodder for the ogre patrols that would inevitably arrive here.

It was Thane Larsgall who came up with motivating inspiration. Striding up to the keg, he brought down his huge hammer with a timber-splitting blow, crushing the barrel and sending a cascade of liquor across the floor. Many of the slaves rose to their feet in fury, but the thane stood there ominously, staring them down, his own expression equally furious.

"Do you think we freed you so that you could have a party at the first chance?" he roared, his tone contemptuous. "There's plenty of this stuff in the city—and plenty of ogres too! If you want your vengeance, follow us to victory. I promise you feasting and drinking for the ages, when this is over!"

Mouse was relieved when the slaves, after a moment's hesitation, began to cheer lustily. A thousand strong they were now as they poured out of the ogre barracks and rushed into the Moongarden corridor toward the ogre city and a destiny for the ages.

* * *

"Here, these come from the weapons room near the dungeon," Tildy Trew shouted.

She and several slaves were bringing out bundles of halberds and heavy swords, dropping the weapons unceremoniously on the floor of the harborside plaza, where they were quickly snatched up by some of the hundreds of slaves Kerrick, Moreen, and Barq had liberated. These still streamed out of the huge pen, through the double doors that Kerrick and the rebels had carried in their sudden attack.

Once again ogre overconfidence had worked to the rebels' advantage. The masters had guarded a cavern of five hundred slaves with a mere two dozen ogres. Apparently the city's rulers had been overly concerned with keeping the prisoners in the pen and not particularly worried about a rescue attempt stirring from the outside. The overseers had been overcome in three minutes of furious battle, and when the bar from the inner door was at last lifted, hundreds of slaves had spilled forth. These included strong, muscular men who had been brutalized by ogres, sometimes for many years. Every one of them was spoiling for a fight.

"This is Black Mike," Tildy shouted to Kerrick and Moreen as the elf led the group in passing out weapons. "He was one of the leaders of the rebellion and he has some ideas what to do."

Kerrick looked at the swarthy human, a sturdy and bowlegged man of Arktos ancestry and evident fierce demeanor. "What do you suggest?"

"We've got to try and rush the city heights right away," cried the man. "They have some massive stone gates in place. Once those are closed, we'll never get up the ramps, and the ogres can hold out for the whole winter up there."

"What about more slaves? Are there more places we can free lots of men who'll throw in with us?" asked the elf.

"Yes—we've already sent men from the gates into the Moongarden and the fish warehouses, also into the lumber yard. They'll have a thousand more recruits for us within an hour, and they'll be bringing all the weapons and tools they can get their hands on."

"Let's get moving upward," Barq One-Tooth said, coming to join the impromptu council.

By now all of the weapons had been dispersed. Kerrick could see hundreds of men milling around on the harbor plaza. Some were swarming onto *Goldwing*, battling the few ogres who were trapped aboard the ship, while others were chasing the merchants from their stalls on the marketplace one level above. The lower two levels of the city were churning in chaos under the onslaught of more than two thousand rebellious slaves.

"You men!" Moreen called. "Will you follow me against the ogre king? To rescue Strongwind Whalebone and to bring down the House of Bane?"

"Hail the King of Guilderglow!" cried Barq One-Tooth. "Long live the Highlanders!"

"And the Lady of Brackenrock!" Kerrick bellowed, exulting in the power of his own voice. "She leads the revolt, in the name of all the Arktos!"

The roars of hundreds of cheering men rose like thunder through the vast atrium of Winterheim. Kerrick found himself shouting along with the rebels, while Moreen held her sword over her head, looking every bit the part of the warrior princess. In a surge of energy, the slaves advanced, and the pair led the frenzied horde in a pell-mell rush across the harbor level.

"They would make a splendid couple, wouldn't they?" Tildy Trew remarked dryly.

Kerrick was surprised to see the slave woman running beside him, keeping up with apparent ease. She carried a long pole, and he noticed that the end was slick with gore. Clearly, she had joined in the revolt with full enthusiasm.

"Who?" he asked, genuinely confused.

"Why, Strongwind Whalebone and Moreen Bayguard," she retorted, without breaking stride. "Isn't that what they both want?"

"Some would call it destiny," the elf replied tentatively, feeling a familiar twinge.

Strongwind and Moreen were the leaders of the Icereach clans, and in their union, mankind would have a real hope of freedom and prosperity. Moreen herself had acknowledged that, and Kerrick had willingly offered to help her. He shrugged away his misgivings and ran, shouting.

The throng of rebels followed the elf and the chief-woman as they raced across the plaza, up the steps to the market level, and onto the ramp leading them higher into the great mountain city. Barq and Tildy ran close to them, and Black Mike surged into the lead, waving a big sword. Kerrick felt a thrill of emotion and knew that there was nowhere he would rather be, nothing else he would rather be doing. Life in Silvanesti, life as an elf, was but a pale shadow of this intensity, this battle frenzy, this joy.

They charged past two more levels, everywhere witnessing scenes of struggle and celebration as the newly liberated humans wrested the city away from their former masters. Amid the chaos was proof of great violence. Bodies of ogres and humans, males and females, young and old of both races were scattered along the promenades, streets, and markets. Here and there pockets of ogre warriors battled stubbornly, each of them isolated in the midst of a storm of raging men, but they were disciplined, especially the red-coated grenadiers. They more than held their own, and in several places they were mounting savage, coordinated counterattacks.

"This is the Terrace Level," Tildy explained to Kerrick as they ran past yet one more level of the ramp. "If we can get above this, we should be able to capture the heights!"

"Onward!" shouted Black Mike, at the head of the file.

They surged up a broad, inclined road, toward the opening leading toward the next level. A thin line of ogre warriors, less than a dozen spanning a fifty-foot gap, stood grimly in their path.

The crash came only moments before the slaves reached that tenuous line. Two huge barriers of stone swung forth on massive hinges, their own weight bearing them outward and downward until they slammed into a framework to form a makeshift wall, nearly crushing the leading rank of humans. Kerrick felt the paving stones shake underfoot from the impact, while many men were knocked from their feet by the powerful vibrations.

The result was clear to the elf and to all the humans, who groaned in unison. The two stone gates formed an impenetrable barrier across the ramp leading to the Noble, Temple and the Royal Levels of Winterheim. Beyond that wall of rubble they heard the cheers of a thousand ogres, roaring in defiance and victory, knowing that—for now— they were safe.

"Sire, the slaves are in full revolt!" cried Lord Forlane, reporting to Grimwar Bane in the throne room. "We have dropped the gates across the ramps above the Terrace Level and blocked them from the heights of the city, but I fear we have lost the harbor, the Moongardens and much below."

"Hold the line at the gates," ordered the king with an angry glance at Forlane.

He knew those stone blocks would be virtually impassable, at least until the humans started using their chisels and picks. There were small gaps in the stone barriers, but these were narrow enough to restrict access to single attackers and could be held by brave ogres. The king knew that under those conditions his warriors could stand against the humans indefinitely.

However, he understood that they needed to do more than simply hold back the slaves—they needed to attack. His judgment told him that he should lead that attack, but he found, to his continuing amazement, that he had no desire to fight, to kill, not right now. He looked at the big human woman, still in chains in the corner of his throne room, and once again felt that urge to talk to her, to try and see this matter from her point of view. Nearby was Strongwind Whalebone, the king of the Highlanders. He looked strangely apathetic for a king, as if he had no fears and no hopes regarding the outcome of this battle. Both people intrigued the monarch of the ogres.

"My husband, allow me to take the axe, to rally your warriors with the symbol of Gonnas. The men will benefit from the knowledge that the sacred talisman has been returned." Stariz spoke for the first time since appearing in the throne room, bearing the Axe of Gonnas.

Grimwar scowled. He didn't trust the queen and for that reason didn't want her out of his sight, but he needed to do something, make some gesture to prove to his warriors that the royal presence was still in command. He glanced questioningly at Forlane, who nodded firmly.

"The queen has a good idea, my lord. The sight of the axe will surely raise morale all along the barricades, and it could serve to terrify the slaves, as well. Your palace guard is ready to move—two hundred ogres, armed and eager for battle. They will follow the axe—er, the queen!"

"Very well," the king ordered, suddenly grateful for the respite from matters of war. He waved his wife away. "Go, go make your gesture, your attack, and see if you can drive them back from the gates. Return here when you are done." He couldn't resist an added, sharp admonition. "This time, do not expose the axe to the chance of capture!"

"As you command, my husband," said Stariz, flinching at his words, then bowing deeply. In another moment she was gone, zealously clutching the axe and followed by Forlane and a retinue of palace guards.

Still agitated, the king started to pace around the throne room. He found his eyes wandering, again, to the solemn figure of the human woman who had been captured with the axe. Her hands had been chained as a precaution, and she was seated on the cube of stone that the queen had wanted to use as a chopping block. A pair of grenadiers, swords in hand, flanked her and watched their charge with determined attention.

The king stalked over and tried glaring down at her, his hands planted firmly on his hips. Several questions had occurred to him, and he decided that it was time for some answers.

"Why did you come here?" he demanded. "Was this rebellion your doing?"

She shrugged. "Wasn't the rebellion inevitable? My companions and I did not come here to incite your slaves to revolt, but surely you must have realized that you couldn't keep that many people under your heel forever. There are more humans here than ogres by far. Think about it!'"

"Why must they revolt?" he asked. "I feed them, allow them to live and breed. Those who work hard are rewarded. It is not a bad life!"

"It isn't close to freedom, even for those who live that blessed existence," she retorted sarcastically. "What about those who suffered the lash or the sacrifices demanded by your pitiless queen? People will not live in slavery forever. As I said, it was inevitable that they revolt."

"Many of them have been killed, and many more will die before this is over!" he argued. "It is pointless!"

"Perhaps to you, but not to them," the woman said quietly. He was startled to see tears in her eyes, and he felt strangely uncomfortable.

"What about you?" Grimwar Bane asked, turning to the Highlander king. "How do you explain yourself?"

Strongwind shook his head with an air of sadness. "I should have died on Dracoheim," he said. "None of this would have happened. They came to rescue me, but I'm not worth all these lives! It was a mad quest, and I would give anything to send them all away from here!"

"Maybe there's more than just lives at stake, whether it be your life or the lives of a thousand slaves," Bruni suggested gently. "What if many are freed because you were brought here?"

"That would be a worthwhile gain," Strongwind agreed wistfully, "but I don't see how it can occur."

"It will never happen," Grimwar Bane interjected sternly. "My grenadiers will prevail!"

"Perhaps the mere chance at freedom is worth the risking of life," Bruni replied sharply. "I know that would be my feeling, if I was out there."

"You are a strange enemy," mused the king. "You say things like that, knowing that I hold your life in my hands. Do you not worry about enraging me?"

She shrugged with elaborate unconcern. "Perhaps I am beyond worries such as that." A hint of a shy smile appeared on her round face It made her look very appealing, Grimwar thought. "In any event, it's the queen's capacity for rage that has me worried . . . not yours."

Grimwar Bane chuckled in spite of himself, before turning to resume his pacing. The queen. Yes, her capacity for rage was worrisome to him as well. Abruptly he turned back to the slave king.

"Did you kill your mistress, the lady Thraid?" he demanded of the human.

Strongwind glared fiercely back at him, the first hint of spirit and emotion that the man had displayed since being brought here.

"I have never killed a woman, be she human or ogress," he retorted angrily, "and I never will, unless I have a chance to drive a blade into your wife's black heart!"

This was an honorable credo to Grimwar. The ogre king had to believe the human, but so many questions remained unanswered. If anything, he had more now than when he began to talk to these maddening humans. How could that woman be so calm? Why did she intrigue him so?

What in Krynn should he do now?

------◆------

Captain Verra was shocked by how quickly his plans had unravelled. The thousand Seagate slaves had been freed, with the loss of every one of the two dozen ogres he had put in charge of guarding the gate. He had never envisioned an attack coming from outside the huge slave pen.

The lumber yards, too, had been swept up in revolt. At least the ogres there had been able to retreat with some modicum of discipline. The rest of his troops he had summoned from their posts on the harbor and market levels, lest they all be destroyed. Now the remnants gathered around him, six or seven hundred red-cloaked brutes, well trained and heavily armed.

"What word of the rebels?" he asked one of his sergeants.

"They have moved past us and up through the city," reported the veteran. "Only a few are left holding the market."

"How far will the main force get?"

" I heard a smash of stone moments earlier, Captain. It seems likely that the gates above the Terrace Level have been closed. Surely they will be stopped there."

The ogre soldier nodded, beginning to form a plan. "There are a thousand ogres from the palace guard above them. If we can attack from below, the wretches will be trapped on the terrace. We'll wipe them out!"

"Aye, Captain—a great plan!" agreed the sergeant, with an eager bob of his tusked face.

"Send a detachment to the Moongarden Road," the captain added. "Two hundred grenadiers should be sufficient. I want them to block the corridor, and if any humans come up from that way they are to be driven back to the food warrens, hunted down, and killed."

"As you command, Sir!"

"Now, form the men into ranks," roared Verra, his optimism recharging. "We'll clean them out of the market and head on up from there!"

His veteran troops responded with precision, forming three long lines. "Forward, my brutes!" the ogre captain bellowed. "Attack without mercy!"

With a roar of enthusiasm, the scarlet-clad grenadiers rushed forward to obey and to kill.

"We can't get through!" Black Mike declared, trembling with rage. "To come so close and be stopped like this! Chislev curse them!"

He and Moreen were gathered with Kerrick and Barq One-Tooth a short distance back from the stone debris that had fallen across the ramp. More humans had joined them, including many house slaves from the ogre dwellings on these levels. They thronged in the passageway but had no way to progress any farther upward into the heart of Winterheim.

Moreen scowled and looked over the makeshift army. Its numbers continued to swell as more and more slaves streamed into the mob from the lower levels of the city.

"We have to do something!" she snapped.

"That's for sure," Tildy Trew said, coming back from the lip of the atrium, where she had been looking down toward the harbor level. "It looks as if the grenadiers have gotten organized. They're on the move. They've already retaken the marketplace, and now I think they're coming this way."

———◆———

Dinekki the bat felt strong again. She had perched on the high mast of the galley and watched the slave revolt sweep across the waterfront. Ogre blood stained the deck below her, and pockets of battle still raged. Nearby, a dozen grenadiers were barricaded in the shipyard, while a hundred humans threw burning brands between the planks of their small fort. Already flames were springing up from the stores of timber. The old shaman shuddered at the thought of all that smoke filling up this mountain cavity.

Now she had pressing business, and once again she took wing. Her flight led her up the wide chimney of the city's atrium, past level after level where slaves still fought their masters or celebrated their newly won freedom.

Higher up, the ogres were still in control, she saw. She spotted the queen wielding her blazing axe and heard the cheers of hundreds of ogre warriors as they beheld their talisman. The ogres on the highest levels were gathering for a downward attack, while other ogres—those in the scarlet cloaks—were fighting their way up from below. There was much killing still to be done, she feared, and it looked as though the main group of rebels would be pincered here on the Terrace Level and annihilated.

The power of Chislev bore her easily, and she offered a prayer of thanks to her benign goddess. When she looked at that flaming axe again, she glimpsed the power of another god there, a deity of pride and violence. Though she sought proof of his dark, evil nature, instead she sensed a power as natural, in its own way, as the might of her nature goddess.

Finally she was at the very top of the mountain city. Winging down a long corridor with a high, arched ceiling, she hurried toward the throne room of the ogre king. She dived through an open door and spied Strongwind Whalebone chained and seated in the corner of the throne room. Bruni was there, too, talking to the ogre king. No one noticed her, just a mere bat, as with a sense of relief Dinekki finally fluttered down and came to rest on a link of chain right next to the slave king's ear.

Mouse looked up and saw a high, vaulting archway and a vast space yawning beyond. Torches
and lamps flickered like stars high above, and
he knew that he was seeing the inside the ogre city. There
was a scent of salt in the air, suggestive of the sea, and the
Arktos sailor knew that somehow, inside this mountain,
the great city's harbor was near.

The bodies of a hundred ogres lay scattered through
the cavern behind them. Mouse and Thane Larsgall had
led the defeat of the defenders of Winterheim. As the war
party surged through the wide tunnel, each detachment of
ogres had been overwhelmed in a brief, furious skirmish.

The war party had been reinforced by hundreds of
slaves liberated from the Moongarden barracks. Along the
way to the city, as they passed other slave pens, caverns to
either side of the passageway that were fenced off by pickets of stout timbers, they threw each gate open, and additional men and women had joined the revolt.

Slyce was still running with the humans, a grin on his
face. The gully dwarf carried a long knife that he had
claimed from a foe, and though at first Mouse was afraid

the little fellow would get injured, he had welcomed the enthusiasm with which Slyce had flung himself into each attack.

The Arktos captain had no idea how many slaves had spilled out of their pens and were charging along with the throng—hundreds, perhaps even a thousand or more. They carried pitchforks and cudgels, hammers and picks, anything that might serve as a weapon. Shouting and whooping, they headed toward the ogre fortress with an air of joyousness, a spirit that Mouse suspected would be violently dashed all too soon. He couldn't help feeling that it had been too easy up until this point.

He saw Feathertail running along in the crush, her eyes alight. She smiled at him, a slash of white teeth in her brown face, and she looked fierce and beautiful at the same time. He wanted to live through this battle, to spend the rest of his life with her, but he knew that if they were to die here it would be a death that would be the stuff of legends.

At last the corridor opened into a wide atrium, but here the momentum of the rush slowed. Mouse pushed himself to the front rank, then stopped and stared in dismay. The exit from the corridor was blocked by a solid phalanx of ogres, six or eight deep, armed with long spears and sheltered securely behind a wall of tall, iron shields. A captain stood with them, and upon his order the formation began to advance at a measured stride.

The slaves outnumbered the ogres here, but the weapons and the narrow frontage all worked to the defenders' favor. Mouse heard murmurs of dismay and a few cries of fear, coming from the slaves who were massed behind him. As if sensing this wavering morale, the captain of the ogres shouted something, and the heavy formation, spearheads gleaming like wicked swords, broke into a trot, still holding those tight, precise ranks.

Mouse raised his sword. "Archers, shower them with arrows!" he called. "Highlanders and Arktos, meet them with your blades and your blood!"

Thane Larsgall was beside him, the man's bearded face creased into an almost bestial smile. He held his hammer high and cried out an ululating challenge. The shout was picked up by the humans of both tribes.

The tromp of the ogre march was a drumbeat in the corridor. Arrows poured down, bouncing from the shields, here and there penetrating the chinks in the enemy armor. No order was given, no signal made, but as if they shared the same mind the humans surged forward against the ogre steel.

Grimwar Bane stared at the captive human woman, who in some ways reminded him of Thraid. She had that same buxom, attractive shape, and her eyes were large and entrancing, even now as they burned with anger and contempt. At the same time, he saw an intelligence there, a depth of knowledge and wisdom that far exceeded any ogress, even his shrewd queen.

"I think I start to understand your feelings," he said, surprising himself with the blunt truth of the statement.

She shook her head in what was almost a gesture of pity. "What does a monster like you understand about anything?"

"A monster?" The king felt genuinely hurt. "I try to rule my realm with wisdom and care. I study, and I learn, and I rule."

"You're a killer of innocents, a maker of war!" she declared, though her eyes narrowed as she seemed to consider his words.

"You are an interesting person," he said. "I regret that we are forced to be enemies by the reason of your birth."

"It's not my birth," she retorted, glaring at him. "It's because you keep coming out of your city and attacking my people, dragging us into slavery or killing us. That's why we're enemies!"

The king flushed. Nobody spoke to him like this! Even in his anger, his response was not the slap or kick that such a remark would normally have provoked. By Gonnas, why did she have to make everything so confusing? He wanted to talk to her, and she insisted upon saying these infuriating things!

Abruptly he spun on his heel, stalked out of the palace, and crossed the promenade to the edge of the atrium. It pleased him to see that the battle was progressing well. The humans were being pushed back everywhere. He should be happy, but he was not. Instead, he was confused.

Absently he started along the promenade, walking, not paying attention to where he was going.

He needed to think. Think!

Stariz made her way back to the throne room, satisfied that the ogres were determined to win for their god and their king—or at least, their queen. Her thoughts, when they turned to her husband, were furious. He was a weakling! He lacked the resolve necessary to destroy his enemies, and thus, unless she continued to protect him, it was inevitable that his enemies would destroy him. For the first time, she no longer felt willing to coddle him.

The Axe of Gonnas was a good weight, a touch of familiar power, in her hands. In the haft of that weapon she felt a sense of immortal violation at having been handled by humans, but at least the weapon had come back to her. She deserved it, for she was the true source of ogre power in the Icereach. The axe was the most potent symbol of that might, and it pleased her to know that it was once again in the hands of its rightful owner.

The guards pulled open the door to the throne room, and she stalked inside, having made up her mind. She took long strides toward the center of the great hall. The two humans were still chained, and they sat motionless while a dozen ogre guards stood around, keeping careful watch on the prisoners. Her foolish husband was nowhere to be seen.

Stariz raised the Axe of Gonnas, twisted the handle, and relished the power that surged forth, flamed forth from that golden blade.

"Hear me, faithful subjects of Gonnas! See the vengeance of your immortal lord! Bear witness to the fate of those who would stand in his path!"

She spun on her heel, enjoying the look of consternation on the two humans' faces as she stalked back and forth before them, chanting her prayers. A bat fluttered through the air, flying away from the man and out the palace doors. She ignored the creature but glared at the human woman who watched the bat, not her, with a strangely thoughtful expression. The man's eyes glowed with malice. She relished that spark of hatred, of pride and resistance, for she knew that she could crush that light, extinguish it forever.

All her hatred, her revulsion at the blasphemy, her fury at the treachery of the slaves, welled within the queen as she raised the sacred weapon. This human woman represented weakness and evil, just as surely as had Thraid Dimmarkull. Stariz had dealt with the Lady Thraid. Now she would do the same with this pathetic human.

"You humans!" she cried. "Behold the vengeance of Gonnas!"

She turned, gestured to the sergeant in charge of the palace guard detail. He hastened forward, dropping to one knee so that he could bow his head.

"Take the prisoners to the temple!" ordered Stariz ber Bane.

"My queen!" objected the guard, looking upward with wide eyes. "The king commanded us to remain—"

"Do you see the king here now?" growled the high priestess, her voice rumbling with menace.

"N-no," replied the ogre hesitantly.

"Then if you know what is good for you, you will bring these two prisoners to the temple of Gonnas so that the Willful One may observe their fate and slake himself upon their blood!"

"The gates are opening!" cried Black Mike, who had been pacing back and forth before the upper barricades. "Stand ready, me mates!" The rebel leader raised his sword and strode up to the gap, other humans pressing behind.

Kerrick looked up to see that indeed the heavy portals that had blocked their advance upward from the Terrace Level were rumbling apart. Before he could call the slaves to rally to the attack, however, the growing gap was filled by a sight that filled him with dismay.

"Behold the Talisman of Gonnas!" crowed Stariz ber Bane.

The golden axe blazed in all of its fiery glory as she advanced, waving it over her head. She brought the weapon down in a sweeping slash, driving the shining head through the rebel leader's skull. Black Mike fell dead, and the nearby humans recoiled with a gasp.

A throng of ogre warriors behind the ogre queen cheered lustily, and as soon as the gap was wide enough they began to press through, stabbing with spears and chopping with their great halberds. Some of the slaves turned and ran. Those few bold humans who tried to stand were quickly cut down, bodies scattered haphazardly as the gates pushed open still wider.

More and more of the brutish attackers crowded into the gap, quickly shoving forward, starting down the ramp, driving the panicking humans before them. A brave woman ran forward, screaming in hatred. She stabbed with a spear, but the weapon was brushed aside by a looming grenadier. That ogre smashed her skull, using the hilt of his sword in an almost casual backhand blow, and she fell like limp doll, her head bouncing roughly off the floor.

Kerrick tried to hold his own ground against the attackers. He chopped at an ogre, forcing the creature back, leaving a gory cut in its face. Beside him, Barq One-Tooth wielded his axe with savagery, while Moreen shouted and cajoled in an attempt to bring more humans into a massed line.

The ogre attack was too forceful. Several more men fell, badly wounded or slain, leaving Barq and the elf alone on the wide ramp. Knowing they would be surrounded in a second, the two fighters had no choice but to fall back. Still they fought hard as they retreated, made the ogres pay for each footstep of ground. Stabbing and chopping in unison, the two warriors forced the enemy to at least measure the speed of their advance.

Nevertheless, the slaves were for the most part milling about in growing panic on the broad avenue next to the atrium, and the ogres pouring through the now wide-open gates waded into them with glee and savagery. The melee roiled across the road, fighters of both sides mingling in hand-to-hand combat. Here and there a formation of slaves made a bold stand, keeping the attacking guards from sweeping across the entire Terrace Level, but in most places they broke and ran. Some fled down the ramps toward the lower levels of the city, others ran through the streets and alleys of the city, seeking shelter from the imminent onslaught.

Kerrick looked for the ogre queen, hoping for a chance to surprise her with an attack. Perhaps he might even regain the axe. Unfortunately, she had not followed the attackers through the gate. She seemed content to urge them on, from the safety of the rear. He saw the gleaming fire of that axe and heard her shrill commands, but he could only curse in frustration.

"It's like Tildy said. More ogres are coming from below," Moreen reported after a quick glance over the rim of the atrium.

The elf shook his head angrily, and it was only then that he noticed the bat fluttering past his scarred ear.

◆━━━◆◆◆━━━◆

Slyce huddled miserably against the wall of the Moongarden corridor. The ogres had charged past and were doing their best to kill all the humans who had brought the gully dwarf to this interesting place. He saw Mouse and Feathertail, humans who had been nice to him, fighting against much bigger ogres. Slyce even tried to help, lunging forward, trying to stab with his big knife, but he tripped and fell, the knife went flying, and the battle quickly swirled past him as the humans were forced to retreat. Now it seemed as if they would be driven all the way back to the Moongarden.

He hid behind the body of a dead ogre, crouching in the space between the corpse and the wall, watching wide-eyed as the melee moved down the corridor, farther and farther away. Finally he was left in silence except for the groaning of a few badly wounded ogres and men.

Slyce scuttled away from the battle and in moments found himself inside the largest place he had ever seen or even imagined. There was more fighting going on here, so he continued to run up a ramp that led away from the big flat space where ogres and humans chased each other around.

Some more fighters started to come up that ramp, ogres marching shoulder to shoulder as if they were chasing him. Slyce scampered farther and farther up, around the wide circles of the ramp, higher and higher into the ogre city. He came to yet another place where there was a big fight going on, but he saw some gates that were open. There were bodies around those gates, but nobody seemed to be paying attention right now. He ducked on through and continued higher.

At least here in the upper part of the city there didn't seem to be any fighting at the moment. There were sure lots of ogres, he noticed. All the humans seemed to be hiding, and the big brutes were running this way and that, many of them carrying sharp weapons.

For once, Slyce was grateful that he was a very small gully dwarf, since he had no difficulty hiding in the shadows when the ogres came rushing past. Still he headed higher until he was at the very top level of this huge place. Here he ran away from the ramp when he heard more ogres coming up from below. Now he was on a wide street, with a ledge and a deep drop on one side, and many fancy buildings on the other side.

There was nowhere else to climb, so he decided to stop and find a hiding place. He saw a big statue of a proud bull ogre wearing a cape and a crown. That stone image would conceal him from the street, and the gully dwarf squatted behind it, wide eyes staring this way and that.

Big doors opened right across the street from him, and to his surprise he saw a person he recognized, all tied up in chains. It was that big Arktos woman—Bruni!—and she marched past with a bunch of ogres on all sides of her. She was being taken with another human, a blond-bearded man, down the street, to the ramp down to the next lower level. A fierce ogress led the way, and she carried the same golden axe that the humans had brought with them from Brackenrock.

They looked terribly frightening. Slyce didn't know what to do, so he simply kept his head down. After they went away, he scuttled across the street into a dark alley that looked like an even better hiding place. Here he curled up against the wall, a little ball of misery, and fell asleep.

———◆◆◆———

"That was Dinekki!" Kerrick said.

"What? Who?" demanded Moreen.

"It sounds crazy, but she's that bat that was flying around here! She was chirping in my ear. I had to listen carefully before I could understand her. She told me that she found Strongwind and talked to him, and he told her something that might help us out!"

He saw the fluttering brown creature swirling about, then watched as it darted away along the Terrace Level promenade. "Let's go!"

"Where?" The chiefwoman was still angry and frustrated. "Explain this to me!"

"No time—come this way," the elf said impatiently. "Follow me!"

Moreen, Barq One-Tooth, Tildy, and a hundred or more armed slaves followed him as he gestured and took off at a trot. The battle on this level of the city had broken into small pockets as the humans had scattered and the ogres clustered around the gates to the higher levels. A few patrols of heavily armed grenadiers could be spotted here and there, attacking the slaves where they found them, but for the most part they seemed content to let the force ascending from below handle the main fight.

The bat wove and bobbed through the air, leading them along, finally circling frantically at an intersection. When the elf got close Dinekki flew off down a side street, and Kerrick led his group of fighters down the lane and into the courtyard of a large building fronting a wall of the city's bedrock.

"This is Thraid Dimmarkull's apartment," Tildy explained. "It's the place where Strongwind was posted for the past few weeks."

The door was a splintered mess on the ground, and Kerrick entered the anteroom in a rush. The first thing he noticed was the rear end of an ogre, who was kneeling next to one of the lady's trunks, rummaging inside. A small pile of valuables, including a lamp, a wine pitcher, and several goblets of gleaming gold, lay on the floor beside the brute, who was obviously looting.

Barq One-Tooth strode forward and split the surprised ogre's skull before he could even begin to fumble for his sword. Meanwhile, Tildy quickly looked in the slave quarters of the apartment. "Brinda, Wandcourt?" she called.

Two humans, gray haired and obviously frightened, came out into the room. Each carried a knife, but they looked around in confusion at the mass of people pouring in through the door.

"What's going on? Is the king dead?"

"Not yet," Tildy said, "but what happened here? Where is the Lady Thraid?"

The male slave pointed mutely toward one of the rooms. They all took one glance in that chamber, the bedroom, and saw the remains of a gruesome murder. The lady's body lay on the bed in a pool of dried blood.

Tildy clucked in sympathy. "She was a trivial creature, but she deserved better than this."

The female slave, Brinda, looked at Kerrick intently. "Are you . . . an elf?" she asked.

"Yes," he replied, "but I've thrown my lot in with the humans. Do you want to join us?"

She patted her knife, sliding it through her belt and stepping closer. "Yes, I do," she said, staring at him with a strange expression.

The bat fluttered around his head, and he followed it into the parlor and pulled the bearskin off the wall. The outline of the door was faint but visible, and when he twisted the bracket of the lamp sconce the secret door rolled smoothly open.

"Get some lamps," he ordered, "and follow me as quietly as possible."

Moreen came right behind him, with Tildy next, then Barq One-Tooth, followed by the throng of armed men and the two slaves of Thraid Dimmarkull. Taking a lamp that someone handed him, Kerrick darted through the door and started up the stairs that spiraled within.

For a long time they climbed urgently. When Kerrick looked behind he saw a dozen lights bobbing through the darkened passage curving below and knew that the file of rebels remained close behind him. There were many more than he could see, as they curled into the distance, masked by the curving walls of this stairway.

Finally the elf reached a landing and held the light up to reveal another door, similar to the one at the bottom. Cautioning the humans to silence, he found the catch and slowly pulled the portal open.

A quick glance showed that he had not reached a palace hall, as he had hoped, but a narrow alley shrouded in shadow. That was better than a busy street, he thought and quickly slipped out the opening.

"Where's Tildy?" he whispered.

She came forward, and together they crept down the alley, looking toward the lights of the promenade. "Do you know where we are?" he asked.

"I think so. Yes, that statue out there is right outside of the palace. If we go down this lane and turn left, we'll be a dozen steps away from the king's front door."

"Well, that'll do," he said softly. In a hushed voice he outlined a simple plan. They would charge out, swiftly and silently at first. As soon as they were discovered they would abandon stealth and put all their efforts into haste.

"With luck, we can take the king by surprise. If we can capture him alive, then we'll have something to bargain with."

"That's as good an insane plan as any I've ever heard," said Tildy, with a wink.

The file of slaves had nearly filled the alley by then, and still more were still backed up in the secret stairway.

"No time like the present," he muttered. "Let's go!"

He drew his sword, took one last look at his file of anxious warriors, and started toward the promenade and the king's palace at a full sprint.

Strongwind Whalebone tugged at the manacles holding his wrists, but the iron links were unbending. He tried to console himself with the fact that his spirit was equally solid, but he saw through that lie with ease. The ogress queen marched along in front of him, and he knew that his time and his luck had run out.

In truth, he was terribly frightened, more afraid than he had ever been in his life. He didn't want to die, yet he couldn't see any way that he would survive. It was not so much for himself that he grieved. The real cause of his despair was the deeper truth, for it broke his heart to know that so many of his friends and countrymen would perish on this mad quest. They would not only fail to set him free, but they seemed destined to bring about only widespread slaughter among the hapless slaves of Winterheim.

Why couldn't they have just left him here to rot? Why hadn't he simply had the sense, the decency, to die on Dracoheim next to the brave Randall? If he had perished then, it would have been but the death of one pathetic man. Now it seemed as though he would bring about the death of whole tribes, the end of humankind in the Ice-reach. For what would the Arktos do without Moreen? That was the greatest sadness of all.

"We had to come for you," Bruni consoled him. She shuffled beside him, chained as stoutly as he was, and seemed to be reading his mind.

"Be silent!" One of the guards cuffed her across the head.

She turned and glared at the brute, then spoke to the king in a quieter tone. Perhaps because the queen couldn't hear, the ogre didn't strike her again.

"There is no point to our life in the Icereach if it means just hiding from the ogres every day of our lives, simply hoping not to get caught, to avoid the next slave raid, to live through yet another ogre attack. Don't you see, we had to try. Besides, we're not dead yet, are we?"

The slave king shook his head. "I would willingly give up my life if it meant the rest of you could go free! The cost is too great! I am but one man, and two whole tribes will be decimated in this vain effort to save me."

"There are many of us who think you're worth the effort," the big woman said. "Do not lose hope."

For Strongwind Whalebone, hope was already gone.

Grimwar Bane returned to the throne room, intending to speak with the human prisoners again. He was startled to see that the captives, as well as his wife and most of the palace guards, were gone.

"Where did they go?" he demanded, fixing a glare on one of the remaining standard-bearers.

"The queen commanded that the prisoners be taken to the temple!" declared the warrior, trembling and dropping to his knees. "Half-Tusk tried to object to her majesty, Sire, pleading that this was not your will, but she threatened him, and he complied! They marched out the door but a short time ago!"

The last words were still echoing from the high walls as the king burst through the doors and lumbered into a jog, hastening toward the ramp down to the Temple Level.

⬦

"Up there—take the ogre barracks!" Mouse cried, pointing to the Moongarden rampart where the slaves had first driven out the overseers.

It broke his heart to realize that they had been driven all the way back from the city, down the long cavern and to the edge of the vast food warren. How many members of his war party had fallen? He couldn't know, and there had been no chance to count the bodies of the dead. How many slaves had been free for just a few hours only to perish in this brutal final fight?

They were at the end of the long tunnel, and there was no further retreat. If the humans went into the Moongarden, they would be surrounded and destroyed with ease. Here, in the ravaged yet still fortified barracks building, they could at least take a defensive position and make a valiant stand.

Feathertail herself was wounded, bleeding badly from a cut in her leg, and Mouse supported her with his left arm as he wielded his sword with his right. All the while the rank of red-coated ogres marched along behind them like a machine, maintaining the steady pace of the chase. Any humans who fell were butchered then relentlessly trampled beneath.

The survivors of the war party and the freed slaves moved through the wide doors that they had smashed only a short while ago. The big room still reeked of warqat, and the shattered barrel lay scattered on the floor.

"Form a line in here!" Thane Larsgall urged.

"Kill as many of the bastards as you can," Mouse added. He eased Feathertail to a seat on a bench some distance from the broken door.

Some men scrambled up stairs to the second floor and took positions on the balconies overlooking the corridor and the downward ramp. The rest joined the rank in the great room, facing the door, waiting for the ogres to start through. Here they would await the inevitable final reckoning.

There would be no escape from this place. All they could hope to do was kill as many ogres as possible before the last of them died.

———— ◆ ————

Stariz pushed open the doors to the temple, leading the way for the guards who dragged Strongwind Whalebone and Bruni of Brackenrock behind. Their chains rattled as the two captives, upon a gesture from the queen, were cast roughly to the black stone floor.

"Fetch my mask and my robe!" demanded the high priestess, and her ogress acolytes scurried to obey.

She drew a breath and looked up at the massive statue, the beautiful black image of Gonnas towering far above her head. This was her lord, she knew, not that pathetic weakling king who could not even bring himself to condemn these hateful rebels. Fortunately, Stariz had divined what needed to be done, and she had the resolve to take action, ruthless action. In a minute the heavy black mask had been placed over her head, the ceremonial robes draped to the floor from her blocky form. She felt pure, whole, and powerful.

She hoisted the axe, relishing the feel of her god's might. The two captives were held flat on the floor, two guards and two acolytes holding each limb, pressing the humans on their backs, spread-eagled and vulnerable. Fire blazed from that golden blade, warming her and terrifying the enemies of her god.

Fingering the haft of the mighty weapon, she looked down at Strongwind Whalebone. All of the hatred, contempt, and resentment of her life swelled up in her heart as she raised the weapon.

"Poor luck, human," she said. "I had planned to wait for this moment—but it seems as though Autumnblight comes early this year!"

The axe came down, and Stariz heard the satisfying sound of the big woman screaming in horror and grief.

Kerrick led the slaves down the narrow alley toward the bright lights on the avenue before him. He had nearly reached that intersection when he tripped over something soft and small and went tumbling headlong.

"Slyce?" he declared, astonished to see the little gully dwarf scrambling out of the way. "What are you doing here?"

"Watching," said the little fellow miserably. "Watch 'em take big Bruni away."

"They took her—where?" asked the elf urgently.

"Come. I show you," said the gully dwarf. "She wit' big ogress lady and shiny axe. Not nice lady, not nice at all."

"No," agreed the elf, sheathing his sword and motioning his comrades to follow. He pictured the ogre queen, and his heart was cold.

"Not a nice lady at all."

"What do you mean by this?" demanded Grimwar Bane, bursting through the temple door. He advanced on his queen, his fists clenched and his face glowering red with fury. He gestured toward Bruni, who was sprawled in chains, held on the black stone floor by two ogress acolytes at her arms, two grenadiers holding her legs. Beyond was the lifeless form of Strongwind Whalebone, cloven by a deep wound inflicted by the Axe of Gonnas, which still glowed in his wife's hands.

"I ordered you not to harm these prisoners! You could not wait to kill the first one, and now this one too? I will not allow it!"

"Yours are the orders of a fool!" shrieked the queen. "Any slut with a silly smile can twist you into idiocy! Now it is this one's time to die, just as I had your whore killed! This time I shall have the pleasure of inflicting the lethal cut myself!"

The axe was over her head, flaming brightly. "Behold the will of Gonnas!" she cried in exultation. She started her swing.

Something halted the downward momentum of the axe. Stariz screamed as the weapon was plucked from her fingers like someone taking a toy from a child. Enraged, she spun around, shocked to see the hulking figure of Karyl Drago, holding the axe and shaking his head at her. The big warrior had stepped out from behind the statue, and now he blinked, almost sleepily, as he shook his head in denial.

"No," said the monstrous ogre. "You are wrong. This is not the will of Gonnas." Karyl Drago held the Axe of Gonnas in one meaty hand, high out of the queen's—or anyone else's—reach.

"Do you know whom you address?" demanded Stariz ber Glacierheim ber Bane. "I am the will of Gonnas, the mouth, the tongue, and the word of our god!"

She stalked away from the hulking Drago and the king, then she spun to confront them both below the obsidian statue of Gonnas that loomed high in the center of the room.

"I am the voice of Gonnas!" she shouted triumphantly. "I am his will, manifest upon the world of Krynn!"

As she shouted the words she knew that it was true, for she felt the power of her god infuse her. She was the Willful One, and she threw back her head and laughed aloud. No one could stand in her path.

"You are a puny fool!" she screamed at her husband.

Extending her hands, she barked a sound of rage and violence. Magic exploded from her fingertips, a blast of fiery power that rushed outward, swatting him aside with one powerful blow. The other ogres in the temple gasped and cried out as the king tumbled across the floor, rolling over and over, finally smashing, hard, against the base of the wall. He gaped up at her in shock and horror, drooling.

"You are an insolent toad!" she spat at Karyl Drago, who was backing away, clutching the Axe of Gonnas. "You are not worthy to touch that sacred relic!"

She extended her hands another time, ready to blast that massive ogre and snatch the talisman from his grasp. Stariz noticed a bat soar down before her—but what could a bat do?

Dinekki's goddess was in her, and she was content. For more than eight decades she had cherished a life upon the Icereach, cold and cruel though that life had often been.

Now she had reached the end of those years, but strangely she was not the least bit sad. Instead, she came to rest on the floor, her claws clicking on the smooth stone. In another instant the spell faded away and she stood, frail in appearance but powerful in spirit, before the enraged, astonished ogre queen.

The old shaman said nothing, merely looked upward with a sly smile creasing her wrinkled face. Stariz shrieked and shrieked, consumed with rage at this mad interruption, and drove a crushing fist downward, smashing the old woman's brittle bones, driving the mortal life from her flesh . . .

Bringing the power of two gods into collision.

The guards at the temple gate were surprised by the sudden determined appearance of the charging rebels, too surprised to pull shut the heavy iron door. They fell, stabbed and bleeding, as Kerrick led Moreen, Barq One-Tooth, Tildy, and at least a hundred freed slaves into the great hall.

Here they stopped, frozen by the sight of a fiery apparition—a giant ogress, in the image of Stariz ber Glacierheim ber Bane, reeling backward, shrieking in unholy pain. Her hand was blackened and blistered, and flames flickered up and down her limbs like hungry scavengers.

Nearby, the body of Strongwind Whalebone lay on the floor, cloven almost in half by a monstrous blow. The elf saw another ragged, broken shape on the floor, and he recognized poor Dinekki—or what was left of her. The frail old shaman's body was torn and broken, as though rent by terrible violence. Smoke rose from her tattered flesh and from the floor around her. An explosion had shattered one leg of the looming black statue that rose above everything else in the room. That obsidian icon teetered now on its remaining leg, and the rubble strewn beside the smashed limb was smoking in the same manner as Dinekki's flesh.

Incensed beyond reason, Kerrick charged the queen, trying to slash with his sword. She didn't appear to notice him but instead staggered away, still screaming, swatting at the flames that burned along her body. Her right hand was a charred stump, blackened and still smoking. He thrust, missing her, and sprang forward to resume his desperate pursuit.

"Don't do that!" cried an excited voice.

"What?" Kerrick asked, stunned by the sudden appearance of his small companion at his side. The elf stopped and stared at the kender.

"That's better," said Coraltop Netfisher. "Just watch. This is getting better and better every second!"

"Bruni!" Moreen cried.

The big woman, still chained, was rolling away from the gaping ogres who had held her. The acolytes fled to the far corner of the temple, while the guards drew their weapons and ran to protect their king.

Together with Barq One-Tooth, the chiefwoman raced across the throne room toward her old friend, who was struggling to stand, her hands chained before her. An ogre guard lunged to intercept them, but when Barq raised his axe the warrior retreated warily.

"Cut these!" cried Bruni, kneeling on the stone floor. She placed her manacled hands on that hard surface, and Barq brought his axe down with one crushing blow, slicing through the iron links.

Magic blasted and a shower of sparks swirled through the air, as Stariz howled in fury and managed to cast another explosive spell at the Highlander thane. Barq One-Tooth flew across the room and smashed into the wall, slumping next to the ogre king, his axe spinning free onto the floor.

"My turn," muttered Bruni, seizing the weapon, and turned to face the looming, burning queen.

The big woman hurled the weapon with both hands. Barq's axe flipped over and over through the air and thunked loudly into the black mask over the queen's face. That obsidian shell broke away, and Stariz ber Bane stood glaring at them, unhurt, her eyes blazing with maniacal fire.

"Blasphemy!" cried the high priestess and queen. She turned toward the tilting statue, raising her arms in a gesture of pleading. "Hear me, O Master! Smite those who thwart your will, who endanger the place of your people in the world! Show us your favor, and destroy those who are your enemies!"

She spun back to face the ogres, humans, and elf, casting back her head with a shriek of crazed sound, half prayer and half laughter. The statue tilted wildly, but Stariz wasn't looking. Her face was distorted by glee and fury, joy and rage all mingled in an expression of insane frenzy.

"This is the will of Gonnas the Strong!" she howled, raising her hands for one last spell.

The statue of the Willful One toppled forward on its one leg. Slowly, like a tall tree breaking free of its ancient roots, it plummeted, smashing down upon the ogress queen with a weight of thirty tons. The brittle obsidian shattered. Black stone chunks tumbled across the floor. Bits flew everywhere, the roar filling their ears.

Of Stariz ber Bane there was no sign except for a smear of dark blood that slowly oozed between the shattered rock, spreading in an oily slick across the floor.

"The queen is dead!" gasped an ogre warrior, one who wore a gold-braided helm that seemed to mark him as an officer.

Others of the guards were tending the king, helping him to stand unsteadily. Two of them offered shoulders for the ogre monarch's support.

For a long time no one spoke. Everyone was too astonished, too exhausted.

"With her passing, let the killing cease," finally declared Grimwar Bane, stumbling for a moment, then shaking off the support of his warriors. He took three steps forward and held up his hands in a sign of truce.

Kerrick's sword was ready, the ogre monarch just a long lunge away from him, but something caused him to hold the blow. Instead, he remained on guard, watching and waiting.

Bruni came slowly forward, wrapping one arm around Kerrick, the other around Moreen Bayguard. Other slaves closed in, swords and spears leveled at the king, as a rank of red-coated ogre guards came forward to flank their monarch,

"What did you say?" asked Moreen, her eyes narrowed.

"I said, let the killing cease," declared Grimwar Bane. He looked at Bruni and nodded quietly. "You were right," he said, "about many things."

"Bruni, what did you say to him?" asked the chiefwoman, in a tone of wonder.

"Well, for one thing, that I was more worried about the queen's rage than the king's," the big woman said with a wry snort. She looked at Grimwar Bane, then stepped forward with an outstretched hand. "I think you're talking about how we waste too much of our energy in trying to kill each other. How slaves, in bondage, will inevitably strive for freedom."

"Yes, yes . . . Bruni," replied the king. "You saw the truth, and you dared to tell me, even when I had your life in my power."

"What about the slaves and all the dead?" demanded Moreen. She gestured toward Strongwind Whalebone's corpse, which was being reverently covered by Barq One-Tooth. "He could have been the greatest leader his people have ever known, and your queen killed him for her own pleasure. Many of your people and ours have died on this day, and your guards are hunting and killing humans in your city even as we speak."

"Send word to Captain Verra!" commanded the king, shaking his head, wiping blood and dust from his face with a beefy hand. "Tell him that I order a truce effective at once. All attacks are to cease immediately!"

"Aye, Sire! It shall be done!" declared the golden-helmed guard. He departed at a run.

"Those slaves are pretty mad," said Coraltop Netfisher, striding right up to the ogre king. "I must say, of course, they have cause to be. You haven't treated them very well, have you now?"

"Who are you?" gruffly demanded Grimwar Bane.

"Oh, me?" The kender all but blushed, then looked sheepishly at Kerrick. "I guess I can tell you now. You see, I'm sort of a . . . well, a god, I guess you could say. Some people would say that, anyway. Lots of folks call me Zivilyn Greentree. I'm not really a great god or a big god or anything, but elf sailors have worshiped me for centuries, all over Ansalon, except I wanted to get out and see more of the world. Kerrick here was kind enough to take me along with him."

"A god? Zivilyn, the Green Star?" declared Kerrick, not sure if believed it . . . not sure if he wanted to laugh, bow down in awe, or cry. "All this time . . . you were, what? Riding with me? Watching me?"

"Well, I had some other things to do. You might have noticed that I wasn't around all the time! Like Chislev Wilder—who is called Kradok by the Highlanders incidentally; did you all know it was the same god? I didn't think so—I was pretty tired of watching you people and you ogres bash each other all the time. Did you know, even Gonnas the Strong was getting sick of it." The kender looked up at the looming form of Karyl Drago. "Isn't that right?"

"That is right," replied the huge ogre, looking up from his beatific scrutiny of the golden blade. "The will of Gonnas is not for more blood."

"The slaves," pressed Moreen, "you'll free them and give them back their lands?"

"Aye. You and they are entitled to everything I can do for them," the king said softly. He took Bruni's outstretched hand. "As you told me, as long as I tried to hold those humans in chains, revolt was inevitable. Many would die. I am tired of fighting and of seeing people die."

"There is room enough here and in all the Icereach for both our peoples," Bruni suggested.

"As of this moment, all of my slaves are free. They may stay here and live as citizens of Winterheim if they wish. I hope that many of them will do so, for I do not know what my city would be like without humans here. Those who wish to may return to their steadings—homes that shall remain free of the threat of ogre raids from this day forward."

"Can we trust you?" asked Moreen warily.

Bruni, still holding the king's massive hand, turned to her oldest friend and replied for him. "Yes, I am certain that we can."

"I think so too," said Coraltop, standing on tiptoes to scrutinize the ogre king's face. "His eyes mean what he says. Not like that queen, may she *not* rest in peace. She was a nasty one, bad temper, had spies all over."

The kender looked at the throng of slaves who were gathering in astonishment. He wandered back and forth with casual glee, studying the humans who had entered the temple in the wake of Kerrick and Moreen. One of them, the gray-haired woman from Thraid Dimmarkull's apartment, dropped her knife noisily and started sidling toward the door.

"Oh, do you know that lady over there, the one called Brinda . . . well, she told the ogres everything that was going on. She even told the queen that Strongwind Whalebone would be going to the market when he did, so that her guards could catch him there." Coraltop looked at Kerrick. "She was supposed to kill you! Wouldn't that have been something—to come all this way, only to get stabbed in the back by a human traitor?"

Brinda screamed and turned toward the door, pushing several slaves out of the way in her desperation to escape.

She didn't get very far.

The Seagate was opened by the combined efforts of ogre and human volunteers, pulling together on the massive capstans, sliding the huge stone barriers to the side. The midnight sun was gone for the rest of the year, and true night had settled across Black Ice Bay. Stars twinkled in the expanse of sky, the tiny sparks reflecting like distant campfires in the smooth waters.

These faint sparkles were swiftly overwhelmed by the surge of yellow flames rising from the great funeral barge. Strongwind Whalebone lay in state at the center of the pyre, while Dinekki rested at his side. The raft slowly drifted out of Winterheim's harbor, into the open waters of the bay, and for a long time those tongues of flame blazed toward the heavens, rising upward in a great column of sparks, flickering spots of light that seemed determined to join the distant specks twinkling in the sky.

Moreen stood on the wharf and watched. She found it easy to believe that the spirits of the two heroes were being borne skyward, toward a place of reward, rest, and peace. Bruni had told her that Strongwind's final wish was that the sacrifice of these lives be more than just about him . . .

and it was. Strongwind Whalebone had been the greatest king that the humans of the Icereach had ever known, for he had been the one who had freed them from their ancestral scourge.

"Goodbye, my friend," she whispered. "I will miss you."

She passed Mouse and Slyce, who were sharing a companionable mug—several mugs, actually—of warqat. Nearby, Barq One-Tooth and the slave girl Tookie were sharing a leg of lamb, the meat freshly roasted in the royal kitchen.

Moreen wasn't hungry or thirsty. Slowly she made her way up the gangplank and onto the big galley.

The chiefwoman found Kerrick on the deck at the stern of the ship, leaning on the railing, watching the embers of the pyre rise into the cool night. She leaned there beside him for a few moments of companionable silence, feeling very tired.

She tilted her head back and saw Grimwar Bane and Bruni up at the edge of the Royal Level, looking down over the vast city. Across the marketplace square, ogres and humans together were picking through the rubble, tending the wounded, gathering the dead for burial.

"This ship the ogres call *Goldwing*," said the chiefwoman. "She was your father's galley, wasn't she?"

"Yes," the elf agreed. "She was called *Silvanos Oak*, back then."

"The king would give her to you, I think. You could sail back to Silvanesti in triumph."

Kerrick smiled thinly and reached out to take her hand. "I think that I don't want to go. I've found a new home," he said. "I've made my life and my destiny here, and here I will remain."

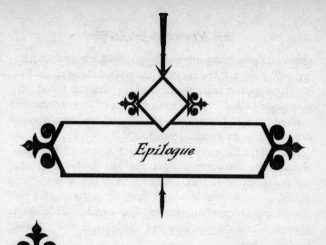

Epilogue

The Kingdom of Icereach existed for more than five hundred years, a unique arrangement of peaceful coexistence between ogres and men, unlike any other time in the history of Krynn. Winterheim was its capital, but great centers of the kingdom were to be found in Guilderglow and the bustling harbor city of Brackenrock, which came to be known as the "Tarsis of the South."

The sons and grandsons of Grimwar Bane, proud half-ogres mingling their paternal heritage with the gentle influence of Queen Bruni, ruled Winterheim for many years, a dynasty that prospered through five centuries of freedom and riches. Through the auspices of the traders of Brackenrock, the ogres traded their gold with the empire of Istar and other realms of far-off Ansalon. In return, the Icereach imported foodstuffs and silks, wines and jewels, and magic aplenty, a steady stream of wonders that the frozen southland of Krynn had never before known.

In Brackenrock, it was the half-elf prince, Coraltop Redfist Bayguard Fallabrine, named for his grandfather and his adopted uncle, who established the rule that saw peace and prosperity among the Arktos for long centuries, long after his beloved mother had passed away in the limited time span granted to those of pure human blood. Her memory dwelled in the annals of history forever, and her husband, called Kerrick the Messenger, lived to a ripe old age of nearly six hundred years.

He might have even lived longer if not for the Cataclysm. That devastating event wracked the Icereach as it did so much of Krynn, bringing forth the glaciers that sealed away Winterheim and Brackenrock and all those other places remote in memory. The kingdom of Icereach vanished, and the glaciers and the Icewall were all that could be seen.

Those magical places remain beneath ice and snow, still warmed by Krynn's internal fires. Perhaps, someday, their brightness will once again emerge to illuminate the world.

The War of Souls
ends now.

The New York Times best-seller from
DRAGONLANCE® co-creators

Margaret Weis & Tracy Hickman

available for the first time in paperback!

The stirring conclusion to the epic trilogy

DRAGONS OF A VANISHED MOON
The War of Souls, Volume III

A small band of heroes, led by an incorrigible kender, prepares to battle
an army of the dead led by a seemingly invincible female warrior. A dragon overlord provides a glimmer of hope to those who fight the darkness,
but true victory —or utter defeat—lies in the secret of time's riddles.

March 2003

The original Chronicles

From *New York Times* best-selling authors Margaret Weis & Tracy Hickman

These classics of modern fantasy literature – the three titles that started it all – are available for the very first time in individual hardcover volumes. All three titles feature stunning cover art from award-winning artist Matt Stawicki.

DRAGONS OF AUTUMN TWILIGHT
Volume I
Friends meet amid a growing shadow of fear and rumors of war.
Out of their story, an epic saga is born.

January 2003

DRAGONS OF WINTER NIGHT
Volume II
Dragons return to Krynn as the Queen of Darkness launches her assault.
Against her stands a small band of heroes bearing a new weapon:
the DRAGONLANCE.

July 2003

DRAGONS OF SPRING DAWNING
Volume III
As the War of the Lance reaches its height, old friends clash amid
gallantry and betrayal. Yet their greatest battles lie within each of them.

November 2003